MARKED

BY SARAH FINE

SERVANTS OF FATE
Marked
Claimed

GUARDS OF THE SHADOWLANDS
Sanctum
Fractured
Chaos
Captive: A Guard's Tale from Malachi's Perspective

MARKED

Sarah Fine

47NORTH

Text copyright © 2015 Sarah Fine
All rights reserved.

Published by 47North, Seattle

www.apub.com

Amazon, the Amazon logo, and 47North are trademarks of Amazon.com Inc. or its affiliates.

ISBN-13: 9781477825853
ISBN-10: 1477825851

Cover design by Cliff Nielsen

Library of Congress Control Number: 2014908971

Printed in the United States of America

For Lam, who is whip-smart and
kind in equal measure

PROLOGUE

The chauffeur drove them home from the hospital, maneuvering the amphibious limousine smoothly through the waist-deep canals in the Back Bay neighborhood. When he pulled to a stop and popped the roof hatch, the oppressive heat stung Cacy's tear-streaked face. The driver held out a hand to lift her onto the dock. She ignored it and scrambled out by herself, her sundress fanning out around her skinny, bruised legs. Her father, elegant and lean in his miraculously unwrinkled three-piece, climbed out after her.

She followed him up the polished stone walkway and stood with him in the vaulted foyer of their home, thinking his face looked as gray and sickly as the disease-filled water lapping at the dock outside. His eyes searched hers. Then he nodded slowly and unclasped the heavy silver medallion from the thin chain he always wore around his neck. The Scope. Door to the Veil, window to the Afterlife. His thumb skimmed over the disk's elaborately etched surface, and the center became shimmery and transparent.

"You'll come see her off with me," he said quietly. His fingers closed around the edges of the medallion and pulled, stretching it into an oval with a gauzy film at its center. He yanked it even wider and held it in front of Cacy, the surface swirling like a giant soap bubble. "It's time you better understood the family business, anyway. Step through."

His voice was so calm it both shocked and steadied her. He'd never allowed her to go into the Veil before, no matter how many times she'd begged. She'd seen her sister and brothers step through the Scope many times, but her father had always told her she was too young. Now she finally had her chance . . . and she was shamefully afraid.

She slid trembling fingers along the glossy skin of the bubble and gasped as her fingertips sank in with a soft slurping sound. "Is this going to hurt?"

The thunder of her father's laughter was too loud to be comforting. "Not physically. Go on. I'll be right behind you."

When she didn't move, he sighed. "Stay next to me, then." He stepped up close and held the silver-framed portal over their heads, then brought it down around them, letting it drop all the way to the floor.

A splintery, bone-hard chill instantly enclosed Cacy. She pressed herself to her father's side and squinted at her surroundings. She was in the same spot, still in the foyer, but everything looked . . . dead. The color had bled from the rich mahogany floors and colorful tapestries that adorned the vaulted corridor in front of them, leaving them a dull gray.

Her father held her shoulders and guided her as she stepped outside the boundary of the shiny metal ring of the Scope. He bent over, picked up the silver-white circle, and pressed at its edges until it was small and solid once again. A moment later, he reclipped the still-glowing disk to the chain around his neck.

Cacy coughed as the icy air of the Veil filled her lungs. Her father's long, narrow fingers closed around her wrist. "You'll get used to it. Come."

He led her along the main corridor of their home, a replica of the nineteenth-century brownstones that used to line the streets of their Boston neighborhood. The originals had all been destroyed fifty years earlier in the Great Flood of 2049.

The plastic heels of Cacy's patent-leather shoes were silent on the hardwood floors, now strangely spongy beneath her feet, though her heart beat a deafening rhythm in her ears as they approached the door of her mother's library. Her father's grip tightened when she began to pull away. He spun around and crouched so that his gaunt gray face was right in front of hers. In the Veil, the shadows under his eyes were deadly deep.

"This is the last time she'll ever get to see you, so I need you to get that scared look off your face, my darling." His strained smile made Cacy's stomach hurt. "Show her your beautiful smile so that she can hold on to it forever. You can cry later."

Cacy sniffled and nodded as he pulled out a silk handkerchief and wiped the tears from her face. Her father stood back and appraised her, and then abruptly pulled her toward the closed door. She flinched as her face plunged into the carved wood. Its surface gave way gently, like gelatin, and flowed closed behind her as she stumbled through.

When she opened her eyes, her dead mother was standing in front of her. Mara Ferry's fingers skimmed along the spines of her precious books. Her smile was as sad as her husband's.

"The Charon himself comes to see me off," she said lightly. She raised her chin and set her shoulders. "I'm glad it's you."

"You know I wouldn't have allowed anyone else to do it." He released Cacy's arm so he could embrace his wife, bowing his head to press his cheek to hers. Her eyes closed, but not in time to stop a tear from rolling down her face, now rounded and full. She was still clothed in her hospital gown and robe, but she wasn't emaciated and ghoulishly pale, as she had been a few hours ago when Cacy had walked away from her bedside for the last time.

Her mother leaned back and kissed her father. "Where is Moros? He Marked me, didn't he?"

Cacy shivered. She'd heard stories about Moros, Lord of the Kere.

Her father nodded and touched his forehead to her mother's. "After all the suffering you experienced, he wanted it to be painless."

"It was."

"I will pay him his commission later. He wishes you a safe journey, but he did not come in person because he didn't want to frighten Cacia."

Her mother inclined her head toward Cacy. "Thank you for bringing her."

He nodded and stepped aside, hovering close.

Cacy's mother turned to her, arms open. "Baby, don't be scared."

"I'm not," Cacy replied automatically, tensing in an effort to stop shaking.

Her mother smiled, and when she hugged Cacy, her body was warm. Cacy snuggled in, unable to hold back her tears. "Don't go," she whimpered.

"I must. But don't ever forget me, all right?" She took Cacy's face in her hands. "I wish I could have seen what you'll become, because I know it's going to be great. And take care of your father for me."

"I will."

"Mara, it's time," Cacy's father said, his voice choked.

Her mother nodded. "I'm ready." She gave Cacy a lingering kiss on the forehead and let her daughter go.

The tortured look on the Charon's face said he wasn't ready to say good-bye, but that didn't stop him. He pulled the Scope off its chain again, flipped it over, and swiped his thumb across it. This time, the center sparked blinding white. He sagged in relief.

"Heaven," he whispered.

Cacy's mother chuckled. "You were worried *Hell* awaited my arrival?"

He straightened. "Never." He gave her a wicked smile. "Well, there was that one time . . ."

She slapped his arm playfully. "Not in front of Cacy." But her arms wrapped over his shoulders, and she kissed him fiercely. Cacy didn't understand the loose, rolling feeling in her belly as she watched them.

Patrick Ferry's hands stroked down his wife's back. The disk flashed between his fingers as he pinched the edges and stretched it wide behind her. He moaned as he pulled back from her kiss and looked into her eyes. "I promise you, I *swear*, I will make sure Heaven is my future as well. I will find you again."

Her mother nodded. Finally, she tore her gaze from her husband's and winked at Cacy. "It is time for my next adventure, my love. Wish me luck."

"Bye, Mommy," Cacy whispered. She sank back against a squishy wall of books, her eyes blurred by tears.

Her father's arms formed a cage around her mother's slight frame. Her mother turned to face the blinding, pulsing door to Heaven in his hands. His chest expanded once more, and then he stepped back and pulled the ring over her, sliding the glowing light all the way down to her feet, letting it swallow her whole. There was a gasp, the last thing Cacy heard from her mother.

With tears streaming down his solemn face, Cacy's father lifted the ring and held it in front of him. A glittering gold coin flew from its center and hit his chest before falling to the hardwood. He scooped it up and turned it over in his hand, then shoved it into his pocket. His payment for delivering his wife to the Afterlife.

One gold coin for a lifetime of lost happiness.

CHAPTER ONE

FIFTEEN YEARS LATER

Eli Margolis shouldered his rucksack and edged his way into the aisle of the crowded bus. The passengers around him were slowly getting to their feet, fanning themselves and plucking at their sweat-drenched clothing. But after twenty-four hours on various forms of mass transport, with his legs crammed into seats clearly designed for much smaller people, Eli was in dire need of a stretch.

He took a step back, blocking the human traffic behind him, making a space for his sister to squeeze herself into the aisle in front of him. Galena's dark-blonde hair was plastered to her temples. The dark circles under her eyes made her look painfully fragile. He laid a protective hand on her shoulder. "Ready?"

She hitched her pack a little higher on her back and looked up at him with a brave smile. "As I'll ever be."

They filed off the bus and onto the dock. The lapping swampy brine that scented the air was both new and depressing. He looked over the heads of the other passengers, scanning the busy transit station. Dock after dock. Every one with an amphibious bus magnetically tethered to its mooring. Every bus disgorging wave after wave of exhausted, hopeful refugees from the West.

Eli tried to draw more humid air into his lungs; he felt like he was suffocating. This place would take some getting used to, but it would be good for his sister. That was why he had come.

Galena pulled her smudged phone from her pocket. "I've got our new address right here," she said proudly, waving the thin tablet in front of him as they headed toward the transit station.

She'd been trying to cheer him up ever since they pulled away from the bus station at the outskirts of Pittsburgh. He still couldn't quite believe they'd gotten seats on an honest-to-God bus, a prize people would kill for. Some of his fellow passengers probably had. And unlike most other travelers, he and Galena had an apartment waiting for them instead of a refugee shelter. All because of her.

He tugged his sister's pack from her, looping it over his own shoulder. "I wish I could go straight there with you. You're sure you'll be all right?"

Galena took his hand, tugging him into the soaring lobby of Boston's South Station. "You worry too much. Someone from the university is meeting me. He's going to help me get settled, and then he'll take me to my new lab. I can't wait to see it!"

Eli smiled. He already knew the lab would be more her home than the apartment, and he was thankful for that. She needed to stay busy.

He held Galena's hand in a tight grip as he scanned the wide-open space of the station's lobby, prepared to meet any threat that came. She looked up at him and rolled her eyes. "*Relax*, Eli. It's a lot safer here. Come on, we can catch a taxi. They gave me an expense account." She tapped the screen of her tablet phone a few times and held it up, showing him a balance that made his eyes widen. She grinned. "See? Not a bad way to start out in a new city, right?"

As their taxi motored through the downtown canals, Eli stared out the window, feeling a bit seasick. This place was so different from the stark, dusty wasteland of his hometown. Flimsy flat-bottomed boats packed the waterways and bobbled in the wakes of amphibious vehicles. The taxi occasionally bumped against the other boats as they wove through the canal. A few people paced the sidewalks next to the low canal walls, using nets to collect garbage floating in the brown-gray water. At first, Eli thought they were public works employees and brightened, amazed that such order still existed. But then he saw a woman pawing through the contents of the net, frantically tucking objects into her own pockets. These people were just scavenging for others' scraps.

The frame of the taxi jerked as the driver gunned the engine and powered the vehicle up a ramp and onto the dry streets of Chinatown. Eli took in the crowded sidewalks, the darting hands of the elderly women at the street markets, the deep alleys between buildings, and the armed guards in front of the noodle shops and apartment complexes. After a few minutes, the taxi came to a stop in front of what looked like an enormous garage. There was no sign on the outside, but the street number matched the address he'd been given. The Chinatown EMS station.

His new place of employment.

He turned to Galena, whose fingers were flying across the screen of her tablet. She'd probably made another brilliant scientific discovery in the last ten minutes. He leaned over and kissed her temple. "I'll see you in the morning, all right?"

She tore her eyes from the screen and blinked at him, then held her arms out for a hug. "Be careful out there, big guy."

"No worries. Text me when you get to the apartment. I need to know you got there safely or I won't be able to focus."

Galena patted his shoulder. "You don't need to know where I am every minute."

Eli pulled back and tipped her chin up with his fingers. "Yes, I do."

"It's going to be different here. It's safe here," she said softly, sounding more like a little girl than a grown woman.

"I hope you're right. But until I know that for sure, have pity on your little brother."

She looked away, probably remembering things he wished she'd forget. He hugged her close again, wanting to go back in time and protect her better than he had, to give her back what had been taken from her in that single brutal night two years ago.

The taxi driver shifted in his seat. "Meter's running."

Eli kissed Galena's forehead. "Later."

He watched as the taxi pulled away from the curb, then strode over to a security screen set into a solid metal door. He tapped the screen to activate it. A second later, a man's face appeared, staring out at him with ice-blue eyes. "That you, Margolis?"

"Yessir."

The metal door clicked, and he pulled it open. The blue-eyed man was striding down the corridor toward him, holding out a hand. "Welcome to Boston! I'm Declan Ferry."

Eli blinked. Declan Ferry was the Chief of the Chinatown EMS station. The one who'd offered Eli this job. And he didn't look a day over twenty-five. If the Chief himself had only been a paramedic for a few years, Eli wondered what the turnover rate was.

Eli shook the Chief's hand. "Thanks, sir. Sorry I look sort of rough. We just got in to town."

Chief Ferry grinned and patted him hard on the back. "Call me Dec. Showers are this way. We have our own filtration system, so running water isn't a problem."

Eli followed the Chief down the hall, forcing himself not to ask a million questions. Running water? He'd never actually seen such a thing. Clean water was like gold in Pittsburgh, and carefully rationed. It was shipped from the East and came in jugs or sealed bags, and every month people were killed in riots, just trying to get hold of a few extra gallons. He hoped he could figure out how to work a shower so the rest of the paramedics wouldn't think he was a complete hick.

The Chief stopped at the door of a small, neat office. He pointed toward a high-ceilinged room at the end of the hall. "When you're cleaned up, come on back here and I'll go over some of our standing orders and protocols. I imagine it's not too different from Pittsburgh, but the canal zones make things tricky sometimes."

"Yessir."

"Call me Dec!" hollered the Chief as Eli headed into the locker room. It was shift-change time, and the room was filled with his new colleagues, some in street clothes, some wearing their uniforms. Instead of rushing to leave or get to their rigs, they were all gathered around a videowall at the front of the room. Eli stood at the edge of the crowd and turned to see what they were watching, expecting to see images of the latest bombing or food riot.

On the screen, a tall salt-and-pepper-haired man in a suit stood at a podium. Dozens of reporters were crowded in front of him, all holding up their tablets to record the event. Behind the older man stood three people: a fit, broad-shouldered man; a statuesque platinum-blonde beauty; and a petite black-haired young woman with huge turquoise-blue eyes. She was staring at the man at the podium, her attention fixed entirely on him.

It was obviously some kind of press conference, but the volume was low and Eli couldn't make out what was being said over the buzz of conversation among the paramedics. A short barrel-chested man beside Eli elbowed him and inclined his head toward the dark-haired woman on the screen. "Mmm, I'd like to spend a night prying *those* gorgeous legs apart."

Eli looked down at his new colleague and forced a tight smile. "I'd prefer to spend time with a woman who actually *wanted* me between her legs," he said, barely suppressing his desire to punch the guy right in his homely face.

That homely face split into a wide grin. "*Aw*, a gentleman. That's cute. I didn't mean anything by it, new boy. I'm Captain Len Ramsey, by the way. Night shift supervisor." He held out his hand.

Before Eli could take it, a wide dark-skinned hand closed hard over Len's shoulder. Towering behind Len was possibly the biggest guy Eli had ever seen, and he wasn't surprised at the flash of fear and pain in Len's eyes. The man smiled at Eli, canines gleaming. "I know you're just working off some frustration, Len," the big man said, "but make sure the Chief doesn't hear you talking about his little sister that way."

Len's jaw went rigid. "Piss off, Trevor," he muttered, shrugging out of the man's grip and stalking toward a row of lockers across the room.

Eli decided he liked Trevor, if only for making Len go away. After introducing himself and shaking Trevor's hand, Eli nodded at the screen. "The Chief's sister?"

Trevor turned to the videowall and barked, "Volume level high."

The voice of a news anchor immediately filled the room: . . . *was packed today as Patrick Ferry, a prominent local philanthropist, and the CEO and owner of Psychopomps Incorporated, announced his retirement, effective immediately . . .*

"Ferry? As in, Chief Ferry?" Eli asked.

"Yeah, the Ferrys are a powerful family here in Boston. That's Dec's father." Trevor pointed to the older man at the podium, then waved his hand at the people behind the guy. "And those are the Chief's brother and sisters."

He pointed at the broad-shouldered man, who was now shaking Patrick Ferry's hand and stepping up to the podium. "That's Rylan. As of today, he's the new CEO of the company."

Trevor pointed at the platinum blonde, who was staring at Rylan Ferry with a cold, pinched expression on her pale face. "That's Aislin. She's moving into Rylan's position as chief operating officer."

Eli raised an eyebrow. "A real family business, huh? What does the company do?"

"Exports," Trevor said in a bland voice. He pointed at the petite woman with the haunting eyes. "And as I said, that's the Chief's little sister."

Eli stared at the woman, whose gaze remained on her father. It was such a protective expression, which was funny because she looked too soft and sweet to do much damage. Still, there was something ferocious in her eyes, a warning, a promise. She shifted uncomfortably from foot to foot, drawing Eli's eyes down her body, which was wrapped in a steel-gray sheath dress that hugged every curve. But as gorgeous as she looked, she also seemed uncomfortable as hell. He wondered why. He wondered if she lived in the city. If she was close to Dec and ever stopped by the EMS station to visit. If she dated anyone but execs and playboys. If she wore underwear under that little dress. If she—

Eli pulled his gaze from the screen. "Does she work at the company, too?" he asked, trying for an offhanded tone.

Trevor chuckled as they watched the young woman hug her father and smile sweetly up at him. "Nah, no way. Cacy works here. She's one of the best paramedics we have. And one of the toughest."

"She works *here*?" Eli tried to imagine that tiny, beautiful woman up to her elbows in blood and gore.

Trevor slapped him on the back. "Yup. Now, pop those eyes back in your head and go take a shower. You stink, man."

Eli wasn't about to disagree. He hitched his pack up and turned for the showers. He'd made it about ten steps when Trevor called out, "Oh, and Eli?"

"Yeah?"

Trevor looked like he was trying to keep from laughing. "I hear you've been assigned as Cacy's new partner. Good luck."

CHAPTER TWO

Cacy plowed past the rows of ambulances parked in the cavernous garage and stumbled through the back door to the locker room, grateful to hit AC again. As soon as she made her less-than-graceful entrance, the guys greeted her with their usual teasing-but-affectionate wolf-whistle welcome. She curtsied elaborately and headed down the hall to the doorway of her brother's office. He looked up from his computer screen and smiled. "Hey. How was the press conference?"

"It went off without a hitch, but it would have been nice if you'd come, too."

Dec ran a hand over his hair, leaving it standing on end. "He has *you*."

She walked into the room and stood next to her brother. He had the same ice-blue eyes as their father, the same inky-black hair of his youth, the same elegantly handsome features. She tapped the Scope hanging from the chain around his neck. "Does he have *you*?"

Dec's face flushed as he looked down at the screen where the scheduling board was displayed. His shift had been over for an hour, but he hadn't yet changed out of his uniform. "It's hard to get the day off when you're the Chief. And you know I do my part.

I shuttled three souls through the Veil during my lunch break. While you and the rest of them were at the press conference."

She pinched Dec's cheek. "Sounds like you need a nap." Ferrys were human, but they required a mere hour of sleep per day, which was the only way she and Dec could maintain their day jobs and still fulfill their family responsibilities.

Dec rose from his chair. "Are they still staring at the videowall in there?"

Cacy shrugged. "Was it that big a deal?"

Dec gave her a look that said she should know better. Normally, the news of a CEO's retirement wouldn't interest their fellow paramedics at all. And they had no idea what the Ferrys' business really was, no idea how the Psychopomps empire touched their lives . . . and maybe their deaths . . . every day. The only thing they cared about was that Patrick Ferry had bought the struggling EMS department from the city and funded the renovation of every EMS station in Boston the year Cacy became a paramedic and joined her brother at the Chinatown station.

It had been her father's velvet revenge after Cacy turned down a cushy white-glove position at his corporate office—and left his side for the first time in eight years. All she'd wanted to do was find her own way, but he'd accused her of abandoning him. So he'd made himself an instant hero to every paramedic in Boston, and Cacy had been dubbed a "princess." She'd had to scrape and fight for every shred of her colleagues' respect.

Every night. For the last seven years.

Dec threw a thickly muscled arm over her shoulders and whispered in her ear, pulling her from her thoughts. "Finally found you a new partner."

She tensed and reached for her own Scope, which suddenly felt heavy around her neck. Her last ambulance crewmate had been killed in the line of duty a month ago. She'd escorted him through the Veil personally. The only problem—when she flipped her Scope and opened what turned out to be a portal to Hell, he'd tried to escape. She'd had to hunt him down and cram him, screaming and clawing, through the portal.

She'd done it tons of times before, just not to someone she'd done shots with.

"Why can't I keep Trevor?"

Dec chuckled. "And here I thought you hated the Kere."

"That's because most of them are bloodthirsty assholes who enjoy the pain they cause. But Trevor's all right. He's different."

"You just want to work with someone who can't die, you coward. Anyway, Trevor misses his day shifts. Your new partner's a regular human, but he seems pretty durable."

"Is he a transfer?"

Dec nodded.

That was good news. It meant the guy wasn't a newbie. It meant he knew what they were facing out there. She relaxed a little. "Which station?"

Dec frowned. "Um."

She twisted from her brother's grasp so she could stand in front of him. "Dec?"

He shrugged. "Wilkinsburg."

"Wilkin-*what*? Where's that?"

He watched her carefully. "Near Pittsburgh."

"You let some freaking refugee desert-dweller into our crew? And you assigned him to *me*? Do you think I enjoy watching my partners die?"

Dec took hold of her shoulders and shook her lightly, a warning in his eyes. "I'm having a hard enough time staffing two-person crews, let alone the four we need to run right. Eli's an experienced paramedic, and—"

"Yeah, if you've got a snakebite or a cactus splinter—"

He clamped his broad hand over her mouth. "You're going to show him the ropes. I'd have taken him on myself, but I'm still trying to get Carol settled in. Len's got a new partner, too, so he couldn't help. You're the next-best thing."

She punched him not so lightly in the chest, and his hand fell away. "I'm the *best* thing," she snapped—and realized she'd fallen into Dec's trap.

Dec grinned. "Go get changed so you can start proving it." He swatted her butt and shoved her toward the locker room. "Be nice, little sister," he said in a sweetly sarcastic voice.

Cacy shot him the finger and stalked into the locker room. She and the other female paramedics had an aisle to themselves. It was the only privacy they got, but the guys—most of them, at least— were really respectful. Besides, Cacy wasn't modest.

Which was good, because she'd just taken off her T-shirt and bra when Trevor appeared out of thin air beside her. "Sneaky bastard," she yelped as she fell against her locker.

He grinned and steadied her with incredibly warm hands. The Kere ran hot, and Trevor was no exception. In more ways than one. The man was six and a half feet of chocolaty hotness. The fact that he was gay hadn't stopped Cacy from enjoying a few elaborate fantasies about the two of them in the back of her rig. The fact that he was a living personification of death . . . well . . . that hadn't stopped her, either.

Trevor patted the top of her head. "Dec told me you finally have a new partner, so I stopped by to give you my condolences."

Cacy's stomach dropped. "Tell me he's not Marked already. It's his first freaking day."

He glanced down at the inside of his forearm, rubbing it like it ached. "Not on my list."

Trevor and the rest of the Kere were responsible for Marking— and presiding over the gory, disease-ridden, pain-filled deaths—of humans who had drawn the short straw of fate. Few Kere interacted with humans as equals, and few had day jobs (they didn't need to, since Ferrys had to split the death commission with them).

Still fewer actually cared about people. That's where Trevor was an exception. For whatever reason, he wanted to stay connected to the humanity he'd lost a century ago when he sold his soul to become a Ker.

Trevor raked his gaze over Cacy's bare breasts. "This is a good look for you, little Ferry. Should I call Len over here?"

"Fuck off," she said, laughing. "Don't you have somewhere to be?"

The grin fell from his face. And that could only mean one thing.

She laid her hand on his cheek. "Hey. How many lives did you save during your paramedic shift today?"

His eyes met hers. "I don't know. We went on twelve calls." He threw his massive shoulders back. "I delivered a baby on the way to the hospital. The little guy couldn't wait to be born."

"How many lives are you about to take as a Ker?" she whispered.

"Nine," he mouthed.

Shit. It was going to be a busy night if the Marked were in the Chinatown emergency response zone. Cacy cringed inwardly but said, "So in the balance, you saved more than you destroyed. It's a good day."

He smiled sadly and pulled her into a hug. "I'm going to miss riding with you, Cacy."

"Bullshit," she mumbled against his chest. "You're thrilled to be back on first shift. You'll get to hit the clubs again."

He chuckled. "But I'll be dancing with tears in my eyes."

"Hey, Trevor, do you know where—? Oh, sorry," said a voice that carried the slightest of western twangs.

Trevor's arms fell away from Cacy as they both turned. The newcomer's emerald-green eyes widened, and his cheeks flushed dark pink. "*So* sorry, ma'am," he muttered, but he didn't seem able to tear his eyes away from her breasts.

Trevor snorted. "Boy, you are so fresh it's sweet. Sergeant Eli Margolis, meet your new partner, Lieutenant Cacia Ferry. Cacia, Eli." He waved his hand back and forth between them.

Cacy put her hands on her hips, praying the men in front of her would attribute her hard nipples to the fact that the room was cold. But in truth, *damn.* The newbie was going to take some getting used to. His short dark-blond hair was streaked with gold and platinum, like the sun loved him. His skin was tanned but not scarred or blistery like so many these days. She couldn't choose which part of him to stare at first, so her eyes just bounced all over, from high cheekbones to square jaw to broad shoulders to lean hips. She almost asked him to turn around so she could admire the rear view.

Her new partner was sex on a stick.

Which sucked, since she had no intention of going anywhere near said stick. Or any other part of him. "You never seen a pair of breasts before, Sergeant Desert Boy?" she snapped.

His tongue darted out to wet his lips as his piercing gaze hit her. He gave her a sweet half-apologetic smile. "None like yours, Lieutenant City Girl."

Trevor threw his head back and laughed. "This is a match made in . . . somewhere. What did you need, Eli?"

Eli's eyes didn't leave Cacy's face. "Her. That's all."

Rebellious little shards of pleasure streaked down Cacy's spine. She shivered and turned toward her locker. "You found me. Give me five minutes and I'll meet you at rig four-three-six."

She actually only needed a minute to get dressed. She needed the other four to freaking *pull herself together.*

"Yes, ma'am," Eli said. She looked over her shoulder to read the expression on his face, but he was gone.

Trevor tugged lightly at the back of her ponytail. "I can't tell if your day just got a lot better or a lot worse."

"I'm not sure, either," she muttered. She'd sworn off guys a few years ago, the night she'd had to escort her last boyfriend to the Afterlife. And Trevor knew that, because he'd been the one to Mark the guy for death. It hadn't been personal. Brian's name had simply come up on Trevor's list, and Trevor had done his job. So Cacy had guided her boyfriend to Heaven, just not the heaven she'd planned at the start of the evening. Then she'd split the commission with Trevor, drunk herself into serious oblivion, and decided getting involved with anyone else wasn't worth the pain.

"Be safe out there, Cace. It's gonna be a long night. Sorry in advance." Trevor leaned in, kissed her cheek, and walked away. Off to wreak havoc Cacy would have to clean up. Off to shed the blood she'd no doubt be washing out of the back of her rig by morning. Off to reap a soul she'd probably have to escort to Heaven or Hell on her coffee break.

CHAPTER THREE

Eli stood by rig 436, pulling at one of the dozens of zippers on his bulletproof, waterborne bacteria–repelling paramedic uniform. It would take some getting used to, like most things in this place. Especially Lieutenant Cacia Ferry.

By the time he'd showered and met with the Chief, Eli had convinced himself it would be no big deal to have her as a partner. He'd worked with tons of female paramedics in the past. He'd never been anything but professional. And this would be just like that. Nothing but professional.

Then he'd come face-to-face with her. Now he would spend the rest of his shift trying to get the image of her breasts, rose-pink nipples pearl-hard and mouthwatering, out of his head.

"Chief's *sister*," he whispered to himself.

A buzzing vibration coming from one of his pockets pulled him from his thoughts. He pried out his cell and looked down at it. *Here safely. Apartment is great! And check out my lab! I think I'll call this handsome fellow 'Danny.' Hope your first day at the job is going well. XOXO*

Danny? In the time it took for Eli to wonder who the hell Galena was talking about, the text dissolved and a picture appeared. His sister was posing with her arm around a broad flat-screen computer, its holographic projections throwing all sorts of odd squiggles across the snapshot.

Of course. Danny. Her new computer.

He smiled, relieved, as he shot back a reply and tucked his phone in his pocket. She'd always worked hard, and she hadn't let what had happened to her slow her down. If anything, she'd driven herself harder after the attack, trying to regain her sense of control. And it had really paid off; this faculty position in the Harvard University Immunology Department was a dream come true for her. Eli just wished she wouldn't spend so much time alone. He hoped there were actual people in that lab facility and not just machines. It'd be nice if Galena made a friend or two.

Eli focused his gaze on the alcove next to the locker room entrance. A videowall there kept up a rotating feed of the different sectors of their station's emergency response zone. He stared at the teeming canals and sidewalks. So many people. So many problems. The population of the city had swollen in the last few years as Boston became one of the few remaining cities with modern conveniences. Electricity. A (barely) functioning police force and fire department. Hospitals still stocked with antibiotics and anesthetics. *Luxuries.*

"Feeling prepared, Desert Boy?" Cacy called as she strode into the garage. Her uniform clung to her body, revealing lush, round hips and shapely legs.

Eli flashed a smile at her and looked back at the videowall, trying to ignore the sudden tightness in his pants. "I'm always prepared, Lieutenant."

Dec had told him about the dangers of the canal zones, and in the city in general. It didn't sound any worse than what he'd faced on the streets of his hometown or during his stint as an Army Ranger.

Cacy yanked open the rear doors of the ambulance and climbed in, where she began systematically checking each compartment in the back, mumbling to herself about self-perpetuating saline gel, chemical defib solution, and fast-acting antibiotic boosters.

The back of the rig dipped as Eli climbed in to join her. She glanced at him irritably and wiped her hand over the back of her neck, drawing his gaze to a delicate platinum necklace that hung there. A circular pendant with some sort of bird etched onto its surface dangled from the chain. She saw him looking and tucked it into the collar of her uniform.

Cacy sat down on the side bench and slid toward the cab of the vehicle. She looked down at the bench and made a face. "Could you grab some Powderkleen and wipe this? I don't know what day shift got up to in here, but I sure as hell don't want to sit in what they left behind."

Eli did as she asked, grateful to have something useful to do. He sneaked glances at her as he worked, admiring the absolute comfort with which she maneuvered around the rig. It was clear she had little tolerance for things being out of place. He was the same way, so it was a relief to have a partner who cared about those details as much as he did. Details saved patients' lives.

She opened the front left cabinet and counted the rounds in the tranq guns. Dec had gone over the rules of engagement with him earlier. Eli had never wielded a tranq gun before, but he figured he could get the hang of it quickly should the need arise. He had plenty of experience with street violence, but in this city, he planned to focus on defending himself against it . . . instead of causing it.

Cacy leaned into the front seat. He wondered if she was aware of the amazing view she offered as she bent over to tap the nav screen by the steering wheel. He gritted his teeth and looked down at the bench, where he'd been scrubbing hard . . . about six inches away from the sticky spot that needed it.

He paused in his work, deciding this might be a good time to clear the air between them. "You don't seem thrilled to have a new partner, Lieutenant. Seems too soon to be personal, but in case it is, I apologize again if I offended you earlier."

"By eye-fucking me in the locker room, you mean?" she asked casually, not bothering to turn around.

He stared at the dangerous curves of her backside. Her tone hinted a challenge, which drew a smile to his lips. "Was it good for you, too?"

Her shoulders shook, and he wondered if she was laughing. But then she made a disgusted sound and grabbed something from the front passenger seat. She turned around and held out a small colorful box. "Want some mockolate? It's the high-end stuff. My father once got us the real thing, and I swear this tastes just like it. You have this kind of thing in the desert?"

Eli peered at the box. "No, can't say I've ever seen that."

"Seriously?" She ripped off the lid of the box and plopped down on the bench. There was a raw, spicy-sweet scent to her that he couldn't quite place, but it made his heart race. He scooted back a few inches and sat on the floor of the rig.

He raised an eyebrow. "You're offering me candy? Does that mean I'm forgiven?"

She gave him a thoroughly seductive smile and plucked a creamy-dark square of mockolate from its crinkled paper nest. "Nope. It means I'm willing to share Len's please-screw-me gift with you."

His mouth dropped open. She took advantage of his surprise and popped the piece of candy between his lips. His mouth snapped shut as deep, earthy sweetness melted on his tongue. His eyes rolled back and he moaned. "Wow."

When he recovered enough to open his eyes, Cacy was staring at him with a slightly glazed look. But then she brusquely crammed the lid back on the box and jumped out of the ambulance. "Don't get used to it," she called over her shoulder.

This woman was giving him a serious case of whiplash. He leaned out the rear of the rig to watch her.

Len stalked into the garage, carrying his med kit. He scowled and raked a hand over his buzz cut when he saw Cacy about to dump the candy into the trash bin.

"*Really*, Cace? That cost a fortune!"

She shoved the box against his broad chest. "Don't spend a cent of your hard-earned paycheck on this stuff, Len. It's not going to get you anywhere with me."

For some reason, her statement lifted Eli's mood. More than it should have.

Len opened the box, peeked in, and grinned. "You ate one. I must be making progress."

For some reason, *that* statement made every muscle in Eli's body tense. He hopped off the rear deck of the ambulance and strode toward them. "Uh, no. That was me. Amazing stuff, Len. Thanks for sharing—with *us*."

Len's eyes narrowed to slits. He opened his mouth to say something but got cut off by the screech of the wireless alert. They turned toward the videowall in the alcove and listened to the dispatcher's voice: *"Mass casualty incident at the intersection of High and Pearl. Multiple units requested. Caution advised. Fire crews and law enforcement not yet on scene."*

Len and Cacy cursed in unison when they saw what appeared on the videowall. Dec had told Eli that the city's surveillance cams, as well as most private home and business cams, were hooked into the emergency call system. When someone placed a call, the feeds from that location were automatically displayed on their screens so they could see what they were up against. It was an impressive system, something they could have used in Pennsylvania. It might have saved some paramedics' lives.

Tonight they were treated to a view of twisted metal and fiery wreckage. Len ran up to the screen and zipped his fingers along its surface, already yelling at his crew. "AV and NMOB collision!" He enlarged the screen capture and flipped it around, giving everyone a 360-degree view of the disaster. "Multiple casualties in the water. Mobilize four-two-zero, four-three-six, four—"

Cacy grabbed Eli's arm and tugged him into motion. "Come on. We're four-three-six."

Eli kept up with her easily as they sprinted for their ride. "AV and NMOB?"

Cacy didn't miss a beat. "Amphibious vehicle and nonmotorized multiple-occupancy boat. Some jackass didn't look both ways and crashed into a boatful of refugees. Third time this month. I'll drive."

"You're the boss, Lieutenant," he said as he split off from her and rounded the ambulance to jump into the passenger seat.

Cacy swung herself up into the cab and punched the ignition code. "Seat belt, Desert Boy."

She tapped the red square on the nav screen, and the ambulance bay doors whooshed open. Eli sat back and watched her slender fingers grip the steering wheel. She glanced over at him. "Ready for your first mass casualty in our fair city?"

There it was. Another challenge. Eli smiled. "I think I can handle it."

"We're about to find out if you're right." She flipped the siren on and hit the gas.

CHAPTER FOUR

Cacy floored the ambulance across Kneeland Street, splashed into the wide mouth of the Main Canal, and gunned the water jets.

And immediately had to pull the throttle back with all her strength.

"Damn sampans," she yelled, rolling down the window and waving her arms at the people on the slow-ass flat-bottomed boat in front of the ambulance. They simply ignored the giant amphibious vehicle with the blaring sirens. "Take the wheel, Eli, will you?"

"What?" He looked at her like he'd never driven an amphibious before. He probably hadn't, since Pittsburgh was pretty much a desert wasteland. She hoped he was a quick study.

"Take. The. Wheel." She was halfway out the window when he scooted over and did as he was told.

As the rig lurched forward, she nearly lost her balance and tumbled out, but Eli's warm hand wrapped firmly around her thigh to offer her some stability. Cacy clenched her teeth. It felt annoyingly fantastic. His grip tightened and he swerved against the canal wall to keep from hitting a speeding uniboat as it zipped between the ambulance and the sampan. Cacy's ribs hit the edge of the window. Hard. That did *not* feel fantastic.

"Jesus! That was close," he shouted. "You okay up there?"

"Just fine," she called, grateful for his hold on her as she leaned forward and screeched at the sampan owners in Mandarin. Their eyes widened and they flipped on the tiny motor at the back of their boat, quickly making way for the rig.

"Did they not understand what the siren means?" Eli asked as she slid back through the window and settled into the driver's seat.

"No, they understood just fine. But we have so many emergencies that they tune us out after a while."

"Then what did you say to get them to move like that?"

"I threatened to cut off their balls and use them as hood ornaments."

"It occurs to me that you might not be kidding."

"Oh, Trevor was right. You are *fresh*." She reached over and tousled his hair. Mistake. It was silk between her fingers and she had this flash of fantasy about running her fingers through it as he did a few things to her that may or may not have involved melted mockolate.

"Jeez! Look out!"

Cacy's hands snapped back to the wheel, and she swerved to avoid an overcrowded NMOB. "Sorry."

"Four-three-six, kindly tell me what the fuck you're doing up there," Len's voice spat over the wireless. His flashers painted their rear view. Freaking tailgater.

Cacy hit the "Reply" key to open the line. "Breaking in the new guy. He likes it rough."

Eli didn't turn to the window quickly enough to hide his smile.

Len treated them to a truly uninspired string of curses until he heard Cacy snoring over the wireless. He hit the "Mute" key so hard the crack resounded through the cab of their rig.

"Now that we're alone again," Cacy said sweetly, "tell me—did Dec go over canal-site protocol this afternoon?"

She swung the ambulance into the High Street Canal, which was barely wide enough for two AVs shoulder to shoulder. Massive skyscrapers jutted up on either side, rimmed by wide sidewalks and a low wall to keep people from falling into the water. Up ahead, she could already see the accident. This was going to be bad.

"He was very thorough, Lieutenant. Both triage and rules of engagement with third-party threats," Eli said briskly as he leaned forward to peer through the windshield, game face on. Cacy could tell he was already trying to spot the victims.

"Yeah, well, the fire crews are so overstretched these days that they only make it to half the calls. It looks like we might be on our own on this one, so keep your eyes open."

Behind them, Len and two other units made the turn from the Main Canal and motored into the High Street Canal. The flashing lights were reflected in the glass storefronts, but they weren't necessary at the moment. The canal and sidewalks were empty. The city's residents knew what happened after accidents and hadn't stuck around.

Cacy took a moment to survey the scene; there were a few bodies in the water, but many of them had been hurled onto the sidewalk or against the canal wall. The AV must have been going ungodly fast. It was overturned in the canal, surrounded by the demolished NMOB. She cursed under her breath as she reversed the water jets and spun the rig around in the last intersection before they reached the wreckage. The canal walls seemed high and close as she backed up the rig to the edge of the accident site, listening closely for the chiming alert that would tell her if she was about to hit organic material in the canal. Like a body.

Len's voice came over the wireless again. "Just heard from Fire and Police. They're on their way but advised it will be a minimum of ten till they're on scene. You want to sit in the rig and wait?"

"With all due respect, Len—hell, no," yelled Cacy, pulling to a stop and reaching for her gloves and goggles.

Eli clearly shared her attitude. He had already zipped on his gloves, strapped on his goggles, and climbed into the back, where he grabbed a med kit and swung open the rear doors.

"Don't forget your tranq gun!" she called, getting on her own gear and jumping into the back. The scent of gasoline burned her throat as she watched Eli vault over the wall and onto the sidewalk, headed straight for a shapeless, bleeding heap hanging halfway into the canal. He made a lightning-fast assessment of vitals, then wordlessly pulled a black tag from the thigh pocket of his uniform and slapped it on the victim's back. Their first fatality.

Eli shot to his feet and ran to the next body.

Reassured he knew how to triage, Cacy sprinted past him, scanning back and forth for threats. Her tranq gun rattled at her waist as she hopped over a severed leg to land beside its owner, a gray-lipped middle-aged woman. The lady's eyes went wide with terror at the sight of Cacy, and she shook her head frantically. Her hands fluttered helplessly at her sides, weakly trying to ward her off.

"Shhh," Cacy said softly. She tapped the insignia on the front of her uniform. "Medic. Hospital. You're safe."

The woman's hands went still. She nodded.

Cacy did a quick vital scan, checked the woman's airway, pinched an oxygen minipump on her nose, and slapped an automatch skin-bandage over the stump of her left leg.

"Three black, two orange, four reds." Len's voice echoed from across the canal. He and the other two units had docked on the other side, where the ass end of the overturned amphibious SUV jutted up onto the sidewalk.

Cacy yanked an insta-cold limbsack from her med kit, carefully bagged her patient's left leg, and left it lying next to the woman. She pulled a red tag from her pocket and stuck it to the woman's chest. She could survive if she got to the med center soon. "Got a red here," Cacy called.

"Me too," Eli said calmly as he injected self-perpetuating saline gel into a male victim with a nasty head wound. Eli lifted his head and met Cacy's eyes, then nodded to his left. A young woman lay on her side, crumpled against the door of a shuttered storefront, her arms and legs canted in the wrong directions. "Another red?"

Cacy scrambled over to the girl and checked her vitals. She was still alive, but only barely. Cacy did some quick mental calculations. They had seven reds in all—victims needing immediate and intensive medical care. And two oranges—those who needed care but weren't as critical. But they only had four rigs, which were meant to transport one patient at a time, two if they were desperate. And this area was too dangerous to leave anyone behind.

Time for the Ferry brand of triage.

Cacy kept her back to Eli and unsnapped the Scope from the platinum chain around her neck. Her thumb brushed over the disk's surface, opening a tiny window to the Veil. She held it to her eye like a monocle and looked at the now-shadowy-and-transparent girl at her feet. Across the girl's chest lay a jagged cross within a glowing orange circle.

Theta, symbol of death.

The girl was Marked. She would not survive. Cacy wondered if Trevor had done it, or if another Ker was responsible.

She kept the Scope concealed in her hand as she turned around. Eli had retrieved the body board from the rig and was hunched over his patient, carefully positioning a head and neck brace in preparation to transport. Cacy put the Scope to her eye and scanned his patient's body. No Mark.

The woman who'd lost her leg was also un-Marked. That made two reds on this side of the canal who would live—but if they didn't get immediate and intensive medical care, the rest of their lives might not be worth living. On Len's side, there was a sea of glowing orange Thetas. At least three Marked bodies lay on the sidewalk, but they were already tagged black. One more floated at the edge of the canal, his clothes snagged on the splintered wreckage of the NMOB. And from the shattered window of the SUV hung its driver, his fat, ringed fingers dangling in the water. The driver's Theta mark covered his entire back, as if the Ker who did it wanted to make double sure the guy was doomed.

Two of Len's red patients were Marked, too, which meant they would die no matter what the paramedics did for them, no matter how good the prognosis seemed. Len was wasting good chemical defib solution on one of them.

"Len," Cacy shouted, pointing to the only un-Marked victims on his side, an elderly woman and a little boy. "Prioritize those two. Take your patients and get going."

Len had known Cacy too long to question her. Everybody knew the Ferrys were never wrong in their triage; they just didn't know why.

Eli twisted around in time to see her snap the Scope back to the chain. He glanced over at the dying girl crumpled against the storefront and gave Cacy a questioning look. He was probably wondering why she was standing there with her metaphorical dick in her hand while an unattended patient lay mere feet away.

She had just opened her mouth to give him some stupid explanation when a deafening crack sounded in her ears. Fiery agony shot all the way through her shoulder. She hit the sidewalk facefirst, gasping, already reaching for her tranq gun with her good hand. Warning shouts from the other side of the canal told her what she already knew.

The canal pirates had arrived.

Cacy flipped onto her back and swung the tranq gun up, pulling the trigger and nailing the bastard who'd shot her before he could do it again. He grunted and pitched over onto the sidewalk, a dart protruding from his neck. Panting with the pain, she rolled to her side and pushed herself to her hands and knees, batting the pirate's improvised bolt gun out of his reach, wishing her code of ethics allowed her to use it on him. She raised her head and looked around.

Where had she left Eli? Had they already gotten him? Had he remembered to grab his tranq gun from the cab?

The body of a pirate landed heavily next to her. Drool flew from his slack mouth, landing in viscous strands on the cement. A dart was sticking out of his cheek.

Eli *had* remembered his tranq gun.

He stood protectively over his patient, his green eyes practically glowing with rage. An empty tranq gun lay at his feet, as did another darted pirate. Eli held the body board in front of him like a shield. Two other pirates had hemmed him in and backed him up against the canal wall, swinging at him with blood-stained rebar machetes. And a third pirate was behind Eli, scalpel in hand, clinging to a ladder propped against the side of the canal wall.

Cacy's chest went tight. She got to her feet, hissing at the pain in her shoulder. This was like a replay of what had happened to her partner a few weeks ago. But her warning shout froze in her throat as Eli kicked the scalpel wielder in the face without even looking behind him. A second pirate slashed at his head, and Eli ducked, then landed a devastating kick to the guy's knee while he used the body board to block the third pirate's machete swing.

Cacy aimed her tranq gun and was squeezing the trigger when a hard body plowed into her, knocking her to the sidewalk again. Her chin bounced off the ground, sending lightning bolts of pain zinging through her head, turning her vision to white static.

A pirate sat on her back and wound his steely fingers through her hair. He yanked her head up and peered down at her. His eyes lit up when he saw the pretty piece of jewelry around her neck.

He examined her face next. "Healthy," he said cheerfully, clearly thinking of the profit he'd make from harvesting her organs.

"Fucking pirate," she spat as blood dripped from her chin. He leaned close to fumble for the zipper of her uniform. She gagged at the stench of his breath. Her fingers scrabbled and stretched for her tranq gun, which lay a few feet away, taunting her. She desperately hoped Len and the others were all right on the other side of the canal. She could only pray Eli had taken out that last—

The weight at her back lifted and she kissed the sidewalk again, then jerked her head around to see if another threat was headed her way. Her attacker lay on the ground, his nose steadily gushing blood. Eli shook out his right hand in a casual sort of way, like he punched canal pirates all the time. Then he scooped Cacy's tranq gun from the sidewalk and shot the pirate in the neck without the slightest hint of hesitation.

CHAPTER FIVE

Eli dropped the gun and turned the pirate on his side so he didn't choke on his own blood. Something deep inside him rumbled, the pressure building, the lid ready to blow. He wanted to kill this bastard so badly that it was almost painful to hold back. But he'd promised himself he was done with that part of his life. He forced his eyes away from the pirate and retrieved his med kit from beside the head-wound patient. The accident victim needed to get to the hospital as soon as possible, but Eli wasn't going anywhere without Cacy, who lay facedown on the sidewalk.

He reached her just as she flopped onto her back, wincing in pain, her eyelids fluttering. Her chin and mouth were bleeding, which ratcheted up his desire to punish the canal pirate to a frightening level.

Eli sank to his knees and got behind her, allowing her to lean against him as he fished in his kit. The flash of a siren brought his head up. Len and the others were pulling out with their patients. Len was leaning out his window, trying to see Cacy. Eli's arms tightened around her. He nodded at Len. *I've got her. You can go.* The night shift supervisor glared back but fired up his water jets and sped toward the hospital with sirens wailing.

Eli gently probed the delicate line of Cacy's jaw and nose. Nothing was obviously broken. She blinked furiously as he shone his biolight into her eyes. "Stop it," she said. "I just need a minute and I'll be fine."

"Pupils equal and round, reactive to light," he commented, determined to stay focused. Before she could protest, he pushed her mouth open and pressed an autostaunch patch to the cut inside her cheek.

"Sorry," he said when he saw the pain in her eyes. He stroked the backs of his gloved fingers down the side of her face, unable to help himself.

"I'm fine," she said, struggling to get up. Her left arm was hanging limp at her side. Their uniforms were bulletproof, but that didn't mean getting hit by ballistic hardware didn't hurt like hell. She would have an enormous bruise.

Eli got to his feet and held his hand out. Cacy took it, allowing him to pull her up. She swayed in place but steadied herself immediately. Her eyes slid over the unconscious bodies of the five canal pirates he'd taken out.

Her full lips curled slightly at the corners. "The desert must have been a rougher place than I thought."

"I'll tell you about it sometime." Eli didn't even try to hide his own relieved smile at the sight of her striding forward to check on one of the accident victims. She was tough.

Cacy touched the neck of the teenage girl who'd been thrown against the storefront. She waved her cardiac wand over the girl's chest and did not seem surprised when it remained silent. "Black," she said quietly, turning back to him.

He met her gaze steadily. "I'll get the stretchers for the others. We can transport two in a pinch, right?"

Cacy nodded. They worked together to get the two patients aboard their rig. Cacy grimly black-tagged the girl. With any luck, the morgue team would arrive before another pirate gang descended to cut her up. Dec had told him the demand was so high for transplants that even freshly dead organs fetched a pretty price in the backstreet clinics.

Cacy drove to Central Medical Center while Eli kept their passengers alive in the back. They rushed their human cargo into the emergency department, handing them off to the harried hospital staff, then drove back to the EMS station, just a block away. Cacy pulled the ambulance into its spot and hunched over the steering wheel for a few seconds. Her shoulders rose as she took a deep breath. Then she sat up quickly, opened the door, and got out.

Eli jumped out of the passenger side and circled the ambulance, blocking her path to the supply cabinet. "I'll clean out the back and refill supplies. You need a break."

She bowed her head and nodded. Her shiny black hair fell over her face, and her fingers rose to touch her pendant. Eli's heart did a funny little kick. She was still giving him whiplash. Tough one moment, vulnerable the next.

He pulled off his glove and leaned close, brushing his thumb lightly along the corner of her mouth. "Is your mouth still bleeding? Do you want me to take another look?"

She shook her head. "I'm fine. I heal quickly. But you're right about me needing a break." She raised her eyes to his, and he felt like he might drown in them. "I won't be long. Thanks, Eli."

It was the first time she'd said his name, and God, it sounded good. "Take your time, Cacy."

She rewarded him with a flicker of a smile before her eyes hooded. His hand fell from her face as she backed away and walked slowly toward the locker room. He watched her go, fighting the urge to scoop her up and carry her.

"Hey, new boy. How'd you like your first taste of EMS Boston-style?" Len swaggered toward him, holding a bottle of Powderkleen and a decon kit. He wore a tight, menacing smile on his face.

"Well, it wasn't boring." Eli walked to the back of the rig and pulled open the rear doors.

Len followed him. "How's my girl?"

Eli bit back the words *she's* not *yours* and looked over his shoulder, toward the locker room. "She got a little beat up, but she seems all right."

Len set the cleaning supplies on the floor of the ambulance. "Cacy and her last partner were attacked by a horde of canal pirates a few weeks ago. An accident a lot like this one. Those bastards have spliced into our feed, and they always show up, looking for easy organ donors."

The memory of that canal pirate trying to rip off Cacy's uniform flashed in Eli's mind. That thug had looked like he had more on his mind than just impromptu surgery. Eli's throat ached as he swallowed hard. "Was she hurt?"

"Nah, not seriously. But her candy-assed partner lost his kidneys and liver before she could do anything about it." Len stared at him with a fierce expression. "You better keep your eyes open, boy. She doesn't need to go through that again."

Eli stared back. "I can take care of myself." *And her, if she needs it.*

Len nodded. "You did all right." He stepped up close to Eli and growled in his ear. "But if you touch her again like you did just now, I'll get you transferred so fucking fast your head will spin."

Every muscle in Eli's body went tight. He'd just fought off canal pirates and saved two patients' lives. Yeah, sure, he'd taken a little extra interest in whether his partner was okay, but *he* hadn't been the one yapping about prying her legs open a few hours ago. Len probably did have the power to get him transferred to a far-flung station, though. It took every ounce of willpower Eli had, but he simply nodded stiffly.

Len took a few steps back, looking smug. "Glad we have an understanding. Now, get on with your decon. You never know when we'll get another call."

Eli gripped the Powderkleen bottle as Len strutted off toward the locker room, but his mind was already drifting back to Cacy. How long had she been at this job? Why had she chosen it over a sweet corporate position at Daddy's company? Why would she risk her life like this if she didn't have to? What made her so tough? She'd probably been raised in luxury, not the hardscrabble existence he and Galena had endured when they were growing up.

He washed down the inside of his rig, grateful for the meticulous, familiar activity. Cacy obviously wasn't interested in Len. The guy was a domineering asshole, despite his excellent taste in mockolate. So what kind of guy *was* Cacy interested in? Eli ground his teeth as he tossed a bunch of enzymatic cleaning cloths into a biohazard bag. He shouldn't even be wondering about that. Not with Len breathing down his neck, not with Cacy being his boss's sister.

But as he tried to chase the memory of her seductive smile from his head, he realized his new job was going to be harder than he'd thought—for the last reason he would have worried about.

CHAPTER SIX

Cacy gave her face a quick wipe as she stared at her battered reflection in the bathroom mirror. Lovely. At least the bruise on her chin would only last an hour or so. She unzipped her uniform and turned around to check out her shoulder. Ugh. *That* bruise, which blossomed like a hideous indigo flower from her shoulder blade, would take a bit longer to heal—maybe the rest of her shift. Its purple tendrils fanned out across her skin, intertwining with the black raven's wings tattooed across her back. The Mark of the Ferry. It kept her safe from the vengeful Kere, some of whom would happily Mark a Ferry for death just so they didn't have to share the commission. The Ferry Mark was one of many conditions set by the ancient treaty between the Keepers of the Afterlife, and Moros, Lord of the Kere.

Cacy winced as she pulled her uniform back on. Her limbs were heavy and aching with fatigue. She wanted to lie down in the back of her rig and get her hour of daily sleep. Or maybe let Eli examine her again. The thought of her new, understated, ass-kicking partner brought a smile to her lips. Maybe he'd let her watch him eat another piece of mockolate. God, the look on his face . . . She wondered what else might make him look like that, because what she wouldn't do to see that expression again. It might even be worth breaking her man-fast, for a few minutes at least. Or maybe several hours.

She shook her head. A fling would be bad, even if it was just meaningless fun. She'd have to work with the guy afterward.

Plus, she had other things to attend to right now. Sometimes duty sucked.

The Scope was frigid in her fingers as she swiped her thumb over its surface. She pulled its edges wide, lowered the ring over her head, and stepped into the Veil. Her feet sank into the gel-like floor as she stepped outside the boundaries of the ring and compacted it into a disk. Then she stretched it open again, creating another portal. This one would take her to the souls she needed to guide.

The skyscrapers were the first thing she saw as her head emerged through the intra-Veil portal, and she stepped out onto the sidewalk next to the High Street Canal. The normally colorful, sweltering atmosphere was dry and frigid in the Veil. The canal was filled with dull-gray boats and AVs, and the sidewalks were packed with shadowy, transparent people, all bustling and scraping and praying and sweating. The Veil muted their voices and scents, the quiet wrapping around Cacy like a layer of ice as they walked through her like ghosts, oblivious to her presence. Oblivious to the nine souls sitting patiently on the low canal wall, shivering silently in the cold.

"Hi, folks," Cacy said. "I'm here to show you where to go." She repeated her statement in Spanish and Mandarin. As a Ferry, she could speak whatever language was understood by the souls she was guiding—but only when she was in their presence. At first it had been a strange experience, hearing those foreign words roll off her tongue, but she had long since grown used to it. And since she mostly guided souls in the Chinatown emergency response zone, she'd actually managed to pick up some conversational Mandarin over the years.

The people in front of her all nodded in response to her re–assurances. Newly departed souls were often oddly numb and passive—until they found out where they were going to end up for eternity. After that, things sometimes got interesting. She flipped her Scope, watching its tiny center as she walked along the line and passed each soul to get a preview of where she'd be sending each one. She always opened portals for the Heaven-bound first, because if she started with the Hell-cursed, everyone else would panic and scatter, scared they'd be next. And then she would have to hunt them down before they became rabid.

The last thing they needed in the Veil was more Shades.

And the last thing Cacy needed tonight was drama. Her shoulder hurt like a bitch, and she wanted to get back to Eli.

Just to make sure he had cleaned up the rig properly, of course.

Fortunately, only one of the souls was headed for Hell—the portly driver of the amphibious SUV, who had recklessly plowed into a boat of refugees. Unsurprising.

One by one, she flipped her Scope and opened a portal to Heaven for each of the souls. Their gasps of pleasure brought a smile to her face. It always made her think of her mother and what she might be doing. Cacy pictured her sitting in a sprawling meadow of flowers, the kind her mother had always had her father import from Siberia, lacy white blossoms with buttery yellow centers.

When it was her turn, the girl whose body had been thrown against the storefront sat unbroken in front of Cacy, looking nervous.

Cacy smiled at her. "You're going to love it there."

"Have you been?" the girl asked in a wispy little voice.

"No. Hopefully someday, though." Heaven was no guarantee, even for Ferrys.

The girl bit her lip. "Okay then." She held still while Cacy lowered the ring of the Scope over her head, letting Heaven swallow her whole. As soon as she was gone, Cacy caught the heavy gold coin that flew out of the Scope's center.

"Hey," called a deep voice behind her. Trevor had come to collect his share of the commission.

"I'm not quite finished yet," Cacy said, eyeing the SUV driver, who was looking eagerly at her. She couldn't tell if it was because he thought he was going to Heaven or if he wanted the gold in her hand. Probably the latter.

Trevor's footfalls behind her were nearly silent, but the heat from his body chased away the chill of the Veil and told her he was close. "You got a little beat up," he commented.

"No shit." She didn't bother to turn around, too busy marshaling her strength for what she had to do next. "Give me a sec."

The warmth disappeared as Trevor gave her space. He probably knew from the flat sound of her voice that she wasn't about to open a window to Heaven.

"Are you ready, sir?" she asked the driver. She held the Scope behind her back, flipped its Afterlife side—the one engraved with a set of scales—faceup, and ran her thumb over the insignia. She grabbed the edges carefully to keep from getting burned by the intense heat now emanating from its center.

"I guess. Are they gonna have clothes there? I'd love to take a shower and get cleaned up." He plucked at his bloody tracksuit and leered at her. "But then again, if there's anybody there who looks like you, maybe I don't want clothes after all."

"Oh, they have *exactly* what you need there." Cacy yanked the Scope wide, swung it over her head, and looped it over the driver before he could say anything else. His scream cut short as she drew the fiery ring all the way down to his feet with a whoosh of acrid smoke. "Whoa. Stinky." Coughing, Cacy stood up and dodged the red-hot coin as it leaped out of the center of the portal. It landed several feet away, cooled instantly on the frigid sidewalk, and she trudged over to retrieve it.

"Your break is probably almost up, and I'll bet your new partner is waiting for you." There was an impatient edge to Trevor's voice, like he had somewhere to be.

Cacy turned around. He was leaning against the very storefront where the girl's crumpled body had landed. His eyes glowed red as he watched Cacy come near. He held out his hand. She dropped four gold coins onto his palm and handed him the fifth. "Split that for me?"

He grinned, baring daggerlike fangs. The Kere looked like normal people in the real world, but in the Veil, there was no mistaking them for human. She was glad he'd kept his mouth closed while the souls were still here.

"No problem, Ferry." He put the coin between his teeth and snapped them shut, slicing it down the middle. He handed one half to Cacy, its edges scalloped with the curves of his fangs.

"Thanks. Are you done for the night?"

He shook his head.

"You said nine! Didn't you do all these?" She waved her hand at the wall where the souls had been sitting a minute ago.

"I got a last-minute assignment," he replied, staring at her with those glowing crimson eyes. She couldn't tell how he felt about it. "Go back, Cace. I'll see you tomorrow."

He turned in place and disappeared.

"At least you could have done me the courtesy of telling me if it was in my response zone!" she shouted at the space where he'd been.

The gold coins were heavy in her pocket as she flipped her Scope again and opened an intra-Veil portal back to the EMS station bathroom. She walked through the jellified closed door of an empty stall and then stepped through the final portal—back into the colorful, warm, messy real world. She sagged against the now-solid wall of the stall.

"—here, Lieutenant?" called Eli, his voice echoing off the tiles.

"I'll be right there," she answered, flushing the toilet.

The bathroom door clicked shut again. *Good boy.* She emerged from the stall and carted her gold into the locker room, where she stashed it in her bag and set the laser snaptrap. The guys were unlikely to go snooping, but if they ever did . . . well. Fingers could be easily reattached with a little vascular glue.

Eli was in the back of their now-sparkling rig when she returned to the garage. He hopped off the rear deck and met her halfway. "I was getting worried that you'd collapsed or something. You hit your head pretty hard, Cacy."

His concerned expression reminded her how beat-up she looked. She tried to give him a reassuring smile. "Good thing my skull is so thick."

"I'll remember th—"

The wireless alert beeped. *"Assault at Tremont and Boylston. One police unit on scene; additional units requested but not available. Casualties confirmed. Four EMS units requested. Caution advised."*

Cacy turned to the videowall in the alcove. A lone police cruiser was pulled up against the curb, wedged in front of a limo with its doors hanging open. Thick red smears covered one of the windows. One figure lay in the street and three others lay on the sidewalk. Another was slumped against the side of a building a few feet away. She ran up to the wall screen and circled her fingers around the area where the victims lay, then punched the center to enlarge it.

And screamed.

One of them was her father.

CHAPTER SEVEN

L en," Cacy shrieked as she sprinted toward the rig. "Three other units. Now!"

Eli ran after her, wondering what on earth had freaked her out like that.

She threw open the door of the cab and jumped in, immediately punching the ignition and opening the ambulance garage doors. The sirens were already on. It looked like she was about to take off without him.

He jerked the passenger door open and leaped into the seat as the rig started to roll forward.

"One of the victims," Cacy choked out, "is my father." She hit the accelerator and lurched into the street, nearly winging a bus.

"Shit. Do you want me to drive?"

Her silence was the only answer he needed. He scooted into the back and started to prepare, thoughts racing. Her father. The CEO. Or former CEO. What the hell had happened? He seemed like the type to travel with an entourage, including a full security detail. But there had been only one vehicle at the scene, plus a police car.

He flicked his eyes up to the front. Cacy was gripping the steering wheel so hard it looked like her bones would split through her skin. Behind them, the shrill sirens of the other units screamed out. As the rig streaked down Kneeland and circled a sprawling shantytown, Eli tried to remember details from the video feed. There had been a lot of blood at the scene, and the limo had been pockmarked with shrapnel.

The wireless came to life. "EMS units are advised that the scene is not yet under control. Please hold your positions."

"Shut the hell up," Cacy muttered as she ran a red light.

Eli leaned forward and touched her shoulder. "Maybe we should take one of the other patients." A personal connection to the patient didn't usually lead to clear thinking. He knew that from experience.

She shrugged him off. Eli wasn't surprised, remembering her face as she'd watched her father give his retirement speech. She'd looked so protective, like it was her job to keep him safe. Whether that was true or not, this had to be killing her.

Eli retreated into the back again and double-checked the contents of his med kit, determined not to let her down.

Cacy screeched to a stop less than half a block away from the intersection where the assault had gone down. Eli peered through the rear window and held his arm out to bar her way as she came barreling through. She hit it with a huff and stumbled back. He turned to her, hating that he had to keep her from her father for even a few seconds. But her own safety was more important. To him, at least. "With all due respect, Lieutenant, this is a hot scene, and I'd rather neither of us got shot."

She flipped open the cabinet to her right, pulled out a tranq gun, and aimed it at him. "With all due respect, *Sergeant*, get out of my fucking way. If we don't hurry, the pirates are going to drag them into the Common."

He held his hands up. "I'm on your side, Cacy. I want to get out there, too. But we can't help your dad if we're perforated." Still holding one hand up, he reached out with the other and popped open the rear door. He picked up his med kit and nodded at her hands, which were still clutching the tranq gun with white-knuckled determination. "At least get your gloves on."

With quick, impatient tugs, she zipped on her gloves and grabbed her kit. Together, they pulled a stretcher out of the back. Eli used his size advantage to push her behind him and was relieved when she didn't fight him. He rolled the stretcher in front of them as they ducked low next to a row of junked cars. The street was eerily quiet. Eli reached back and pressed Cacy against an amphibious sports car with busted-out windows and dried blood on the seats.

"Wait a second." He raised his head and took in the scene. "The cop's gone, but his car's still there. I don't see anyone else, though. Maybe he chased the attacker off?"

Cacy peeked around Eli's shoulder. Her gaze focused on a lean man hunched against the stamped-concrete wall of the building at the corner. Her father. Patrick Ferry. He was still wearing the dark suit he'd worn to the press conference. His head was bowed, and his gray-streaked hair hung over his face. Eli felt nothing but relief as he watched the man's chest expand with a shuddering breath. It wasn't too late.

On the street in front of them lay a man with a gaping wound to his head, his gray matter scattered on the asphalt. A definite black-tag. A few feet away lay a woman with glazed eyes set in a deathly pale face. She was alive, but in shock. Red. Two other men were crumpled on the ground in front of Cacy's father, both red-tag status. One of them was bleeding profusely from a neck wound, while the other was curled into a ball, moaning softly. Possible gut wound. They'd probably been trying to protect their boss. It looked like all of them had been shot, but Eli couldn't figure out how it had gone down. Why had they left the safety of their bulletproof limo?

Footsteps thunked along the pavement behind them, accompanied by the squeak of ungreased stretcher wheels; Len and the others were on their way. Cacy twisted out of Eli's grasp and was at her father's side in less than a second. Eli took a moment to check the vitals of the other victims before handing them over to Len and the other crews. He looked up in time to watch Cacy wave a shaking cardiac wand over her father's chest. It beeped.

"Daddy. I'm here."

Patrick Ferry moaned. The fingers of his left hand, lying limp at his side, flexed. "My . . . darling," he rasped. His head rose briefly from his chest but then bobbed back down, too heavy for his weakened body.

"Tachycardic," she whispered as Eli squatted down next to her.

"The others have been shot. Is he bleeding? Did you assess for trauma?"

"I . . . I don't know," she said, her eyes filling with tears.

Eli's hands closed gently around her shoulders. "Cacy, move aside and let me help him."

She scrambled backward, and Eli got to work. Patrick Ferry's lips were gray with shock. The streetlight above them reflected off the blood that soaked his dark suit. *Shit.* He yanked the man's shirt open to reveal a puckered hole in the lower-right quadrant of his chest.

"Cacy, hand me an autostaunch." Eli held his hand out as he leaned around to check for an exit wound. "Wait. No. Make it two."

Cacy let out a low sob and began to dig in the med kit as Eli maneuvered his patient onto his back. "Shears too, please."

Cacy handed him the shears and bandages. Eli cut the perfectly tailored suit away from her father's arms and chest, wishing to God she didn't have to witness this. The soaked fabric soon lay in a pile next to them. He hoped the autostaunches would do their job and keep Patrick Ferry from bleeding out before they could get him to the hospital.

Eli glanced up and saw Len and the two other teams carting victims away. He could tell by the urgency of the paramedics' movements that the patients were at serious risk if they didn't get to the CMC fast enough. He focused on prepping Cacy's father for the same journey. He clipped an oxygen minipump to the man's nose and a blood-pressure ring to his neck.

The cardiac wand chirped. A disruption in the patient's heart rhythm. Patrick Ferry's eyelids fluttered. He turned his head toward his daughter. His hands shifted restlessly at his side, and his eyes went wide. "No," he mouthed.

Eli whipped around to see Cacy staring back at her father, her full lips open in a silent scream. Her eyes were wild. She clutched her round pendant in her hand. Tears coursing down her beautiful face, she looked down at the engraved metal disk as if it had betrayed her.

Eli's hand shot out, and his fingers closed around her wrist. He yanked her close and spoke right into her face. "It's going to be all right, Cacy. I'm going to take care of him. But you've got to help me."

He released her arm. "Get over here and help me get him on the stretcher." He kept his voice firm, trying to snap her out of panic mode. Cacy obeyed him, and together they lifted her father onto the stretcher.

Eli looked down at Cacy as they jogged toward the rig. She was steering the stretcher while he injected chemical defib into her father's chest. She looked shaky and pale, like she'd seen a ghost. "You're going to drive, all right? I'm going in the back with your dad."

She nodded. They loaded her father into the ambulance. Eli grabbed the suction device and got to work, but when he looked up again, Cacy was still standing in front of the open rear doors, staring at her father. She touched her tearstained cheek and looked blankly at her fingertips, like she hadn't known she was crying.

"Cacy, dammit, get up there and drive!" Eli reached forward and slammed the rear doors in her face, praying she would understand.

The driver's side door opened, and Cacy climbed into the cab. A second later, they lurched into motion.

Eli's heart pounded as he worked. He'd never wanted to save a patient more than he wanted to save this one. Anything to chase that pain out of Cacy's eyes. It shouldn't have mattered as much as it did—he'd only just met her—but he didn't have time to analyze his feelings.

Patrick's breathing was rapid and shallow, his heart rate fluttering and unsteady. Eli turned up the oxygen on the minipump and grabbed an oropharyngeal airway, in case his patient lost consciousness.

Suddenly, Patrick's eyes opened and fixed on Eli with a burning intensity. His lips began to move. Eli tilted his head and bent close, trying to catch the whispered, faltering words. He understood only one, but it was enough to send his own heart rate sky-high. ". . . Galena."

Eli leaned away and stared at Patrick, who looked back at him like he knew exactly who Eli was. Like he could see straight through him.

Why had Patrick Ferry just said Eli's sister's name?

Cacy slammed on the brakes and cursed at the traffic. Eli caught himself against the ambulance bench and broke eye contact with Patrick. The cardiac wand screeched.

Cacy's father had gone into cardiac arrest.

From the front seat, Eli heard a broken, hitching sob. And all he could think was *No. No. I will not let this happen.*

His hands flew over the equipment; he inserted the airway in less than five seconds, injected self-perpetuating saline gel, positioned the autocompression device to keep the heart going, suctioned beneath the autostaunch, and checked blood-pressure-ring readings. They weren't good.

His eyes flicked up and caught Cacy's in the rearview mirror. "Eyes on the road," he barked. "I've got this."

But he didn't.

Cacy pulled up to the front of the hospital and cut the sirens just as the piercing scream of the cardiac wand fell silent.

CHAPTER EIGHT

By the time Cacy crawled into the back of the ambulance, Eli was already shouting for hospital staff and wrenching her father's stretcher off the rear deck of the rig. He plowed through the double doors of the emergency department, hauling the stretcher by himself instead of waiting for the nurses to help. Cacy's father lay still and pale atop it, the autocompressor doing its futile work.

Cacy already knew it was too late. She'd seen it with her own eyes, through the lens of her Scope. Her father had been Marked.

She climbed off the back of the ambulance, thinking vaguely that she should follow, that she should be doing *something* for her father. But her legs couldn't hold her up, and she collapsed to the ground.

"Cacy!" Eli jogged back through the emergency department doors. He gathered her in his arms and climbed into the back of the ambulance, clutching her to his chest. "Did you hit your head when you fell?" he asked.

"No," she whispered. He tried to lay her on the bench, already reaching for his biolight. It was clear he was planning to examine her, like she was one of his patients. But that wasn't what she needed. What she needed was something to hold on to, something to keep her from falling, from tumbling over the edge of the world.

Her fingers curled around the thick muscles of his shoulders, hanging on tight. She buried her head in the crook of his neck. His fingers nudged under her chin and tipped her face up to his. He gave her a long, searching look. Then he sat on the bench and wrapped her in his arms.

"I told them you were his daughter. They said they'd give us a status update as soon as they could."

She nodded.

"I'm so sorry, Cacy." His voice was rough. "There's still a chance—"

"No," she choked. "Don't, Eli. He was dead when we pulled into the ambulance bay. You know that."

He didn't argue. He might be optimistic, but he obviously wasn't stupid. Instead, he held her tighter. The warm, clean scent of him filled her up, keeping the darkness at bay for the moment. She couldn't push him away. She needed this feeling of safety too much.

"I feel like I failed you," he said.

She shook her head. "You were amazing, and you did all you could." She didn't want him to feel bad. Her father had been doomed before they even arrived on the scene. A black void of sorrow opened its mouth wide in front of her, threatening to swallow her whole. She hid her face against Eli's body, not wanting him to see her fall apart.

Eli sighed and laid his large palm against her cheek, his fingers burrowing in her hair. His other arm held her against him, like he wasn't going to let anything happen to her. She was surprised how good it felt. They were practically strangers. And she planned for it to stay that way, in all the ways that counted. But for now . . . she focused on the deep rise and fall of Eli's chest, the whoosh of air from his lungs, the pulse in his neck. She counted the beats, pinning her thoughts to each number so she wouldn't picture the doctors with her father, their fruitless attempts to jolt his silent heart back into motion.

They sat like that for a long time—quiet, alone and yet together. Eli held perfectly still for her, like he knew one move would remind her of where she was, of what they were waiting for. She pressed her palm over his chest and took refuge in the solid strength of him. Maybe, if she could stay there forever, the darkness wouldn't find her. Maybe she could hold off the moment when her father's death became real just a little longer—

The swooshing sound of an automatic door opening stole her breath. Eli's arms became steel around her. His heart pounded beneath her hand. Hers felt like it had stopped.

"Ms. Ferry?" asked the doctor as he strode forward to look into the back of the ambulance. He was a wispy little fellow, and Cacy had delivered many a patient into his competent care. She knew the message he'd come to deliver by the well-practiced mournful tone of his voice.

"Dr. Umber," she said, proud of the evenness of her voice as she pulled away from Eli.

"I'm sorry," the doctor said. "We were unable to restart your father's heart."

Cacy nodded, sparks and spots crowding her vision. The only thing keeping her from hurtling into a black abyss of helpless sorrow was Eli. "Can I see him?" she asked, fighting to keep her fragile control from breaking.

The doctor looked hesitant. "He hasn't been cleaned up—"

"I can handle it." She hopped off the back of the rig, feeling surprisingly steady, then looked down and realized she was holding Eli's hand in a white-knuckled grip.

Dr. Umber stepped back and gestured toward the hospital doors. "The forensic team is on its way, but I don't see the harm in a few minutes."

They walked down the stark-white hall of the emergency department and into the operating theater where they'd worked on her father. Eli didn't try to get his hand back, and she didn't let it go.

Her father lay on a table, covered up to his neck with a crimson-stained sheet. His face was white and bloodless. His eyes were closed. His cheeks were sunken. Cacy stared, trying to reconcile this image with the understanding she'd had of him. Immortal. Timeless. Strong.

"Do you need me to call Dec?" Eli asked. "Give you some time alone?"

Dec would already know; Len would have called him. But she nodded and finally released Eli's hand. She had to get her father's Scope before the forensic team arrived. She had to get ready to help her brothers and sister deal with the enormous fallout. And she had to get some distance from Eli. She had to make sure she didn't start to need him.

"Yeah. Thanks. For everything."

He gave her shoulder a quick squeeze and headed out.

When the door to the operating theater slipped closed behind him, Cacy reached out and pulled the sheet away from her father's neck.

His Scope was gone.

"Motherfuckers," she whispered as she pulled the sheet back up. Someone had already taken it. She reached into his pocket and pulled out his phone. The forensic techs would be pissed if anything was disturbed, but Cacy didn't care. She needed to find out why this had happened. She flipped open the scanning port in her phone and aimed the needlelike beam at the matching port in her father's phone. It took all her concentration to begin the transfer and keep her hands steady until the upload was complete, and then she slipped her father's phone back into his pocket. She looked down at her phone's display, hoping to find out who he'd talked to and met with recently, anything that would give her clues. But it was password-protected. She'd have to give it to Rylan and see if he could figure it out.

She started toward the door, but it flew open just as she reached it.

Dec strode toward the table, and Cacy followed him, pointing to their father's neck. "His Scope's gone."

Dec's face didn't change. "Of course it is, Cacy. He gave it up this afternoon."

It felt like she'd been punched in the gut, and she wrapped her arms around herself to stay upright. *Of course.* She hadn't been thinking straight at all. Their father had retired this afternoon, and he'd given his Scope, the symbol and source of his power, to Rylan. She suddenly knew that if they turned over their father's body, the raven tattoo would be gone.

"I called Rylan and Aislin," Dec said quietly. "They're on their way. And I met Eli in the hall. I sent him back to the station."

He put his arm around her shoulders and pulled her into a hug, never taking his eyes off their father's face. "We'll do this together."

If he hadn't been holding on to her, Cacy would have fallen down. "I don't know if I can, Dec."

"Trust me—you'll regret it forever if you don't." Dec was speaking from experience. He hadn't come into the Veil to wish their mother good-bye all those years ago.

Dec reached out and lifted the sheet. He swore when he saw the wound. Cacy stared at the hole, the size of a bottle cap, with ragged edges. Something inside her stirred, huge and dark. This was no way to treat a great man. "Dec, the Kere violated the treaty."

Dec sighed. "If he formally gave up his Scope, he gave up his immortality. He was fair game."

She wrenched herself away from him. "That's bullshit. How is this *fair*?"

He backed away from her and crossed his arms over his chest. "Life isn't fair, Cacy, and neither is death. Stop acting like a child."

Angry tears burned in her eyes. "Stop acting like a heartless asshole."

"Cut it out," snapped a voice filled with arctic chill. Awesome. Aislin had arrived.

Cacy whipped around and glared at her older half-sister, who stood, lean and elegant, in the entrance to the room. She wore a light-blue silk suit that perfectly matched her eyes. Her hair was coiled into a neat bun at the base of her neck, not a strand out of place. Her expression was absolutely composed, as usual. "Declan is right, and this is not the time to fight. Three of our Psychopomps employees are in critical condition, and one is dead. Father would want us to fulfill our duties to him and them, not engage in childish name-calling."

Aislin gave Cacy a look that said, *You disappoint me*, which was also as usual, then approached their father's bedside and pulled the sheet back up to his chin. Cacy blinked. She must have imagined the tremble in her sister's hands, because when Aislin turned around, she was steady as an iceberg.

Her eyes focused on Cacy's neck. "Where's your Scope?"

Cacy's hand flew to the chain. "I . . . Shit. I must have dropped it on scene."

Aislin looked at her as if she were the silliest, most idiotic creature on the planet. And for once, Cacy agreed with her. "Once we've escorted Father, you will retrieve it," Aislin said in a flinty voice. "And pray it's still there."

Cacy didn't have the energy to defend herself. Her fingers were curled around the chain where her Scope had hung since the moment she turned sixteen and accepted her birthright. Without it, she felt naked. Helpless.

"Father!" Rylan clutched at his ebony hair as he burst through the door and ran to their father's side. His eyes were full of tears. "No, no, *no*," he said through clenched teeth.

Cacy touched his arm. Apart from her, Rylan had always been closest to their father. "I'm sorry, Ry."

He pivoted and pulled her against his chest so tightly she could barely breathe. "They said you were there, Cace. Are you all right?"

"I wasn't there when it happened. I took the call, though, and brought him here."

He looked down at her, rage burning in his dark eyes. "We need to talk, then. I want to go over everything you saw."

"Rylan, with all due respect, that is ridiculous." Aislin didn't flinch when Rylan rounded on her, his fists clenched. "Going after the human culprit is police business."

"I didn't ask for your counsel." Rylan stood tall, his arm around Cacy's shoulders, glaring at Aislin.

"Do as you wish," she replied icily. "*After* we take care of our father."

Rylan's fingers coiled painfully around Cacy's arm, but she didn't move. He stared at Aislin like he wanted to kill her. Or fire her. Cacy was in favor of both at the moment. Rylan didn't need to be reminded of his duty to their father, and Aislin was a bitch for implying he'd ever shirk his responsibility.

"Come on, guys," said Dec quietly. He stood next to their father's head, still staring at his gaunt face. "Let's just go. We can fight later."

Rylan nodded at Dec and let go of Cacy. He unsnapped the ornate Scope of the Charon from the chain around his neck and ran his thumb over the raven etched on its surface. Jaw set and eyes steely, he pulled the ring wide. He held it as they climbed into the Veil one by one, silent and grim, preparing to say good-bye to their father for the last time.

CHAPTER NINE

Eli parked the ambulance in its spot at the EMS station. He sat in the driver's seat and stared through the windshield, seeing nothing but Cacy's face. His chest felt hollow. With a sigh, he reached into his pocket and pulled out his phone. It wasn't even six in the morning, an hour before shift change, but he needed to hear his sister's voice right now.

She picked up on the second ring. "Eli?"

"Hey," he said softly. "I thought I'd be waking you up."

She chuckled. "Oh, no, I never got to bed. I got back from the lab an hour or so ago, and I've been doing some unpacking. Campus security is great, if you were wondering. They drove me door-to-door."

He smiled. She knew how much he worried about her. "Glad to hear it."

After a few moments of silence, Galena said, "What's up?"

Eli leaned his head back against the seat. "It's been a long night. I've got this new partner—"

"I hope there's no hazing at *this* EMS. Is he nice?" Now she was the one who sounded worried.

"*She* is all right. A good paramedic."

"And?"

"And I think tonight might have been the worst night of her life." Eli closed his eyes, trying to erase the image of Cacy's grief-stricken face. But he couldn't shake it, so he told Galena everything that had happened.

When he was finished, she said, "You feel guilty. Even though you did the best you could."

"I want to make it better for her, but I wouldn't even know where to start. I don't even know her. Not yet." He was surprised to hear himself emphasize that final word.

"And despite that, you want to be there for her." Galena didn't question it, didn't make him feel stupid for his feelings. He loved that about her. And she was right. He couldn't stop reliving those moments when Cacy had been in his arms. Despite the horrible circumstances, he'd felt like he'd been right where he needed to be. But he wanted to do more.

"I wish I could rewind this entire night and . . . I don't know. Be better. Faster. Smarter." It wasn't the first time he'd felt that way.

Galena made a sympathetic noise. "Eli, you take too much responsibility for things beyond your control. Sometimes stuff simply . . . happens. What matters is what you do now. I'm sure she'll appreciate you just being there." Her voice faded to a whisper. "I know I did."

"I will *always* be there for you." He rubbed at the ache in his chest. "Hey, you ever heard of the Ferrys?" *And do you know why your name was Patrick Ferry's last word?*

She laughed at the abrupt subject change. "No, is that some paramedic superstition around here?"

"Ha ha. I'm not talking pixie dust." He spelled the name. "They're an important family in town, and they own this company called Psychopomps Incorporated. Ever heard of it?"

"Uh, no. Should I have?"

Eli relaxed a little. He had probably been hearing things. After all, it had been loud in the back of the ambulance and Patrick

Ferry's voice had been so weak. Plus, Boston was a big place. Even if Cacy's father had said "Galena," he probably hadn't been talking about *his* Galena. "No. No worries. I was just wondering."

A bang on his window jerked Eli's head forward. Len peered up at him, waving a bottle of Powderkleen.

"Hey, G, I have to go." Eli raised one finger at Len. "My new supervisor's got some issues." One of them being Cacy, but he didn't have time to get into that. "Love you, sis. Thanks for the advice."

Eli clicked off his phone and opened the ambulance door. Len shoved the bottle in his face. "You've got some work to do, Sergeant. Your rig's a dump."

Eli took the bottle and leveled a somber look at the night shift supervisor. "Cacy's dad didn't make it."

Len gave him a curt nod. "That lets Cace off the hook, but not you."

"It wasn't an excuse," growled Eli. "I just thought, since you claim to care about her, that you'd want to know."

Len's eyes narrowed. "Oh, I already knew. And so do the others. They know you're the medic who let Patrick Ferry die."

Eli's stomach dropped. He hadn't thought of it that way. On his first night on the job, he'd lost one of the most prominent men in Boston. The Chief's father. Would Cacy feel the same way? Sure, in the shock right after it happened, she'd told him he'd done everything he could, but would she feel differently tomorrow? Would the Chief?

Eli avoided the stares of his new colleagues as he cleaned out the rig. He scrubbed until his hands were raw, wishing it were enough to bring Patrick Ferry back. As he worked, he overheard a few guys talking about the attack, speculating about what had happened. Apparently, they hadn't caught the person who did it. The police officer had chased the assailant into Boston Common, the wild, overgrown swampland at the edge of their emergency response zone. It was pretty much a lawless hideout for canal pirates, so the officer, alone and without backup, had given up before going too deep.

The killer was still on the loose. No big surprise, but Eli had hoped the Boston police would be more effective than law enforcement where he came from. Apparently, they were as understaffed and underequipped here as everywhere else.

Eli used an entire bottle of Powderkleen on the rig. By the time he finished, his nose and throat felt burned by the chemical scent. Len had walked by a few times to tell him what a crap job he was doing. Eli had put his head down and gritted his teeth to avoid succumbing to the temptation to turn Len into a bleeding pile of human wreckage on the garage floor.

He finally punched out after what felt like the longest shift of his entire life. His fellow paramedics were already shunning him, his supervisor had it in for him, and for all he knew, the Chief might blame Eli for his father's death. What a shitty start to his new life in the East.

As tired as he was, though, he didn't head straight home. At the hospital, he'd noticed Cacy's pendant was no longer around her neck. It must have fallen off in the chaos of getting her father to the ambulance. No matter what she thought of him, she'd probably be glad to have it back.

He caught a bus to Boston Common. A few people got off at the same stop, and all of them scattered quickly, jogging away as if someone might leap out and drag them into the swamp. Probably a realistic fear. Eli scanned the edge of the Common. A low fence had been built around it, as if that would keep its inhabitants inside.

In her excitement about moving to this city, Galena had read him an entire book of Boston history on the bus ride from Pittsburgh. Apparently, every year, the water crept a little closer to the center of town, and the city tried to keep up by building more canals and reinforcing its buildings. Unfortunately, it had let some of the "less desirable" neighborhoods flood, so the residents had ended up homeless and unprotected. Many of them lived in the nearby shantytown that used to be the city's theater district.

Eli turned in place at the corner of Tremont and Boylston. The sulfurous stench from the swamp was stronger now that the sun was rising, along with the temperature. A trickle of sweat snaked down his back. People were starting to emerge onto the streets, their eyes darting anxiously back and forth, their footsteps hurried. The road was potholed and fissured. The building Patrick Ferry had fallen against appeared to be abandoned. His blood was still pooled on the sidewalk and smeared across the stamped-concrete wall. This was clearly a terrible part of town, a world away from the gated, guarded Back Bay a few blocks away. Galena had told him that the city had even built a bypass around the Common to enable people to avoid it. So why had Cacy's father come here?

A police cruiser was parked at the corner, and the area was loosely taped off. Eli waved his paramedic badge at the officer eyeing him from inside the vehicle. "I'm looking for something my partner dropped when we responded to the call. Is it all right if I poke around?"

The officer nodded at him. "Just stay outside the tape."

Eli searched the ground, praying someone hadn't snatched up the shiny piece of jewelry. It had looked valuable, and it was obviously really important to Cacy. Her fingers often drifted up to touch the pendant, and the Chief wore one exactly like it. Maybe it was a family heirloom or something. Eli squatted down at the edge of the road.

There, amid the shattered glass of the amphibious sports car, he saw it. Eli reached out to retrieve it but drew his fingers back with a gasp as a bolt of sensation zapped across the palm of his hand, so cold it almost burned him. He stretched his arm out again, ready for the feeling this time. The medallion was small but much heavier than he'd expected it to be. He plucked it from the glass and closed his hand around its frigid surface, relieved to have found it.

While the bus carried him to the place he would be calling home, Cacy's pendant continued to send icy spikes of pain across his palm. He would have expected it to be warm by now, clutched as it was against his skin. Instead, it seemed to pulse with cold. Bizarre. He shoved it into his pocket.

He got off at a stop next to Harvard and followed the map in his phone until he reached the low, square apartment building. He punched in the security code Galena had texted him and pulled open the door. The apartment was spare and basic, and probably would remain that way. Neither of them had the time or inclination to decorate. He padded silently around the small space; Galena was probably grabbing a few hours of sleep before heading back to her lab.

Eli tossed his rucksack to the floor in the empty bedroom. Galena had taped a sign to the door that said *Eli's Room, Keep Out!* in childish handwriting, like they were still kids and this was their clubhouse. He walked over to examine the barred windows. They were sealed shut. Damn. It was stifling in here, and he could use some fresh air.

He threw himself onto the bed, which sagged under his weight. Galena had made it up for him, and he smiled at her thoughtfulness. He should be thinking about sleep, since he had another shift tonight and he'd have to be sharp. But the cold fire of Cacy's pendant was almost literally burning a hole in his pocket. He pulled it from his pants and examined it. A set of scales was etched on its surface in amazing detail. He turned it over to see a fierce-eyed bird, wings spread as if in midflight. Engraved below the bird's feet were three words, but Eli couldn't quite make them out. He held the disk close to his face and brushed his thumb over the letters.

A low yelp flew from him as an icy pulse shot through his fingers and frigid shocks traveled up his arm. He squinted, trying to make sense of what he was seeing. The pendant was now a ring with a transparent, swirling center. Heart racing, he clutched the edges to hold it up to the light, but it expanded in his grasp until he held a large hoop in his hands.

"What the hell?" he whispered. His skin tingled as the room began to swim in front of his eyes; he realized he was holding his breath. His chest expanded as he drew in a lungful of the cool air flowing from the hoop. He peered through its center and could still see his room, but everything looked different—gray and dull. And . . . oddly familiar, like something from a dream, like a memory he couldn't quite touch. His trembling fingertips penetrated the skin of the swirling bubble, sending a shiver throughout his body. He reached forward until the cold engulfed his entire arm, turning his skin pale, and he suddenly needed to see what lay on the other side of the ring. Already knowing this might be the stupidest thing he'd ever done—but unable to fight the bone-deep curiosity and his certainty that he'd seen all of this before—Eli stepped through the ring.

CHAPTER TEN

Cacy and her siblings stood in the dead chill of the Veil, watching as Rylan compressed his Scope and pulled it wide again. She didn't know where her father's soul would be waiting, but the Scope always took them where they needed to go. It always knew.

That knowledge didn't save her from the wave of pure confusion that sloshed over her as she stepped through the intra-Veil portal. Dec's eyes went wide, echoing her surprise. She had expected to arrive at their Back Bay brownstone. Or their father's posh office at Psychopomps Inc., where he'd pretty much lived for the last fifteen years. Or that meadow in Siberia where he'd scattered her mother's ashes.

She had not expected to arrive in front of a boxy apartment building on a dingy street. "Where the fuck is this?" she asked.

"Cambridge, my salty-mouthed darling." Her father walked toward her, arms outstretched. "Thank you for coming." His embrace was strong, which brought her tears to the surface all over again. "And thank you for trying to save me," he said in her ear. "Please tell your partner he did an admirable job as well. He has my . . . gratitude."

"Daddy," she choked. "How—?"

"Father," said Rylan, moving forward and clapping a hand on his shoulder. "Tell us what happened. We have to catch whoever did this to you!"

Their father released Cacy from his embrace and gave Rylan a firm hug. "Forgive me, son. Hashing out the details of the human crime that led to my death is not how I want to spend my final moments with my children."

He pulled back and took Rylan's face in his hands. "You are the Charon now. You will make the hard choices from now on." His pale, burning eyes bored into Rylan's. He drew him close again, clutching his eldest son's head against his shoulder as if Rylan were a little boy and not the most powerful Ferry in the world.

He took a few moments to embrace each of his children in turn, whispering secret, final words into their ears.

He saved Cacy for last. "Cacia," he said as he held her tight. "You want vengeance, I know. But I need you to do something else for me. Protecting the future is more important than righting the wrongs of the past."

"Aren't they the same thing?" she whispered fiercely.

"Not today." His voice was so quiet she could barely hear him.

He let her go and turned to Rylan. "Show me my future, Charon."

Rylan's face blanched. So did Dec's. Aislin was already so freaking pale it was hard to tell for sure, but she still looked utterly calm, like she was in an administrative meeting instead of saying good-bye to her father forever.

Cacy stared at the Scope in her brother's trembling hand. She knew what he was thinking. What if they were about to send their father to Hell?

"Children," chuckled their father. "You have so little faith in me?" His expression became serious. "Whatever the outcome, you do it, and you do it fast."

Rylan drew himself up straight. He flipped the Scope in his palm so the scales were facing up and brushed his thumb over its surface. Cacy held her breath . . . and nearly fell to the ground with relief as the center of the Scope glimmered white, shooting a beam of crystal-bright light into the sky. Dec looked at the ground and blinked. A tear hit his boot and slid to the soft cement beneath his feet.

Rylan smiled as he pulled the portal to Heaven wide. A huge weight had just been removed from his shoulders, Cacy could tell.

"Say hi to Mommy for me," she whispered, squinting into the blinding light, trying to make out the sparkling, swirling images within.

Patrick Ferry smiled as his eyes fell on her and then rested briefly on each of her siblings. "I love you all, and I will miss you, but you do not have to worry about whether I am happy."

He stepped into the portal. Rylan pulled it shut behind him, but not before catching the shining gold coin that came flying from its center. He snapped his Scope back onto its chain, then held the gold coin up and slowly turned in place, his smile morphing into a grimace.

"Here it is, you bastard!" he roared. "Come and get your commission!"

"Rylan," Aislin said sharply. "Do you really—?"

"Shut up!" he snapped as he held the coin high. "Come on, the Kere are usually so cutthroat. Moros or one of his lieutenants come calling within hours if a Ferry tries to stiff them on the commission. They only care about lining their pockets. So where is this guy? I want to see what kind of coward would Mark our father. I want to see—"

"Control yourself and *think*," Aislin snapped. "If the Ker is a coward as you suggest, why would he show himself now? Be logical. This likely proves it was an unauthorized Marking, but we won't learn anything else tonight."

He and Aislin glared at each other. Fire and ice.

Breathing hard, his eyes full of rage and sorrow, he tossed the coin at her feet. "You can keep this then," he said, his voice cracking.

Aislin plucked her Scope from the platinum chain at her neck, opened it wide, and stepped through. The abandoned coin glinted dully on the sidewalk where she'd been.

As soon as her sister disappeared, Cacy dropped to the curb and pulled her knees to her chest. She waited for the desolate emptiness of grief to swallow her, but it didn't. She knew her parents were together now, and as fucked-up as the circumstances were, that knowledge would allow her to go on.

"What now?" asked Dec. His boots were next to her legs. One of them was still streaked with the narrow path of his tear. His hand rested gently on her head, and she leaned against him and closed her eyes.

"I apologize for calling you an asshole," she said quietly.

"Already forgiven. I shouldn't have called you a child."

"It's okay. You know that."

"It's not okay," said Rylan. "None of this is *okay*. I'm going back. I'm going to find out what the hell happened."

Remembering her father's final advice to her, Cacy said, "Father didn't want—"

"Father is gone, little sister," Rylan said, grasping her arm and wrenching her to her feet as Dec took a step back, looking uneasy. "I'm the Charon now, and I will see justice done."

Staring into Rylan's dark eyes, seeing the anger and hurt and determination there, she totally understood. If their father, who had led their family for the last century, could be slaughtered so easily, what did that mean for Rylan? What did that mean for the rest of them? He would need to be strong and decisive in the coming days. He would need to confront Moros, the leader of the Kere, and demand an explanation. He would need to reassure all their associates that he was in control of the business. He would need to make sure justice was done on the human side, as well. They were, after all, the wealthiest family in Boston. If he didn't put up a show of strength, who knew what could happen?

It could be open season on Ferrys.

Cacy nodded at Rylan, and he released her arm and stepped back, straightening his suit with brisk movements. "I'd better return to headquarters and get the next steps straight with Aislin. We need to present a united front." He winked at Cacy. "In other words, we'll duke it out and be just fine."

She grinned. "I won't object if you knock a few of her teeth out."

"*Cacy,*" chided Dec. For reasons she would never understand, he'd always gotten along with Aislin.

Rylan stroked Cacy's cheek. "I'll see you soon, all right? We'll get dinner at Lombo's." He flipped his Scope and opened himself a portal.

"That would be nice." She waved at him as he stepped through the glassy bubble and pulled it shut behind him.

Dec held out his hand, and Cacy took it. "Are you going straight home?" he asked as he unsnapped the Scope from his neck.

"I need to go get my Scope. What if someone found it, Dec?" She shivered, her fingers traveling to the delicate chain where the empty setting hung. Although she dreaded going back to the scene of her father's murder, she didn't want to give Rylan anything else to worry about.

"We'll find it. Remember when that canal pirate snatched mine while we were working that building collapse?"

She laughed grimly. Dec had suffered a deep scalpel wound to his neck, but the loss of his Scope was what had upset their father the most. She couldn't imagine how much gold he'd shelled out to get Dec's Scope off the black market.

"I'm going to go look for it. Hopefully it's still there," she said.

Dec squeezed her hand. "Don't go alone. Maybe you could call Trevor."

She clenched her teeth. "No, thanks."

Dec's eyes widened. "Whoa. Did you guys have a falling out?"

"What if he's the one who Marked Father?" It felt weird, saying her fear aloud, but she realized this terrible thought had been rattling in her brain ever since she'd seen the jagged Theta mark on her father's chest.

"No. No way." Dec shook his head and let go of her hand. "He would have warned me. Or he would have refused."

Every once in a while, a Ker did refuse a job—but only at a terrible cost. She'd heard the rumors and stories at family gatherings since she was a little girl: Apart from the fact that refusing to Mark caused the Kere intense physical pain, Moros also punished them severely for their disobedience. They usually lived to tell about it, but they were never quite the same.

Cacy remembered the sound of Trevor's voice as he'd told her he'd gotten a last-minute assignment. She asked Dec, "Are you sure?"

Trevor was Dec's closest friend, but she wasn't sure the Ker would be willing to endure the terrible suffering that came with refusal, even for her brother. At the moment, she wasn't sure she knew Trevor at all.

Dec set his jaw. "Absolutely. Let it go, Cace. It's pointless to try to figure out who did it tonight." He looked away from her, like he was ashamed of his own words.

"I guess that's why *Ry's* the Charon," she said.

Dec nodded without looking up. "Maybe, but—"

The smell of rot hit her a split second before the Shades attacked. A screeching roar split the silence as an oozing gray hand closed around her throat, its eerily strong fingers digging in. Wheezing for breath, Cacy kicked back but made no contact. The Shade knocked her to the ground and pressed her face into the gelatinous cement. Cacy reached back, buried her fingers in the Shade's rags, and rolled over. It shrieked and yanked at her hair, trying to claw her eyes with its ragged fingernails. She elbowed it in the side and twisted to punch it in the face.

Out of the corner of her eye, she could see Dec fighting off two other Shades as they wrestled for the Scope in his hand. She lunged for them, but the Shade beneath her grabbed her leg and clamped its teeth on to her calf. It couldn't break through the surface of her uniform, but it held her in a punishing vise grip all the same.

Cacy jumped and brought her other leg down in the center of the Shade's chest. Her foot penetrated its rib cage and sank in, but the Shade didn't seem to care that she'd just stomped on its long-silent heart. It released its toothy grip on her calf and grabbed her belt, jerking her down to her knees. Before she could lean back, the Shade grabbed her neck and tore, blazing an agonizing trail of fire along her throat.

She gave a wet cough as her blood poured onto the Shade's face. It shoved her aside, uprooting her foot from its chest and twisting her ankle in the process. It rose to its feet and held up its prize—her broken platinum chain—in front of its rotted-out eyes. But then its horrible grin opened wide to become a roar of rage.

It didn't turn to attack her again, though.

All it wanted was a Scope, and she didn't have one.

Cacy lay on the ground, panting, pressing her hand over the gushing wound in her neck, watching helplessly as the Shade joined the other two fighting Dec. She tried to scream but couldn't.

Dec shouted in pain. Then all three Shades shrieked and took off running.

"Dammit!" Dec took two steps after them, then paused and turned to Cacy. "I'll come back, I swear. They got my Scope."

He took off after the Shades, legs and arms pumping hard. In her mind, Cacy ran with him, just as desperate and determined.

Myths about zombies had a basis in reality. Dec had to get his Scope back or the Shades would open a portal into the real world.

But Cacy wasn't running with him. She couldn't help her brother. She could barely help herself. Chest heaving, she dragged herself across the sidewalk to the stoop in front of the apartment building where her father had awaited his fate. She rolled onto her back and stared at the clear black sky, wondering how long it would be before her brother returned. A hard chill of fear coursed through her. She needed to get back through the Veil, back to the real world, so she could heal properly. Wounds inflicted in the Veil festered and stayed open here.

Her eyelids fluttered, and her head felt like it had been packed with gauze and stuffed in an insta-cold limbsack. The frigid air of the Veil sank deep into her bones. She'd often thought about the horrors of being trapped here, in this in-between world, cut off from color and warmth, cut off from other people. No wonder the Shades were rabid and desperate.

Of course, most of them had been destined for Hell, so this place was probably a step up. But it wasn't enough to keep them from wanting to go back to the warm, real world. Which was exactly what Cacy wanted at the moment.

"God, what a shitty night," she rasped.

A distant shriek startled her from a drowsy haze. She tried to scoot to a sitting position but found she was too weak. So she lay within the chill, waiting to discover who would find her first. Her brother, or the Shades.

CHAPTER ELEVEN

Eli walked slowly through his apartment, Cacy's pendant clutched tightly in his hand. After he'd stepped through it, it had shrunk back down to a tiny, unassuming size at the slightest touch. But it wasn't cold anymore; it had grown warm. He concluded he was either going crazy—or Cacy had a lot more going on than an average woman.

He reached for the doorknob of Galena's room, wondering what she would think of the pendant, whether she could make any more sense of it than he had. But the knob just squished in his hand. He turned his back and leaned against the door, only to fall through it and land with a splat on his ass.

Galena's bed was mussed. The sheets formed a lump in the shape of her body, but Eli could barely see her. She looked like a ghost, transparent and hazy. He leaned forward to touch her, but his hand swept right through her.

His teeth began to chatter, and the walls felt as if they were about to cave in on top of him. He had to get out of this place. It made him feel like something awful was about to happen. He needed air. With great squelching steps, Eli ran right through the door of his apartment and down the hall to the entryway. An echoing screech from outside froze him in place. He ducked and peered between the bars over the tiny window in the door to the building. What he saw made his heart turn as cold as the air in this dead, gray world.

Cacy Ferry lay on the front steps in a black puddle. Her throat had been torn open. Her eyes were huge and dark in her starkly pale face. And suddenly, nothing else mattered.

"Cacy!" He plunged through the door and sank to his knees next to her, pulling her slender, shivering body against his chest. "Cacy. Look at me."

She blinked up at him and let out a raspy whimper. "Eli?" He lifted her from the ground as another shriek rent the night. It sounded like it was coming from only a few blocks away. His arms tightened around her.

"Inside," she whispered. "Get inside."

He carried her up the steps, through the door, and back to his apartment. She felt so light and fragile in his arms. His shirt was now soaked with her blood. She wouldn't last long if he couldn't stop the bleeding. All his questions and confusion evaporated in the face of this one essential task: keep Cacy alive.

He had no intention of letting her down again.

Still cradling her in his arms, he slid through the door of his bedroom.

And jerked to a stop.

From between the bars over his sealed bedroom window, a pair of glowing red eyes looked back at him. Eli was struck by a powerful sense of déjà vu.

"What is it?" Cacy asked quietly, her voice a little steadier than it had been just seconds ago. She turned her head toward the window and tensed. "Oh God." Cacy looked even paler now.

The eyes disappeared.

"Was that what I heard shrieking outside?" Eli asked.

Cacy shook her head, and her eyelids fluttered closed. "But it was probably looking for someone who lives in this building."

Eli walked cautiously to his bed and laid her on top of the sheets. He leaned over and peeked out the window, but the streets were empty. "Cacy, I live in this building."

A shadow of anxiety flickered in her eyes. "We . . . have to . . . get back." Her words came in gasping, halting syllables.

He held out her pendant. "Using this?"

Her eyes went wide, full of questions, but she nodded. With trembling fingers, she reached up to take it from him, but she couldn't seem to get a good grip on it. Eli sat down next to her and wrapped his arm around her waist, letting her lean against him. He held the pendant, and she swiped her thumb across its raven etching. It immediately turned to a warm, pulsing ring.

"Help me open it," she whispered.

He did as she asked, pulling the ring wide, opening up a window to the colorful world he'd left a few minutes earlier. She guided the ring over their heads, and he helped her slide it over their legs. Warm, humid air hit his skin. Cacy's head lolled on his shoulder, and he supported it carefully as he laid her down to examine her. She'd finally passed out. He was surprised she'd been able to stay conscious and lucid for so long.

The gaping wound at her pale throat looked slightly smaller than it had a minute ago. And, oddly, it had stopped bleeding. Faint blue veins stood out on her closed eyelids. But she had lost a lot of blood. He grabbed her wrist and felt for her pulse, sagging with relief as he found it, strong and steady, beneath his fingers. He fished his first-aid kit from his rucksack.

Moving quickly, he pressed an autostaunch over her neck wound and pulled her arm into his lap. Her sleeve was too tight for him to push it up and get access to the vein. Wincing, hoping she wouldn't get upset when she found out, he unzipped the front of her uniform and peeled the blood-soaked material from her body. God, she wasn't wearing a bra. All he needed. Focusing attention on her now-bare arm, he injected her with self-perpetuating saline and a vial of plasma to rehydrate her.

Anxious about the wound on her throat, Eli carefully removed the autostaunch bandage to check it once more. He froze. The deep gash was almost completely closed.

"You are *not* a normal woman," he said softly, brushing his fingers across her chin, which now showed no signs of its earlier collision with the pavement. Still shaking his head, he went to the bathroom to get a few enzymatic cloths. He stripped off his bloody shirt and wiped himself down, already looking forward to a shower tonight at the station.

With a few more cloths in his hands, he returned to his bedroom. He spent a few seconds in the doorway, staring at the woman on his bed. Her torso was streaked with blood, and there were smudges of it on her cheeks, but she was still the loveliest thing he'd ever seen. As briskly as he could, he cleaned her off. Her skin was warm and temptingly smooth beneath his hands. Eli ran his fingers over the skin of her shoulder blade, where he'd expected to find a horrible, deep bruise from where she'd been hit with the bolt-bullet, but all he saw was pale, creamy flesh. She had an intricate tattoo of a raven on her back, identical to the raven etched on her pendant. And now he could read the words below the raven's feet: *Fatum Nos Vocat.*

He'd have to ask Cacy what it meant. It was only one of a million questions he had for her, including what the hell kind of world her pendant contained and why it seemed familiar to him. But right now, he was just relieved. She would live.

He reached into his bag and pulled out a T-shirt. He pushed her head through the neck and threaded her arms through the short sleeves, then laid her back on the sheets.

He lowered his head over her nose and smiled as the soft warmth of her exhalations tickled the side of his face. Her breathing was rhythmic and deep. She sighed and turned over, her breasts resting against his arm, her jet-black hair spreading across his pillow, her spicy scent making him dizzy. Her full lips parted. Her cheeks were flushed. She was sleeping. Maybe dreaming. In his bed. Wearing one of his shirts.

He shifted uncomfortably and tugged at the waistband of his pants. Cacy had sent him from emergency triage mode to raging erection in two minutes flat. He got up, stripped down to his boxer briefs, and grabbed a pillow from the bed before allowing himself one final glance at her face. He went out into the living room and collapsed onto the couch, mentally cataloging first-aid supplies in alphabetical order to get his mind off the woman sleeping in his bed. He hadn't gotten past chemical defib solution before his exhaustion got the better of him.

CHAPTER TWELVE

Cacy's eyes flew open. Without moving, she took in her surroundings. Blank walls. A barred window. A thin sheet covering her body. She looked down. She was wearing an oversized T-shirt. She pulled the fabric to her face and inhaled its clean, masculine scent.

Eli.

This was his apartment. He'd cleaned her up and taken care of her. She closed her eyes as the previous evening's events came crashing back. Her father had been standing right outside this building, waiting for his children to find him and guide him to the Afterlife. And a Ker had been peeking in Eli's bedroom window like a freaking Peeping Tom. What was going on? This couldn't be a coincidence, but now it was too late to ask her father what it meant.

Cacy sat up and slid herself out of bed, snatching her Scope from the windowsill. She could get a new chain to replace the one the Shade had torn from her neck, but the Scope itself was irreplaceable. Somehow, Eli had used it last night. That wasn't supposed to be possible for humans who didn't bear the Mark of the Ferry, but there was no other way to explain how he'd found her in the Veil. But thankfully, he had, because if Dec hadn't—

Her cell phone buzzed at her hip. She pulled it from her belt and nearly cried with relief when she saw her brother's number.

"Dec."

"Oh, thank God," Dec gasped into the phone. "Your throat looked so bad."

"It healed up on its own. I'm fine."

"I came back to get you, and you were gone. How did you get back?"

She bit her lip. "I . . . um . . . found my Scope. It was in my pocket the whole time." She hated to lie, but she didn't know what was going on yet, and she didn't want to get Eli into any trouble. It would be much easier if Eli didn't know anything about the Ferrys . . . and if the Ferrys didn't know anything about what he'd done.

Dec was silent for a few moments before saying, "Well. That's great, then. Obviously, I got mine back, but the motherfucking Shades nearly tore my arm clean off, so Trevor's here, making sure it heals up straight." His wound must have been much worse than hers.

"Hey, Cace," Trevor called. "No worries. I'm taking good care of him."

Now it was Cacy's turn to be silent.

"Don't be like that," Dec whispered sharply.

She could hear the strain in her brother's voice, so she relented. "Tell him thanks. Are you really okay?"

"I'll be good as new in a few hours. I'll see you at the station at shift change."

Cacy ran a hand over the now-smooth skin of her neck. "Have you talked about funeral plans with the others?"

Dec cleared his throat. "I talked with Aislin a few minutes ago, to fill her in on the situation. She said she had it under control. She'll . . . um . . . be glad you found your Scope."

"You mean she went on and on about what a screwup I am."

"Cacy . . . I know it must have been hard for you, being the one to find Father. Having to take him to the hospital."

Cacy's cheeks burned. "Eli was the one who took charge. I was useless."

"Yeah, well, you're going to have to look out for Eli tonight. Len called me."

His tone of voice made Cacy's stomach hurt. "What did that little worm do this time?"

"He called to tell me he thought it might be better if I transferred Eli to Mattapan."

Mattapan had the highest paramedic casualty rate of all the EMS stations in the city. "And you're not going to do that," she said.

"No, I'm not. But Len said the guys are talking. They think he's incompetent. That he could have done something more to save Father."

Cacy shot up from the bed, sending the sheets sliding to the floor. "What? You should have seen him last night, Dec! The guy's a fucking badass. He's smart and decisive and—"

Dec chuckled. "I guess you don't mind having a desert-dwelling refugee as a partner after all."

Cacy sank back down. "You should have seen him with Father. He . . . didn't give up. He wouldn't let *me* give up."

"You saw that he was Marked, didn't you? You knew he was going to die."

"Yes," she whispered. "I needed to know."

"Damn, Cacy."

"I'm all right. I just don't want anyone to give Eli shit for this. He did an amazing job, and he deserves better."

"I'm sure it'll all get sorted out," Dec said. She heard him inhale sharply, then Trevor murmuring an apology in the background.

"Go. Focus on getting better. I love you."

"Love you too."

Cacy tucked her phone back into her pocket and looked down at herself. Her bloody uniform hung from her hips. Eli had just taken off the top part, but he'd steered clear of anything below the belt. She smiled. He probably thought she would have been embarrassed if he undressed her all the way. Even though he had an undeniably sexy edge to him, Eli seemed like the wholesome type. She pushed the formfitting fabric down her legs, wondering what he'd been thinking as he undressed her.

"Get a grip," she whispered. "He probably thought you were bleeding to death." She tucked the Scope into the pocket of the T-shirt and frowned as she considered all the things Eli had seen last night. Way too much, actually, and not because he'd practically seen her naked. He'd been in the Veil. He'd seen a Ker, even though he couldn't possibly know what it actually was. He'd witnessed her heal supernaturally fast. He must be utterly freaked-out.

She opened the door to his bedroom and walked into the living room. He lay on the couch, looking pretty unfreaked. He was sound asleep, one arm folded over his face, one hand resting on his chest, which was rising and falling with each slow, deep breath. Cacy tiptoed over to him, her eyes sliding down his chest to the narrow trail of hair that started below his belly button and dipped into the waist of his boxer briefs. *Oh.* Her fingers twitched with temptation. Getting involved with him would be violating her strict no-guys policy, but after what she'd been through in the last twenty-four hours, she needed some serious distraction. And, staring at the generous bulge in his briefs, she was willing to bet he would do the trick.

A door behind her creaked open, and Cacy whirled around so fast she nearly fell backward onto Eli. A tall woman with dark-blonde hair emerged from the bedroom across the hall. "Hi there," the woman said quietly, her eyes dipping to Eli's body and back up to Cacy. "What are you doing in my apartment?"

"I'm . . . um . . . Eli's partner." *And who are you?*

The woman frowned, a thin line creasing the space between her big green eyes. "Oh. Okay. That was fast." She tilted her head. "Then why is he sleeping on the couch? Did you get into a fight already?"

Cacy looked down at Eli's half-naked body and let out a high-pitched giggle before clapping her hand over her mouth. "No, no, his *paramedic* partner. I'm Cacy Ferry."

"Ferry?" The woman's mouth opened, like she was completely at a loss. "Um, I mean, I'm Galena. I'm Eli's sister." She offered her hand.

Cacy shook it as she stared at Galena's face. She had such beautiful, sad eyes, just like Eli's, only dark where his were bright. "Welcome to Boston."

Galena grinned. "I can't tell you how happy we are to be here. Coffee?"

Cacy looked down at Eli again, but he seemed to be out cold. "Sure. Thanks."

Galena padded into the tiny kitchen and pulled a box of coffee pellets from the counter. She dropped one into a cup and pulled a jug of water from the counter. She held it up and shook it back and forth, the water sloshing heavily. "We've got running water from two to four p.m. *every* day. I love this town!" she crowed as she filled the cup then popped it into the microwave.

"So," she said, looking at Cacy through her lashes. "Eli called me early this morning."

Cacy stared at her. "Okay."

Galena fiddled with the bottom of her shirt. "He told me you lost your dad. I'm so sorry. He felt awful about it." She looked like she was about to cry.

"Thanks." There was no way Cacy wanted to talk about it. "Eli did the best he could, and he was really there for me."

"That was all he wanted. He was worried about you."

"Yeah?" Again, Cacy's eyes were drawn to the gorgeous male sleeping on the couch. He'd been the *only* person to comfort her last night. Her brothers had tried, but their grief had been fresh, just like hers. And Eli was solace and distraction wrapped up in one.

When she turned back to Galena, the woman was watching her with a knowing look. Cacy's gaze dropped to the floor. She didn't want to know what Galena saw, and *really* didn't want to know how many women she'd looked at that way. Eli was entirely edible, so of course there had been others. And it was only a matter of time before he started hooking up with women here. And that was fine. Totally fine. Cacy had no claim to him, as long as he showed up to work and did his job.

Galena offered Cacy a cup of steaming coffee. "Eli doesn't date that much these days. He works too hard." Galena put her own cup in the microwave. "And he worries too much. He needs to have some fun."

Cacy took a sip from her cup and tried not to wince at the bitter, stale brew. "I could use some fun myself."

Which sounded pretty dirty, even though she hadn't meant it that way. Her eyes drifted back to Eli's abs, to the thick muscles of his biceps. Well, maybe she had. Just a little.

"Just don't hurt him," Galena said. "Don't hurt my brother. He's been hurt enough."

Cacy tore her eyes away from Eli to look at Galena, somewhat shocked at the woman's sudden, harsh tone. "Galena, I have no intention of doing anything with your brother except working. We're colleagues."

She sounded more like she was trying to convince herself than anyone else, but Galena simply smiled and retrieved her coffee cup from the microwave. "I have to get ready for work. Long day ahead of me."

"What do you do?"

"I spend the day surrounded by disease," Galena said brightly. "Nice meeting you, Cacy. I'm glad we got to talk."

With that, Galena walked into her room and shut the door behind her. Cacy stared at the place where she'd been, replaying what had just happened as she finished her coffee.

A pair of large hands closed over her shoulders, startling her. Coughing and spluttering, she barely managed to set her cup down on the counter without spilling it. She turned around and stared up into a pair of vivid-green eyes.

"Sorry," he said. "And good morning."

"You didn't sleep very long," she said hoarsely, inhaling the heady scent of his bare skin.

One corner of his mouth curled upward. "Neither did you."

"Yeah, but I'm—"

"You're what?" He took a step closer, the warmth of him making her sweat. She turned around to rinse her cup in the sink . . . and remembered they had no running water until later this afternoon. She reached for an enzymatic cloth.

By the time she'd composed herself enough to give him a joking answer, Eli was gone. Cacy had just finished cleaning out her cup when he emerged from his room, wearing jeans and a T-shirt. She felt a flash of disappointment. Eli smiled at her as his eyes did a quick slide down her body. She followed his gaze and was abruptly reminded that she wasn't wearing any pants.

"I'm sure Galena will let you borrow something," he said, brushing past her and reaching into a cardboard box for a chipped mug.

"Thanks. I guess I should get going." *Or stay and let you distract me.*

He set the mug on the counter. "Can we talk first?"

Shit. Cacy took a few steps back. Pants or not, it was tempting to take off running, just to avoid that piercing gaze of his. "Eli, I'm kind of tired . . ." A lie. But a necessary one.

"Please. You have to know how weird last night was." He moved a little closer and reached out. She held her breath as his fingers skimmed over her neck. "You should have died last night. But now it looks like it never happened."

She leaned away from his touch. "Maybe it didn't."

His jaw ridged with tension. "One moment, please." He strode into his bedroom and emerged holding a crumpled mass of bloody sheets and clothes. He dropped them at her feet. "Am I imagining *this*? Do you think I'm stupid?"

His voice was harsh, both with anger and a hint of hurt. Cacy opened her mouth and closed it again. "N-no, of course not. I just—"

"Eli, I'm headed out . . . Oh." Galena stood in the hall, staring with wide eyes at the pile of bloody laundry at Cacy's feet. She cleared her throat and backed up unsteadily.

Eli cursed under his breath and rushed over to her. He wrapped his arms around her, gave her a tight hug, and escorted her past the kitchen, blocking her view of it with his body. As he guided her to the front door, he whispered reassurances Cacy strained to hear.

After kissing Galena on the forehead and telling her to have a good day, Eli stalked back into the kitchen and scooped the clothes and sheets from the floor. "Galena's sensitive," he muttered as he tossed the bundle into his bedroom.

"She's afraid of blood? Isn't she some sort of doctor?"

"She's a researcher. She doesn't work with people—I mean, patients. She works with test tubes and centrifuges and a computer she's named Danny." He stared at the floor for a few seconds, then lifted his eyes to Cacy's and closed the distance between them. "Now. No more distractions. I have some questions."

Cacy's heartbeat kicked into a dangerous little rhythm as he towered over her, and she wasn't sure whether it was her desperation to escape or her body's reaction to being this close to him. She folded her arms over her chest. "I have trouble thinking when I'm not wearing pants."

Eli laughed, a deep, husky sound, and took a few steps back. "I guess we have that in common. I also have trouble thinking when you're not wearing pants."

He retrieved a pair of sweats from Galena's room and tossed them down the hallway. She caught them clumsily and stared at them. Had he just admitted he was attracted to her? *Could* she distract him and avoid his questions? She was well aware he wasn't dumb. But he *was* a man. And . . . Cacy hadn't touched one in three years. With her last boyfriend, she'd been young and naive. She hadn't considered how fragile regular humans were, how easily their hearts could stop beating. She hadn't even contemplated how it would feel if she had to guide his soul—until it happened. But since then, she hadn't been willing to risk getting attached and having to push her love through a door *she* didn't plan to walk through for a long time. She hadn't met someone yet who was worth that risk.

Her fingers balled into fists around the sweatpants as she stared at Eli. This wasn't about attachment. She wouldn't let it be. It was about escape. Pure, mindless escape from things she couldn't face right now.

She let the pants fall from her hands and walked slowly toward him. The friendly smile on his face faltered, and his eyes flickered with uncertainty.

Cacy stood in front of him and slid her hand up under his shirt, over the hard ridges of muscle on his belly and chest. He inhaled but didn't stop her. She watched his pulse beat at his throat and pressed herself close, smiling as the thick length of his cock grew rigid against her.

"Maybe now's not the time for thinking," she murmured.

Eli's fingers slid along her cheek and down her neck, sending shivers to all the right places. He nudged her chin up with his fingers so she was looking at him and lowered his head until their foreheads were touching. He closed his eyes and brushed his thumb across her mouth. Cacy put her arm around his waist and ground slowly against him, shaking with the desire building inside her, feeling his body respond, needing him to give up the fight, needing to feel his bare skin against hers.

Eli let out a slow breath through parted lips. Cacy tilted her head up, craving his kiss, hungry for a taste of him. Instead, he bent down and scooped her from the floor. Cacy wrapped her arms around his neck as he carried her through the living room. She buried her face in the heated skin of his throat, closing her eyes as her heart raced. This wasn't about distracting him. This was about distracting herself. Right now, she didn't want to think. She only wanted to feel. To forget everything else for a while.

Eli lowered her legs to the floor, the warmth of his touch sliding along her calves and thighs before disappearing. Cacy opened her eyes. They weren't in his bedroom. They were at the front door. He took her face in his hands. She flinched at the diamond-hard glint in his eyes.

"I don't know what kind of game this is," he said. "Maybe you're trying to get me fired, or maybe castrated by your brother and the rest of your paramedic buddies. Maybe you think I let my dick do the thinking for me, that I would give up my shot in this city for a fuck." She winced at the harshness of his words and tried to pull away, but he wouldn't let her. Instead, he leaned closer. "Maybe you think you can make me forget what I saw. Or maybe," he said, his tone softening as he stroked her cheek with his thumb, "you're messed up inside by what happened to your father, and you need to think about anything but him. But whatever you're thinking, I know very well this means nothing to you."

She looked away, unable to meet his eyes.

He sighed. "All right. I'm not playing." His arms fell away from her, leaving her cold in the humid air of the apartment. A few seconds later, he pressed the sweatpants into her hands as she stared at the floor. His voice betrayed his exhaustion as he said, "Are you okay to get home by yourself? Can you call yourself a car?"

Cacy shook her head. No way would she call a company car. The driver would almost certainly run squealing to Rylan or Aislin that he'd picked up Cacy, wearing someone else's clothes, in a low-rent part of town. She considered trying to use her Scope to get home, but that required a level of concentration she didn't have right now.

"There's a bus stop right at the curb."

She nodded, focusing her attention on the chipped, peeling paint at the lower corner of the front door. With trembling hands, she yanked the sweatpants on as Eli walked back to the kitchen counter. In her entire life, she'd never felt so ashamed.

He returned to open the door. "Are you going to work tonight?"

"Yeah," she whispered hoarsely.

"Good," he said quietly. "Maybe we can get a fresh start."

She raised her head and looked at him. He gave her a sad smile. Then he took her hand and pressed a bus token into her palm.

"Thanks, Eli. I-I'm sorry."

He nodded, inscrutable. It was too much. Aislin was right. Cacy was a screwup. And today she'd outdone herself. She'd exposed the Ferrys' secrets by losing her Scope, and now she'd hurt someone who had only been kind to her since the moment she'd met him. Cacy turned around and fled without a backward glance.

CHAPTER THIRTEEN

Eli watched Cacy jog down the hall. The front door to the building slammed shut behind her. He strode up the corridor and watched out the narrow window as she sat down on a bench, pulled her knees to her chest, and lowered her forehead to her knees. Her shoulders shook as she hugged her legs. Eli stared at her with clenched fists and a hollow feeling in his gut. But he didn't move.

A few moments later, a municipal bus, its shrapnelproof plating rattling loud enough to wake the neighborhood, pulled up to the curb. Cacy pushed herself to her feet, wiped at her face, and disappeared through its open doors.

Eli returned to his apartment and collapsed onto the couch, his body aching all over. He should be furious at her, but the look on her face had told him she hadn't been trying to hurt him. She hadn't been trying to get him in trouble. She'd just been trying to take something she thought she needed. And, damn, for a minute there, he'd considered giving it to her. The way her lips had brushed the skin of his neck, the way her body had melted against his, the smooth curve of her thighs, how she'd touched him with shaking hands . . . he could have lost himself in her. He almost had. He'd almost thrown her down and taken her right there on the floor.

But there were many things wrong with that idea. Getting fired, for one. Not to mention taking advantage of a woman reeling from the grisly death of her father only hours before.

"Shit." He shouldn't have been that harsh. But he'd been so frustrated, and not just sexually. After everything they'd been through last night, she'd done nothing but evade him. He'd stumbled into another dimension, or whatever it was, with a piece of her jewelry, and he could almost swear he'd been there before. Then he'd found her there, too, and for a few horrible minutes, he'd been sure she was going to die in his arms. Instead, she'd healed miraculously, like nothing he'd ever seen before. She'd obviously been worried about that red-eyed creature peeking in his window, but not enough to tell him what it was. Her avoidance of his questions was maddening. She was hiding something—a big something.

The phone in his pocket buzzed. He pulled it out and looked at the screen. Galena.

Here safely. Will try to be back before you leave. Cacy???

Eli sighed as he typed. *Gone. Sorry if she caught you by surprise.*

Not what I meant. She's pretty.

Eli groaned. *And off-limits.*

She likes you.

Eli stared at those three words. How could she? They'd met on the worst night of her life. And she'd just made herself vulnerable to him and he'd callously sent her out the door with a few cruel words, a bus token, and a borrowed pair of sweats. What a gentleman he was.

He punched at the tiny letter icons on the screen of his phone. *Not anymore.*

Her response brought a reluctant smile to his lips. *6 p.m. You. Me. Darts. I'll kick your ass.*

Unlikely. His fingers slowed as he looked around the room uneasily. *Where's the board?*

They'd packed light for this move, and they'd sent their stuff ahead of them, courtesy of the university, so that it would be waiting for them when they arrived. But Galena had done most of the packing, because Eli worked so many extra shifts.

In the box marked "Essentials." See you at 6.

He tucked the phone back in his pocket, nestled back into the couch cushion, and laid his arm over his eyes. He needed to get some rest or he would be slow at work tonight. And he needed to be fast. Smart. Better than he'd been last night, because now he had something to prove. But as he tried to lull himself to sleep by counting vials of self-perpetuating saline in his head, his thoughts kept wandering in Cacy's direction. What would it be like for her to return to work? Would she be able to hold it together the next time they responded to a violent scene? Would being in the back of the ambulance bring back horrible memories for her? Would she let him in and answer some of his questions, or push him away?

Eli ground his teeth and turned over, laying a pillow over his head. Part of him was looking forward to getting back to work. He'd always loved, even craved, those moments of total focus, when everything dropped away except the patient in front of him. In that place of complete concentration, he didn't have to think of his parents and how he hadn't been there when they died. He didn't have to think of the city crumbling around him. Of Galena, of her pain. Of the blood on his hands. Of *anything* but cardiac rhythm, oxygenation, and respiration. Saving someone else's life had been the best excuse in the world to ignore his own problems. For the last two years, he'd relied on that excuse.

Work was his haven. He'd thought it would be no different here, that by putting his head down and working hard, he could get over uprooting his life in the West and coming to this strange, swampy place.

Now things were probably irreversibly screwed up. The low whispers from last night, the narrow-eyed, suspicious glances . . .

All the other paramedics seemed to think he could have done more for Patrick Ferry. That he could have saved him.

Eli wondered if they were right.

He replayed the call over and over again in his mind, running through every choice he'd made. Had he been too aggressive with the chemical defib? Should he have pushed the saline earlier? Had he moved Patrick too roughly?

"Eli."

Had he missed some sign? The guy had been talking before he coded, and his final word . . . had Eli gotten distracted when Patrick said Galena's name?

"Eli. Wake up."

Eli sat up with a jolt, sending the pillow flying to the floor. Galena stood next to him. She looked worried. "I just got in. You'd probably better get going. We'll have to take a rain check on those darts."

"What?" Eli asked, wiping sleep from his eyes and reaching for his phone. Holy hell, it was five minutes to seven. He was going to be late. "Shit!"

He jumped from the couch and ran to his room, shoved his feet in his boots, and tied the laces with impatient jerks. He grabbed Cacy's bloody uniform and ran for the door, giving Galena a quick kiss on the cheek as he sprinted past her.

The bus ride to Chinatown took forever, and by the time Eli jumped onto the curb, he had convinced himself he'd probably only be there long enough for Dec to fire him and send him right back home. He punched the security code into the keypad and opened the door to the station.

Cacy was standing just inside. Her long hair was pulled up in a ponytail, and she was wearing a fresh uniform. Eli swallowed hard, trying to think of something to say. Without meeting his eyes, she snatched her bloody uniform from his hands and pushed a flat cardboard box at him. He grabbed hold of it to keep it from falling to the floor and watched, speechless, as she spun around and jogged toward the locker room.

Eli stood there for a few seconds, trying to figure out what had just transpired. Then the most amazing scent drifted to his nose. He flipped open the top of the box and peeked inside.

It was full of some sort of pastry. Tubes of fried dough filled with a white cream.

Still trying to figure out what the hell kind of game she was playing now, Eli strode into the locker room. The place was pretty full; he'd arrived only twenty minutes late, and a lot of the first-shift paramedics were still hanging out.

"Eli," Cacy called cheerfully, pushing her way toward him as if she'd only just seen him come in. "You brought us cannoli!"

At the sound of the word "cannoli," Eli was immediately sur-rounded by hungry paramedics. The box was lifted out of his arms. A few people slapped him on the back.

Trevor snatched a fat pastry from the box. "Nice, Eli." He grinned and shoved the entire cannoli into his mouth as everyone else clamored for their own and called out their gratitude between bites.

"Aw! From Mike Junior's! You went all the way to the North End?"

"Dude. Good call."

"Thanks, man. We never get the good stuff."

Eli smiled vaguely as most of the guys thanked him for some-thing he'd had nothing to do with.

Cacy edged up to him, a paper-wrapped cannoli in her hand. "That was really sweet of you, Eli. Thanks for picking up my favor-ite comfort food. It was exactly what I needed tonight." She said it loudly, like she wasn't afraid for others to hear her.

The other paramedics looked at Cacy with care. They stood up straighter when they saw her smile. Their eyes drifted to Eli, and several of them nodded. His cheeks burned as he nodded back.

A small knot of guys in the corner appeared uninterested in the rapidly disappearing pastries. Len was among them. His mud-brown eyes stared hard at Eli.

"Hey," Cacy said, patting Eli's shoulder. His heart sped as his eyes met hers. "How about you change and meet me at the rig?"

Eli opened his mouth to speak, but "Thank you" was the only thing that came out.

She gave him a small smile and took a bite of cannoli, closing her eyes as she savored it. Most of the blood flow to Eli's brain was choked off as he watched her lick cream from her lips. He turned and walked quickly away. He desperately needed a cold shower.

He was standing under a chilling spray, teeth gritted, thoughts racing, when he heard the squeak of boots outside his shower stall.

"If you think you can cover up your incompetence and tardiness with a few cannoli, you're stupider than I thought."

Len. Probably staring at Eli's naked ass at this very second. Eli switched off the water and reached for his towel. He wrapped it tightly around his waist before turning around. "I . . . uh . . . thought it would be nice."

Dressed in the uniform that accentuated his wide, muscular chest and gorilla arms, Len was leaning against the tiled frame of the stall. "Nice won't cut it around here, hick. You actually have to be able to do the job."

Eli raked a hand through his dripping hair. "With all due respect, Captain, you must have seen my record. You know I can do the job."

Len gave him an ugly smile. "What I know is you let a great man die. So you're on thin ice. And if you touch his daughter, you're going to fall through. You get me?"

"I did my best with Mr. Ferry. And Cacy is my partner. I just got here last night, sir. Give me a chance to prove myself."

It took every ounce of patience he had to get those words out. His fists balled at his sides. One quick jab, and Len would be on the floor, his blood flowing down the drain. One second of satisfaction for a whole lot of hassle. Not *quite* worth it.

Len frowned, like Eli's thoughts were written across his forehead. "Prove yourself by showing up on time, ready to work. You'd better be in uniform and at your rig in three minutes." Len pivoted on his heel and walked stiffly away.

Eli rushed to his locker, pulled on his uniform, and raced out to the garage. Cacy was in the back, cataloging supplies. She didn't look up as he climbed in. A cannoli on a paper towel was sitting on the bench next to her.

"I saved one for you," she said. "I thought maybe you'd never tried one."

"You'd be right." His stomach growled loudly as he picked it up. With everything that had happened, he hadn't eaten since last night. "Look, I really appreciate what you did, but . . . uh . . . why did you?"

"It was the least I could do." She was leaning over the stretcher, tucking plastic-wrapped suction catheters into an overhead cabinet.

He stared at her, willing her to look at him, his hunger turning to a sick, queasy feeling as his words from this morning replayed in his head. He'd never felt like such an asshole. "Cacy, I'm sorry. I shouldn't have been harsh—"

"Of course you should have." She turned her back and opened one of the front cabinets. "I crossed the line. And you were right. About some things, at least."

Her voice was brisk. Cool. All business. Like her friendliness in the locker room had been an act. He waited, wondering if she had more to say. Would she tell him which part he'd gotten right? Would she tell him what the hell had happened last night? How she was still alive despite having her throat ripped open? Didn't she owe him some explanation for what he'd seen? Especially the eerily familiar red-eyed *thing* that had been peering through his window?

After a few minutes of silence, it was apparent she wasn't going to tell him anything.

"So . . . how are you doing?" he asked, offering her another opening.

Cacy sat back and pulled a tray of atropine into her lap, counting the vials. With her gaze focused on the tray, she said, "I'm fine." Her eyes flicked up to his. She nodded toward the cannoli. "You're not hungry?"

She looked back down, not waiting for his response.

He didn't want her to think he was turning down her gesture of goodwill, if that was actually what it was, so he took a huge bite of the cannoli in his hand, snapping his teeth through the flaky shell. The sweetness was overwhelming. He finished the whole thing in a few seconds. His stomach still felt hollow.

He watched Cacy, waiting, crumpling the paper towel in his hand, squeezing it tight. She didn't look up or speak to him again. She had completely shut him out. And why shouldn't she? She'd lost her dad, gotten hurt, and reached out to him, albeit in the most achingly dangerous way. And he'd pushed her away. He hadn't been nice about it, either. He'd asked for this. He should be grateful for it. She could have been vengeful and petty. She could have gotten him fired. Easily. She could have doomed him—it was clear that most of the paramedics were loyal to her. She could have destroyed his reputation, his job prospects, his chance at making it here. But instead, she'd saved his ass.

As he stepped off the back of the ambulance and tossed the grease-spotted paper towel in the garbage, Eli tried to be thankful. She'd protected him, covered for him. So why did it make his stomach hurt?

He turned back to the ambulance, where Cacy had pulled out a tablet and was tapping away at its screen. And then he realized what was bothering him about her. As blank as her expression was, as briskly professional as she was acting, her eyes were red. Like she'd spent most of the day crying.

He didn't have more than a moment to dwell on why he cared, though, because the alarm screeched and the videowall lit up. A fire in an apartment complex. Eli ran for the rig, hoping the next few hours would be an adequate distraction. The last thing he needed to think about was how badly he wanted to comfort the Chief's sister.

CHAPTER FOURTEEN

Cacy and Eli rolled a stretcher through the yawning doors of the emergency department. "Full-thickness burns to both hands, forearms, and the left thigh. Partial-thickness burns to the face and thorax. Compound fractures of the right femur and left radius and ulna, secondary to a jump from three stories up," Cacy yelled. A young resident poked his head out from an examination room, cringed, and came jogging toward them, waving a nurse over as well.

As Cacy passed off the arson victim to the hospital staff, Eli went back to the rig. She found him waiting for her in the back, calmly wiping down his uniform with an enzymatic cloth. It was six in the morning. Cacy had never had such a busy night. And it wasn't over yet.

She took a shuddering breath. "Can you take the rig back to the garage? I have to stay here."

Eli was frowning as he tossed the cloth into a biohazard bag. "Are you all right?"

Not really. "I'm fine. I want to go visit the Psychopomps employees who were with my father yesterday night."

"Do you want me to come with you?"

Yes, she did, even though it was the last thing she should want, and the last thing he should be offering. After the way she'd acted yesterday, she was surprised he was willing to spend an extra second with her. And after the way he'd sneaked into her thoughts today, despite all her grief and her family responsibilities, she shouldn't even be contemplating spending an extra second with him.

But . . . she'd been dreading this visit to her father's staff all night. It had produced an undercurrent of anxiety as she went on call after call, a drumbeat of sorrow, a weight of responsibility. She wanted to figure out what had happened to her father, and talking to the people who had been with him when he was attacked seemed like the best place to start.

Looking at them would bring it all back for her, though. As much as she hated to admit it, she didn't want to be alone when that happened.

Eli hopped down from the rear deck and turned back, waiting for her. He tilted his head. "Did I misread you? Do you want to go by yourself?"

She shook her head, completely confused by her intense relief at the thought of Eli at her side—and at his willingness to be there. "No, I appreciate it."

They walked side by side through the crowded lobby of the hospital. Cacy spotted a familiar long-limbed figure lounging next to a spindly old woman shaking with chills and pale as paste. The platinum-haired Ker, looking wickedly handsome and completely relaxed, was looking at the woman fondly, his arm across her seat back.

Probably because she represented a nice portion of his income for the night.

The Ker winked at Cacy as she walked past. She gave him a tight-lipped smile. "Hey, Luke."

Luke loved to kill with disease, which was easy enough since it was so rampant and virulent these days. He specialized in the slow, painful spinning out of a life, and worse, he liked to *watch* as it happened. He reminded Cacy of a spider.

Luke licked his lips. "Maybe I'll see you later?" He looked down at the woman, whose eyelids were fluttering faintly as she slumped in her seat. "In an hour or so?"

Eli was close enough for Cacy to feel him tense, and she wanted to kick Luke for being so careless. "I'm busy," she said through gritted teeth. *Find someone else to ferry your victim, asshole.* "We'll have to catch up some other time. Take care of your *aunt*." She gave the old woman a pointed look.

Luke's eyes flicked up to Eli, and his gaze glittered with curiosity, and maybe a little hunger. "Always do." He patted the un–responsive woman's shoulder. "Catch you later, Ferry."

Cacy nudged Eli toward the elevators, eager to get him away from Luke. But Eli gazed steadily at the Ker for a second before he followed Cacy's lead. As they headed down the main corridor, he asked, "Friend of yours?"

"More of a business associate, really."

"His aunt looked in pretty bad shape."

Cacy sighed. "He'll take care of her."

She hit the button for the top floor as soon as they boarded an elevator. Psychopomps Inc. owned a special unit, a suite of rooms within the hospital devoted to the care of regular human employees and retired Ferrys who had given up their raven marks. There was even one room devoted to obstetrical care. Cacy had been born there.

All three of the employees who had survived the attack were in the unit. The fourth, her father's driver, Chad, had died at the scene. Cacy rubbed her arms, fighting the chill despite her long-sleeved uniform. She glanced at Eli from the corner of her eye. His tanned face had paled a shade or two.

"You okay?"

He blinked, like his thoughts had drifted somewhere else in the last minute or so. "Of course. You?"

She shrugged. "I know all of them pretty well. It hurts to think of them being hurt like this." Debra, her father's personal assistant, had spent hours in surgery and no longer had a spleen and part of her colon. Alex and Peter, her father's bodyguards, were in even worse shape. Alex was still in a coma. He'd lost so much blood that they feared he would be permanently brain-damaged. Peter was going to receive a spinal transplant, which was the only chance he had to walk again. "We're taking good care of them. But they've sacrificed a lot for our family."

Eli leaned back against the elevator wall, watching her carefully. "Have the police talked to them?"

"They won't until Rylan gives the okay."

Eli's brows shot up, and he chuckled softly. "Does Psychopomps own the police force, too?"

Even though the Ferrys' influence was an open secret among the people of Boston, most were too in awe of her family to say that type of thing to her face. Cacy fixed her gaze on the emergency call button on the elevator's control panel. "Just a twenty percent share."

Eli let out a low whistle. "And I'm sure you guys would never dream of abusing that power."

Cacy lifted her chin. "We take care of the people in this city. In more ways than one." She internally kicked herself for saying that last part, but she wanted Eli to understand her—and her family.

Eli opened his mouth to say something, but before he could, the elevator dinged and the doors slid open.

They stepped into the hushed corridor of the Psychopomps unit, complete with its own medical staff and five large rooms, all with state-of-the-art equipment. Cacy approached the nurse at the central desk, very aware of Eli's warm, solid body next to hers. Just knowing he was there gave her the reassurance she needed. "Hey, Helen, I'm here to see my father's staff."

The matronly gray-haired nurse nodded. "Alex is still comatose, Ms. Ferry. Peter just got his morphine and is pretty sleepy. Debra's probably most able to tolerate a visit right now." She pointed toward a room at the end of the hall. "She's in there."

"We won't be long," Cacy assured her.

Eli hung back near the door as Cacy walked in to find Debra staring at the videowall, watching some old movie. "Hey, Deb," Cacy said softly.

Debra turned her head and smiled weakly when she saw Cacy. "Hey," she said in a voice as brittle as an eggshell, "you just missed Aislin."

Cacy stiffened. "Are you up for another visit?"

Debra nodded. "You want to know what happened."

Cacy's cheeks grew hot, and she stared at the knitted blanket folded over Debra's feet.

"It's all right, Cacy. I know this is hard for all of you. It's hard for me, too." Deb laid her head back on the pillow, her wavy brown hair fanning out around her. "I loved your father," she said quietly.

Cacy sat in the chair next to Debra's bed, looking back at Eli for a moment. His gaze was riveted on her, like she was the only thing in the room. It filled her belly with a warm feeling for which she was both grateful and uneasy. She looked away quickly. "I want to know how it could have happened, Deb. That's all. Why were you there?"

Debra shrugged, her thin shoulders rising in sharp angles. She winced and relaxed slowly. "Your father had a meeting in Cambridge, and he wanted to take only one car. We were supposed to take the bypass, but Chad made a wrong turn and ended up taking the long way, out by the Common."

"Was Father upset?"

Debra shook her head. "He was on the phone the whole time. I don't think he even noticed."

Cacy steeled herself for the answer to the next question. She almost didn't want to know. "What happened next? Can you talk about it?"

Debra's face twisted a little. She was trying not to cry. "I didn't even know what was happening, Cacy. It went down so fast. Chad pulled over and opened the window to the backseat. He said we had a flat, and he opened the door and got out. A second later, a guy was shooting into the car and we were all scrambling. I don't think Alex and Peter even had a chance to draw their weapons."

"I'm sorry, Debra. I'm so sorry you got hurt." Cacy offered her hand, and Debra took it and gave a feeble squeeze.

Debra shut her eyes tightly, but tears were leaking from the corners. Cacy stood up and kissed Debra's forehead. "We'll take care of you. You don't have to worry about anything."

"I know. Aislin said the same. I'm grateful to your family, Cacy."

Cacy patted Debra's hand and turned away, a leaden ball of guilt settling into the pit of her stomach. "I'll check in later this week to see how you're doing, all right?"

"Sure."

The visit had the anticipated effect; she missed her father more than ever. She made her way out into the hallway and collapsed against the wall outside, wrapping her arms around her body. Eli sank down next to her, nudging her shoulder with his, letting her know he was there. She didn't move, didn't speak, just soaked up his warmth and let it drive away everything else. Even though it only made the guilt weigh more heavily on her, she stared into Eli's eyes, focusing on their color, that deep green, and how they glinted with what she was sure was concern.

Only for a few seconds, she promised herself. *Then I'll pull myself together and leave him alone.*

"Cacy?"

She jerked her head up to see Rylan striding over from the central desk. She scrambled to her feet, and Eli did the same. Rylan leaned around Cacy and extended his hand, staring with unholy intensity at Eli. "I'm Rylan Ferry," he said. "You are?"

"Eli Margolis. Nice to meet you, sir. I'm Cacy's paramedic partner."

Rylan's eyes widened briefly before he said, "Margolis, huh? And I take it from your accent that you're not from around here?"

"No, sir. Just transferred in from Wilkinsburg."

Rylan released Eli's hand and returned his attention to Cacy. "I didn't expect to see you here."

Cacy tightened her ponytail. "I'm not the only one. Aislin was here, too. I met with Debra. She told me what happened."

When she finished relating the story, Rylan said, "Cacy, I've talked to the police. None of the limo's tires were flat."

A hard chill went through her. "Then why would Chad stop in that neighborhood?"

"Maybe because someone paid him to do it." He glanced over at Eli. "Would you excuse us for a minute, Eli? Cace and I need to discuss some family business."

Cacy cringed at Rylan's dismissive tone. It was one of the reasons Cacy had taken the paramedic job instead of working at Psychopomps. She hadn't wanted to lose her ability to talk to people who didn't have as much money as her family did.

Eli didn't look offended. He nodded at Rylan before looking at her. "You want me to wait?"

She shouldn't ask it of him. "Would you?"

He walked over to the lounge area and settled himself onto the couch. She turned to Rylan. "Now, what do you need to tell me?"

CHAPTER FIFTEEN

Eli stared at the muted videowall in the lounge, seeing nothing but black spots. He'd been fighting to stay upright and calm ever since they'd arrived. He hated hospitals. Everything about them. They smelled of hopelessness and pain. He knew it was ironic, considering how many of his working hours he spent elbow deep in other people's blood. But out in the field, it was action, decision, movement. Sitting in the hospital felt like being at a grave. Somber, silent, mourning for what had happened. He'd spent three weeks in the hospital with Galena after the attack, and when they'd left, he swore he'd never set foot in another.

And yet, here he was.

All because of Cacy. The vulnerable slope of her shoulders, the sheen of unshed tears in her eyes. She hadn't wanted to come, either, but she had clearly felt like she needed to. And he wasn't okay with making her do this alone.

From the corner of his eye, Eli watched Cacy with her brother, who towered over her. He appeared to be giving her orders, which made Eli even more tense. Rylan looked to be in his midthirties, and was obviously used to being in charge, used to being waited on. He had the kind of commanding attitude Eli would have expected from someone with that kind of money and power. But Cacy didn't act that way at all. She acted normal. Like she wasn't too good for anyone, like she was up for anything.

At least, that was how she'd seemed in the hours he'd known her before her father died. She'd been quiet tonight as they went on call after call. Totally professional, totally focused. You'd never guess what she'd been through in the previous twenty-four hours, and it was like that weird encounter between them at his apartment had never happened.

He should have been happy about that.

"I'm ready when you are," she said as she walked up to him. "Sorry about that."

He stood up. "No problem. Are you finished here?"

Her eyes darted up to his, and she wrapped her arms around her middle. "Yeah."

He tried not to look too relieved. "Cool. You hungry?" He almost cringed as the words crossed his lips. Did he really want to get more entangled in her world? Did he really want to spend more time with her, seeing as every moment spent in her presence made him want a little more from her?

For the briefest moment, her mouth curved into a tiny smile, but then she bit her lip. "I should be getting home."

Eli folded his arms over his chest, over the stupid ache there, thinking that he and Cacy were a fine pair, staring at each other with their arms wrapped protectively around their bodies, as closed off as two people could be. "Me too, I guess."

As they rode down the elevator together, another thought occurred to Eli. "Hey, do the police have the video captures from that intersection during the assault? They must have everything on camera."

Cacy shook her head. "That was part of what Rylan just told me. After a little pressure, the police admitted that fourteen minutes of video has been deleted from their databases. It was an inside job." Her face blanched. "That's not public information—please don't tell anyone."

Eli moved to stand in front of her, making sure she was looking at him. "You can trust me, Cacy."

For a moment, she gazed into his eyes, and he wanted to reach out to her, to comfort and reassure her, feel the softness of her skin, and help her shoulder the weight of her sadness. The impulse was so strong his hands actually rose from his sides. But before he could touch her, she turned away, looking like she'd rather be anywhere in the world but standing next to him. As soon as the elevator doors opened, she was talking fast and walking faster. "Thanks, Eli. I shouldn't have asked you. Thanks again. I'll take the rig. You can head home. See you tonight. Bye!"

She hopped into the rig, slammed the door, and drove away without waiting to hear his response. Eli stood in the ambulance bay, rubbing the back of his neck, his mouth half-open, thinking maybe it was good she didn't give him a chance to speak, because he had no idea what to say.

CHAPTER SIXTEEN

Cacy smoothed the skirt of her black silk dress and shifted in her chair, wishing she was at home in her PJs rather than crammed into a law office with all her relatives. She sat up straight, focusing on the antique books behind the polished wooden desk and reading the spines one by one. This was how it had been for the last few days. No matter where she was, she counted, cataloged, kept her hands and thoughts busy. It was the only way she'd kept herself from falling apart.

Work had been a total necessity, and she'd buried herself in both her jobs. She hadn't even had time to visit Debra, Alex, and Peter since that first day. The city had been terrorized by a string of arsons, many of them in the Chinatown emergency response zone. Cacy had spent her nights saving as many lives as she could—and guiding the souls of the ones she couldn't, the ones who'd been Marked. There had been many. So many that she and Dec, along with the rest of the Ferry clan, had been working nonstop. Their bank accounts were swelling, but Cacy was just tired of all of it, and disgusted by the sight of the Kere, who were so pleased with the bedlam, delighted by the suffering. Normally, Trevor would have been the exception, but she hadn't seen him since the night of her father's death. She wondered if he was avoiding her.

Or maybe he was as busy as everyone else. The other paramedics looked ragged and demoralized, shell-shocked by the chaos. Except for Eli. He simply did his job. Did it really well, in fact. Never complained. Never got freaked-out. Never slowed down. It left her wondering what his life had been like to that point, if the last few days hadn't left him exhausted and reeling like everyone else.

Every time she returned from a "coffee break" spent in the Veil, Eli had already cleaned the back of the ambulance, refilled their supplies, and gassed up the rig so she didn't have to. They hadn't spoken much since she'd made the mistake of letting him go with her to the hospital. She'd needed it to be that way; she'd felt terrible about what had happened between them and anxious about what he'd seen. But he hadn't asked any more questions. He hadn't pressed her for information. Hadn't acted mad or resentful. He'd just . . . been there. She'd never felt so in tune with anyone. When they were on a call, they were in perfect sync. A great team. It was both completely satisfying and impossibly frustrating.

Because being that close to him was harder than she'd ever expected. She found herself wanting to reach for him and lean her head on his shoulder. She wanted him to put his arms around her, and she pictured burying her head against his chest. But she didn't want him to think she was using him—or that she would put his standing with Len and Dec in jeopardy. She also didn't want this sense of *connection* she felt with him to grow any stronger. So she'd kept their interactions professional. She'd thought it would get easier.

It hadn't.

Dec plopped down in the seat next to her, pulling her from her thoughts. He tugged at the collar of his dress shirt, looking so uncomfortable that Cacy almost laughed. Almost.

"See?" he said quietly. "I made it on time, like I promised."

Rylan sat on Cacy's other side, looking dignified and solemn. He'd been as busy as everyone else since their father's death, but not guiding souls to the Afterlife. He'd been making sure everyone knew Psychopomps Inc. was still in business. Making sure the Kere and the Keepers of the Afterlife knew the Ferrys were still able to uphold the treaty, still strong enough to stand in the gap between the two warring sides. Humans did *not* need another war between the Kere and the Keepers.

Cacy glanced over at her eldest brother. He winked at her. But the pale-purple circles under his eyes told her it was all taking a toll on him. Yesterday, they'd been given word that Moros was in town. Probably making sure Rylan was still in control, keeping the gold flowing to his Kere. She didn't envy Rylan this responsibility. Cacy tucked her arm under Rylan's and squeezed.

Aislin sat on the other side of Dec, her platinum-blonde hair in its perfectly round bun, her dress perfectly unwrinkled, her demeanor perfectly composed. But like Rylan, there were circles beneath her distinctly red eyes. No way. Had her ice-queen sister actually shed some tears? Cacy hadn't thought that was possible. But then again, she hadn't spoken to her sister since the night of their father's death when Aislin had coldly refused Cacy's offer to help with the funeral arrangements.

All around them, the rest of the Ferry family sat in ornate carved chairs or stood at the edges of the room. At least fifty people had showed up for the reading of Patrick Ferry's will and the naming of his executor, the person who would be in charge of seeing the will honored. More would have come—there were at least a thousand Ferrys living in Boston—but everyone assumed Rylan would be executor, so that part was a formality. Most of her uncles and aunts and first cousins were here to suck up to him, and to see if any money or property had been left to them.

Mr. Knickles, their family's portly little lawyer, bustled into the room, followed by two bodyguards, who remained by the door. He skittered to his desk and set down a rectangular silver plate. His eyes flicked along the front row, where Cacy and her siblings were seated. He looked nervous.

He cleared his throat. "I have verified the electronic signature of Patrick Ferry and can attest that this will is authentic, as I witnessed its recording," he said in a reedy voice. "Copies will be available after the official viewing for those who have the executor's approval." They'd all been stripped of their electronic devices before entering the room.

Cacy nudged Rylan with her shoulder, and though his eyes were focused on the rectangular plate, a tiny smile played on his lips.

Mr. Knickles looked up. "Everyone ready?" He nodded and tapped the silver plate. Cacy held her breath as a three-dimensional image of her father sprung from its surface. Even though she'd prepared herself, it made her chest ache to see him again. Rylan's arm tensed beneath her fingers. As their father smiled and squared his shoulders, Cacy realized he was wearing the same suit he'd had on the day he was killed.

"Dearest family," he said. "I am sorry to be speaking to you like this, under what I am sure are the *saddest* of circumstances for you." His lips curled into a sardonic smile. He had once told Cacy it was hard to love a person unconditionally if you had too much to gain from his death. "But I assure you, if I am with my beloved Mara, I am happy. There is no need to spare me another thought, apart from the wonderful, happy memories I share with each of you.

"Now, to the question of my executor. Ah, such a job I would not wish on anyone." His smile turned regretful, but his eyes glinted with a hint of mischief. Most people wouldn't be able to spot it, but Cacy had spent years memorizing every nuance of her father's expressions, trying to figure out how to distract him from the gnawing hole of sadness her mother's death had opened within him. Her mother had asked her to take care of him, and Cacy had taken that job very seriously. Now, her heart sped as she saw that look in her father's eyes. It meant he was about to say something no one expected.

Please don't make Aislin the executor. Cacy made a pleading expression at the 3-D image, as if that would make him change his mind. To her surprise, he smiled, like he'd seen her. His eyes weren't directed at her, but she wondered if he'd predicted she would know something was up.

"I ask that each of you respect my executor and follow my wishes to the letter, no matter how you feel about them. I have done my best to be fair, and my holdings are extensive, as are my secrets. Respect my executor and you respect me and my memory."

Cacy glanced around. Most people looked bored. They were waiting for this part to be over with so that they could hear if they'd been gifted one of the Charon's houses or yachts or jets or subsidiary businesses. She was suddenly gripped with the desire to run from the room. This was too much like scavengers gathering around a carcass. *Her father's* carcass. She pulled her hand from Rylan's, gripped the arms of her chair, starting to push herself up to go, and cast one final glance at her father's tall, lean form.

His eyes burned with incredible intensity as he said, "My executor is named as follows: Cacia Sybil Mara Ferry."

Cacy fell back into her chair as if her father had shoved her. The room was completely silent. She looked around. Fifty pairs of eyes were riveted on her. Aislin's eyes were wide and shiny with shock and anger. Cacy swung her head around to Rylan, who was looking back at her with concern on his face. "You all right?"

Cacy nodded numbly and stayed in her seat as her father went on to detail how his fortune would be divided. She should have been listening, since apparently she was in charge of making sure his wishes were honored, but she couldn't hear anything past the clamoring thoughts in her head. Why? Why had her father done this? Why not Rylan? Why not Aislin, for fuck's sake? Why her?

Was this just another attempt to pull Cacy into the corporate fold? Another form of velvet revenge?

She stared at her father as his lips kept moving, his words whooshing past her like the wind, waiting for him to take it back, to say he was joking. But he didn't. And soon it was over. Everyone filed out of the room, leaving her sitting with Rylan, Dec, and Aislin in the front row.

"Ms. Ferry," said Mr. Knickles, nodding at Cacy. "I know you must depart for the funeral mass, but will you please remain for a few minutes so you can look over the list of beneficiaries and sign off on their electronic copies?"

"Sure," Cacy said, putting a hand to her churning stomach.

Aislin stood up abruptly. "I have to meet the priest and finalize the hymn list for the service. I'll see you all at the cathedral." She spun on her heel and marched from the room. Dec gave Cacy an apologetic look and a kiss on the forehead before following Aislin out.

Rylan put his arm around Cacy's shoulders and pulled her close. "Aislin's going to get over it. Let her get through the funeral, and she'll settle down. She's been working hard to make it—"

"Perfect. I know." Cacy tilted her head up so she could see her big brother's face. "How about you? I thought it would be you. I swear I didn't know anything about this, Ry. I would have told you."

"I know. And it's all right, Cacy. If it wasn't going to be me, I'm glad it's you. I trust you, and you can always come to me if you have questions. Father hid his secrets well, but he trusted me with most of them. I can help you out if you come across something you don't understand."

She sighed. "Thanks. I'm going to take you up on that. Business isn't my thing. That's why I'm a paramedic."

Rylan grinned. "He was really proud of you, you know. He talked about it all the time. You and Dec. How you were out there doing good."

"Really?" Cacy blinked at the sting of tears. She'd always thought her father had resented her decision.

"Yeah," said Rylan, his voice husky. "Now come on. Let's get this done, and then we need to get going. We can't be late for the service."

CHAPTER SEVENTEEN

Eli sat in a pew, surrounded by strangers, wondering whether being here was a good idea. He had worn his nicest shirt and jeans, but every other guy he could see was wearing a suit and tie. Sun filtered through the elaborate stained-glass windows, casting colors across the deep-brown stone floors. The high domed ceiling had a coppery shine to it. He'd gotten here early, giving him the chance to count every arch, as well as the chance to get more and more nervous as the time for the service drew near. Why had he even come? It was his day off. He could have been sleeping or out exploring the city. Instead, he was at a funeral. For a guy he didn't really know.

Then his reason for coming walked up the aisle at her eldest brother's side, her head held high. Her eyes swept across the crowd. She nodded at people in every row and reached out to grasp several outstretched hands and hug a few particularly tearful folks. Her brother did the same. As they approached his row, Eli's heart beat so loud in his ears that he was surprised other people couldn't hear it. Cacy's hair was loose and curled around her shoulders. She wore a plain black dress. She looked achingly beautiful and heartbreakingly sad. He stared at her without blinking.

Hoping she would look at him.

Praying she wouldn't.

Totally confused.

Just as he'd felt every second he'd spent with her. He'd never been so tied up in knots around a woman. She didn't seem to be doing it to him on purpose. She'd been completely professional. When he arrived at the station, she was always there first, laughing and chatting in the locker room. She'd greet him enthusiastically in front of everybody and disappear out to their rig. Whenever he tried to talk to her, she was polite but always cut the conversation short with an excuse about having to restock supplies or fill out postaccident reports. After a day or two, he'd stopped trying to find a way to ask her about that night at his apartment, because she seemed totally determined to pretend it never happened. Not that they'd had much downtime to talk, anyway. They'd had at least a dozen utterly harrowing calls over the last week, and Cacy had been nothing but cool and decisive. Which was great. Fine. She seemed all right, dealing with her father's death like a champ. Eli was glad for her, really.

So why did he want her to look at him? Not just a glance, but a *real* look, like she had given him the night of their first shift. Why did his whole body tighten up every time she brushed against him, straining for more? Why did he look forward to work, not because he could use the barely controlled chaos to avoid thinking about his problems, but just because he knew she would be there? Why had he offered to go with her to the hospital, and why did he keep hoping she'd ask him to go with her again? And why was he here now, even though he obviously shouldn't be?

Cacy was a row away now, looking like some modern-day princess, delicate but unbreakable. She did not look pleased when her eyes settled on someone a few feet to Eli's left. Eli cast a sidelong glance at the tall olive-skinned man down the row. Ex-boyfriend? Estranged cousin? The man was staring at Cacy and her brother with an amused smile on his face. He nodded at them. Eli turned back to see Cacy's reaction, and that was when she spotted him. Eli swallowed hard as everyone else in the room became invisible, as he wordlessly tried to let her know he was only there for her. Only to support her. Not to upset her. Not to ask anything from her. Only to be there for her if she needed him.

Cacy smiled. A real smile. One he hadn't seen since the first few hours he'd spent with her. She rose up on her toes to whisper something in her brother's ear. Rylan Ferry turned sharply in Eli's direction, a look of shrewd curiosity on his face. Eli's stomach dropped. But then Rylan smiled too, and Cacy nodded at Eli before walking on.

The mass was painfully long, and the woman sitting next to him was wearing so much perfume that Eli's head began to pound. Even so, he was unable to take his eyes off Cacy. As the mournful, heavy hymns played, filling the enormous space with echoing sound, Eli stared shamelessly. And he noticed a few things. She seemed most relaxed with Rylan, staying close to him and whispering in his ear every once in a while. She also seemed comfortable with Dec, who sat on her other side. But with her sister, it was a different story. Neither woman acknowledged the other. Not even a look. It was like both of them were trying to pretend the other didn't exist.

The service ended, and the Ferry family filed to the back of the cathedral. It looked like the only way out was through the receiving line. Eli wiped his palms on the legs of his jeans. The woman next to him gave a little *hmph*.

Someone behind him chuckled. "You look like a fish out of water, my friend."

Eli turned to find it was the olive-skinned man who had spoken. The man's thick black hair was slicked back away from his face. Eli was no fashion expert, but he knew enough to realize the guy was loaded. The pea-size diamond stud in his earlobe kind of gave it away, as did the glittering cuff links at his wrists. Eli was wearing a basic button-down shirt. No tie. He didn't own one. Just as he was thinking it would have been smart to buy one for the occasion, the man smiled politely and said, "Did you know Patrick Ferry well?"

"No, not at all. I work with his daughter." Eli stepped out into the aisle and let the man out ahead of him, hoping to put some space between himself and the snotty lady with the headache-inducing perfume. As he did, he noticed the man was wearing gloves. Odd, since this time of year the daytime temperature of the city rarely dropped below a hundred degrees.

The man inclined his head toward the back of the cathedral, where the family had gathered. "You must mean Cacia. Yes. I had heard that she and her brother Declan declined corporate positions. Interesting choice."

They shuffled silently up the wide aisle, waiting their turn to give their condolences. Eli was glad the well-dressed man was quiet now; he wanted to watch Cacy without distraction. She was beginning to look tired, like the day was taking a toll on her.

Eli's fists clenched as he noticed Len several feet ahead of him, dressed in a suit that fit him like a sausage casing. He was flanked by two other paramedics, Gil Young and Manny Vieira. Despite being truly green, they both acted like hot shit back at the station and were constantly sucking up to Len . . . and constantly looking at Cacy like she was a piece of meat. The group of them reached Dec, giving him manly slaps on the shoulders and nodding at everything he said. Then they reached Cacy. She held out her hand for Len to shake, but he leaned forward and pulled her into a hug.

"Motherfucker," Eli whispered before he could stop himself.

The glove-wearing man in front of him bowed his head, and his shoulders started to shake with silent laughter. He glanced back at Eli. "Your paramedic station must be a fascinating little microcosm."

Eli gave the man a tight smile but didn't take his eyes off Cacy, who was patting Len on the back and looking stone-faced at the ceiling as he hugged her. "Sorry. I just—"

"You don't have to explain anything to me. I believe I feel the same way. It doesn't look like she finds him very . . . comforting."

The gloved man stepped forward to greet some people Eli didn't recognize. Since they were in the receiving line, he assumed they were other members of the Ferry clan, which, by the looks of it, was very large. And every single one of them wore a pendant, exactly like Cacy's.

Eli followed the gloved man through the line, noticing how the family members paled as the man shook their hands. By the time it was Eli's turn, many of them actually smiled at him. Probably because the gloved man had passed them.

The gloved man reached Aislin Ferry, who stared at him coldly but took his hand without fear or hesitation. "I heard you were in town," she said smoothly. "So kind of you to come pay your respects."

"I wouldn't have missed it," the man said softly. "Your father was a great man. A good leader." He glanced in Rylan Ferry's direction.

"He was taken too soon," Aislin said, her voice taking on an edge.

The man's eyes swung back to her. "Indeed. So tragic. I'm sorry, my dear, for your loss." He released her hand and moved on to Declan Ferry, who shook his hand without flinching but didn't say a word.

Eli shook Aislin Ferry's hand and muttered his condolences. Her eyes swept down his body, noting his shirt and jeans. "You must work with Declan and Cacia," she said, not unkindly.

"I do," Eli said. "I started less than a week ago, but they've been kind to me." He didn't mention that he'd met Patrick Ferry, too, under the worst possible circumstances.

She gave him a sad smile, like she already knew. "Thank you for coming."

Dec held his hand out when Eli stepped up to him, and suddenly the reality of being here hit Eli hard. He was the one who'd failed to keep Patrick Ferry alive. And now he was face-to-face with the man's son. "Chief. I—"

Dec reached out and took Eli by the shoulder. "You did everything you could have for him, Eli. We're all grateful. It was nice of you to come." His hand dropped away. "Listen, we're having a less formal get-together at Bart's tonight. Do you know it? Off Summer Street in the South Boston canal zone? You should come. You could get to know some of your colleagues a little better."

Eli nodded, somewhat distracted by the sight of Cacy engaging in a sharply whispered conversation with the gloved man. "I-I will. Thank you, sir."

Eli stepped to the side to allow the next mourner to shake Dec's hand and ended up standing right behind the gloved man, who was leaning over Cacy in a way that made Eli want to tell him to step off. He could see Cacy's eyes over the man's shoulder. Instead of looking fearful, like some of the other mourners, Cacy looked mad enough to punch the guy. She spotted Eli and closed her eyes for a second, like she was composing herself. When she opened them, she said, "Thank you for coming, Moros. It's an *honor* to Father's memory."

The gloved man bowed his head and moved on to Rylan Ferry. Eli stepped toward Cacy, knowing he was supposed to say some condolences now. But it was like his tongue was glued to the roof of his mouth. Everything he'd been saying to all the others suddenly seemed shallow and stupid, and he didn't want to say anything like that to her. All he could do was hold out his hand and hope she understood how sorry he was. Her hand, slender but strong, slid into his, sending an honest-to-God electric current shooting up his arm. "You're here," she said, giving his fingers the slightest tug, enough to make him step forward.

Before he realized what she was doing, she wrapped her arms around his neck and hugged him. Right in front of her brothers. In front of her whole family. Stunned, his heart pounding like a jack-hammer, he tried not to think of the delicious press of her breasts against his chest, hoping she wasn't aware of what her touch was doing to his body. At a funeral, of all places. His hands landed awkwardly on her back as he started to catalog ambulance supplies in his head to keep from embarrassing himself in front of the wealthiest, most powerful family in the city.

Cacy's arms tightened, like she was holding on for dear life, and Eli's hand slipped up. His fingers grazed the bare skin at the back of her neck, and then the only thing he could think about was how he would stand there forever if she'd let him.

Something about touching her this way loosened his tongue. "I'm so sorry, Cacy. For everything."

The heat of her breath tickled his ear. "Please don't be. Are you coming to Bart's tonight?"

"I . . . don't know." Eli's eyes darted over to Dec, who had frozen midhandshake to stare at him and Cacy. Cold dread sluiced through Eli's veins.

Cacy must have felt Eli tense, because she let him go, her hand skimming down his arm to take his hand again. "Come. Most of the station's going to be there."

"I'll try," Eli said hoarsely, pulling his hand from hers. Dec's icy, predatory stare was focused on Eli alone now. The Chief nodded to his left, and Eli realized they were holding up the line. And that everyone was watching him. Eli blinked and looked down at Cacy, whose gaze was riveted on him, so intense it burned. "I'll try," he repeated. Then he turned away before he drowned in Cacy's eyes.

He started to leave, but a hand closed around his arm. Rylan Ferry. Eli had nearly brushed past the new patriarch of the family without saying a word. Not the smoothest of moves. He opened his mouth to apologize, but Rylan just shook his hand, staring into Eli's eyes with a look as intense as Cacy's. But while hers held warmth, heat even, his was like Dec's, ice-cold. "Nice to see you again," Rylan said. "Thank you for coming."

Like it had been when they met at the hospital, the man's handshake was iron, but he wasn't putting any kind of bullshit macho squeeze action on Eli. It was simply firm. Confident. Eli thanked him, pivoted on his heel, and wove his way through the crowd, wondering what the hell had just happened.

By the time he plowed through the door of his apartment, Eli had convinced himself that going to Bart's was a bad idea. Dec and Rylan Ferry had given him the definite we'll-kick-your-ass-if-you-touch-her vibe. Given their power and connections, it could easily have been more of a touch-her-and-they'll-find-your-body-in-the-canal vibe instead.

The problem was that if Eli went tonight, he *would* touch her. He didn't think he'd be able to stop himself. He'd never felt anything so perfect as when she'd been in his arms. The world had dropped away. The ultimate distraction. The ultimate temptation.

Why had she looked at him like that after ignoring him for days? Had it just been some sort of grief reaction? Would she go back to being distant? Part of Eli hoped she would. It would make it a lot easier for him to keep his job.

He sighed as he kicked off his boots. "G? You here?"

A startled squeal came from Galena's bedroom, and the door flew open. "Eli! I didn't know when you'd be home." Her eyes widened. "Are you okay?"

He nodded. "I don't know if I should have gone to that funeral."

Galena bit her lip. "I'm sorry I didn't get back from the lab in time to go with you. I'm getting really close to a breakthrough, though. I can feel it. I got caught up with Danny and—"

"It's all right." Eli smiled at her. He really hadn't minded. He knew how Galena got when she was on to something.

She shook her head. "Not really, because I have to ask you a big favor."

"Oh, you think I'm keeping score or something?" He walked into the kitchen, searching for something to eat.

"No," she said, turning to watch him paw through the cabinets. "Never. But . . . wait here." She went back to her room.

Eli found a nutrition bar in the last cabinet he opened and was taking his first bite when Galena emerged again, carrying a garment bag. "So," she said, "I got invited to give a speech at this big university fund-raiser."

Eli nodded as he chewed. The university should want to show off its most promising new faculty member. Lots of places had wanted her. Her research was so hot that offers had started coming in before she'd even finished her doctorate. But Harvard was the best funded and had offered her a state-of-the-art lab. It had been an easy choice.

"And," she continued, glancing up at him nervously, "I want you to be my date."

She unzipped the garment bag, revealing a tuxedo. He inhaled a few crumbs of the nutrition bar and began to cough.

Galena's brow furrowed. She looked down at the tuxedo and back up at him. "Please?"

Eli waved his arms, trying to let her know he wasn't turning her down. He'd just been struck by how badly he wished he'd known about that garment bag before he'd left for the funeral. "No problem," he said hoarsely, reaching for a bottle of water. He opened it and took a sip. "I'll go."

Galena's face lit up. Her blonde ponytail swirled around her head as she jumped up and down, clutching the garment bag to her chest. "Oh, thank you! I don't think I could do this alone. The administrator who called me said there would be several hundred people there, and you know I get nervous in crowds."

Eli stepped forward and hugged his sister. "I'm so proud of you. I wouldn't miss it for anything."

"You should see the dress I got! They gave me such a generous allowance. They even sent the tux over for you! I didn't even have to ask! They knew it was a rush thing—it's tomorrow night."

"I guess Harvard really has it together," Eli said, taking the garment bag from her hands. "Are you in for the night? Want to play darts or something?"

Galena frowned. "Shouldn't you have plans, little brother? Your first night off in a new city?" Her eyes narrowed when she saw his expression. "You can't hide anything from me, Eli. Spit it out."

"I got invited to a thing. But I'm not going to go." He stalked back to his room to hang the bag in his closet.

Galena followed him. "Why not?"

"Because Cacy will be there."

"So? Didn't you just say you were *invited*?"

He gave her a sidelong glance. "Sure, it was the Chief who invited me. But that was before . . . God, I don't even know what happened really. Cacy hugged me, I guess. But it felt . . ." Eli sighed, unable to describe what Cacy's embrace had done to him. "It happened in front of her entire family. There I was, this poor hick in jeans, and she . . ." He shook his head.

Galena leaned against the wall and folded her arms over her chest. "Oh, you're going."

"That would be a very bad idea. You should have seen the way they looked at me."

"Eli Benjamin Margolis, when have you ever let anyone intimidate you?"

She sounded so much like their mother that Eli laughed, even though it made his chest hurt a little. "Never. It's just—"

"You want to see her again." Galena stepped forward and laid her palm against his chest.

He wanted to say no, but Galena smiled, no doubt feeling his heart pounding at the thought of seeing Cacy tonight.

"You want to see her again," Galena repeated, looking utterly satisfied with herself. "If you don't go, I'm going to call her and tell her secrets about you. Like your incomprehensible fear of needles."

"If you feel that strongly about it, maybe you should come with me." He put his hand over hers, holding it to his chest as he watched her face fall. "Come on, G. You need to interact with some actual humans, not just computers and single-celled organisms." Galena hadn't been able to stomach going out since the attack, and Eli hadn't pushed her. But she was going to have to face it at some point. It couldn't be good for her to be alone all the time.

Galena's gaze was glued to his chest, on his broad hand covering hers. "I'm so busy, Eli," she said quietly. "Maybe another time." Then she arched an eyebrow mischievously. "But *you* better get going. You can't let her down."

His hand fell away, and so did hers. "Let her down? What makes you think she'd notice?"

She smiled sweetly. "Trust me, Eli. I saw the way Cacy looked at you when you were passed out on the couch."

His heart kicked into a hard rhythm again, and he was glad Galena couldn't feel it pounding as he asked, "How did she look at me?"

Galena shook her head. "You can go see for yourself. I can't wait to hear how it goes. I'm headed back to the lab. But when I call you in an hour, you'd better answer, and there had better be someone there who can vouch for your whereabouts. Get cracking, bro, you've got some friends to make. Have fun," she sang as she walked through the living room and headed out the door.

Eli stood in the hallway, furious but strangely grateful to his pain-in-the-ass sister. She'd given him the excuse he needed to go get himself in serious trouble.

CHAPTER EIGHTEEN

Cacy sat back from her tablet phone and sighed. She'd spent the afternoon since the funeral mass dealing with dozens of cousins who'd felt they were slighted in her father's will. Then she'd spent an hour wading through her father's files using the passwords Mr. Knickles had given her. Rylan had offered to do it with her, but as grateful as she'd been, she'd known he had other things he had to do. Plus, Cacy had wanted to be alone with all of it for a little while. She wanted to know why her father had chosen her. His words from the night of his death echoed in her mind. *Protecting the future is more important than righting the wrongs of the past.* Words he'd said to her while standing outside Eli's apartment in Cambridge, of all places. What had he been trying to tell her?

She'd searched his incredibly long list of property holdings for an address in Cambridge, thinking maybe he'd bought another condo complex or business. Nothing. She pulled up the copy of the data she'd snagged from her father's phone and scrolled through his calls. Both Rylan and Dec had called him in the half hour before the attack, and the calls were only minutes apart. She took a look at his private calendar next, searching for discrepancies between it and the public calendar maintained by his secretary. On the day before he died, the press conference and family lunch were clearly marked. He'd also had dinner with Rylan at Lombo's. Those were the only things listed, so Cacy clicked to the next day, since he'd been killed around one in the morning. There, slated for 12:01 a.m., was a notation: *M. Final Decision.*

Cacy stared at the words until her vision blurred, her heart bumping frantically against her ribs. Had that meeting been in Cambridge? And who was *M*? Had that person been responsible for her father's death? Her eyes narrowed as she closed the calendar. She already had an appointment with her number one suspect.

She checked the time and her heart skipped a beat. Time to go. The paramedics had wanted to have their own informal send-off of Patrick Ferry, so she and Dec had to show. Not that she would have missed it. She loved most of her colleagues and appreciated their loyalty to her father, no matter how much shit they'd given her the first few years she'd been a paramedic. She was so determined to be there on time that she'd asked Moros to meet her at the bar so she could ask him some questions before he left town again. Normally, the youngest daughter of the Charon would have been beneath the notice of the Lord of the Kere, but getting named the executor of her father's estate had made all the difference. Not that her father would approve of how she was going to use her new authority.

The sun was still smoldering, hovering at the rim of the skyscrapers, when Cacy made it to Bart's. The humid air was filled with the briny swamp scent of the canals—part rot, part chemical burn. She wrinkled her nose as she walked beside the canal wall, watching the sampans and motorboats and amphibious vehicles weaving and bumping in Friday afternoon rush-hour traffic.

Cacy swung open the door to the bar and took a deep breath as the smell of beer and whiskey rushed over her. She smiled and nodded to the hostess as she headed for the back room where her father had often met with local patrons. He'd bought the bar expressly for this purpose.

A few guys were already gathered at the long mahogany bar, including Len, who had changed from that awful too-tight suit he'd been wearing earlier, thank God. Her skin had crawled as he'd embraced her in the receiving line. It wouldn't have been considered dignified to knee a mourner in the balls, though, so she'd let him hug her and counted the seconds until it was over.

Len pushed away from the bar when he saw her, the eager, horny look on his wide face making her stomach hurt. She looked past him, searching for the one face she actually wanted to see. Eli wasn't here. She wondered if he would come at all—and wouldn't blame him if he no-showed. But this morning, when she'd seen him standing in the pew, looking so out of place and yet so perfect, it was like warm honey had been poured over her soul. He'd come to a funeral, dressed in what Cacy was sure were the nicest clothes he owned. On his day off, too. Maybe he'd come to honor her father's memory, or out of misplaced guilt for not being able to save a patient. But when her eyes had locked with Eli's, Cacy had been sure he'd come to the funeral for her and her alone.

After dealing with all the wrenching pain of the day, and Len, and Moros . . . she'd practically wrapped herself around Eli and begged him to carry her away. She hadn't been able to hold back any longer. She hadn't been able to think about the risks. She had completely given in to the need that had been building in her for the last few days. The need to hold on to him, to feel the solid beat of his heart against her chest, like it was strong enough to keep hers going. She hadn't cared that everyone was staring. In that moment, Eli had been the only other person in the cathedral.

Oh God. Len was approaching her, arms open. Cacy stepped back and folded her arms across her chest. "Hey. You're early," she said, trying to sound friendly . . . but not too friendly.

His arms dropped to his sides. "So are you. Can I buy you a drink?"

"No. I'm meeting someone in the back. I'll be out in a little while."

Len frowned. "In the back?" It was obvious where his thoughts were going. He looked her up and down like she'd walked in here naked instead of in a skirt and a tank top.

Cacy flipped him off. "A business associate of my father's, Len. What's wrong with you?"

Len's frown deepened to a scowl. "I thought maybe—"

"Yeah? Well, as usual, you thought wrong." She gave him a thoroughly disgusted look before turning toward the hallway. "Not that it's any of your business, but don't worry about it. I'll be right out."

The corridor leading to the back room smelled of booze and cigarettes. She ran her fingers along the dark wood paneling as she walked, wondering how many times her father had walked this path, if his hands had skimmed over the same places.

Moros was waiting for her in the last room on the left. The small room contained a liquor cabinet and a desk surrounded by antique wooden chairs. The Lord of the Kere lounged in one of them, a low tumbler of amber liquid in his gloved hand, his feet propped up on the desk.

Cacy walked in, knocked Moros's legs to the floor, and seated herself behind the desk. He was thousands of years old, so she figured he should know better than to put his feet on the furniture.

"Have some respect," she said calmly, and turned to pour herself a few fingers of Scotch from a heavy cut-crystal decanter.

When she looked back at Moros, he was giving her a lazy smile, but Cacy read the sharp admiration in his eyes. "No disrespect intended, Cacia."

Cacy took a sip of the deep, smoky liquid and closed her eyes as it burned all the way to her belly. She sat back down. "Thank you for meeting with me."

Moros shrugged. He'd changed from his designer suit and was now wearing black slacks and a tailored gray silk shirt that matched the steely color of his eyes. The diamond in his ear had been replaced by a small silver hoop, and his hair was stylishly disheveled. He was pretty sexy for an ancient guy. Of course, he looked no older than Rylan, but even so, he wasn't really her type. He returned her appraising look with one of his own. "How could I say no? Anything to honor the memory of my good friend." His eyes slid down her body. "And such charming company. Your request intrigued me."

Cacy lowered her gaze to her glass, watching the liquid sparkle in the warm light of the Tiffany lamp on the desk. "I want to know why he was killed."

Moros sighed. "My dear, you should know better than to ask me that. Your father would never have asked me such a question."

Her head snapped up, and she met his metal-gray eyes. "He hadn't been retired for twelve hours before he was Marked by one of your Kere. Father trusted you to be just."

"Our ways are not your ways, Cacia. But believe me when I say there is justice in what we do." He shifted in his chair. "And in what I *intend* to do," he muttered, then took a sip of Scotch. "We *were* friends, you know. Not merely business associates. I'd known him for over a century. After Rylan and Aislin's mother died, I was the one who introduced him to Mara. She was my chief archivist's daughter. Did you know that?" He leaned back in his chair again and hooked an ankle over his knee.

"No," Cacy said quietly, gazing into her glass.

"You look just like her," Moros said, his voice betraying his sadness. "I think your father never recovered from her loss. He was lucky to have you, though. It kept him going when he needed it most."

Cacy stared at the desk and blinked. "Were you that close?" Had their midnight meeting been a social call? Somehow, Cacy doubted it. *Final Decision* didn't sound very social.

"What do you know of our ancient history, my dear? What did he tell you of your heritage?"

It was obvious he wanted to take the long way around answering her questions, but since she'd called this meeting, she would indulge him for the moment. She downed her Scotch, feeling it burn all the way down her throat, then said, "I know that, centuries ago, there was no buffer between death and the Afterlife. The Kere delivered the souls to Heaven or Hell themselves."

"*Thousands* of years ago. Almost two thousand years ago now." He frowned, like he remembered it well, like it still hurt him. "We were slaves then, my Kere and I. Like dogs. Roaming the Earth like beggars." He was gripping his glass so tightly that Cacy was surprised it didn't shatter.

"You rebelled."

Moros nodded and took a slow sip of his drink. "What do you think happens when death does not come for those who should die? And I know you are familiar with the Shades, so you know what happens when those who have died are not delivered into the warm embrace of their final fate." He closed his eyes as if savoring, but Cacy wasn't sure of the source of his pleasure—thoughts of zombies wreaking havoc, or the fine alcohol. "It was chaos on Earth *and* in the Veil. No balance anywhere. Those fated to live were dying too soon, and those fated to die lived on as undead monsters. The Keepers of Heaven and Hell tried to compel us, of course—to rule us with threats and torture as they had for so long. But we'd had enough. They showed a remarkable lack of foresight when they refused to treat us as their equals."

"They agreed to a treaty. To pay for your services, to reward you for delivering the souls to them. But they insisted on an intermediary."

"Those were but a few of the terms, and the only ones that need concern you." He stood and leaned over the desk, helping himself to another few fingers before waving the bottle in her direction.

She held up her glass, and he poured as he spoke. "They did not trust us to show restraint if there was money to be made from human death. They never believed we had any good in us, you see. They thought we were a *necessary evil*." His voice had taken on a dangerous edge, but then he chuckled again. "So the Charon was created as an intermediary, as a watcher, and, I suspect, so that the Keepers did not ever have to behold my face again. Thus your proud race began, my dear. I have worked with twenty Charons since that time, some peacefully, and some . . . not so much. But I have dealt with all of them justly."

Cacy swirled the Scotch in her glass as Moros sat down again. Had Moros veered from his sense of justice to have her father killed before his time? The list of those fated to die was generated by Moros's ancient sisters, the Fates themselves, who were said to live in complete seclusion and isolation within the Veil. Cacy's father had told her no one but Moros knew where they were. There were even stories that they didn't exist, that Moros himself made the list and used the Fates as a cover for his own actions. That he alone decided which humans to doom and which to spare.

That had been why the Mark of the Ferry had been created, so Ferrys could operate without fear of reprisal from Moros and the Kere. It was forbidden for a Ker to kill a Ferry who was still in service—only the Charon himself could sentence a Ferry to death, and it hadn't happened in over a century. Moros had been religious in upholding that part of the treaty, probably because the Keeper of Hell himself would hunt him down if he didn't. No Ferry had ever been killed in the line of duty, though some had been roughed up by the Kere or permanently maimed by Shades. When Ferrys retired from duty and gave up the raven mark and their Scope, though, they became regular mortals again, as vulnerable to death—and the Kere—as the next person. But with as much of a chance at life, too. Or, at least, that was the way it was supposed to be.

"I guess I'm wondering if everyone's still honoring the treaty. No one came to collect the commission on my father."

Moros's eyes glinted.

Cacy smiled innocently and dropped her bomb. "You were planning to meet with my father the night he died. You were negotiating about something."

He gave her a small, cold smile. "What a clever little thing you are," he said. "He never made it to our meeting. I never saw him that night. And if you're wondering, no, I did not Mark him myself."

Cacy's eyes narrowed. "But you know who did?"

Moros stared back at her, then stood abruptly. "It has been lovely spending time with you, Cacia. Thank you for the drink." He set his glass down on the desk.

Cacy stood as well. She wasn't done yet. "What's in Cambridge?"

For the first time, she seemed to have truly caught the Lord of the Kere off guard. He turned stiffly to face her. "What did you say?"

She swore she could see the faintest of red flames in his eyes.

"I think you heard me." Her mind was spinning. She was desperate to know why her father had been there but had no desire to draw any attention to Eli. A Ker had been looking through his bedroom window that night, but it hadn't Marked him. And yet Cacy doubted it was a coincidence.

Moros leaned across the desk toward her, no longer trying to hide the inhuman red glow in his eyes. "I don't play games, little girl, so stop being coy. If you want anything from me, you will pay me . . . in information, or through another method of my choosing. I think we have established that I do not work for free." He did not break eye contact with her as he took his gloves off and set them on the desk in front of him.

Cacy fought the urge to back herself up against the wall. The danger of Moros's touch was the stuff of myth and nightmares, and his threat was clear as he laid his palms flat on the deeply grained wood and spread his fingers.

"I'll tell you this," she said, her words tumbling out in a breathless flow. "Father was in Cambridge that night. *After* he died. It's where we found him when we entered the Veil to guide his soul."

Moros seemed to be trying to look straight into her mind. The intensity of his gaze nearly burned her, but she didn't look away. He leaned forward even further, his body now halfway across the desk, his face only inches from hers. "Cacia, why do you think your father made you executor? It was a shock to your family. I heard them talking about it at his funeral."

She stood her ground. "I think . . . I think he trusted me. He trusted that I would take care of his affairs."

The red glow faded to smoldering cinders within the steely gray. "You don't think he trusted your older siblings?"

Cacy's brow furrowed. "I-I'm sure he did. But it was just the two of us in that house for so long after my mother died. We were close."

"He worked with Rylan and Aislin every day. He wasn't close to them?"

She shrugged. She wasn't about to air her family's dirty laundry, but it was an open family secret that Rylan and Aislin had been at each other's throats for years. "He did work with them every day. But maybe that's why he thought I would be the better choice."

Moros paused, then said, "Well, I shall consider trusting you, too."

Cacy looked up to see Moros pulling his gloves on and tried to make her sigh of relief as subtle as possible. But he was leaving, and she hadn't yet gotten what she needed. She opened her mouth to stop him, but he shook his head and said, "As stimulating as this has been, I have other things to attend to. But believe me, we will meet again. Soon." He turned in place and was gone.

Cacy fell into the chair behind her like someone had kicked her legs out from under her. She reached forward and chugged the remaining Scotch, relishing the painful pleasure as it scorched her throat. She had spent all her courage facing down the Lord of the Kere. While she had no real answers, she had gotten something useful out of him. He *had* planned to meet her father that night to make some sort of major decision. And he obviously knew what was important about her father's presence in Cambridge, but he didn't trust her enough yet to tell her what it was.

Something about the whole conversation bothered her, though: he was supposed to know just about everything, but he seemed to want information about the circumstances surrounding her father's death as badly as she did.

At least he would contact her again soon. Moros was known for keeping his promises. It was one of the reasons people were afraid of him. *One* of the reasons.

Cacy stood on wobbly legs, opened the door to the meeting room, and walked down the hall toward the noise of a party in full swing. This would not be a solemn memorial to Patrick Ferry. This would be a balls-out send-off. Cacy wasn't sure she was up to it, but she owed it to the guys. She put a hand to her stomach, which was empty except for the warm curl of Scotch steadily winding into her bloodstream. She knew she should eat something soon, or she wouldn't last long.

She threaded her way through the crowd and was immediately spotted by Dec, who waved a half-empty bottle of whiskey at her. "Cacy!" he shouted. Everyone else turned toward her and whooped.

"Thanks for coming, guys. Here I am," she called, raising her arms. Someone pressed a beer bottle into her hand, and she put it to her lips and downed it in one long chug while everyone cheered. She lifted the empty bottle and shouted, "To Patrick Ferry!"

Everyone went nuts. Cacy accepted another beer and listened to a few other guys toast her father and his memory, cheering raucously in all the right places. But her eyes searched the crowd.

Where was Eli? Had he decided not to come? Her heart sank, and she realized how much she'd wanted to see him.

"Hey, Cace."

She looked up to see Trevor standing next to her. Every muscle in her body tensed, and his relaxed smile disappeared. "Looks like I'm guilty until proven innocent," he said as he clinked his beer bottle against hers and took a drink.

She leaned close to him, feeling the incredible heat emanating from his immense body. "Did you Mark him? You said you'd gotten a last-minute assignment. Was it him?"

Trevor looked down at her, his eyes so brown they looked black in the dim light of the bar. "You think I would do that? Mark your father without a heads-up? We're *friends*, Cacy."

"You're a Ker," she blurted out.

His lips formed a tight line. "Now I see how it is with you. I thought you saw me as a person, but I'm thinking you see me as something less than that. Well, here's some news for you. I Marked your father's *killer* that night. He had a nasty run-in with a tree branch deep in the Common. He was just a street punk, Cacy. Not much more than a kid. I found three Afterlife coins in his pocket, if that tells you anything." When he saw her mouth open, he snapped, "I didn't know he was going to kill your father, if that's what you're going to accuse me of next."

Her cheeks burned as she looked away, picking at the label on her beer bottle. Trevor was right; she did have some prejudice against the Kere. But Trevor had never been anything but a friend to her. "I'm sorry. I should have trusted you."

He lifted her face with gentle fingers. "Listen, Cace, I know how much this hurt you. If I can find out more about it, I will. I've already told Dec that. I turned the Afterlife coins over to him, but we all know it's impossible to trace them. So we only know one thing for sure—the human who killed your dad was someone else's puppet."

Something occurred to her, and she was just tipsy enough to say it out loud. "Does Moros know who Marked my father? Did he give the go-ahead personally?"

"Moros gives all the assignments. Why would you doubt that?"

"I'm wondering if he's as much in control of his empire as he wants people to think."

"That's a dangerous thing to say."

She forced herself to stand tall. "Even more so if it's true."

"Everything all right here?" Eli appeared behind Cacy, and in the close-packed space of the bar, he and Trevor formed a Cacy sandwich. Eli put his hands on her shoulders, and she automatically sank backward into his solid warmth.

"Everything is completely all right," she said as she stared up at Trevor, who was looking at Eli with frank curiosity, like he couldn't believe someone would challenge him like this. "We were wondering who would suck more this year in interleague soccer—Fire or Police."

Trevor smiled, though Cacy caught the flash of red in his eyes. She'd struck a nerve with her concerns about Moros. "Police," he said. "They're barely hanging on. Catch you later, Cace. Eli." He nodded at them and turned to wave at some paramedics who'd just come through the door.

Cacy twisted to look up at Eli, amazed at the ecstatic, skipping beat of her heart. "You're here," she said.

He grinned as his eyes searched her face. "That's the second time you've said that to me today. You always seem so surprised."

She barely knew how to explain what was going on inside her. The past hours had been full of worry and responsibility and sorrow, but seeing him made it all go away. "I haven't really given you any reason to show up, and yet here you are."

He laughed. "If that's what you think, you don't see yourself very clearly." He tucked a stray lock of hair behind her ear, sending little shocks of pleasure shimmying through her.

"Can I buy you a drink, Sergeant Margolis?" She slid her arm around his waist, suddenly certain she wanted him to be by her side for the rest of the night. Bad idea, maybe, but she couldn't make herself care.

He raised his head and looked around, obviously trying to spot someone among the horde of half-intoxicated paramedics pressed in around them. But a second later he was smiling at her again. "I'd love that."

They wound their way through the crowd, Cacy fielding slaps on the back. When one landed on her ass, Eli instantly slipped in behind her and guided her in front of him. She hopped onto a barstool, and he claimed the one next to her. He was still wearing jeans, but he'd changed into a black T-shirt that fit him so well it had to be a crime. Cacy tried to direct her thoughts away from what it might be like to peel it off him.

"What can I get you?" asked the bartender as he set two beers in front of the guys next to them.

Cacy looked at Eli inquiringly, but he just shrugged. "I'll have whatever she's having."

"Aw, come on, Eli," she began, but then she saw the look on his face and realized he might not actually know what he liked. "Two Jamesons, water back."

The bartender nodded and turned away. Cacy bumped Eli's knees with her own. "Let me guess. You didn't get out much in Whatsitburgh?"

"No such thing as bars there. At least, not for ordinary people. Water was rationed so carefully that no one could afford anything beyond the basics."

Cacy bit her lip. He said it matter-of-factly, but she felt like a jerk. She'd known they were better off in the East, but she hadn't known how bad it had gotten everywhere else. "I'm glad you found your way here."

His smile was sad. "I didn't, not really. It was my sister. She's the brains of this outfit. She got offered this once-in-a-lifetime position at Harvard. Our parents died a few years ago, so we didn't have anything keeping us in Pittsburgh, and had every reason to leave."

Cacy reached out and took his hand. "Then I'm grateful to your sister."

The bartender came back and set their glasses down. Cacy swiped her phone over the scanner embedded in the edge of the bar counter, which brought up her bill. "Add a round for the guys," she said.

"Round on the house!" the bartender shouted, and a roar went up all around them.

Eli laughed, and Cacy noticed he had a dimple in his cheek when he smiled big enough. She reached out and touched her finger to it. Eli stopped laughing and put his hand over hers, keeping it there for a moment. Then he pulled it away from his face and wrapped her fingers around her glass. He picked up his own and held it up. She did the same.

"To fresh starts," he said, in a light voice that belied the intense look in his eyes. He clinked his glass against hers and threw the whiskey back.

Cacy had her glass to her lips when Eli started to cough. She set it down and clapped him on the back.

"Man, that burns," he wheezed, his eyes wide.

"You've never had Jameson before?"

"I've never had alcohol before," he admitted, his cheeks turning red. Cacy suddenly found herself thinking about how much fun it might be to introduce Eli to *all* her vices.

"So, you're a mockolate virgin, a cannoli virgin, *and* an alcohol virgin? Is there anything else you want to tell me?"

He chuckled and nodded at the bartender, who set another glass in front of him. Eli's smile was so sexy it nearly made her fall off her chair. "You'll have to get to know me a little better for that."

Cacy reached for her glass and tapped it against his, surprised at how badly she wanted to get to know him *a little better*. "It's a deal."

CHAPTER NINETEEN

Eli downed his fourth drink quickly, noting with gratitude that his throat no longer felt like it was about to explode. The tingling looseness in his arms and legs was pleasant, and he didn't think he'd smiled or laughed this much in years. But that wasn't because of the alcohol. Cacy was still next to him, sitting close enough for her hair to tickle his arm. He'd never talked about himself this much before, either, but she seemed to want to know, and he realized he wanted her to. Every time he tried to move the conversation in her direction, though, she turned it around on him or changed the subject. It occurred to him that she was being evasive again, but it was hard to hold on to those thoughts right now, because the rest of her was so damn distracting.

The bare skin of her shoulder was warm against his bicep as she leaned over and peeked into the glass clutched in his hands. "Another?"

He looked down at her full pink lips curling into a sensuous smile. Her eyes were bright. "I may be reaching my limit. I think you might be, too, Lieutenant."

"My metabolism would astound you," she giggled, waving at the bartender, who sauntered over with the bottle, like he'd been waiting, and refilled her glass.

"I'll bet it would," Eli muttered, recalling how her body had healed itself from what he'd believed was a fatal wound.

"Mmm?" She laid her head against his shoulder and put her hand on his knee. Eli clenched his jaw. She was touching him way too much, which was bad in all kinds of ways. For the five hundredth time in the last hour, he looked around the room, searching for Len or Dec, wondering if they'd noticed.

"I was just thinking there are a lot of things about you that would probably astound me," he said more breathlessly than he intended as her hand slid up to his thigh. "Cacy . . ." *Don't do this to me. I won't be able to say no.*

She raised her head and looked straight into his eyes, like he'd said his thoughts aloud. For a moment, he wondered if he had. She was close enough for her spicy scent to fill him up, warm enough for him to lean in to her, tempting enough to draw his entire body tight with desire. No matter what she wore, she always looked sexy, but tonight, she had on a tank top that left little to his active imagination. Her skirt ended midthigh and flared at the bottom, which was both incredibly cute and painfully sexy. And with the rush of alcohol through his veins, he was having an increasingly hard time keeping his hands off her, which was why they were gripping his glass like they were held there with vascular glue.

The heat and longing in her gaze made his teeth grind. She opened her mouth to say something, and all he could think was, *Anything. Anything you want, and I'll give it to you. Just ask me. Please ask me.*

Suddenly cheers went up in the crowd, and the pounding music went silent. A wiry guy wearing all black leaped onto the bar, holding a violin. He flashed a wide grin and pointed his bow down at the Chief, who was looking disheveled and holding a near-empty bottle of whiskey in his hand. Dec lifted it in a salute.

The violinist tucked the instrument against his chin, and the bar got quiet. He laid the bow against the strings and began to play what Eli soon recognized as "Danny Boy," the lonely, lilting swell of the music rising over the hush of the crowd. He looked at Cacy, whose easy smile had dissolved. Eli glanced around him at all the somber, sad faces. Then he stared down at the bar, once again replaying his moments with Patrick Ferry, wishing he'd been able to save him.

The song ended, and there was a moment of silence. Then the musician drew his bow along the strings with a screeching dissonance and launched into some sort of jig, stomping on the bar with his hard-heeled boots. The depth of the sound increased, and Eli leaned over to see a bagpipe player standing on the other side of the bar, his fingers flying.

"Dance!" shouted the men around him. "Time for a dance, Chief!"

Dec had his arms up in the air like he was in no mood to argue. "Where's my sister?" he yelled. "I need Cacy!"

"I knew this would happen," she laughed. "Right here, boys. Here I come." She rose from her barstool, resting her hands on Eli's shoulders and leaning so close that her breasts brushed against the side of his face. He was barely able to suppress his moan. He turned his head away to look at the fiddler on the bar, who was playing like his life depended on it.

The pressure of Cacy's hands disappeared, and Eli looked around to find her. She'd climbed onto the bar, and now her shapely legs were right in front of his face. His eyes traced from ankles to thighs. If he lifted his gaze a few inches, he'd know if she was wearing underwear. He glanced at the guys around him, who were gaping at her with naked appreciation, and found himself praying she was.

Her face was glowing beneath the lights of the bar. She was looking down at him, that heat still in her eyes, and she winked. Her white teeth flashed as she grinned and began to dance, her heels clacking against the bar rhythmically, providing the perfect percussion for the fiddle and bagpipes. Her feet were moving incredibly fast, just a blur. She inched her way across the bar, her feet never stopping, and abruptly dove forward into the out-stretched arms of the guys at the edge of the bar. Eli shot to his feet, trying to see her, desperate to know if she was all right, but then a space cleared and she was there with Dec, who was dancing now as well. Their backs were straight, their shoulders squared, and their feet clacked a precise beat against the wooden planks of the floor as they hopped and spun in time with the music.

The men and women around them were dancing as well, but none of them held a candle to the Ferrys, who looked like they'd been dancing that way all their lives. Both of them were smiling, but their eyes were shining with unshed tears. Dec's black hair was plastered to his face, while Cacy's flew around her as her brother lifted her up and swung her around.

All Eli could do was stare. Cacy's cheeks were a lush pink, and her smile was so beautiful it hurt him. Her movements were sure and graceful, lithe and strong. He'd never seen anything so lovely, and he'd never wanted anyone as badly. The crowd was packed tightly around her and her brother, and Eli leaned so he could keep his eyes on her, needing to see her as much as he needed to breathe. His heart pounded in time with the music. His head pounded, too, saturated with desire. His breaths came quick and deep, and suddenly he was dizzy with his want of her, and he had to get away from it. Because, as he stared at Dec, at everyone else crowded around her, he realized he wasn't part of her world. And it hurt too much.

Eli staggered toward the exit. He couldn't reach it fast enough. Cacy had sucked all the air from the room. He stumbled through the door and drew deep lungfuls of swampy Boston air. His head was spinning as he walked unsteadily to the canal wall and leaned against it, the image of Cacy's bright eyes and wide smile taunting him.

"God, I shouldn't have come," he mumbled, staring down at the cloudy brown water lit up by the streetlights. He'd spent all week being driven crazy by her remoteness and mystery, and now he'd spent all evening being driven crazy by her raw, sexy charm. Maybe that was it. No matter what she was up to, no matter her mood, no matter what was going on for her, Cacy just drove him crazy.

And he needed to get over it. She was a freaking princess in a family that ruled the city. She had brothers who could bury him, and who probably would if they suspected Eli was messing around with her. Even worse than that, she was hiding something from him. Something big. Maybe the whole family had had some type of genetic enhancement that allowed them to heal supernaturally fast. Or maybe they'd all sold their souls for eternal youth, and that was why the Chief looked twenty-five, though Eli had discovered the other day that he'd been the head of the Chinatown station for the last fifteen years. And none of that explained the pendants every single member of the family wore around their necks, or why Cacy's was apparently a portal to some parallel dimension.

Eli hung his head and closed his eyes, but that made him feel like he was falling, so he opened them again. Maybe he should let himself get transferred. Maybe what he needed was to get away from the Ferrys, and especially Cacy, who'd been on his mind every waking second since he'd met her. Many sleeping seconds, too. His dreams of her had left him spent and aching. And he'd only known her for a week. He didn't think he could take much more.

"Dammit," he snapped, pulling himself up and turning to go. Deep in the bar, a raucous cheer went up, and despite his frustration, he paused. Half of him was clawing to go back in there, to watch her some more. Another part of him wanted to go far beyond just watching. That part wanted to push her up against a wall, ruck her skirt up, and plunge into her. Hard.

He'd taken one heavy step toward the door of the bar when it opened. Len, Manny, and Gil stepped out, their eyes focused on him. "Hey," Len sneered. "I guess Cacy finally got tired of babysitting your sorry ass."

Eli stopped short. Len was probably right, but it still pissed him off. He chuckled, half-surprised to realize he no longer gave a fuck what Len thought about him. "Jealous, sir?"

Len stepped up close to him, bumping Eli's chest with his own. The guy was at least five inches shorter, but a lot wider. Eli took a few lazy steps back, still chuckling quietly while his pulse beat hard in his ears.

Len's smile was pure ugliness. "I guess it's my turn with her, eh? She looks good tonight, doesn't she? Pretty drunk, too. Maybe I can bend her over the bar once Dec's passed out." He high-fived Gil.

A rush of pure rage roared through Eli. "She doesn't want you. Don't touch her."

Len's face twisted. "Are you threatening me?"

Eli smiled, now past caring about anything this asshole could do to him. Len had crossed the line, and Eli wanted to hurt him very badly. "Yessir, I am."

It was almost a relief when Len swung at him. Eli ducked instinctively, and Len staggered. A reckless anger burned through Eli, and when Len charged again, Eli drew back and slammed his fist into Len's jaw. Len hit the pavement with a curse. He stood up and spat blood onto the concrete as he massaged his jaw. "Boy, you are not long for this world."

He, Manny, and Gil charged Eli all at once, fists flying. Eli braced himself and took Gil out with a solid roundhouse kick, but Len doubled Eli over with a blow to the stomach, and Manny grabbed Eli's hair and wrenched him off balance. Eli drove a knee hard into Manny's ribs, and Manny let go of him with a grunt. But Eli barely had time to take a breath before Gil jumped on top of him, making him stumble back against the canal wall. Eli bent sharply and flipped Gil over his shoulders, but he didn't even have time to straighten up before Len hit him like a freight train, driving his shoulder into Eli's chest. Len lunged and jerked Eli's legs up, sending him plummeting over the canal wall. Eli's head cracked against the cement as he fell. His world turned black.

CHAPTER TWENTY

"Fight!" someone shouted, cutting through the wall of music around Cacy. "Fight!"

The cry was coming from near the exit. Dec stopped dancing and plowed through the crowd. Cacy followed. When she emerged from the bar, her breath caught in her throat. Dec dove forward, shouting "Len, no!" just as the night supervisor sent Eli flying over the wall and into the canal below.

Cacy sprinted toward Len, who spun around, rubbing his shoulder, right before she punched him in the face. He bent over, clutching at his nose, and she kneed him in the balls, sending him to the pavement. She kicked him in the side and hissed, "If you touch Eli ever again, I swear I will tie you up, drop you in the Common, and laugh when they find your body."

She leaped over him and hit the edge of the wall. Eli was standing in the chest-deep water a few feet below her, clutching his head. He looked like he had no idea what had happened to him. Dec was shouting to the other paramedics to block the boat traffic upstream so that Eli didn't get crushed against the wall by an errant AV.

"Eli," Cacy called. "Hey."

Eli looked up, blinking and shaking his head. He spat a mouthful of water into the canal, making Cacy's heart sink. "Cacy?"

Cacy looked over her shoulder. "Trevor! Get your ass over here and help me!"

Trevor, who'd been standing on the wall and stopping traffic several yards down, jogged over.

"Help me pull him out," she ordered. "You're the only one who's strong enough."

"We're getting a rope—"

"We can reach him. I want him out of that fucking water *now*. Dec! You too!"

Dec appeared at Trevor's side, his hair sticking up at funny angles like he'd raked his hand through it. "He's gonna need—"

"I know what he needs," Cacy snapped. "Get him out, and I'll take care of him."

Dec and Trevor looked at each other for a second. "I'll hold your legs," Dec offered. "You're stronger."

Trevor nodded and bent over the wall without another word. Dec knelt at his feet and wrapped his muscled arms around Trevor's calves.

"Eli, lift your arms," Cacy called. The way he was standing there, dazed and staring, he'd obviously hit his head. Cacy was terrified he'd lose consciousness and sink into the disease-infested water again. Every second he spent in that toxic soup shortened his life. She wanted to scream in frustration. She wanted to murder Len and his two little sidekicks, who both lay groaning on the pavement.

Eli looked up again and shakily raised his arms, allowing Trevor to grab his hands. "Hang on tight, man," Trevor called as he started to pull. The massive muscles across Trevor's back flexed as he lifted Eli from the water. "Shit, you're heavy."

Cacy leaned over the wall herself, reaching for Eli. She caught his arm and pulled, too, bringing Eli back over the canal wall with a final, wrenching heave. He rolled from the wall onto the sidewalk, coughing and gagging.

"Eli," she said softly, kneeling by his head. Brown rivulets of canal water snaked through his blond hair. He blinked furiously; the water was probably burning his eyes. "We have to get you back to the station. Can you stand up?"

"Cacy, I can call a unit to transport him," Dec said as he squatted beside them. He discreetly pulled his Scope from his neck, opening it just enough to look at Eli through it. He snapped it shut quickly. "He's not Marked," he mouthed.

But that wouldn't save him from being desperately ill, from suffering permanent disability or organ damage. It only meant he wouldn't die.

Cacy looked into her brother's eyes, willing him to understand her feelings. She *needed* to take care of Eli. "It would take at least fifteen for them to get here, and another fifteen to get him to the hospital, where he'll sit for hours because he's not critical. But by the time they get to him, he will be. I'm going to take him back to the station." She tapped her Scope.

"What are you doing? He'll be nearly invisible there. If you lose track of him, he'll be trapped there." Dec looked at her like she'd lost her mind.

She laid her palm on Eli's back. "He's solid and visible in the Veil, Dec. I don't know why, but I've seen it myself. It's a long story."

Dec's mouth dropped open for a second. "Regardless of what you and he *can* do, let's think about what you *should* do. You're not supposed to use it like that," he whispered. "He might see—"

"He's barely conscious, and I don't really care, anyway." She glared at Dec. "You think Rylan would sentence *me* to death over something like this? No way. And I'll take anything less than that with a smile on my face. Help me get him up."

Dec's face was solemn as he wrapped his arms around Eli's chest and helped him to his feet. Eli lurched away from him and retched into the canal, sending an icy bolt of panic through Cacy's gut. She pulled the Scope from the chain around her neck.

"Not here," Dec snapped. He turned to the small crowd that had gathered behind them. "Take these three inside and get them cleaned up," he ordered, waving at Len, Manny, and Gil. "We'll take care of Eli."

As the crowd shuffled back and some of them started to help Len up, Dec and Cacy ducked under Eli's arms and carried him toward the alley next to Bart's.

"I can walk, guys," mumbled Eli, trying to pull away from them. "I'll be fine. I'll just go home and shower." He lifted his head, winced, and leaned heavily against the brick wall behind him.

"You can't," Cacy said, praying he wasn't about to fall over. "You've probably been infected with half a dozen bacterial diseases. And you obviously have a concussion. You're coming with me."

She brushed her thumb over her Scope, opening a window to the Veil. She looked at Dec. "I've got this. He can walk, so I can handle it."

"I guess I'll go manage the fallout." Dec stalked out of the alley.

Cacy pulled her Scope wide and stepped up close to Eli. "Hey, I've got you. Just stay close to me, all right?"

"You're the boss," he said, lowering his head onto her shoulder. He smelled like a cesspit, but Cacy didn't care. She lifted the Scope over their heads and lowered it around them, then helped Eli step over its edges. He shivered, soaked and chilled in the frigid air of the Veil.

"Hang on, baby," she whispered. She flipped her Scope and focused hard on the locker room of the EMS station, pressing her thumb against the warm metal engraving, willing it to open a window to where she needed to go.

"Oooh. Pretty."

Cacy's head jerked up from her Scope. She'd recognize that raspy voice anywhere and knew it signaled trouble. Her arm tightened protectively around Eli's waist. Despite the icy dread oozing down her spine, she smiled confidently as she swiveled her head around, looking for the owner of the voice. "Well, thanks. I love compliments."

The voice *tsk*ed. "You're not my type. But *he* is." Glowing red eyes stared at Cacy from the depths of the alleyway.

Eli tried to lift his head but didn't quite succeed. "Cacy?" he whispered.

"Shhh. It's all right." Cacy backed out of the alley, dragging Eli along with her. He stayed upright, but just barely. She turned toward the alley as the Ker stepped into the open. Cacy's hand rose to Eli's neck, and she held his face against her shoulder. "What's up, Mandy?"

Spiteful and unnecessarily cruel, Mandy exemplified everything Cacy hated about the Kere. She clicked her lacquered red claws together and cocked her hip as she eyed Cacy and Eli. Her stilettos left little holes in the squelchy cement as she shifted her weight. "Cacy Ferry. Is this a *live* human? And are you planning to share?"

Cacy scoffed, working hard to hide her fear. Not for herself. Mandy couldn't touch her. But Eli . . . what if she was here to Mark him? Could she be persuaded not to? "He smells like a sewer. You want him?" She skimmed a hand down Eli's soaked shirt and flicked the filthy water toward Mandy, who skipped back with a squeal. "I didn't think so."

Eli shivered and stood up straight, still leaning heavily on Cacy. She twisted around until she was between him and Mandy. Eli flinched. He had probably seen Mandy's glowing red eyes. Shit.

Mandy grinned and licked her lips, revealing her glistening fangs. "Hi, gorgeous." She turned to Cacy. "Oh, hell. I'll take him, smell and all."

"Don't even think about it," Cacy snarled, cursing herself silently as Mandy's eyes widened with interest. Eli's hand, knuckles bleeding and raw, slid over Cacy's collarbone. He pulled her back against him, like he was trying to protect her. It made her heart ache.

Mandy's eyes glittered with predatory curiosity as she looked them over. After a few seconds, she stuck her bottom lip out. "I have business to attend to, anyway. Places to go, people to Mark. But I'm thinking we need to hang out, Ferry. You keep very interesting company. I'll see you soon." She turned in place and was gone.

Cacy sagged, and so did Eli. He'd probably used the last of his energy to get through that encounter. She turned so she could support him, sinking into the sidewalk under his weight.

"What was that?" he said into her hair.

Cacy didn't answer. Maybe Eli wouldn't remember this. There was a decent chance—with the hit to the head he'd taken, the postconcussive amnesia might keep him from recalling things that happened in the hours after the injury. On the one hand, she hoped that was the case. On the other, she didn't want him to be hurt that badly.

She clutched him against her as she slid her thumb over her Scope again, opened the portal, and yanked it wide, relieved when it revealed the station locker room. Eli leaned against her, his eyes half-shut. She pinched his chest, and he twitched. "Don't you dare pass out on me."

"Hey, be gentle," he mumbled against her neck, sending a shiver down her spine.

She peeked through the hoop. Thankfully, the locker room was empty. It was hours into the shift, and the paramedics who weren't at the bar would all be in the garage or out on a call. Eli sighed as the hoop descended over him and the warmer air of the locker room hit his goose-bumpy skin. He opened his eyes and scanned the room. "How the hell did we get here so fast? Weren't we just outside the bar?"

She guided him to sit on a bench and snapped her Scope back to the chain. "I called a taxi," she explained. "You must have blacked out. I'll be back in a second, all right?"

She held her breath while she watched him consider that, then let it out as he lowered his head into his hands. Concussion. Definitely.

Mentally reviewing all of Eli's possible injuries, she sprinted to the supply cabinet and grabbed everything she needed. By the time she made it back to him, supplies piled in her arms, Eli was standing up and swaying in place.

"I want to take a shower," he said to no one in particular. "I'll be fine once I get this gunk washed off me."

He clumsily stripped off his shirt, revealing his tight, defined torso. Cacy caught her breath. Even covered in canal water and smelling like hell, he looked like a god. Too bad he wasn't actually immortal. "Eli, I need to treat you, or you're going to get very sick, very soon."

"I'm fine. I'll be fine." He stumbled away from her, leaning against the wall with his shoulder as he lurched toward the shower room.

Cacy followed. She couldn't stop him unless she wanted to hurt him more, which was tempting, but not likely to be good for him in his present state. "Eli. Stop. Slow down. Okay. Stop now."

He ignored her, walking unsteadily toward the last stall on the left. He fumbled with the button of his pants as he leaned against the tile wall of the shower room. His fingers couldn't seem to manage it, though. He raised his head and looked at her, clearly embarrassed. "A little privacy, please?"

Cacy laughed. "Stop being such a jackass. Do you realize what a crappy patient you are?"

"You're not the first person to tell me that," he said quietly.

Cacy heaved an exaggerated sigh and set her supplies down on the bench in the shower stall. "You're driving me crazy."

For some reason, Eli seemed to find that really funny, but he stopped laughing and sucked in a sharp breath as she reached for his pants. He caught her wrist. "Um, maybe you shouldn't—"

"Eli. You're drunk and concussed. You just took a bath in toxic canal water. Let me help you, or I'm going to hurt you." She shoved his hand away and unzipped his jeans, pushing them down his lean hips, trying to ignore the tight feeling low in her belly.

"I think I'll keep this layer," he said, nodding at his boxer briefs. Not that they hid much.

"For now. Get in there and sit down," she said breathlessly, trying not to stare.

Eli sank down onto the bench, and Cacy scooped up the antibiotic eyedrops. She stood between his legs and tilted his head up. "Look at me. Keep your eyes open."

He smiled, staring at her with the sweetest expression on his face. "No problem."

She stared into his eyes for a moment, relieved to see his pupils were of equal size and reactive to the light. It took a few moments to tear her gaze away.

She administered the eyedrops and thoroughly swabbed out his ears and nose. He obediently swallowed the concussion-safe extra-strength analgesic she gave him, and then he put his hands on her hips. "Shouldn't you be getting the same treatment?" he asked. "You got water all over you."

She gave him a small smile. "I'm immune to those diseases," she said gently. Normally, she would have put up a show of taking all the medications herself to keep from raising suspicions, but she was worried about Eli and didn't want to waste time engaging in a charade. And . . . there was a sneaky little part of her that wanted him to know everything about her.

He nodded, like he'd expected her to say something like that. While he gargled with the antibiotic rinse, which would kill any remaining bacteria in his mouth, Cacy turned on the shower. "The only thing we have left is the systemic antibiotic."

"Oral?" he asked, and Cacy almost giggled at the hopeful note in his voice.

"I'm afraid not. You need a massive dose, and the only way to do it is through injection." She held up the capped injector pen.

He shook his head. "I'll take my chances. I've got a healthy immune system."

She touched his face, running her fingers along his cheekbone. "Don't tell me you're afraid of needles, Sergeant Margolis."

He stood up, put his hands on her shoulders, and guided her out of the shower stall. "Can we talk about this sometime when I don't smell like a sewer?"

He turned his back to her, facing the showerhead. When the steaming spray hit his face, he moaned. Cacy tucked a bar of anti-bacterial soap into his hand and took a step back. For a moment, he seemed to forget she was there. He twisted so that the water was on his back, and Cacy stood there, mouth agape. The water streamed over his dark-blond hair, down the planes of his handsome face, and fell in rivers across the hard ridges of muscle on his abs. Cacy locked her knees as the rush of warmth between her legs nearly sent her to the floor.

"I'll get a towel," she squeaked, then spun and headed down the hall, cursing Eli all the way. She grabbed a towel from the rack and walked in a slow, determined stride up the hall.

She peeked into the shower room to see Eli leaning against the wall, his hands spread against the tile on either side of the showerhead. Lather streamed down his legs and pooled at his feet. The muscles of his back were flexed, like he was trying to hold himself up. Without even thinking about it, she dropped the towel, tucked the capped injector pen in the back pocket of her skirt, and

ducked under his arm, soaking herself in the process but not caring at all. She took his face in her hands.

"Hey," she said softly, "are you still with me?"

He squinted, like he was working hard to bring her face into
focus. "Just a headache."

She threaded her fingers through his hair and found the knot
on the back of his head. Both of them winced at the same time.
"We can scoot over to the hospital for a scan after we clean you up."

"No hospitals." He leaned his head on her shoulder. "Please. I
hate those places. The front door is as far as I go."

The pleading in his voice pricked at Cacy's heart. He'd been
willing to walk into the hospital when *she'd* needed him. For him
to be unwilling to go there himself, something must have happened to him. She wasn't sure she wanted to know what. It hurt
enough to know that it had, which told her she was in some trouble. She already cared about him too much. Somewhere, deep in
the back of her mind, part of her was screaming to back off, to stay
professional. But it was easy to ignore right now, with Eli here and
needing her.

She let him lean on her, the warmth of his breath on her neck
drawing her nipples tight against the fabric of her tank top. "You
can't stay in here forever." *But I wish we could.*

He groaned. "A few more minutes. It feels so good." He raised
his head and opened his eyes, and it was like he was just fully
understanding she was in there with him. "You're . . . wet."

She smiled at the dawning realization in his eyes. "It's all right.
I don't mind."

His gaze dropped to her breasts, which were easily visible
through the thin white fabric. "You're very wet."

Watching his gaze go from dazed to hungry gave her an idea.
"I am very wet," she said, and that was true in more ways than one.
She lifted her chin so their lips were a few inches apart. "Does that
bother you?"

His laugh was low and rough. "It bothers me quite a lot, actually." She looked down to see the head of his cock peeking over the waist of his soaked boxer briefs. *Oh.* She was trying to distract him, but now all she could think about was touching him. With her hands. With her mouth.

Focus, Cacy.

"Do you want me to leave?" she asked, moving a little closer. His breath smelled like whiskey and the minty antibacterial mouth rinse.

"Cacy . . . are you playing with me?" He lowered his head until their noses were almost touching. Water from his hair dripped onto her face.

She licked her lips and slowly reached forward, touching the tips of her fingers to the head of his shaft. She skimmed over the top slowly, feeling him jerk in response. He let out a breath and wrapped his hand around the back of her neck. The look in his emerald-green eyes set her on fire, but she couldn't tell if they held anger or desire. Maybe both. His lips parted, and then he pulled her close and kissed her, his lips crashing down on hers with a desperation she could taste. He wrapped his arm around her waist and pressed her against him, allowing her to feel the thick jut of him against her belly.

She slid her arms around his neck and ran her tongue along the seam of his lips as her world tilted on its axis. It had been a long time since she'd been with a guy, but even so, it had never felt like this. All the safety of being near Eli was there; it was like the rest of the world took a full step back and fell silent, unable to touch her when he was with her. But there was danger as well. The heat of his smooth skin, the tension coiling in the muscles of his arms and chest, the shaking need she felt as his hands slid under her tank top and up her back. He kept himself under such control, but Cacy could tell there was something wild lurking beneath the surface. She wanted to be the one to bring it out.

She kissed him deep, relishing the thrust of his tongue against hers. He moaned and backed her up against the wall of the stall, causing the capped injector pen to poke her. Through the mindless desire spiraling within her, the need to feel him as close as possible, it reminded her how she had gotten to this madness in the first place.

Better get this over with. As healthy as he appeared, Eli was human, and he would be incredibly sick if he didn't get the heavy dose of antibiotic in her back pocket very soon. As much as she was desperate for him and afraid he might hate her in a minute, it had to be done. It was probably better this way.

Still kissing him breathless, she pulled out the injector pen. Eli's hands were busy, one now tangled in her hair, one cupping a breast. He rubbed his thumb over the tight bud of her nipple. She gasped and saw stars behind her closed eyelids. He growled and rocked against her. It sent a hard thrill right through her that his control was starting to break. She wanted it. She wanted him. She wanted to be the one who drove him crazy. But getting involved with him was probably a mistake, and if she let this go on much longer, they would hit the point of no return.

She ran her free hand down his back, his muscles taut under her touch. Her fingers wiggled beneath the waistband of his boxer briefs and inched them down over his hips. His erection sprang free and rubbed against the bare skin of her belly, making them both moan. Eli's hand dropped to her thigh, where he started to draw her skirt up. *Oh God.* The throb between her legs made her tremble. She wanted him to lift her up. She wanted to wrap her legs around his hips. She wanted him inside her.

As he bowed his head and kissed her neck, his fingers slipping along the seam of her panties, she bit down hard on the inside of her cheek. The pain was just enough to keep her sane and focused. She skimmed her other arm around his waist, flipped the cap off the injector pen, and, with a regretful, silent apology to Eli, stabbed it into the round, hard muscle of his butt.

Eli jerked in her arms and froze. Cacy pulled the pen away from his skin, pressed the lid closed, and cleared her throat. "It had to be done, Eli. You needed it."

His hand was still on her breast, and he rolled her nipple gently between his finger and thumb, sending jolts of pure pleasure straight to her core. He raised his head and made sure she was looking at him. "I guess the joke was on me? This was all a distraction so you could jam a needle in my ass?"

This was it. Her out. She could pull away and make light of it. And thank God he hadn't gotten her panties off, because if his fingers had slipped between her legs, he would have felt exactly how much she wanted him, exactly how ready she was, exactly how far this was from a joke. Maybe he'd buy that it was just a trick. Sure, he would hate her, but it would protect them both. She had secrets to keep. He had a life to live. And he was probably safer leading it away from her. *Especially* now.

His hand slid down her belly and around her hips, and her body responded automatically, flexing forward, hungry for him. "Are you going to lie to me, Cacy?" His voice was low in her ear, and she shivered.

All right, maybe he wouldn't buy it after all.

"Cacy? Eli?" Dec's voice echoed off the tiles.

Cacy spun herself away from Eli and stepped out of the stall. Dec's eyes went wide. "What are you doing?"

Cacy held out the spent injector pen and pointed to the small pile of used supplies at her feet. "I was making sure you didn't lose a good paramedic to botulism, cholera, leptospirosis, or typhoid. You?" She licked her lips, hoping they weren't too swollen from Eli's kiss. God, that man could kiss. She folded her arms over her chest.

Dec nodded, but his eyes skimmed over her dripping-wet clothes and hair. "Is he all right?"

"I'm fine, Chief," called Eli from the stall, sounding perfectly friendly, though Cacy could detect the edge in his voice.

"Glad to hear it," answered Dec. He looked back at Cacy. "Concussion?"

"Mild. Pupils equal and reactive to light. Oriented to person, place, and time." She continued to rattle off information about Eli's physical and mental condition, hoping to bore Dec into leaving them alone. She hadn't yet decided what she wanted to say to Eli, and she knew they weren't done talking. But Dec stood there, listening, annoyingly attentive.

"I can call a company car for him. He doesn't need to ride the bus home," Dec said when she was finished. "Are you sure he doesn't need a scan?"

"No scan needed, sir," called Eli. The water switched off.

Cacy picked the towel up from the floor and held it out to Eli without looking in his direction. He took it from her. She heard the wet slap of his boxer briefs hitting the floor of the stall and had to force herself not to turn toward him.

Dec was staring at Cacy with a distinctly suspicious gleam in his eye. "You went a bit over and above tonight," he said softly.

She glared at him. "He's my partner."

"You punched our night supervisor. And kneed him in the balls. And kicked him. You broke one of his ribs, Cace."

She shrugged. "I'll send him flowers. What are you going to do, fire me?"

"Don't tempt me," he growled.

Eli stepped from the stall, the towel slung low on his waist. Cacy swallowed hard, rocked by her lingering, unsated desire. But Eli didn't look at her. His eyes were focused on Dec. "I'm sorry about the fight, Chief."

Dec gave Eli an appraising look. "Manny has a cracked rib, too. And Gil's pretty banged up. You took three of my paramedics off the roster for Monday. Want to tell me why?"

Eli stared at Dec's feet. "Manny and Gil were self-defense, sir. Len is more debatable." Eli didn't see it, because his eyes were on the floor, but Cacy saw Dec working hard not to laugh at Eli's cryptic assessment. She wondered what the fight was really about. Eli raised his head. "I'd appreciate it if you gave me another chance, though I'll understand if you want to transfer me."

Cacy's mouth dropped open. "You are *not* getting transferred."

Dec put his hands on his hips, any humor erased from his face. "Isn't that my call?"

Cacy clenched her teeth. "You're *not* transferring him. I know Len, and this was his fault. Three against one! How is that fair? And I bet—"

Dec held up his hands. "*Cacy.* It's been an incredibly long day for all of us, and I think it's time to go home. We'll talk about it tomorrow." Dec was using his superpatient voice, which meant he was one smartass comment away from losing his shit. Cacy didn't argue further.

Eli touched her shoulder. The look on his face was so sad that it stole her breath. "Thanks for looking out for me, Cacy. I really appreciate it." His hand fell away from her, and he walked down the hall and into the locker room without a backward glance.

CHAPTER TWENTY-ONE

Eli turned down Dec's offer of a company car and took the bus, unable to stomach more exposure to the Psychopomps empire. It only reminded him how far he was from Cacy's world. He leaned back against the hard vinyl seat and closed his eyes, trying to will away the throb in his head. And in other places. He was still trying to figure out which parts of this evening had actually happened. Thoughts swirled and gusted in his brain, splitting apart and leaving odd gaps. He remembered the taste of whiskey. The flash of Cacy's smile. The aching sight of her dancing with tears in her eyes. The satisfaction of his fist smashing into Len's face. The sick, tilting feeling of falling. Glowing red eyes. A bone-splintering chill and the comfort of Cacy's arm around his waist, pulling him close. All of it was hazy and seemed only half-real.

But those moments in the shower . . . he was pretty certain *they* had been branded into his memory forever. He'd been out of it, dizzy and hurting, barely able to remember how he'd gotten there, but Cacy's touch had made it all go away. While her hands were on him, while her smooth skin was beneath his fingers, all he could think of was her scent, her taste. *Her.*

And apparently, all she'd been thinking of was injecting him with an antibiotic.

But . . . he'd been certain there was real desire in her eyes, certain he'd felt the eager quiver of her body as he'd touched her. It had been enough to make him forget everything else, to make him willing to risk everything for a chance with her. Then it had all turned out to be a distraction. *Another* distraction. That's what Cacy was all about. Drawing attention away from what was really going on.

He couldn't handle it anymore. He'd been seconds away from taking her right there in the shower stall. Seconds from getting caught by her brother.

On Monday, when he returned to work, he was going to ask Dec to transfer him. Or to place him with a different partner. No matter how much he loved working with Cacy, his feelings for her were going to get him in trouble. Knowing she felt nothing for him made it both better and worse.

He trudged up the hallway toward his apartment, but the door opened before he could reach it. "Oh, thank God. I was worried!" Galena came jogging down the hallway, took the bag of ruined clothes from him, and ducked under his arm.

"What are you talking about? You knew I'd be late." He leaned against her gratefully.

"Cacy called me. She got my number from your emergency contacts. She told me what happened."

Eli winced at the mention of her name. "And I'm sure she made it sound worse than it actually is."

Galena laughed as she helped him through the doorway of their unit. "She said you'd make it sound better than it actually is." She guided him into his bedroom and pointed to his uniform, which had been the only clean thing he had to wear home. "Do you need help getting that off?"

"I'm not an invalid," he snapped, then instantly regretted his tone. "I'm sorry, G. It's been such a long night." He fell back on his bed.

"Are you not going to be up for tonight?" she whispered.

Tonight? Oh, shit. The fund-raiser. He squeezed his eyes shut. No, he wasn't up for it. "I wouldn't miss it. After some sleep I'll be good as new."

Galena leaned over and kissed him on the forehead. "You are the best little brother ever."

Because I have the best big sister. He sighed as he heard her walk away and shut the door. With shaking hands, he unzipped his uniform and peeled it off, then collapsed back on his bed and welcomed the smothering blanket of unconsciousness that descended over him.

He dreamed of Cacy. That spicy scent, her warmth, so real. He let it take him, didn't even try to fight it. He didn't have the strength. And he wasn't sure he wanted to. Her hands were on his face, on his arms, stroking. *I'm here,* she said. *I'm here.*

He smiled, wishing it were true, because that would mean he meant something to her. She smoothed the hair from his face, kissing his eyelids and nose. *Be all right,* she whispered. *Please be all right.*

He felt her body against his, her arm around his waist, her head on his shoulder. He let the lush heat of her roll over him, thinking this was all he wanted from her—this closeness, this warmth. *Don't go,* he wanted to say. *I'll do anything. Just don't go.*

Her breath was on his neck. *I'm here.*

He sank into the feeling, the dream of Cacy pressing him into a deep ocean of rest.

CHAPTER TWENTY-TWO

Cacy's head jerked up as her phone buzzed. Her fingers fumbled to silence the thing as quickly as possible. Silencing her pounding heart was another matter entirely. For a moment, she kept perfectly still, until she was assured she hadn't been detected. Then she looked down at her phone. A text from Aislin.

Come to Psychopomps. We need to talk.

Cacy grimaced. She wanted to talk to Aislin about as much as she wanted to drink canal water, but maybe her sister had some information about the Ker who'd Marked their father. Or the missing footage of the attack. Maybe the mystery had been solved.

She tucked her phone back into her pocket and allowed her eyes to return to the man sleeping next to her. The text had been the wake-up call she needed.

This was the last place she should be.

Her plan had been to check in on Eli only to make sure he was still breathing, still alive.

For the second time in less than a day, she'd broken the rules and used her Scope for something other than her formal duties as a Ferry. She'd sneaked through the Veil and into his room. Where he'd been sleeping. Naked.

Too much temptation. She'd climbed through the Scope and entered the warmth of the real world. She'd been sitting next to him all morning, watching the rise and fall of his chest, the pulse-beat in his neck. But it hadn't been enough, so she'd held his hand and felt its warmth, touched his face and heard him sigh, kissed his cheek and watched his lips curve into a heartbreaking smile. She'd wanted to run her hands over him so badly she'd balled them into fists.

Cacy stood up and pulled the sheet from the foot of the bed. She spread it over him, regretfully covering his gorgeous—if some-what bruised—body. His breaths were even, and his eyes moved beneath his lids as he dreamed. His temperature had remained steady, judging by the lush warmth of his skin and the healthy color in his cheeks. No fever. No chills. "You'll be fine," she whispered, mostly to reassure herself.

She stared at his face, that peaceful expression, knowing he wouldn't look like that the next time he saw her. He'd probably scowl. He'd probably turn away. He had every right to. It seemed like she hurt him every time they were together, without meaning to.

I'd better leave before I do it again.

On impulse, she leaned over and kissed his forehead, letting her lips linger against his skin, an intimacy she did not deserve. She straightened and pulled her Scope from around her neck. It was a familiar burden in her palm as she opened a portal into the Veil, and then another that took her back to her apartment. From there, she took a company car to Psychopomps.

The grim expression on the face of Walter, the weekend recep-tionist, instantly told her something was wrong. "Good afternoon, Ms. Ferry," he said. "Your sister is expecting you."

Cacy nodded at him as she reached the elevators and hit the button for Aislin's floor. As the COO, Aislin oversaw the activities of the fifty thousand Ferrys of Psychopomps Inc., as well as their relationships with both foreign governments and supernatural entities. She'd just taken over the job from Rylan, who had been in the position for two decades. Cacy wondered if her smooth, flawless older sister ever felt like cracking under all that pressure.

Actually, as much as she despised Aislin—a side effect of years of neglect and cold disapproval—Cacy suspected her sister would do a good job. By all accounts, Aislin had been a devastatingly effective vice president of foreign exchange. She'd not only run a successful international money-laundering operation, which melted down the Afterlife coins into bars ready to sell on the open market, she'd also propped up the currencies of half the governments in the world by getting them to participate. And she'd been doing it since Cacy had been a little girl.

The elevator doors slid open, revealing the cool green-and-blue decor Cacy had come to associate with Rylan. Apparently, Aislin had been too busy to change anything yet. Cacy stepped into the room, wondering if she was imagining the chill that rode over her skin. She'd always felt welcome here when Rylan was the chief operating officer, but that was far from the case now, even though her sister had "invited" her. Cacy shivered and rubbed her hands over her bare arms.

Aislin was standing next to the long conference table in the central meeting room of the suite, in quiet conversation with two people, a round-faced young woman with flaming-red hair, and a dark-haired man with a stunningly sculpted face. He looked to be in his early thirties but was probably forty years older than that.

All of them were staring at a giant hologram of the Earth floating above the table. The bright-yellow deserts and dustlands of the central United States, southern Europe, and parts of southern Asia were stark in comparison to the verdant green of northern Canada, Russia, and the archipelago of Greenland. Sizable orange spots dotted the globe, denoting areas of high population density. Most people had migrated to the larger cities, some of which were newly established in the wake of the massive flooding and catastrophic climate change of the mid-twenty-first century. The big news lately was that the Arctic Circle colonies were about to declare independence from Canada, despite threats of armed suppression. Cacy had no doubt Aislin was keeping close tabs on the situation, should the need to reassign resources arise.

After all, with war came death, and with death came profit.

"I expected you half an hour ago, Cacia."

Cacy jerked her gaze from the globe to stare into her sister's glacial blue eyes. "Did you expect me to get here by magic?"

Aislin arched an eyebrow, and Cacy was suddenly quite sure Dec had tattled on her about using her Scope to transport Eli last night. She made a mental note to set a laser snaptrap in his desk drawer later.

"I expected you to take my summons seriously."

Cacy rolled her eyes. "Look, I'm here. Did you want to complain about what Father left you in his will or something?" As she watched the color rise in her sister's pale cheeks, Cacy knew she had gone too far, but she couldn't force herself to take it back.

Aislin bowed her head and took a measured breath. "Cavan," she said evenly, turning to the dark-haired man. "I apologize for the interruption. As I was saying, please return to the Lucinae and tell them we will keep them informed of the situation. Ask them to keep us apprised of any unusual Kere activity, and be sure to convey that their payments will remain unchanged."

The Lucinae were the intermediaries of new souls, in charge of shuttling them from the Spring of Life into the bodies of babies all over the world. They would no doubt be nervous about the sudden and unexpected death of Patrick Ferry and wanting reassurance that the Ferrys and the Kere were at peace.

Cavan, obviously Psychopomps' ambassador to the Lucinae and probably a cousin many times removed, nodded to Aislin. "Their leader will be happy to hear it from you." He touched his

Scope and bowed respectfully, then walked to the elevators without even acknowledging Cacy's presence.

Fair enough. She hadn't exactly been on her best behavior.

Aislin watched Cavan go, then said, "We'll meet in my office." She gestured to the redhead, who Cacy recognized from family gatherings. Shauna was a first cousin, the daughter of one of Patrick Ferry's youngest sisters. She was usually at the reception desk in the lobby.

When Cacy gave her sister a questioning look, Aislin said, "Shauna is training to be my executive assistant. She will attend all my business meetings."

"Business meeting. Wow, I feel so important."

Aislin strode toward her spacious office. "You are as important as any member of our family, and you are also, for some incomprehensible reason, Father's choice as executor."

"You really have a gift for stating facts. How about you tell me something I don't know."

"D-do you want me to record the meeting, Aislin?" Shauna's voice was a symphony of uncertainty.

Aislin rewarded Shauna with a surprisingly fond smile. "No need. Just listen." Shauna took a seat in the corner while Aislin waved toward the seating area and sat down in one of the chairs, waiting for Cacy to follow suit. Aislin took a moment to straighten her skirt and cross her legs at the ankles before aiming a cool gaze at Cacy. "I didn't want to tell you this over the phone. Debra and Peter passed away early this morning, within a few minutes of each other."

Cacy's vision went hazy, and she sank into one of the chairs. "What?"

Aislin gave Cacy a searching look, then her eyes drifted to the window, to the late afternoon sun baking the city outside. "Debra died from an accidental overdose of some kind of anticoagulant. The hospital is claiming it was a medical error. Peter died from a reaction to the pretransplant medications. Foul play is a strong possibility."

Cacy shot up from her chair. "A *possibility*? Does Rylan know about this?"

Aislin turned sharply to Cacy. "Of course he does. He went to guide their souls this morning, and I accompanied him."

"Well? Did Deb or Peter say anything? Could they tell you what happened?"

Aislin's expression said she thought Cacy was very naive. "Both of their deaths appear to have been accidental. However, the timing was highly suspicious and, like with Father, no Ker showed up to accept the commission."

"What about Alex?" Cacy asked.

"He remains in a coma. The chief neurologist is concerned it's irreversible."

Cacy's fists clenched. "That's probably the only reason he's still breathing."

Aislin didn't disagree. She was silent for a full minute before asking, "Have you received any inquiries about Father's will?"

Cacy scoffed. "Only about a thousand or so."

"He changed the will the day of his death. Did you know that?"

"I know he was wearing the same suit in the recording that he did on the day he died."

Aislin nodded. "But you don't know what details of the will he might have changed?"

Cacy took a step closer to her sister, suspicion burying itself like a tiny seed in the fertile soil of her mind. "Why so interested, sis?"

Shauna, who'd been sitting quietly in the corner, flinched. Aislin, however, did not.

Instead, she rose slowly and gracefully from her chair to face her sister, and it pissed Cacy off to no end that Aislin was able to tower over her as they stood face-to-face. Cacy raised her chin and glared at her older sister.

"Cacia, I am merely wondering if anyone was unexpectedly cut out or added. In other words, I want to know if anyone has cause to be disgruntled. Or *devious*."

Cacy couldn't be certain, but she could have sworn there was a hint of accusation in her sister's pointed stare. She glanced over at Shauna. It suddenly seemed very smart for Aislin to have a witness who was on her side.

As much as Cacy didn't want to believe it of her sister, Aislin had better reason than anyone to be devious—and to pump Cacy for information. Aislin, only a few years younger than Rylan, was probably angry at losing the CEO position to him. She was the one who'd argued that they shouldn't pursue their father's killer aggressively, all in the name of "logic." She was obviously enraged that Cacy had been named executor. Could Aislin have had something to do with their father's death? And with the deaths of Deb and Peter?

No. Not possible. Aislin was a bitch, but she wasn't evil.

Was she?

Cacy shrugged, deciding that keeping her mouth shut might be the smartest move.

Aislin let out an impatient sigh and crossed her arms over her chest. "You are as contrary as ever." She nodded at Shauna, who rose and opened the door to the office, then looked over at Cacy expectantly. An invitation to leave. The meeting was over.

Fine with me. Cacy stalked to the door without a backward glance. She was eager to escape the corporate headquarters and go somewhere to think about all this for a while. And, as ashamed as she was to admit it, she was also worried about Eli and wanted to check on him again. Maybe just a quick call to Galena—

"Cacia? One more thing, please."

Cacy didn't turn around, but she did stop walking. Maybe Aislin would say something, anything, to erase the horrible suspicion that had planted itself in Cacy's mind. "Yeah?"

"Try not to embarrass our family tonight. Dress like an adult instead of a wayward child."

Aislin was right to think Cacy was naive. Cacy had actually believed her sister would say something useful or constructive. With a bitter laugh, Cacy saluted Aislin with her middle finger and headed for the elevator.

CHAPTER TWENTY-THREE

Eli," Galena whispered. She brushed his hair off his forehead as he slowly opened his eyes. A sheet had been draped over him. He drew a deep breath and could swear the scent of Cacy had followed him from his dreams.

He sighed. "Time to don my penguin suit?"

She nodded, then bit her lip. "Are you sure about this? You should probably get some more sleep."

"What time is it?"

"Almost seven."

Lord, he'd slept for almost fourteen hours. "No," he said, pushing himself up. He swung his feet to the floor and blew out a long breath, wishing the pounding in his head would go away. "Can you get me some painkillers from my med kit, though?"

"I've got them right here. She said you'd need some." Galena held out a cup and the pills.

Eli squinted down at them. "Did she call again?" He shouldn't have cared, but . . . he did.

"Yes. I was at the lab, and she asked me to come back and check on you."

Eli raised his head sharply and winced. He took a moment to down the pills and drank the entire cup of water. He'd never tasted anything so pure. He looked down at the cup.

"It was delivered shortly after I got home." Galena took the cup from him and reached out to run a gentle hand through his hair. "Cacy's looking out for you, Eli. She sounded really worried."

Eli rubbed at the ache in his chest. "Yeah. She's been a good partner." It had been damn sneaky of her to use his desire for her to distract him. But now that he thought about it, it had also been damn smart. So why did it hurt to think about?

Because you want more and you can't have it.

He scrubbed a hand over his face and stretched, pasting a smile on his face as he looked up at Galena. Maybe this event tonight was exactly the thing he needed to get his mind off Cacy.

"Give me half an hour to get ready." He blinked and looked at his sister more closely. She'd put her hair up and was actually wearing makeup. She didn't need it; she was beautiful no matter what, but she was looking at him so hopefully that he had to say something. "You look gorgeous, G. People aren't going to listen to your speech, because they'll be too busy staring."

Her face lit up. "You're so charming. I needed to hear that." She kissed his cheek and skipped from the room, calling, "Wait till you see my dress!"

Eli headed for the bathroom, where he shaved, and got dressed. The tuxedo fit him perfectly. Maybe Cacy's family would look at him a little differently if they could see him now.

He stepped out of the bathroom and stopped dead. Galena stood in the living room, shifting her weight from foot to foot, watching him nervously. She was wearing a low-cut, flowing dark-purple dress. She looked perfect in it, but it was clear she wasn't sure about that. "You look amazing, G. Are you sure you want to be seen with me?"

She smiled and walked forward to fiddle with the tie he'd clumsily knotted. "You don't look half-bad yourself, Eli. All the ladies will be jealous of me." Her smile fell a bit. "How's your head?"

"Those pills fixed me right up. I'm good to go."

Her look of relief meant the world to him. "My speech is ready," she said. "They're sending a car."

"Well then, let's go have a good time."

Eli blinked as he got out of the car. He'd expected this event to be at one of the university buildings, but instead, it was at one of the downtown hotels. Armed guards stood at either side of the doors while suited attendants helped people from their cars. Eli reached down and offered Galena his hand. She looked a little unsteady in her high heels, but she was practically glowing with happiness and excitement. He tucked her arm in his and led her through the doors, following the other guests to a huge banquet room. One of the attendants came rushing up to them before they stepped through the wide entrance.

"Dr. Margolis? You're at the head table. This way, please."

Eli's heart beat a little faster as he followed his sister to the front of the cavernous room. A massive chandelier hung from the high ceiling, thousands of crystal droplets gleaming. Ornately set tables surrounded a huge dance floor. A string quartet was playing just at its edge, the strains of classical music wafting over the milling crowd dressed to glittering perfection. Eli resisted the urge to tug at his collar and sniff at his armpits. He didn't belong here.

The head table was larger than the others. The centerpiece appeared to be an honest-to-God tree, its narrow trunk sprouting right up from the table. Hanging from it were crystal beads. Galena grinned when she saw them. She touched one. "That's cholera," she whispered. She stroked another. "That's typhoid."

They'd made crystal decorations in the shape of bacteria, to honor Galena and her research. Eli shook his head. He'd known her research was cutting-edge, but he hadn't known she was this important.

Galena looked up at him. "Eli, dance with me. I'm too nervous to sit here and watch people come in."

Eli smiled. "Think our moves are good enough for prime time?"

She nudged him with her shoulder. "Mama taught us well. Come on. I need this."

Eli led her to the floor, his hand over hers, thinking he'd do anything to keep Galena smiling tonight. She'd worked hard to get here. She'd been through so much. She deserved this.

He lifted his arm, and she spun into him. There was nobody else on the dance floor, and a few people turned their heads to watch. Eli spent a second wondering if it was bad manners to dance during the cocktail hour, but only a second. Galena's grin erased his worries. As long as she didn't care, he didn't either. Plus, it was easier to forget where they were when they were spinning and laughing and dancing steps they'd learned as children in their family's kitchen. He might not be able to dance like Cacy and Dec, but he knew his way around a waltz. He'd never thought it would come in handy before tonight.

Eli was just beginning to enjoy himself when the music stopped abruptly and the room grew silent. Galena tensed as she looked toward the entrance. Eli followed the line of her gaze. His stomach dropped as he watched Aislin and Rylan Ferry walk through the archway, both strikingly good-looking, making the other guests around them look paunchy and old by comparison. Eli craned his neck, and sure enough, Cacy and Dec were right behind them.

"Damn," Eli mouthed. Cacy walked forward with her head held high, just like she had at the funeral. Tonight, her hair was up, pinned in looping curls on top of her head. Tiny jewels held her shiny black locks in place. The other women in the room, all of whom were wearing long, intricately designed formal dresses full of ruffles and flounces of fabric, were staring at Cacy in outright shock, but the men's stares conveyed another sentiment entirely. One that made Eli want to collectively punch them . . . even though he was looking at her the same way. Cacy's silver dress was a simple design, cut straight and low across her breasts, a black band cinching tight just below them, with a skirt flowing over her hips and ending at midthigh. Eli was suddenly reminded of moments last night when he'd been running his hands over those thighs. His groin tightened at the thought.

He swallowed hard. He could not catch a break. Though he should have known she might be here. It was a fund-raiser, after all, and the Ferrys were the wealthiest family in the city. The crowd began to clap as the Ferrys took their place at the front table directly across the dance floor from the head table. One of the chairs at that table had been draped in black fabric, no doubt in memory of Patrick Ferry. Aislin, Dec, and Cacy sat down while Rylan faced the room and bowed, mouthing his thanks as the crowd quieted.

The quartet began to play again as Eli continued to stare. Galena's hand brushed his shoulder. "She looks beautiful, doesn't she?"

Eli turned to Galena. "Don't make me answer that."

Galena looked down at his chest. "Do you want to leave or something?"

"No, G. It's no big deal." *Lie, lie, lie.*

A waiter passed by with a tray of flutes filled with sparkling wine, and Eli snagged one and drank it down. Galena gaped at him. "Is that a good idea? You have a concussion."

Eli set the glass back on the gaping waiter's tray and cleared his throat. "Don't worry about me. Are you ready to give this speech?"

Galena spun around and grabbed a glass for herself. The waiter paused, holding out his tray. Galena swallowed the wine as quickly as Eli had and set her glass next to his. "Completely ready." She giggled. She'd never had alcohol before, either.

She tugged him back toward the dance floor, which was a little more crowded now. "My speech is before dinner," she whispered. "Forget about the Ferrys and distract me until then."

Eli groaned inwardly as she pulled him closer to Cacy, which made it pretty damn hard to forget about her. Not that his body would ever let him. Just looking at her drew his muscles tight with want. She was engaged in conversation with Rylan, who looked troubled. Eli's feet moved automatically, guiding Galena through the steps, but every time they turned, Eli's eyes were on Cacy. A few minutes later, Cacy paled slightly and stood, her hand on Rylan's shoulder. Eli dipped Galena so he could see what Cacy was looking at, and was surprised to see the gloved man from the funeral approaching her with outstretched arms. He bowed to her, took her hand, and gestured toward the dance floor.

Eli's heart began to pound as they approached. The man had a satisfied smile on his face. He twirled Cacy onto the floor and pulled her close, his gloved hand skimming over the raven's wings that covered her back. Eli's jaw clenched. Galena touched the side of his face and turned her head to look. "Oh, that's Mr. Moros."

Eli arched an eyebrow at her. "You know him?"

She nodded. "He was the university representative who came to Pittsburgh to meet with me. He's the one who offered me the job, and he's been helping me get settled here as well. He's a nice man. Weird about those gloves, though. I've never seen him without them. You think he has some kind of skin condition?"

Eli lost his rhythm, and his footsteps stuttered. "Sorry." He'd have been willing to bet his life that Mr. Moros was more than a university representative. The entire Ferry family, with the exception of Patrick Ferry's children, had seemed terrified of him. And the four Ferry siblings may not have been scared, but they hadn't seemed happy to see him, either. Eli had pegged him as a rival businessman.

Someone tapped Eli on the shoulder, and he turned to find Mr. Moros standing right next to him, Cacy on his arm. She didn't look happy. They couldn't be *together*, could they? The thought made Eli's stomach knot.

Mr. Moros flashed a wide smile at Galena. "Hello, my dear. You look lovely tonight."

Galena blushed. "Thank you for making the arrangements. This is my brother, Eli."

Mr. Moros nodded and turned to Eli. "Yes, yes. We met un–officially at my dear friend's funeral. Such a sad day. I'm Jason Moros." He held out his gloved hand, and Eli shook it, noticing the worry on Cacy's face as he did. "May I dance with your beautiful genius of a sister?" He turned to Galena. "I just want to go over the specifics of your speech, my dear. I'm sure you've had yet another breakthrough since I last spoke to you."

Galena seemed perfectly willing, so Eli let his arms fall away from her as Moros took her hand and twirled her around. Cacy's hand slid into Eli's, and she looked up at him cautiously. "How are you feeling?"

"Great. Thanks for sending over the water." His fingers laced with hers before he could think about it. He should be walking her right back to her table—Rylan and Dec were both staring at them now—but he couldn't make himself let go of her hand.

Her eyes dropped to his chest. "No problem. I'm glad you're all right. Should we dance?"

He sighed. "What the hell," he muttered, pulling her close. What did it matter? Eli was guessing he'd be transferred away from Chinatown by Monday night. He'd never see Cacy again, so he might as well enjoy the moment for what it was.

She gracefully fell into step with him and followed his lead easily, but Eli expected no less. Apparently she did, though. "You can dance," she said softly, like it was a total surprise.

"My mother taught us."

"She did a good job."

Eli shook his head and tried to ignore the tightening in his throat. "My parents passed away in the outbreak of the H3N2 virus about five years ago. It happened while I was overseas. I ended my career in the army so I could go home to Galena."

Cacy's smile died. "I didn't realize you lost both of them at once."

He twirled her around and pulled her back, treasuring the feel of her curves against his body. "It's all right. Galena got sick, too, but she pulled through. I think it's driven her ever since. She wishes she could have saved them."

He looked around for Galena, who was smiling and chatting with Moros as they danced.

Cacy was watching them, too. "What did you say your sister's research is about?"

"The human immune system."

Cacy's hand tensed in his as he whirled her around again. "Can you be more specific?"

"All I know is that her research involves how vaccines can be modified to boost people's immunity to contagious diseases. It's cutting-edge stuff, I guess. She's pretty brilliant."

Cacy's eyes narrowed as she watched Galena and Moros, but she didn't say anything else. The song ended, and Moros and Galena were now coming toward them. It was time to let Cacy go. But when Eli tried to let go of her hand, she held on.

"Listen," she said softly, "I'm sorry about last night. But . . . I need you to know . . . it wasn't just a ruse." She squeezed his hand, and Eli got the sudden impression she was only saying a fraction of what was on his mind. Then she turned abruptly and walked back to her table, leaving him standing alone in the middle of the dance floor.

CHAPTER TWENTY-FOUR

Cacy was wound tight as hell by the time she made it back to her table. Her thoughts were on fire. First, she'd never seen anyone look as good in a tux as Eli did.

He was here with his sister. An immunologist. Apparently, a fairly prominent one. And that was the second thing that had Cacy on edge—Moros seemed really interested in Galena, and it raised her suspicions into the red zone. This could not be a coincidence; it had to be what Moros didn't want to tell her when they met at Bart's. It was all coming together in Cacy's mind . . . Moros's plans to meet with her father in Cambridge, her father standing in the Veil outside Eli's apartment, the Ker looking in Eli's window, and now this. Cacy felt like she was standing at the precipice of a huge cliff, about to tumble into something vast and dangerous.

She sank into her chair and reached for a glass of wine as Moros patted Galena's shoulder and pulled out her chair before seating himself next to her. Cacy glanced at her siblings. Rylan and Aislin were watching Moros, too, but Dec's eyes were scanning the crowd. "He brought friends," he said quietly.

Cacy followed the sweep of his gaze and spotted a few Kere sitting at a table near the rear of the room. Luke looked slickly handsome in his tux. The female Ker next to him was wearing a god-awful flouncy pink dress, like she was doing her best to look soft and human. Her name was Jill and, like Luke, she had a fondness for illness. Hemorrhagic fevers, specifically. Next to Jill sat a young guy with brown hair. Cacy didn't recognize him. He was either a Ker . . . or a very unlucky human.

"Since when do the Kere attend fund-raisers?" Cacy whispered.

Before Dec could respond, a gaunt, ridiculously tall man with huge glasses skittered up to the podium at the front of the room. "Ladies and gentlemen," he said in a low, nasally voice. "It is my pleasure to welcome you here tonight to celebrate excellence in higher education . . ."

As he talked, Cacy watched Eli. His hand was curled protectively over Galena's as he listened to the speaker. Every once in a while, he glanced over at his sister with a worried glint in his eyes. Cacy sighed. He'd given *her* that look a few times, and it had felt amazing, like he would lay his life on the line for her.

". . . and to show you how well your contributions are spent, please welcome Harvard's newest brilliant addition to its immunology department, Dr. Galena Margolis."

Galena rose to the sound of polite applause and walked to the podium. The audience quieted quickly, no doubt expecting yet another boring speech from a dry academic. Galena tapped the display on the podium a few times, and a three-dimensional squiggle appeared next to her, swirling slowly. It looked like some type of single-celled organism.

She smiled at it like it was a good friend and said, "When I began my research five years ago, I dreamed this day would come. Every night, I prayed for it. Every day, I worked for it beside my wonderful colleagues. Every spare moment, I thought about it. No matter what happened in my life, I clung to that dream. I was fortunate to have the support of my loving family"—her eyes found Eli's—"along with the University of Pittsburgh, and I'm thrilled to be continuing my work here at Harvard and sharing my hopes

with you all tonight. I am proud to have finally made enough progress in my research to be able to say this with some confidence: My
friends, imagine a world without contagious disease."

Cacy sat bolt upright in her chair. As Galena talked about her
research and its potential, how her method for creating customized
automutating multicure vaccines might end viral and bacterial
outbreaks forever, Cacy realized exactly why Moros was interested.

Eli's sister was about to put a serious dent in the death industry.

In the last fifty years since the great floods, new viral and bacterial illnesses had emerged every year, mutating at rates that pre-
vented development of effective vaccines. Nearly a billion people
had died. This wave of early death had created a boom for the
Ferrys and the Kere, filling their vaults with gold from the Keepers
of the Afterlife, letting them live in luxury while the rest of the
world teetered on the brink of disaster. If Galena had really discovered the way to create vaccines that mutated right along with
the illnesses for each specific person, she might cut the worldwide
death rate by at least a third. That meant a major, immediate loss
of income for the Kere.

And the Ferrys.

Trying not to be too obvious, Cacy looked over at her siblings. Aislin's body posture was even more rigid than usual. Rylan
was staring at Moros. And Dec . . . he was staring at Galena with
an intensity Cacy had never seen before. She knew her siblings
well enough to know they understood the significance of Galena's
research. What wasn't clear: Had they known about it ahead of
time? And how did they feel about it?

Galena finished her speech, and the applause was significantly
louder this time. Eli stood up, holding his arms out to Galena. She
stepped into them and accepted his hug with a sweet, relieved look
on her face. Cacy tried to ignore a twinge of envy. She knew that
being in Eli's arms made a person feel safe, and she could use that
feeling right now.

Waiters carrying their loaded trays came up the paths between tables, and everyone settled into conversation.

"Well," laughed Rylan, raising his eyebrows. "That was interesting."

Dec cleared his throat and sat back. Every line of him was practically vibrating with tension. "Very. I'm out of here." He drained his wine in one gulp, set his glass on the table, and stalked out of the hall. As he passed by the tables in the back of the room, Cacy noticed that the Kere were gone, too.

Without a word, Aislin rose to her feet and crossed the room. Moros saw her coming and stood up. He had a charming, relaxed smile on his face, but his eyes were intense with emotion as he watched her approach. After a slight bow, he held out his arm and escorted Aislin out of the room.

"What is that about?" asked Cacy, her hands closing hard over her knees. It would be just like Aislin to try to make some sort of slimy deal with Moros. When one vulnerable mortal was poised to singlehandedly deliver a massive financial blow to some of the scariest and most powerful creatures in the known world, that deal might involve breaking some of their ancient rules. Like only Marking someone who was fated to die. Like not interfering with the course of human events. If Aislin was able to negotiate directly with Moros to kill Galena and keep their profits high, she might be able to get the family shareholders to overturn their father's succession decision and put her in place as the CEO.

A perfect corporate coup.

Rylan couldn't possibly be oblivious to Aislin's plotting, but he showed no signs of anxiety as he picked up his fork and speared a potato. "Cacy, I wanted to talk to you about Deb and Peter." He gave her a sidelong glance.

"I already know they're gone," she said quietly. "Aislin called me to headquarters today."

"Did she tell you we suspect foul play?"

Cacy nodded. "She said she went with you to escort their souls."

"More like she insisted on coming with me."

Cacy stared at a twinkling blown-glass squiggle hanging from one of the branches of the centerpiece. Had Aislin not trusted Rylan to go by himself? Or had she been afraid Deb and Peter might say something incriminating? At that exact moment, Eli glanced over at them, and his eyes met Cacy's. She suddenly wished everything else would disappear and leave her alone with him, if only for a few minutes. But with this new—and utterly mind-blowing—complication, it didn't look like that was going to happen anytime soon.

Rylan chuckled, a stark contrast to his dire statement of a second ago. "He looked at you that way at the funeral as well. Any chance you're off the wagon?" She'd told Rylan all about how she'd sworn off men when he'd tried to set her up with one of his bodyguards.

"No. I'm still riding it." She tried to smile, but it felt painful.

Rylan took a sip of wine and put his arm around the back of Cacy's chair. "You could do worse."

She slapped his chest lightly. "What's that supposed to mean?"

He looked down at her, his brown eyes soft. "It means I think you've been lonely, and Eli seems like a very nice young man. It looks like he cares about you. Maybe you should get to know him a little better."

In spite of herself, she smiled. "I would. I mean, I want to. But after tonight—"

Rylan's expression hardened. "Are you worried about who killed Father, or are you worried about someone trying to stop Dr. Margolis?"

"Both," Cacy said, her eyes wandering back in Eli's direction.

Rylan fingered the stem of his wineglass. "If you knew I was taking care of it, could you relax and allow yourself to have some fun for once?"

She leaned her head on his shoulder. "Maybe."

"Well then, I'm handling it. But I could use more information. Have you uncovered anything in Father's files? Maybe who he met with in the week before he died. His financial records. Any hint of where he stood on this Dr. Margolis thing. It must have been on his mind—and his agenda." He obviously remembered their father's soul had been near the Harvard campus in the Veil. And he clearly recognized the implications of Galena's scientific discoveries. But there were things Rylan didn't know—the Ker looking in Eli's window, for one. He also hadn't heard their father's final words to Cacy . . . *Protecting the future is more important than righting the wrongs of the past.*

She knew exactly where her father stood—on the night of his death, her father had told her what he wanted her to do. He wanted Cacy to worry less about figuring out his death and more about protecting Galena. She was almost certain that was what he'd been trying to tell her. Patrick Ferry had a reputation as a calculating, ruthless Charon, but in the last fifteen years, he'd also plowed billions into charity and been unrelenting about obeying the rules of the treaty. About making sure what happened was *meant to be.* Cacy thought she knew why, too. Her father wanted to make sure he got to Heaven. He'd been trying to get back to Cacy's mother.

Cacy looked up at Rylan, so strong, so burdened by managing a complicated corporate and supernatural empire, possibly while his own COO was trying to undermine him. Part of Cacy wanted to lay everything in her big brother's lap, just hand it over to him and focus on Galena. But part of her also wanted to figure it out herself—she wanted to prove she was worthy of the responsibility her father had given her. Like everyone else, Cacy didn't know why he'd trusted her with managing his estate or protecting Galena, but she did know Patrick Ferry never did anything without a reason.

She hugged Rylan. "I have to finish going through his records. He didn't talk to you about Dr. Margolis and her research?"

Rylan shrugged. "I guess he wanted to keep that one to himself until a decision was made."

She'd suspected something like this before, but now she knew exactly what *Final Decision* must have meant. Her father had been planning to meet with Moros to decide what to do about Galena Margolis. "Did you know he was planning to meet with Moros in Cambridge the night of his death? That's where he was headed when he was killed."

Rylan's arm grew tight around her shoulders. "How do you know all this?"

"After I talked with Debra, I met with Moros," she admitted.

Rylan turned to her and clutched her shoulders. "Cacy, you are getting in way over your head. He could be responsible for all this. Do you know what he could have done to you?"

She bowed her head and pulled away. "I can handle it. I'm a grown-up, Ry."

He chuckled and put his hand on her shoulder again, and this time it was warm and protective. "But you'll always be my little sister. You haven't been swimming in these waters as long as I have, Cacy. Compared to me, you are a child. I was at Father's side for nearly eighty years. Long enough to see what Moros is capable of. He may not be able to Mark you, but he can hurt you in ways you can't possibly imagine, no matter how much you think you know. Chances are we've got a conspiracy on our hands, and it could involve absolutely anyone. Even if Father was Marked by Moros or one of his Kere, I'm betting someone at Psychopomps bribed his driver and deleted the footage. Please, let me handle this."

A child. The words echoed in her ears. She didn't feel like a child. She hadn't felt like a child since her mother died and left her alone with her grieving father. Rylan had been too busy climbing the corporate ladder to pay much attention to what was happening at home. Aislin too. And Dec had just been promoted to Chief at the Chinatown EMS station when their mother died. They hadn't been the ones who helped their father stumble to bed after drinking bottle after bottle of whiskey to numb his pain. They hadn't borne the responsibility of making him happy again. She might only be twenty-five, which *was* young for a Ferry, but she was no child. Cacy brought her wineglass to her lips, staring into the sparkling ruby depths. "Message received, Rylan."

Cacy walked the soft gray streets outside Eli's apartment building. She was still wearing her party dress, which had been stupid, because she'd started shivering as soon as she'd entered the Veil.

She wasn't allowing herself to go into the building—or into the real world. She wasn't allowing herself to stalk Eli, no matter how badly she wanted to. But she was too worried about him and Galena to go back home. She'd called Moros as she left the fund-raiser and demanded another meeting. Until then, she would stand guard. She wasn't sure exactly what she would do if a Ker showed up, but she would figure it out. She was prepared to involve the Keepers of the Afterlife if she had to.

Her high heels kept sinking into the squishy sidewalk, so she leaned against a bench and pulled them off. A soft, slurping sound on her right made her instinctively duck behind the bench. Someone was coming through a portal.

Another Ferry.

But there were no souls around here who needed to be guided to the Afterlife.

A shimmering ring was hovering about half a block away, and from it emerged one of the last people she would have expected to see. He lowered the ring to the ground and stepped over its boundaries before picking it up and compacting it in his hands. His gaze raked the area around them but didn't slow as it passed the bench where Cacy was hiding. He hadn't seen her.

Still looking back and forth, he climbed the steps to Eli's apartment and sank through the front door of the building. Cacy stood up, stunned.

What the hell was Dec doing?

CHAPTER TWENTY-FIVE

When Eli got to the EMS station for his shift on Sunday evening, Dec was waiting for him.

"I need you in my office for a minute, Sergeant," he said, then he turned and walked down the hall.

Eli followed, steeling himself. He was going to get transferred—he just knew it; he'd been thinking about it all weekend, trying to force himself to be okay with it.

After the fund-raiser the night before, where he'd danced with Cacy, held her in his arms again, seen her gorgeous smile, and listened to her say words he'd needed to hear—that it wasn't just a distraction, that she wanted him, too—he'd understood this would be painful.

He wondered if Dec would give him a chance to say goodbye to her, or if he was going to ship him off to another station immediately.

Dec gestured to a chair in the corner of his cramped office. "Have a seat, Eli."

Eli sat. Dec remained standing. His expression was somber. "I've talked to Len, Manny, and Gil. They said you had a few things to say about Cacy that night at Bart's. Len said you were bragging about how you planned to fuck my little sister while I was too drunk to notice."

Eli shot to his feet before he could stop himself, blood pounding in his ears. "They're lying, sir. I'd never say that about *any* woman. And Cacy—"

Dec stepped forward, looking Eli hard in the eye. "What about Cacy, Eli? Anything you want to tell me?"

Eli looked away and sank back down in his chair. "I would never hurt her, Chief. And I have more respect for her than I can say."

"You're saying my night supervisor is lying. You'd swear to it." Dec's voice was quiet but dangerous.

"I would swear to it." Eli kept his gaze rooted on Dec's boots.

"Then tell me what happened."

Eli sighed. As much as he hated Len, the asshole was a decent paramedic, and Eli had no desire to ruin a career. "Just stupid guy talk, sir. I can't really remember." He pointed to where he'd hit his head.

"I think you remember more than you're saying. But it's damn honorable of you to protect them after what they did to you."

Eli's head shot up. "What?"

Dec smiled grimly. "Someone overheard you and told me what happened."

Eli sagged with relief. He could deal with being transferred, but he didn't think he could live with Dec thinking he'd said those awful things about Cacy.

Dec's smiled dropped away. "Now tell me your intentions toward my sister."

Eli's eyes widened. "I . . . I don't have any intentions toward her."

Dec folded his arms over his chest. "I thought you were an honest man, Eli. Let's try again. I've seen the way you look at her. I saw the way you danced with her at the fund-raiser. Nice party, huh? I'll bet you'd never seen anything so fancy. A man could get used to that, am I right?"

Eli's hands curled into fists. He was barely able to think past the rage rising within him, but he managed to choke out, "Are you suggesting I'm interested in Cacy because of her *money*?"

"I know your life has been hard, Eli. It must have occurred to you."

Yes. It had. But not how Dec was implying. Which made what the man was saying impossible to take; if it weren't for Cacy's money and her family, maybe Eli would have had a chance with her. He stood up slowly this time, forcing himself to keep his fists at his sides. "I like you, Chief. And I respect you. But if you think my feelings for Cacy have *anything* to do with money, you can go fuck yourself."

He started to push past Dec, knowing he was about to get fired but not caring anymore. He needed to get as far as possible from the Chief before he exploded.

Dec's arm shot out and barred the door. "You *do* have feelings for her."

Eli froze.

Dec smiled and held his hands up in a conciliatory gesture. "I needed to know. She cares about you, Eli. She hasn't been involved with anyone for a long time, and I don't want to see her get hurt."

"Sir?" Eli's voice was only a hoarse whisper.

Dec shrugged and ran a hand over his hair, making it stand on end. "She's my little sister, Eli. You can't blame me for being protective. You have a sister, too. Galena . . . You understand that."

Eli nodded, trying to decipher the way Dec's expression changed as he said Galena's name. Dec gave him a quick smile. "You're a good man. You could be what Cacy needs. Just don't let her push you away, all right? She can be tough sometimes."

Eli laughed, his tension draining away. "Sometimes?"

When Eli entered the garage, Cacy was waiting in their rig. "Late again?" she asked, but her voice was friendly. Her eyes lit on him and lingered, drawing him toward her.

"I was talking to your brother," he said as he climbed into the back, pulling the doors of the rig shut behind him. Even though her hair was in its usual ponytail and she had her uniform on, she looked as devastatingly beautiful as she had last night.

Cacy sat down on the bench, looking wary. "What did he say?"

Eli sat next to her and looked at the floor of the rig. His hands curled over the hard edges of the bench. "He wanted to know my intentions toward you."

After a few moments of silence, Cacy laughed, a shaky little sound. "Do you have intentions, Sergeant Margolis?"

He raised his head to look at her. "I might have a few."

Cacy's face was a bewildering array of emotions. For a moment, it lit up. Then that light died, smothered by something darker that he didn't understand. Was *she* worried he was after her money? Or was she involved with someone else? Dec said she wasn't, but Cacy was a grown woman and probably didn't tell her big brother everything. Could it be that Moros guy? Did she feel guilty that she'd kissed Eli that night in the shower? As his heart sank, Cacy wrapped her arms around herself like she was trying to keep it together. She drew in a sharp breath. "Eli—"

"No." He shook his head. "Don't. I'm sorry. You've been through so much in the last week. I shouldn't have said anything. I'm sorry for making this awkward."

They stared at each other. Eli remembered each of the intimate moments they'd had, every single one followed by a veritable tsunami of awkwardness, more than he'd ever experienced with anyone. From the twitch of her lips, Cacy was thinking the same thing. They burst into laughter at the same time.

Cacy clutched her stomach, laughing so hard there were tears in her eyes. "Yes. *Please* don't make this awkward." Her smile was real. Her tears were happy. Eli had never wanted to kiss anyone so badly.

He forced the thought away and chuckled. Then he said a word that should have been a relief, a gift, but was instead like a leaden weight on his chest. "Friends?"

Her smile faltered. Eli thought he'd messed up again until she slipped her hand into his and squeezed. "Absolutely."

She laid her head on his shoulder. It wasn't everything he wanted from her, but it was perfect nevertheless. His heart swelled as she laced her fingers with his, and he reached up and cupped her face with his hand. The delicate burden of her head on his shoulder made him feel weak and strong at the same time, like he would do anything for her, like he could be anything she needed, even if it meant just being her friend. But it also made him feel vulnerable, because she could hurt him now—*really* hurt him—and she didn't even know it.

He smiled a rueful smile and kissed the top of her head, realizing he'd felt like this for a while, maybe since the first time he'd laid eyes on her. And every moment since, as he'd watched her get hurt and get right back up, as she'd looked out for him like no one outside his family ever had, as she'd touched him in ways that set him on fire . . . now he was so wound up in her he wasn't sure he'd ever be able to get loose.

Eli had a feeling this was going to be the most complicated friendship he'd ever had.

CHAPTER TWENTY-SIX

Cacy sat with Eli, her head on his shoulder, her heart in his hands. He had no idea. And she couldn't tell him now, not when his sister's life hung in the balance and it was Cacy's family who would benefit from Galena's death. Cacy had no intention of letting Eli's sister die, but until she knew Galena was safe, it didn't seem right to get involved with Eli. If something did happen, he would probably think she'd played a part in it and would hate her forever. More importantly, she couldn't afford to be distracted by her feelings for him now. Too many people had died already.

None of that stopped her from wanting to get involved with him. Actually, "involved" was a tame word compared to what she wanted from Eli. Part of her was thrilled that her brothers had given their approval—but the other part wondered why. Especially after seeing Dec at Eli's apartment last night. She'd carefully followed him in, but he was nowhere to be found. Cacy had always trusted Dec—but now she wondered if his alliance with Aislin was strong enough to lead him to spy for her. Aislin wasn't the type to get her own hands dirty, but Dec was a different story entirely. He was practical and tough—and had the medical knowledge to kill Peter and Debra and make it look accidental. If Aislin and Dec had teamed up with Moros or any of his Kere, Galena's soul could be

Marked and crammed through a portal to the Afterlife in a matter of minutes, and no one would know if she was fated to die that way or not. She'd never finish the research that promised to deliver a miraculous cure for all infectious diseases.

After a night spent in the Veil, standing guard in Eli and Galena's cramped living room, shivering, wanting nothing more than to step through her Scope and crawl into bed with Eli to feel the delicious heat of his skin, Cacy went home and crashed for an hour. Then she'd spent the day wading through her father's records and dealing with more whiny Ferrys who thought they'd been neglected in the will. She'd gone to meet with the families of Debra and Peter, quietly making sure each of their dependents was set for life. And all the while, looming on the horizon, was her meeting with Moros, which had been scheduled for tomorrow afternoon.

Her stomach churned even thinking about it.

Moros would demand payment for a favor like the one she was going to request. But she didn't know what else to do. Her father had given *her* this responsibility. He had trusted her to see it through. And Eli . . . he had already lost his parents. He couldn't lose his sister, too.

The ambulance bay doors yawned wide as a rig pulled into the garage. It would be a busy night. Len and his crew were out of commission, so they were short-staffed. They could get a call at any moment. And yet, she and Eli sat there, hoarding as many seconds as they could get, unwilling to relinquish the moment. She'd never known a guy she could sit with comfortably in silence, enjoying the simple pleasure of being together. It was as satisfying as it was frustrating.

Eli shifted and gave her shoulder a squeeze. "We've got to get prepped."

"I know," she whispered.

"I guess we asked for this when we beat up our colleagues."

She nodded.

"Hey." He took her face in his hands. "Will you . . . meet me tomorrow? You know, for dinner before our shift or something? As friends," he added quickly.

Her meeting with Moros was at Bart's early the next afternoon. Maybe she'd be able to resolve everything then. Maybe it really would be as simple as that. Maybe that would mean she and Eli could relax and actually get to know each other better. The thought made her smile. "Yeah. I've got a business meeting in the afternoon, but let's meet up at Bart's at five?"

The alarm sounded. Eli got up from the bench grinning, and it made her heart soar. She wanted to put that look on his face a lot more often.

"Perfect," he said. "Now, let's go save some lives."

Cacy paused outside Bart's and looked out on the canal. As usual, the smell was dreadful, but the view was fascinating. Uniboats, sampans, and amphibious vehicles bumped and zoomed along, churning up the cloudy water in muddy brown whirlpools. There was a certain beauty in the chaos, a certain order in the mess. Just like in the world of the Veil. As long as everyone played their part, things would come together as they should. But when people were tempted by greed, when power went unchecked, things fell apart. Her father had taught her that. He'd believed in the mission of the Ferrys, to serve as witnesses and intermediaries. He'd told her the Ferrys were, ultimately, servants to fate. Cacy believed that, too.

She would get through this meeting . . . and then she would see Eli. Last night had been as busy as they'd feared but they'd worked side by side, hour after hour, in complete sync. They'd saved nearly a dozen lives. In fact, for the first shift in years, Cacy hadn't lost a single patient. It was a strange switch from the carnage of the past week. But to be successful, they'd worked their asses off, and so they hadn't had another chance to talk. At the end of their shift he'd said good-bye with a long hug, and she'd greedily absorbed the strength and warmth of his arms, needing his touch as badly as she needed oxygen.

"Stop stalling," she whispered, drawing herself up and turning toward Bart's. She pulled open the heavy wooden door. It was early, so there were only a few guys at the bar, hunched over their beers.

Cacy nodded to the hostess and walked down the narrow, dark hallway, her shoes sticking in the tacky leavings of a recent spill. Moros was waiting for her in the last room on the left. This time, his feet were planted respectfully on the floor. He gave her a lazy smile as she entered the room. He'd already poured her a drink. "Cacia, you look lovely today."

Cacy looked down at her T-shirt and jeans. "You have interesting standards."

He shrugged and sipped his Scotch, closing his eyes and savoring. "You asked to meet me."

Cacy shut the door behind her and leaned against it. "I want to know what you're up to with Galena Margolis."

He laughed. "Nothing untoward. She's a beautiful woman, but not really my type."

"You know what I mean," Cacy said quietly.

His eyebrows shot up. "Do I? Why don't you tell me what you want, my dear."

"You knew about Galena's research before she came here, didn't you?"

He smiled. "Of course. You think I wouldn't be aware of something so significant? I've known about Galena for a long time. I knew what she would accomplish before she did."

A chill passed through Cacy as she realized just how powerful Moros was. "You were meeting with my father about her. To make a decision."

He set his glass on the table. "What, exactly, are you suggesting?"

"That she could put a major dent in our cash flow, and that you two were deciding what to do about that. About her."

His eyes flashed red. "What makes you think there's a decision to be made? Perhaps she is fated to die. I'm the only one who knows my sisters' will."

"True, but why would you be focused on her if she was fated to die soon? You said her work was significant—you wouldn't be worried about it if it was all for nothing. So I think she's fated to live, unless someone intervenes." *Just like Father was.* "Is that what you and Aislin met about?"

He smirked. "You could ask her that yourself."

Cacy's eyes narrowed. "Galena's fate should be allowed to unfold naturally. Without interference. No matter who would benefit from her death."

Slowly, he rose to his feet. "Are you here to scold me, little Ferry? Or," he said with a chuckle, "to threaten me?"

Cacy shook her head, her heart beating so hard it nearly deafened her. "I'm here to ask a favor."

He canted his head to the side. "I'm listening."

"Spare her. Protect her. Don't let her be Marked before her time."

He sighed. "Only my sisters and I know the time. You cannot say it is not now."

She met his gaze. "No, I can't. But regardless, I'll pay you to resist twisting her fate to preserve your profits."

"And yours."

"I care about a lot more than just money."

A gentle smile rendered his face beautiful for a moment. But his words made her heart drop. "I understand. Her brother. Galena is not the only one you wish to protect."

Cacy looked in his eyes, not able to deny it. "I am offering you my entire inheritance."

Moros took a step toward her. "As considerable as your fortune is, my dear, it wouldn't make up for the financial loss Galena's discovery will cause. Imagine our income dropping by a third. It would be like the Worldwide Depression of the twenty-first century for our people. Surely you learned about that in school? My Kere are accustomed to certain luxuries. They will not be happy. I have no doubt they would be tempted to start a full-scale rebellion. It will take work to protect Galena."

"But you can control them, can't you?"

His jaw tightened. "Of course."

"Then I'm asking you to do this. Please. I'll give you anything."

"Anything? Oh, my dear, you have no idea what you're saying."

She gazed at him steadily. Her voice shook more than she would have liked as she said, *"Anything."*

His tongue traced across his bottom lip as he began to remove his gloves.

Cacy's pulse pounded in her ears. She'd been raised on the stories that Moros could kill with one touch, that he could ruin and destroy with the merest brush of his fingers. "You can't kill me. The Keepers of the Afterlife would crucify you." Big words that didn't match the crack and tremble in her voice.

Moros *tsk*ed and waved his gloves at her. "I have no intention of killing you. Why would you say such a thing?"

"I . . ."

"I am merely accepting payment for the favor you've requested from me." He laid his gloves on the table next to his Scotch.

Her back pressed flat against the door as her breath became ragged with fear. "Will it hurt?"

"Always."

"Will I be the same after?"

"Never." His voice was quiet yet deadly.

She stared at the long fingers on his hands. "Will you promise me she will be protected?"

He gave her a small smile. "You have my word."

Cacy pushed herself away from the door and took a step forward, despair and hope at war in her body. She had no idea what he was about to do to her, but she believed Moros would keep his word. And with Eli and Galena protected, it would be worth it. "Then do what you want."

Moros walked slowly around her, the heat from his body pouring off him in waves. And despite that, all Cacy felt was cold dread. He moved in front of her, the red glow in his eyes burning right through her. She bowed her head, waiting for him to strike.

"Are you ready?" he asked, his voice just a rasp.

"Just do it."

His hand closed hard around her throat.

It was like being hit by a wrecking ball.

Cacy's back arched as everything inside her shattered. Her thoughts, her heart. As her mind sparked and stuttered, her vision went black, overloaded by millions of split-second images that blurred together. Faces streaking by, some she knew and some she didn't, smiling, crying, twisted with rage. Places she recognized and many she'd never seen. Darkness. Bright, blinding light. Hands on hers, over her own pregnant belly. A sleeping child in a darkened bedroom. Deep-green eyes, staring into hers. She couldn't fully translate any of the images, but she could feel them. *All* of them. At the same time. Sorrow, hatred, shock, disgust, rage, despair, joy, excitement. A longing so painful she cried out. Love so deep it buckled her knees. Pain so jagged it robbed her of any control. Loss so profound she wanted to die. Her arms splayed out helplessly as every conceivable feeling plowed through her body, causing it to seize and shudder. The entire world disappeared as wave after wave of raw emotion tossed her mind, shredding all her plans and hopes, drowning her in sensation.

Then everything stopped. Moros opened his fingers and stepped back. Cacy crumpled in a heap on the floor, a rag doll too ruined to raise her head. All the things she'd seen still jabbed at her soul like tiny bolts of lightning.

"That was . . . magnificent," he whispered hoarsely. "Thank you."

Cacy lay there for several minutes, unable to move, barely able to draw breath. Her entire body vibrated with agony, like all her limbs had been pulled out of joint. Finally, she summoned enough strength to speak. "What did you do to me?"

The wooden chair creaked as Moros sat down. "I tasted your future."

Excruciating pain shot through her arms and shoulders as she pushed herself up. "Don't you already know my future?"

He nodded, his usually neat hair now disheveled, his breaths still coming deep and heavy. "But now I have experienced it for myself. Ah, you feel things so deeply, Cacia. The *sensation* of it . . . Not many people willingly allow me to do that."

She could certainly understand why. It wasn't just the physical pain. It was the feeling of being split wide open at the very core of her soul, torn apart, and carelessly glued back together with no regard for where things were supposed to go. She shakily got to her feet, leaning against the door to keep from falling. "Is that all? Have you had enough?"

He stroked a hand lazily down the arm of his chair. "More might permanently damage you."

"That was really my future?" Right now she wasn't sure she could endure another minute, let alone a lifetime. But there had been flashes of beauty in all that pain. Moments of ecstasy. It felt far out of reach now, though. "Do I still get to have it?"

He peered down at her, a million secrets glinting in the dark depths of his eyes. "You might."

"You will keep your promise," she said, ashamed of the broken, childlike tremor in her voice. The images were subsiding now, fading, like a movie she'd already seen.

Over. It felt like her life was *over*.

Moros nodded, a tiny smile curling his lips as he lifted his glass once again. "Of course."

Cacy closed her eyes to keep her tears from falling. "All right."

It took her a few tries to open the door, but she managed to do it and stumble into the hall. A yawning chasm had opened in her heart, like her life had already been lived without her, like it wasn't really hers anymore. She wanted to scream, to weep, to hide.

Eli's face floated in her mind for an instant. She was supposed to meet him soon. But she didn't want him to see her like this, broken and used, her entire future just a tasty snack, a momentary pleasure, for the Lord of the Kere. It felt like she had nothing new to share anymore, no mystery, no excitement left to offer.

CHAPTER TWENTY-SEVEN

Eli sat down at the bar and ordered a soda. He shifted nervously in his seat and told himself for the thousandth time that this was no big deal, that he was simply getting together for dinner with a colleague.

The bartender set a fizzy soda in front of him with a smirk. "You want a straw with that?"

Eli shook his head, gave the guy a sarcastic smile, and waved his phone over the scanner at the edge of the bar to pay. He kept his eyes on the row of bottles in front of him as he drank, but every time he heard the door open, he tensed in anticipation. And every time he realized it wasn't her, he sagged with disappointment.

The bartender returned and set a glass of clear liquid in front of him. Eli looked up at him in confusion. The bartender nodded toward the other end of the bar. "Courtesy of the lady."

Eli's eyes followed the bartender's and landed on a pretty blonde wearing bright-red lipstick. She winked at him. Eli looked away and pushed the drink toward the bartender. "Unless that's water, I can't. I have to be at work in a few hours."

The bartender looked at him like that was irrelevant. "Buddy, she won't buy drinks for just anyone."

Eli's eyes traveled back to the blonde woman. There was something familiar about her, but he couldn't place it. She licked her lips and leaned forward over the bar, giving him a view of breasts barely contained by her tight, low-cut shirt. It did nothing for him.

The door to the bar opened and shut again, and this time Eli turned to look. But it wasn't Cacy. Where was she? Had she decided not to come? Had he been too forward? Too awkward? Had she been afraid he couldn't take a hint? He suddenly felt stupid for even asking her to meet him. She'd made it clear she didn't want to get involved with him, so why had he invited her to dinner?

"Because I'm an idiot," he mumbled, pushing away from the bar and turning to go.

Cacy stumbled out of the back hallway, pale as death, one arm wrapped around her middle, one on the wall to hold herself up. She raised her head, her glassy eyes riveted on the door.

Eli started forward as she lunged through it. He strode after her, but by the time he made it out of the bar, Cacy was gone. He looked up and down the street and into the alleys on either side of the bar, wondering if she'd used that pendant around her neck to disappear into that gray, cold world it contained. "Damn."

What the hell had happened to her? He stalked back into the bar and looked toward the back hallway. She said she had a business meeting this afternoon. Had she been meeting someone here? A shadow in the doorway of a room at the end of the hall caught his eye. Someone was back there. Someone who'd hurt Cacy. His fists clenched.

As if he'd heard Eli's thoughts, Jason Moros appeared in the last doorway on the left, leaning casually against the doorframe as Eli strode down the hall. "Are you looking for me, Mr. Margolis?"

Eli's throat was tight as he opened his mouth to speak. "Were you just meeting with Cacy Ferry?"

"What business is it of yours?" Moros asked, then smiled like he knew the answer.

"Because I just saw her, and she could barely walk."

Moros shook his head. "She'll be fine. This business can be cut-throat at times, my friend." Eli could swear the guy's eyes flashed red.

Eli took a slow breath, forcing himself to stay calm. "Did you hurt her?"

Moros sighed and held his hands out in a conciliatory gesture. "Mr. Margolis. Why are you still here? Your woman needs you now."

Eli's mouth dropped open. "She's not my—"

Moros stepped forward suddenly, his smile revealing star-tlingly sharp canines. "Trust me. I know more about her now than she knows about herself."

Eli ground his teeth at the thought of Moros knowing *anything* about Cacy, let alone everything. The guy radiated menace. Cacy could handle herself, but Moros seemed like he didn't play by any rules but his own.

Moros tapped Eli's chest with a gloved finger. "I'm on your side, Eli. There is more going on here than you understand, but there is one thing you can count on. She. Is. Yours."

Eli stepped back, his thoughts racing. "She's the only one who can tell me that."

"Oh, she told me as much just now. But if you want to hear it from her, you have to go to her." Moros nodded toward the front door of the bar. "She lives in the Kingston complex. Number 3401."

Eli turned to look toward the door. If he went to her, would she let him in? Or would she shut him out? He looked over his shoulder to ask Moros how the hell he knew where she lived, but he was gone. Eli slowly turned around and peeked into the room Moros had met Cacy in. Empty. The guy had disappeared. A hard chill went through Eli. What was Cacy involved in?

He jogged down the hall. The blonde from the bar stepped into his path just before he hit the door.

"You didn't like your drink?" she asked, pouting.

"Thank you for the thought," Eli said quickly, already trying to edge past her, worried he'd miss the next bus. "I work nights and don't drink before shifts. Sorry."

He took a step to the side, but so did she. Then she put a surprisingly warm hand on his chest. "I live close by," she said softly, tossing her hair over her shoulder. "You could make it up to me." Her nails scraped gently against the fabric of his shirt.

It made his skin crawl. His hand closed over her wrist and pulled it away from him. "I'm already late," he said firmly.

She smiled. "Your loss." She turned and walked away, hips swaying, stilettos clicking against the grimy hardwood.

Eli rolled his eyes and turned on his heel, following the firm tug deep in his chest. As much as he distrusted Moros, the guy was right about at least one thing. He needed to get to Cacy and make sure she was all right.

The ride to Cacy's apartment felt longer than the trip from Pittsburgh. He leaped off the bus and pulled his phone from his pocket as the armed guards in front of the building eyed him with suspicion. Cacy's phone rang and rang. And then switched to voice mail. Eli cursed and tried again, with the same result.

He shoved his phone back in his pocket. The guards didn't seem like the types to be forthcoming with information. He ran a hand through his hair and looked up at the high-rise.

"Eli Margolis?"

Eli spun around to find Aislin Ferry standing right behind him, holding a shopping bag. "Ms. Ferry. I-I'm—"

"Looking for Cacy?" She gave him a cool smile.

He nodded. "I don't think she's feeling well. I just saw her at Bart's. She was meeting with Jason Moros, but she left the meeting looking . . . bad. I'm worried about her."

Aislin's expression tightened. She tucked her arm in his and nodded at the security guards as she led him through the doors of the luxury complex. "Have you been here before?"

Eli looked down at Cacy's older sister as she walked him through the marble lobby. "No, ma'am."

She laughed. "Aislin, please." She came to a stop in front of the elevator and hit the up arrow. "Does she want to see you right now?"

Eli sighed. "Honestly? I'm not sure. But if she wants me to go, I swear I'll go. I just need to see that she's all right."

Aislin's eyes were so like Dec's—nearly impossible to read. But her voice was kind as she said, "Judging by her behavior at our father's funeral, I suspect she wouldn't mind seeing you."

The elevator doors opened, and they stepped inside. Aislin pressed the button for the thirty-fourth and thirty-fifth floors.

"You live here, too?" Eli asked.

"We all do," said Aislin. "We own the building."

Of course they did.

When the door opened at the thirty-fourth floor, Aislin turned to him. "Don't let her push you away. Even if she tries." She gave him a gentle shove.

Eli stepped through the elevator doors, which closed immediately. He wasn't in a hallway as he'd expected—he was in another lobby. And there was only one door. Was Cacy's apartment the only one on this floor? He rubbed his palms on his jeans and walked up to the door, pressing the viewing screen before he could think better of it. He stood directly in front of the camera lens embedded in the door so she could see it was him. He didn't know if that made it more or less likely that she would open the door.

From inside, he heard footsteps. Cacy's face appeared on the screen. "Eli? How did you get in here?" she asked, her voice strained and hoarse. Her eyes were red. It made his chest hurt.

"Let me in, Cacy," he said softly.

She stared at the screen for a moment, her eyes huge and shiny. The door clicked. He yanked it open and stepped into an airy living space that still managed to be cozy, decorated with warm, lush colors and soft, inviting fabrics. It reminded him of Cacy herself: casual and irreverent, but undeniably classy and entirely unique.

She stood before him wearing a robe, her wet hair tangling over her shoulders like she'd just stepped from the shower. She was looking at him strangely, almost fearfully, like she was frightened of what he might say. Even though every fiber of his being was screaming for him to take her in his arms, he held himself back.

Cacy wiped a stray tear from her face. "I'm going to call in sick to work. Sorry."

"You don't have to tell me what happened, but I need you to tell me if you're okay."

She smiled, but it didn't quite reach her eyes. "I had to complete some negotiations, and they . . . drained me. You didn't have to take the bus all the way over here. It's out of your way."

She ran a trembling hand across her neck and shuddered, which drew him toward her. "I don't care about that. I needed to see you."

She held up her arms. "And now you have, and I'm fine."

His jaw clenched. "With all due respect, Cacy, you don't look fine."

"Eli, I just need to rest. I'll be back at work tomorrow." She took a few steps toward the door, like she was about to show him out. "We'll reschedule our dinner plans then, okay?"

"No. It's not okay. Not at all."

Her brow furrowed. "I'm sorry for standing you up."

"I'm not upset about that—something happened in that meeting with Moros. I don't know what, but I know things are going on, Cacy. So many things that I don't understand." He stepped toward her and grasped her shoulders. "But, see, I don't care. I only care about you."

She closed her eyes and put her hands on his chest. "And I don't want you to have to care about any of it."

His grip on her arms tightened. "Why?" He suspected he knew, but he needed her to say it. She was protecting him, but from what, he didn't know.

"It's not your problem," she said quietly.

"What if I want it to be?" he snapped, Moros's words echoing loudly in his mind—*she is yours*. "What if it is, whether you like it or not?"

"Eli, you don't understand."

"Then make me understand, dammit!" he shouted, his patience evaporating under the heat of his frustration. "Tell me how I'm supposed to stay away when all I want is to be close to you. Tell me how I'm supposed to walk out that door when all I want is to hold you. Tell me how I'm not supposed to worry about you when that's all I can do! Please explain it to me, Cacy, because I'm not getting it."

She pushed weakly on his chest, so different from her usual fierce way—he would have expected her to punch him, and the fact that she didn't only worried him more. He took her face in his hands. "Tell me what to do," he said softly, "because I'm lost. I'm totally in the dark. I'm naive and clueless, but the one thing I'm *not* is a guy who walks away."

She laid her cool palms over the backs of his hands. "You're making this so hard."

"Good. We're almost there, then." He ducked his head until they were nose to nose. "My plan is to make it impossible."

His lips met hers before he could think better of it. He'd meant to be gentle, but as soon as he tasted her and inhaled her raw, spicy scent, his good intentions were burned to ash. Her fingers curled over his hands, and she made a vulnerable, helpless noise that only fueled the inferno inside him. He crushed her against him as he deepened the kiss, sliding his tongue forward to claim her mouth. Her lips parted, letting him in, and her hands traveled to his shoulders.

She wasn't pushing him away. Not at all. In fact, she was up on her tiptoes, trying to get closer. Everything inside him roared, his blood beating a furious rhythm in his ears. His hand slid to her ass and pressed her hips to his body. The delicious pressure made his hardening cock throb with want. How often had he dreamed of this since meeting her? His fingers spread over one of the soft mounds of her rear, only the thin fabric of her robe separating his skin from hers. Even that was too much.

"Eli," she gasped as he lowered his head to kiss her neck. "You shouldn't . . . We shouldn't . . ."

"Tell me why not," he murmured against her neck, scraping his teeth along her skin and pushing her robe off her shoulder. Because right now, he couldn't think of anything he needed more than this, more than the feel of her body, more than the taste of her in his mouth. He needed it more than his next breath, and he suspected she needed it, too, no matter how she was trying to convince him otherwise.

"I . . ." She moaned as his hand closed over her breast, his thumb circling her taut nipple. "Don't stop." She pressed her hand over his. "Please don't stop."

Yes. It was the surrender he wanted. Every cell in his body craved her, that need taking him over. With barely controlled ferocity, he backed her up to the table in her dining area and lifted her, still kissing her breathless. Her robe, hanging from one shoulder, was still tied at her waist, but the silky fabric parted as she spread her legs to allow him to stand between them. His palm skimmed up her thigh until soft curls tickled the tips of his fingers. They inched up further, greeted by the softest, most delectable flesh he'd ever touched, already slick with desire. She smelled incredible, of spice and earth, and he needed to taste her. He needed to claim her.

Slowly he sank to the floor, his tongue tracing the hollow of her throat, the curves of her breasts, the flat expanse of her stomach, all the way down to the ebony curls between her legs. She lay back on the table, and he kissed the inside of her thigh while pushing her legs farther apart, to bare the petal-pink folds of her sex. Something primal shifted and spread its jagged wings inside him, unfurling along his limbs, flowing like liquid steel through his veins. He drew his tongue up the center of her and then thrust it inside, growling with satisfaction as she arched her hips and drew in a shuddering breath. She curled her legs over his shoulders, her fingers gripping the edges of the table. She let out a hitching gasp when his finger circled the mouthwatering nub of her clit, and he kept his eyes on her as he lowered his mouth over it and sucked. Cacy sighed his name and pressed toward him, all resistance gone.

He throbbed with the need to bury his cock inside her. But first he wanted to feel her come, to drive her over the edge. He slowly sank two fingers into her, awed by the tight, silken feel, still drunk with her taste. Cacy let go of the table and clutched at his hair. He followed the rhythm she set for him with the rise and fall of her hips until she arched up, fierce and sudden, every muscle in her body locked, her mouth open in a scream of pure release.

He nearly came just from the sight of her, head thrown back, hair spread across the table, her full lips. Saying. His. Name. Her inner muscles contracted around his fingers as she cried out again. Desire crashed over him like a brutal wave, pulling him beneath the surface where no rational thought could survive. He rose above her. She was laid out like a feast before him, and his pulse hammered with his one thought—*Take her take her take her.*

CHAPTER TWENTY-EIGHT

The look on Eli's face as he loomed over her was everything Cacy needed. It reminded her that she was worth something and made her determined to take back what was hers. Before he'd come to her door, she'd thought Moros had wrecked her forever, but as soon as she'd seen Eli peering into her door camera, his jaw set and his eyes full of concern, the cracks in Cacy's torn heart started to close. His fierce refusal to leave was the thread that started to stitch her up. Each kiss, touch, and caress helped knit her back together. And now, with his hands firm on her thighs, his body shaking with need for her, the rigid column of his flesh evident against the front of his pants, all she wanted was for him to claim her, completely, nothing held back. To help her reclaim her life, her future.

While Eli's green eyes searched her face, she slid her ankles around his hips, trapping him against the table, then unbuttoned his pants and slid down his zipper. She sat up, pushing his boxer briefs and pants down over his thighs. His cock sprang free, the hot flesh nudging her belly. He closed his eyes and lowered his head. "Be sure," he whispered, his fingers stroking down her cheek.

Her hand closed around him, and he drew in a sharp breath. With her other hand, she pushed his shirt up until he reached over his head and pulled it off. His beautiful, hard body was still bruised from his encounter with Len and his minions, but he looked no less strong for it.

"I'm sure." *More* than sure. She kissed him, guiding him until the tip of his cock breached her. She gasped at the sensation. Relief—this was something she'd been craving since she'd met him. Pain—just the sweetest edge streaked through her as her body stretched for him. Surprise—it felt even better than she'd expected.

Cacy flexed her hips, her legs contracting around him, forcing him to lean on the table as he sank into her, pulling a groan from deep in Eli's chest. She hung her head and closed her eyes, focused only on the feeling of fullness. Eli's hands held her hips in a vise grip as he watched her with half-lidded eyes hazed with need. Once again, he was in control, holding back that wild creature she knew he kept chained inside.

Needing to break his composure, she reached down to stroke his balls, drawn up tight and hot between his legs. Then she slid her fingers further down, to the smooth strip of skin just behind. One stroke and Eli jerked against her, his jaw clenched. His kiss turned fierce and metal-edged as his stomach muscles trembled.

"Don't you dare hold back, Eli," she whispered against his mouth. "Take what you want."

His eyes opened, and he pushed her back onto the table. His gaze predatory, he thrust into her, hard and deep, one stroke she felt all the way inside. Cacy cried out as he hooked his forearms under her knees, his fingers clamped over her thighs, pinning her against him. The pressure was intense and overwhelming. She gripped the table as he pulled back and drove forward again, hitting her in just the right spot and sending waves of molten pleasure crashing over her. Eli growled as his grasp on her tightened, keeping her trapped and vulnerable and begging for more as he breached her body over and over.

Cacy hung on as Eli took control, setting a devastating rhythm that had her rocking against him, taking him deeper, sending helpless moans rolling from her throat. The table creaked beneath the force of his movements.

Eli had ignited a fire in her core that was burning away everything but him, melting her bones, fusing her soul to his, and branding her forever. She reached for him, and he leaned closer, releasing one of her legs so he could brace himself with his palm, which only added weight and depth to his penetration. She whimpered as his tempo increased, keeping time with their hot, panting breaths. She clutched at him as he flexed and pulled back, every thrust sending her higher. It was ecstatic, this feeling of being completed and whole, no longer fragmented, no longer torn. Just filled, healed, chasing an ocean-deep pleasure that was almost in her grasp.

"More," she gasped.

Eli was nothing if not accommodating. He buried himself inside her, every muscle taut with effort and emanating heat, ready to explode. She could feel it in him, the wildness, the desire, as powerful as an avalanche, more explosive than a volcano, and yet controlled somehow. She wanted him to let go. She wanted him to lose himself in her.

She wrapped her hand around the back of his neck and pulled him down until his bare chest touched hers. Her teeth scraped his skin at the junction of his neck and shoulder, and her name burst from his lips, a warning. He was so close. She could sense him trying to hold himself back again, but he didn't have anything to worry about. She was right there, hovering at the precipice of an orgasm so raw and powerful she knew it would change her forever.

As the tension inside her ratcheted to its final, almost painful degree, she closed her teeth over his skin, biting the rigid muscle of his shoulder. He slammed against her, all of his muscles contracting, filling her with throbbing heat. It was all she needed. She screamed with her release, all systems melting down, every cell sizzling, every nerve ending sparking and flashing. Her body convulsed around his, milking him dry, and, over the rush of blood pounding frantically in her ears, she heard him saying her name.

After he picked her up and carried her, boneless and panting, back to her bedroom, Cacy lay on Eli's chest, listening to the powerful, steady beat of his heart. Amazing. After Moros had touched her, she'd been certain she would never feel whole again, but now, just two hours later, she'd never felt more complete. It was like Eli's touch filled in the gaps, reordered the chaos. It almost made her forget the pinprick memories of her future, and that Moros had already felt everything she would ever feel.

She ran her hand up Eli's muscled arm and rested it on his chest. His skin was incredibly warm. She turned her head and kissed him, right over his heart.

His fingers were tracing lazily along her back, outlining her raven tattoo. "This is beautiful," he said softly. "What does *Fatum Nos Vocat* mean?"

She tensed. Pure reflex. He sighed and shifted like he was going to get up, but she wrapped her arms around him and refused to move. "It means 'Fate Calls Us.' It's our family motto." She raised her head. "Eli . . ."

His expression was a mixture of hurt and hope. "You don't have to tell me everything, Cacy. I know there's a lot. But—"

"I *want* to tell you everything." Ferrys were allowed to tell those they trusted most, those who were permanent parts of their lives. Eli hadn't told anyone about the things he'd seen. He was a good man. And in her heart, she knew she wanted him to be in her life. So he needed to understand a few things about the life she led.

His vibrant emerald eyes grew wider. "You do?"

She looked down at their bodies pressed together, as close as two people could be. "Don't you think I owe you that?"

The corner of his mouth curled up ruefully. "Not necessarily. I came into this without expectations. Only hope. I'll take whatever parts of you you're willing to give."

She reached up and stroked his face, then scooted up his body and kissed him. "This meant something, Eli. A lot. *You* mean a lot to me. It's just that I've never told an outsider about my family before, and after a lifetime of keeping it to myself, my first instinct is to keep the secrets."

He touched her lips with the tips of his fingers. "You mean a lot to me, too. Which is why, if you need some time, I can wait. But you can trust me, Cacy. I would never hurt you, or your family."

Cacy's eyes lingered on his face, the heat of his expression, the set of his jaw. Just looking at him made her heart fill with gratitude. "I want you to know me. And I know I can trust you. But it's all going to sound strange."

The depth of his laughter shook her. He took her face in his hands. "I've seen you heal from a fatal throat injury. I've seen you walk through some sort of portal into a parallel dimension. I've been hijacked by your jewelry."

"What?" Now she was laughing, too.

"Your pendant. When I touched it that night, it turned into a ring that just kept growing. Like a window to another world."

She blew out a heavy breath. "You shouldn't have even been able to open it."

"What is it, exactly?"

"It's called a Scope, and it's only supposed to open for those devoted to its service. It's a portal to the in-between, the Veil." She laid her head on his shoulder and slipped her forearm under him, her fingers hooking over it and holding on tight. What would he say when she told him everything? Would he think she was evil?

"In between what?"

Here goes. "In between life . . . and the Afterlife. Like a no-man's land. Regular humans are not supposed to be able to go there. Unless they're dead."

He rolled to his side and propped himself on an elbow, looking at her carefully. "And what you're saying is that you're not human?" His voice was very even, like he was trying to stay calm.

He didn't seem angry or scared. But she'd never seen a look so intense. "I am human. Mostly. I just have a few extra features. It's part of being a Ferry."

"Like, you pay enough money and you can be immortal?"

She shook her head. "No, like, I'm an intermediary between life and death, like the rest of my family. I guide souls in the Veil to the Afterlife. Heaven or Hell. The Scope shows me which one, and I . . . help . . . the person get there."

He chuckled. "Oh, I get it. *Ferry.*"

Her mouth dropped open. "That's all you have to say?"

He grew serious again. "What do you want me to say? I've known there was something up with you from the first night I met you. It didn't stop me from falling for you."

"What I'd like to know is how you ended up in the Veil yourself. Only souls of the dead are solid there. Live people are transparent, like shadows. Like ghosts."

His expression didn't change, but his skin grew a shade paler. She watched his throat move as he swallowed. "Would someone be solid there . . . if he had died before?"

"What are you talking about?"

He fell back onto the pillow and stared up at the ceiling. "A few years ago, Galena and I were attacked by a street gang while we were walking home from a movie theater. They took our money. And they . . ." His jaw clenched. "That's not all they took. A bunch of them held me down while they raped Galena, and when I got loose to try to help her, one of them jabbed me with an electro-shock baton. Over and over again."

Cacy laid her head on the rock-hard, tense muscles of his arm. "Oh God, Eli."

His eyes stayed riveted on the ceiling. "It stopped my heart."

She stayed very still. Thinking of what he and Galena must have gone through reopened the chasm in her heart, and she was sure it would hurt to move. "Do you remember what happened next?" she whispered.

He shook his head. "I don't remember anything but the worst pain of my life, and waking up in an ambulance. The paramedic was still holding the defib paddles and leaning over me. He said 'I guess it wasn't your time.'"

Eli turned to her, and the raw honesty in his face intensified the ache in her chest. "For a long time after that, I wished it *had* been my time. Galena was beaten up really bad and totally traumatized." He shifted beneath her and turned his face away. "They hurt her so bad. And I couldn't protect her. I could barely face her after that, even after we'd both physically recovered. I failed her."

Cacy touched the side of his face, bringing it back toward hers, rubbing her fingers against the light stubble on his cheeks. "I doubt she thinks that. I've seen how she leans on you."

He closed his eyes and set his forehead against hers. "I wasn't strong enough to keep her safe. I'll never live that down."

Cacy wrapped her arm around his neck and pulled him to her, burying her fingers in the thick golden hair on the back of his head. "You're human. You did your best. You *died* for her, Eli. You laid your life on the line. And you know what? That doesn't surprise me one bit, because that's who you are."

He kissed her shoulder. "I guess the one good thing about having died is that it made it possible for me to help you that night. That's it, right? It's because I've already died. I've already been in the Veil."

She tightened her grip on him. "I think so."

His lips brushed against her neck, feather-light. "Then I'm okay with it." He raised his head. "Seems like a big job, being a Ferry." His forefinger brushed over her Scope.

The icy prickle at her neck told her that the Scope had responded to his touch. His gaze flicked up to hers. "So when people die, you're who greets them?"

"Me or one of my family."

His hand closed around one of her breasts, and his thumb skimmed over her nipple. He smiled at her sharp intake of breath. "I don't think I'd mind dying too much if you were waiting for me."

"Stop talking like that," she said breathlessly. "You're not going to find out for a long time."

He nudged the Scope with two fingers, and it opened a little wider, raising goose bumps all over Cacy's skin as she felt the chill of the Veil seep through. She lifted it from her chest to compact it again.

A flash of orange in the shimmery center of the Scope immobilized her.

Eli frowned. "What's wrong? I'm sorry if I—"

"No. *No no no no no.*" She gasped, her heart beating against her ribs so hard that it hurt. She held up the Scope and looked through it again, praying she'd been seeing things. But it was still there.

A neat *X* in the center of a circle.

On Eli's chest.

He'd been Marked.

CHAPTER TWENTY-NINE

Cacy was staring at Eli the same way she'd stared at her father just before he died. She sat up and scooted away from him, pulling her Scope from its chain and stretching it wide. Her hands were white-knuckled as she clutched the thing and scanned the room.

Eli sat up. "What is it?"

"You've been Marked," she choked out, nodding at his chest.

Eli looked down at his chest, which looked like it always did. "What are you talking about?"

The Scope snapped shut, and Cacy clipped it back to the chain. She blinked and wiped her eyes. "The Ferrys aren't the only ones who roam the Veil. We work with creatures called the Kere. Moros is their leader, and he has some serious explaining to do."

She jumped from the bed and began rooting through their discarded clothes. "Did you talk to him back at the bar?"

Eli swung his legs from the bed, trying to decipher what she was saying. "I did. He told me to come to you, that you . . ." *Are mine.* He shook his head. Now didn't seem like the time to get into it. She was already half-dressed, and he was still sitting there naked, staring at her like an idiot.

"That bastard. It's just the kind of thing he would do." She yanked her shirt over her head. "Did he touch you?"

As he reached for his pants, Eli remembered how Moros had poked him in the chest. "He did, but only for a second—"

"That's all he needed. This is all just a fucking dirty trick. He lied to me. He's used what he knows about me to design the ultimate distraction."

Eli had never hated another word more. His hands shot out and closed around Cacy's arms. Her eyes went wide as he pulled her to him. "Is that all I am to you? A distraction?" he asked.

After what they'd just done together, after she'd screamed for him, after she'd shaken in his arms with the aftershocks of their lovemaking, after they'd shared secrets neither of them had ever told another person, he'd been pretty damn sure he was more than that.

Her face crumpled. "No. That's why his plan is so *evil*." Her palms flattened against his chest, but she didn't push him away. Instead, she kissed him, right over his heart. A tear landed on his skin and slid down to his belly, a tiny river of sorrow. "I don't want to lose you. I can't lose you like this. Not now," she whispered.

Her hair was silk as he stroked it. "You won't lose me. I'm not going anywhere."

"You don't understand." She sucked in a breath. "You've been Marked, and now I have to figure out what to do."

His arms tightened around her. "Don't you mean *we* have to figure it out? Tell me what's happened. I don't understand half of what you've said in the last five minutes."

Her hands skimmed around his waist and locked behind his back. "The Kere are like the grim reaper. They Mark the people fated to die. They choose how they'll die, and then they cause their deaths."

Eli's heart beat with a new urgency. "Wait. Wait. Are you saying I've been marked for *death*?" It didn't make sense. He felt fine. In fact, he'd never felt more alive.

Cacy nodded stiffly, her hair brushing his skin. "Why would he do this now? I thought we had an agreement!"

He nudged her chin up so he could see her face. "What did he agree to?"

She bit her lip. "To keep Galena safe."

"What?" He stepped back from Cacy, alarm bells sounding in his head. "What does she have to do with this?"

As Cacy explained how his sister could present the single biggest threat to the death industry since the discovery of antibiotics, Eli got dressed, nearly ripping his shirt as he pulled it over his head. His rage grew with every word she said. "Are you telling me you've known about this?" he snapped. Galena was his responsibility. Cacy had prioritized her family's secrets over Galena's life.

Cacy shook her head and held her hands up, begging him to understand. "Only since the fund-raiser. And I've done everything I could—"

"You should have told me!" He stalked toward the door, his heart pounding with fear for Galena. Death could come for him, fine, but he had to protect his sister. He reached the door and stopped. What the hell was he supposed to do? He was up against things he couldn't even see.

When he turned around, Cacy was right behind him, pale but determined. "I understand that you're mad. But don't leave, Eli. If you go out there, you're going to die."

He touched his chest, the place Cacy's gaze kept drifting to. "Based on what you just said, I'm going to die no matter what I do." Eli wondered why he wasn't terrified. Maybe because it didn't seem real. His heart beat against his hand, steady as ever.

She winced. "Please. You might have some time. You'll be safer if you stay here. I have to go back to Moros, or maybe . . . I don't know. I have to do something."

"Didn't you tell me he's the one who Marked me for death? What if he does that to you?" Even through his anger and confusion, Eli's concern for Cacy got the better of him.

She touched his face. "Moros can't hurt me. Not . . . not too much, anyway. But I'm going to ask my brother for help first."

"You think Dec can do something?"

"No. I'm going to Rylan. He's the Charon. Our leader. He can go straight to the top if he thinks Moros has abused his power."

"I'm coming with you."

"No. You'll be safer here. No one knows you're here."

Eli took her face in his hands. "Do you really think I'm going to sit here and wait? You've told me my sister is in danger. You've told me I don't have much time left. Plus—both Moros and your sister know I'm here. He told me where you lived, and she showed up at just the right moment to help me get into the building. They practically shoved me into your arms."

Cacy closed her eyes and laid her hands over his. Her grip was strong. "I'll deal with Aislin later. I'm not going to let this happen, Eli. I bargained with Moros for Galena's safety. He's broken a vow. He will pay." She wrenched herself away from him and pulled her phone out. "But you're right. If they know you're here, you should come with me. We're taking a company car."

Had she just said she'd bargained with Moros for Galena's sake? Was that why she'd looked thrashed when she left the bar? "What did he do to you, Cacy?"

"It doesn't matter. I'm all right. But we bargained fair and square, and he cannot renege like this." She punched a button on her phone and put it to her ear. She ordered the car and gave him her hand. "It'll be here in a few minutes." Their fingers laced, both of them holding on tight. "Ready?"

No. Not at all. But never in his whole life had Eli backed down from a challenge. And this time, he had Cacy by his side. "Yeah." He pulled her close and kissed her. "Let's go."

CHAPTER THIRTY

After what felt like hours, the elevator doors finally opened. Cacy hesitated, peering in carefully to make sure no one was waiting to ambush Eli.

"Hey," he said with a nervous smile as they stepped in, "seems like I could just as easily be struck down by natural causes. I think I nearly died of a heart attack back in your apartment." He winked, but Cacy knew it was for show. Ever since she had broken the news to him, he'd taken on an air of quiet desperation that made her ache. Unlike any normal person, he hadn't received the news with horror or fear. No weeping, complaining, or raging about how unfair it was. Just concern for his sister. And for her.

It made her all the more determined to find a way to save him. He wasn't fated to die. She knew it. Moros had completely double-crossed her. And based on what Eli had said, she would bet her fortune that Aislin was in on it.

Cacy tucked her arm in Eli's, staying as close to him as possible as the elevator descended. "First, that's not funny, and second, that's not how it's going to happen."

"No?"

Cacy shook her head. "You have to be fated to die before a heart attack or some other natural cause could kill you. So if the Kere have gone rogue, they'll have to bring about your death directly, with their own hands." The elevator arrived at the lobby, and Cacy peeked out the doors, then led Eli into the lobby. "Which means they're going to come after you. And they're going to have to come through me."

"Whoa." He came to a full stop in the middle of the room. Strains of classical music floated in the air, along with the sound of water flowing in a fountain in the corner. "You're not going to endanger yourself for me. It's not worth it."

Cacy stomped her foot and yanked on his arm. "You don't get to say what's worth it to me," she snapped. "That's my decision." She rounded on him, got up on her tiptoes, and kissed him fiercely. When she pulled away, he looked a little stunned, as did most of the other people in the lobby. "Now get moving."

Eli didn't argue, to her relief. But his gaze swept the lobby with a cold vigilance that hadn't been there before. His thoughts were transparent to her. Before, he'd thought he might simply drop dead from a brain aneurysm, but now that he knew his death would come violently—and soon—he was going to fight back.

She led him out of the front doors of the apartment complex, nodding at the guards and pushing Eli ahead of her toward the bulletproof limo at the curb. The guards stepped out on either side of them, reading Cacy's tension and scanning the street for threats. "Thanks, guys!" she called as the driver shut the door behind her.

Eli sat next to her, looking with amazement around the black leather interior of the limo. He rubbed his palms on his jeans. "Are you sure your brother won't just toss me to the sharks?"

She leaned her head on his shoulder. The clean, masculine scent of him filled her up and she pressed in closer. "Don't worry. Rylan will be all over this. He'll go straight to the Keepers of the Afterlife, and they will *destroy* Moros. The Kere can't get away with this—Marking people who aren't fated to die is strictly forbidden."

Eli tensed as they passed a crowd of men on the sidewalk at the edge of the canal zone. But they didn't even look up as the limo chugged down the ramp and deployed its water jets. "I thought you and the Kere worked together. Like a team."

Cacy scoffed. "The Kere only work with us because they have to. Thousands of years ago, they reaped and delivered the souls themselves. But they demanded payment for their work, and that came with a few conditions."

"Ferrys." Eli's eyes were fixed on the canal, assessing every potential threat.

"Yes. We split the payment and the work with them, but they're ruthless and greedy. If they can marginalize us or make it seem like we can't control the empire, the Keepers of the Afterlife might decide we're just useless bureaucracy—that the death industry should be left to fully inhuman creatures like the Kere. But Rylan won't let that happen."

Eli pulled out his phone and smiled as he read the screen. "It's Galena checking in. She's home safe from her lab."

Cacy kissed his shoulder. "Tell her to stay put, all right?"

Eli nodded as his fingers tapped at the screen. Cacy's heart squeezed painfully as she watched him swallow hard and type *I love you.* He blinked a few times and stuck his phone in his pocket. This had to be hurting him.

A uniboat raced by and sideswiped the limo, which swerved into oncoming traffic. The driver yanked the wheel back just as an amphibious bus passed. Eli gripped the seat hard and cursed under his breath. "Are we almost there?"

"It's right up here." She pointed to the fortified skyscraper in front of them, the tallest in the city. The headquarters of Psychopomps Inc. and all its subsidiary holdings—the banks and cover businesses through which the gold coins flowed and were converted into local currency. All Ferrys and Kere had accounts, and Psychopomps managed their money. For a small fee, of course.

The Kere resented it, but they had never been organized enough to set up an alternative system. They were too busy reveling in their wealth and causing chaos and pain.

The limo pulled up at the curb, and the driver popped the roof hatch and offered Cacy his hand. She ignored it and leaped out onto the small dock. "Hey guys, we need cover."

The burly armed guards looked surprised at her request but obeyed. The offices were in the safest part of town, and Ferrys were supposed to be protected. But with the upheaval of the past week, Rylan had posted guards, which was fine with Cacy as she ran side by side with Eli through the glass doorway of the tower.

Cacy breathed a sigh of relief as soon as they hit the air-conditioned interior of the lobby. "We'll be safe here. A Kere attack here would be in blatant violation of the treaty."

She waved at Shauna, who was staffing the front desk, and pointed to the special elevator that ran to the Charon's office. It was the only way up. "Is he in?"

"Of course, Cacy," Shauna chirped. "Go on up. I'll tell him you're coming." She punched a button on her earpiece and turned away.

Cacy squeezed Eli's hand as they hopped into the elevator. He was standing up very straight, and for the first time since being told he was Marked for death, he actually seemed a little scared. Eli looked out through the glass walls of the elevator as they ascended past floor after floor of the Psychopomps dominion. "Cacy, you know I'm not after your money, right?"

"It hadn't occurred to me," she said honestly.

He turned to look down at her, a sly smile on his face. "I guess you're the only one it didn't occur to. But I'm glad you feel that way." The backs of his fingers stroked her cheek.

Cacy tilted her head up, and his lips were against hers in less than a second. His strong arms wound around her waist. She threaded her fingers through his hair as her body molded to the firm contours of his, and all she could think was, *Alive.* That was how he said he felt, and that was how he felt to her. Like nothing could stop him. Like nothing could get the best of him. Like he could go on and on. And he would. She would make sure of it. There was no way she was going to give him up.

Eli's hand slid up her back as his tongue dueled with hers. Their uneven breaths were loud in Cacy's ears . . . but not loud enough to miss the ding of the door opening or the awkward throat-clearing that followed it. They both froze in place, then slowly separated, and looked over to see Rylan at the open elevator doors, eyebrows raised.

"Shauna let me know you were coming up," he said, his eyes wandering back and forth between Cacy and Eli. "Would you like to come in, or would you prefer to ride up and down for a while?" He gave them an indulgent smile, which crinkled the corners of his eyes.

"We were taking advantage of the moment," Cacy said breezily, twining her fingers with Eli's. She tugged him into the opulent suite but slowed as she noticed how much it had changed in the past two weeks. All her father's tapestries were gone, replaced by abstract paintings in cool greens and blues. The curtains had been removed from the windows, allowing the piercing rays of the setting sun to fill the space.

Rylan looked around at his office like he was seeing it for the first time. "I guess it looks pretty different, huh?"

Cacy swallowed the lump in her throat and tried to keep her voice light. "A bit. But you're the Charon now, so it's yours."

Rylan, dressed casually in khaki pants and a buttoned shirt with no tie, ushered them into the inner chamber of the suite, his personal office. He gestured for them to be seated, then stood behind his desk. "What can I do for you?"

Cacy glanced at Eli, who looked steadily back at her. "Eli's been Marked. We think Moros himself might have done it." When Rylan's brow furrowed, Cacy added, "I've told him everything."

Rylan gazed at her for a moment, as if taking in the significance of her statement. Then he sank into his desk chair and pulled his Scope from its thick chain. He brushed his thumb over it, opened it just wide enough to allow him to look through, and held it up, peering through the center of it at Eli's chest. He winced and snapped it shut. "When did this happen?"

"About three hours ago."

He pursed his lips and nodded. "Why do you think Moros did this? It could have been any of the Kere."

"Because I saw him this afternoon. I spoke to him at Bart's," Eli said. He gave Cacy a sidelong glance. "He touched me, right where the Mark is."

Rylan crossed his arms over his chest, flipping the heavy Charon's Scope like a coin. "You sure it was him? Hard to imagine Moros hanging out in a place like that."

"No, it was him." Cacy sighed. "He was meeting me, all right? I went to ask him to protect Galena."

Rylan caught his Scope in his fist. His elbows hit his desk as he leaned forward. "You went to Moros. After I told you not to."

Cacy cringed, feeling more of a screwup than ever. She'd thought she was saving Galena, but it looked like Cacy hadn't done anything but hand Moros the best way to hurt her. Why he'd want to do that confused her, but maybe he was threatened by her. Or maybe . . . oh God, what if he was using her to distract Rylan?

Rylan nodded stiffly as Cacy's eyes lit with realization. Rylan probably knew it all along—Moros wasn't doing this to hurt Cacy. He was doing it to get to Rylan. She hung her head. Eli squeezed her hand.

Rylan sighed. "You let him touch you, didn't you? You let that bastard touch you. Now he knows everything about you,

Cacy. Your dearest hopes and worst nightmares. Your *future*." He dropped the Scope on the desk and stared at it, then looked up at Eli. "I'm sorry you got dragged into this, Eli."

Eli merely nodded in acknowledgment.

Cacy scooted to the edge of her seat. "Ry, I'm sorry about all of it. But no matter what stupid thing I did, this Marking can't be right. It's too convenient. Moros is abusing his power, and he has to be stopped."

"Yes." Rylan heaved a weary breath. "Yes, I suppose this is clear enough. It would be very convenient if Galena died, and it would only help facilitate that if everyone interested in protecting her was dead or chasing their tails."

He ran a hand through his hair. "I hate to tell you this, Cacy, but Mr. Knickles was found dead this morning. Home invasion. I guided his soul a few hours ago."

Their family lawyer? That harmless, hard-working little man? But he'd been privy to her father's will—a will he'd changed the day of his death. "This has to be a conspiracy! All these people couldn't be fated to die! Father, Debra, Peter, Mr. Knickles . . ." She looked over at Eli, her heart thudding in her chest. She couldn't bear to add him to the list. Not yet. Not ever.

Rylan stood up and walked to the window. The setting sun bathed his tall figure in orange light and cast his shadow long and gray on the wall. "I'll have to go to the Keepers." He turned and shot a glance at Eli. "Moros can't get away with this. I'll arrange a summit. He'll have to come and answer for his actions."

He strode back to his desk, where he lifted his Scope and examined it. "I'll go now." His eyes landed hard on Cacy, filled with regret. "It's going to take some time to arrange."

It felt like a boulder had settled onto her chest. She knew what he was saying. Eli might not have that much time. Galena might not, either. She wanted to burst into tears, but that wouldn't help anyone. "Okay," she said, nodding. "All right."

Rylan closed the distance between them and put his hand on her shoulder. "I'll do everything I can to put this right. I'll do it as quickly as I can. You have my word."

She laid her hand on his. "I know." She stood up. So did Eli. The look on his face told her he understood more than had been said. The weight of the boulder crushed her heart.

Cacy hugged Rylan and let him walk them back to the elevator. He shook Eli's hand with a grim look on his face and turned to Cacy. "I'll check in as soon as I can and let you know what I've arranged. I'll let them know about this situation, and it's possible they'll intervene immediately, but . . . they're notoriously hands-off. There's only one time in history they've actually taken action."

Cacy nodded. That one time had led to the rise of one of the world's largest religions. The hope that the Keepers would leave their thrones and directly intervene on Earth was exceedingly slim. They would be willing to punish Moros if they found him guilty, but they wouldn't be willing to undo the deaths he had caused.

"Where are you headed now?" Rylan asked them as Eli pushed the down button.

Cacy glanced at Eli. She was hoping he'd come back with her to the apartment, but she knew he couldn't. She wasn't the only one who needed him. Eli took Cacy's hand. "I need to go check on my sister," he said. "I need to make sure she's okay."

Rylan folded his arms across his chest. "I'll tell you what. Call her now. We'll send a company car to bring her here. We'll keep you both safe."

The weight in Cacy's chest lifted. That her brother was willing to shelter Eli and Galena, and go to the Keepers, meant he thought he had a strong case against Moros. But . . . "What about Aislin?" she asked.

Rylan frowned. "What do you mean?"

"Can you trust her? She insisted on guiding Peter and Deb with you, like she was afraid they would say something. You saw her with Moros the other night, how cozy they were. And she led Eli up to my apartment earlier. Right around the time he was Marked, or right after. She brought him right to me."

Eli cleared his throat. "Cacy, I don't think she—"

Cacy shook her head. "No, Eli, you don't know her like I do. What if they're working together to kill Galena?"

Rylan rubbed the back of his neck and made a pained face. "It's hard for me to believe Aislin would betray us like that, but maybe she thought it was what Father wanted. We weren't really clear . . ."

"He didn't want this, Ry. I know he didn't. He told me to protect Galena. And that's what I'm going to do."

By the expression on Rylan's face, she could tell he was hurt their father hadn't confided in him, and Cacy half regretted her words. But he also looked worried, like he didn't know what it meant that their father had said that to Cacy, and angry because of the position it had put him in. Another screwup to add to her long list. Why had she kept this to herself? Why hadn't she confided in Rylan before now?

"I'll deal with Aislin directly," Rylan said flatly, pulling his buzzing phone from his pocket. "It's Shauna. She's bringing up my dinner. She always orders too much, so I'm sure there'll be plenty if you two are hungry." He turned back to the phone. "Yes. Bring it up."

Cacy took a step toward her brother as he put his phone away. "I'm sorry I didn't tell you about Father's wishes earlier."

He held his hands up and took a step back. "It's fine. Father had his reasons for everything. I only wish he were still around to explain them." He gestured at Eli. "Call your sister now. Tell her you're sending a car for her. She'll feel safer if she hears it from you."

Eli nodded and pulled his phone from his pocket. Galena picked up quickly, and his instructions were calm and matter-of-fact. He didn't explain much, just let her know that some people he trusted were coming for her, told her he loved her and would see her soon, and signed off.

Eli met Rylan's steady gaze. "She'll be waiting for them."

Rylan turned to go back into his office, pulling his Scope from his neck with tense, agitated movements. He might be furious with Cacy, but he was going to do his best to get her out of this mess. Her heart swelled with admiration and gratitude.

She put her arms around Eli's chest and rested her head. Mark or no Mark, his heart beat firm and unrelenting in her ear. It was the best and most hopeful sound in the world.

His voice hummed deep in his chest as he said, "Thank you for helping me and Galena. You have no idea what it means to me." He kissed her forehead, his lips lingering on her skin for a long, bittersweet moment. "In case I don't get to say this to you later—"

She laid her fingers over his lips. "None of that. We'll have plenty of time to say everything we want to say."

He smiled against her fingertips.

The elevator dinged and opened, revealing Shauna balancing a wide cardboard flat that held several grease-spotted paper bags. The smell of garlic and ginger instantly filled the room. Ry had always loved Chinese food.

Shauna bobbled her burden as she stepped out of the elevator, and Eli rushed forward. "Let me help you with that."

"S-sure," she stammered, looking at him like she was surprised he was being nice.

Eli lifted the flat and put it on a nearby conference table, and Cacy's eyes trailed him automatically, unwilling to let him out of her sight. When he turned back, his eyes went round. She spun to see what had upset him.

Shauna stood in front of them, pale and trembling, aiming a gun at Eli's chest.

CHAPTER THIRTY-ONE

Eli had no time to do anything except shove Cacy to the side. There was a sharp crack, then searing agony in his chest and a wrenching scream from the woman who owned his heart. He stumbled backward as a second shot hit him hard and high, sending him crashing to the floor. Cacy's cries hurt him more than the bullets. Over the roaring in his ears, he heard her shrieking for Shauna to put the gun down.

But Shauna didn't. She kept advancing, lowering her gun only enough to aim at his head. Cacy's chest pressed against his face as she hunched over him, protecting him with her body. A haze of red descended over his vision, painting Cacy's creamy skin with a bloody tint. He tried to push her out of the way, terrified she would be hurt, but found he couldn't move his arms. When he tried to draw a breath, the air was too heavy. His mind was oddly detached, running through his likely injuries. Collapsed lung. Internal bleed—

Cacy jerked away, and the overhead lights blinded him. "Stop her!" she shouted, and another gunshot rang out. Then Cacy was leaning over him again, phone to her ear, tears streaming down her face, her speech so fast and breathless he could barely understand. But he heard Dec's name. He heard *hurry*. He heard *please*.

His eyes traced her face as his brain buzzed from a lack of oxygen. Cacy tossed the phone to the side and ripped his shirt open from the neck. She yelled something to someone standing over him. Rylan. A gun was hanging loosely in his grip. He walked out of Eli's narrowing field of vision.

Splinters of fire stabbed through Eli as Cacy put her hands on his chest. She sank her fingers into his wounds, trying to stop the bleeding. Even if he'd had the breath to tell her it was hopeless, he wouldn't have. As much as she was hurting him, he didn't want to stop her. Here she was, black hair hanging around her delicate face, her full lips parted, a light dusting of freckles over the bridge of her nose. All he wanted to do was stare.

She reached out and took something from Rylan's outstretched hand. A med kit.

"Hang on, baby," she said. "Hang on for me."

Anything for you.

Still keeping one hand pressed hard against his chest, she ripped the kit open with her other hand and clipped an oxygen minipump to his nose. A needle pierced his arm the next second, a tiny pinprick in an ocean of knives. "Don't you dare leave me. Don't even think about it."

Never.

She bent low over him, her shirt soaked with his blood, her fingers still jammed inside his chest. Her forehead touched his, her turquoise eyes now the only thing he could see. "Dec will be here soon. I'm so sorry, Eli, I thought we were safe."

I am safe. You're with me.

"I'll protect Galena, I swear."

I know.

"This is my fault. All my fault. I'm sorry," she sobbed.

I don't regret any of it.

Her tears hit his cheeks, burning him. He was on fire. Drowning in flame. Sinking deeper into it. He tried to open his mouth and say everything it was too late to say, but Cacy rose up above him, a new panic in her eyes, her mouth moving with words he could no longer hear. He strained to keep his eyes open, unwilling to relinquish the sight of her, but it was impossible. Night closed in around him, wrapping him up tight, leaving him with a single echoing thought.

I love you.

CHAPTER THIRTY-TWO

Cacy was still working frantically long after Eli's eyes fluttered shut. His lips were tinged with blue even though the oxygen minipump was at its highest level, but the bleeding seemed to have slowed. And he was strong. So strong. She could get him through this. No way would she let him go now.

The clatter of wheels drew her head up. Dec and his partner, Carol, rolled a stretcher through the open elevator doors.

"Oh God," Dec said, taking in the scene.

Shauna was splayed next to the wall, lying loose-limbed. Rylan stood over her, phone to his ear, engaged in a tense conversation with the police. The gun he'd used to shoot Shauna lay on the side table next to the Chinese food. He'd come out of his office, eyes blazing, and shot their young cousin without any hesitation.

Dec pointed his gloved finger at Shauna. "Carol, take care of Shauna—the female victim."

He knelt next to Cacy and put his arm around her, gripping her shoulders gently.

She jerked away, keeping the heel of her palm jammed against Eli's chest to keep pressure on the severed ends of his subclavian artery. "Penetrating thoracic trauma to the upper left quadrant," she choked out. "Severed subclavian, penetrating trauma to the upper right quadrant of the abdomen, likely transection of the hepatic artery. There's"—she shifted, and her knees slipped in the pool of Eli's blood that surrounded them—"hypovolemic shock. He's—"

"Cacy," Dec said softly. "Stop."

"Shut up and help me!" she shrieked as she shoved Dec and tried to grab his med kit. "I need two more vials of plasma, the atropine, and the cardiac wand!"

Dec's arms surrounded her like a steel vise. He was trying to pull her away from Eli.

She slapped at him with her free hand. "Stop it! Goddammit, Dec! Why the fuck aren't you helping me?"

Dec yanked her back to the floor and sat with her between his legs, holding her tight. "You can stop now," he said quietly in her ear as he held her. "It's time for you to stop."

Cacy kicked at him, arching and struggling, painting the legs of Dec's uniform with the blood from her hands. Eli's blood. "Let me go! He needs me!"

Dec didn't react as she clawed at his arms. He calmly held her, firmly enough so she couldn't get loose, so she couldn't get to Eli. Did he *want* Eli to die?

"Why aren't you helping? Why?" she sobbed.

Dec sighed, his arms trembling with the effort of keeping her still. His voice was as unreadable as his expression as he said, "He's been dead for several minutes, Cacy. You just didn't notice."

The breath escaped Cacy's lungs in a long, slow whimper, taking the last of her strength with it. A void opened in front of her, a future full of nothing, a sorrow too deep to survive. Black and hungry, it yawned wide, threatening to swallow her.

And this time, Eli wasn't there to keep her from falling in.

CHAPTER THIRTY-THREE

Eli opened his eyes to gray dustland lit with moonlight, stretching endlessly to a black horizon. He shivered as his feet sank into the spongy dirt. His chest ached, but when he looked down at himself, his skin was smooth and unbroken. He put his hand over his heart. It was silent but throbbing with a pressure that was nearly unbearable, like something was trying to break free.

"You come from a desolate place, my friend." Jason Moros appeared next to him, impeccably dressed in a suit and tie, his dark hair slicked back from his face, his eyes glowing red.

A bolt of pain sliced through Eli, but it wasn't physical. He'd wanted to see Cacy. Expected to see her. And instead, here was Moros. The man who'd ordered his death. "Get away from me," Eli shouted, surprised at how animalistic he sounded.

"You were just as fierce the last time we were here. Most souls I meet are completely passive."

"I don't know what you're talking about," he said, though he wasn't sure that was true.

Moros shrugged. "You wouldn't remember. But the last time you died, I was there, too. You got right in my face, wanting to know where your sister was. My appearance did not scare you in the slightest." His smile revealed dagger-sharp fangs. "Your future was so uncertain, even then. My sisters and I were on the fence. That was why I came to meet you in person."

Eli moaned at a sudden tearing sensation in his chest. "Lucky me."

"I wouldn't say that." Moros's smile became tainted with sadness. "I decided not to Mark you that night. And as soon as I made that decision, I saw your future. It was . . . a good one."

"You saw *this*?" growled Eli, barely able to fight the urge to leap on Moros and tear his throat out.

Moros frowned. "No. This was not supposed to happen."

Another shock of agony sent Eli to his knees. It was as bad as being hit with an electroshock baton.

"Ah, the transformation has already started." Moros bent so Eli could see his glowing eyes. "You'll be a Shade soon. Cacy is on her way, I'm sure. She feels so deeply for you that she will find you easily. Do you really want her to see you like this?"

Eli moaned, thinking he didn't care how Cacy saw him, if only she would appear and hold him one last time.

"It was a Shade who tore her throat open the night you found her in the Veil, and that's what you're becoming. I've never seen it happen quite so fast, though. Soon, you will be rabid."

"No."

"There's another way, Eli. You don't have to go out like this." He paused for a moment. "You weren't supposed to go out like this," he said quietly.

"Why did you do it?" Eli pushed himself back, sitting on his heels and fisting his hands against his thighs. "I wasn't your enemy. I'm not important."

Moros chuckled. "Ah, there's the irony. You *weren't* important in the grand scheme of things, my friend. But now . . . now you have a chance to be."

Eli's heart was still aching for Cacy. He rubbed slow circles over his chest. "What are you talking about?"

"Become a Ker. Become one of mine. Think of it, Eli. You will be wealthy beyond your pitiful imaginings. You will be one of the most powerful creatures to walk the Earth. And you will live forever. As long as you obey me."

Eli winced as jagged shards of pain cut loose and rolled through his arms and legs. "I must have something you want, if you're offering me such power. I thought you wanted me out of the way."

Moros clenched his fists, and his eyes glowed bright crimson. "I didn't Mark you. It was unauthorized. One of so many unauthorized Markings lately. And when I find out who did it, they will pay," he rasped through jagged fangs. His fingernails elongated into claws, curling slightly at the tips. He looked like the monster Cacy had described him to be.

Moros turned his face toward the starry sky and took a deep breath. "I am merely trying to undo the damage that was done," he said, more gently and in control this time. "I am trying to do what is right."

"Cacy said the Kere kill people."

"Death is an inevitable part of life, boy."

"She said they *like* to kill."

Moros met his eyes. "Some of us do. Some are more . . . tempered in their passions. You might enjoy it more than you think." He gave Eli a knowing look. "Some people deserve a certain kind of death. But you know that better than anyone, don't you?"

The look in his eye told Eli that Moros knew way too much about him.

Eli summoned all his remaining strength and pushed himself to his feet. He looked out on the barren wasteland of a childhood home he thought he'd never see again. "What if I don't become a Ker?"

"A Ferry will arrive soon to open a door for you." Moros chuckled. "Which do you think awaits you, Heaven . . . or Hell?"

Eli closed his eyes, memories assaulting him. "I don't know."

"Really? I think you have a good idea. How do you think Cacy will feel if she has to shove you through a portal to eternal damnation?"

A hard, heavy throb pressed against his chest, like his silent heart was about to burst forth. It was so sudden and painful that Eli couldn't stop his cry of agony. These were the shittiest choices he'd ever been dealt. Turn into a Shade and possibly harm the woman he loved. Stand still and force her to send him to Hell. Or become a Ker . . . "She'll hate me if I join you."

Moros shrugged. "Cacy's opinions of my kind are no secret. Most Ferrys feel the same. Their blind prejudice is not my concern."

"Galena," said Eli quietly. "What will she—?"

"She doesn't have to know. You will look human enough. Your differences won't be apparent for years, when people will notice that you do not age. However, there are so many genetic and chemical enhancements these days that it will take decades for anyone to even wonder about it. And who knows, perhaps your sister will invent eternal youth by that time!" He laughed before growing solemn again. "As a Ker, you will be better able to protect her until I can root out the rogue elements in my ranks. Right now, it appears she is in significant peril. As is Cacy, particularly because she will defend your sister to the death."

And that sealed it. Eli could never leave Galena or Cacy without knowing they were safe. No matter what he had to sacrifice, including his relationship with Cacy. "I'm in. How do I sign up?"

Moros grinned, his fangs glistening in the moonlight. He pulled the glove off his right hand. "Simple. You give me your soul."

He punched his hand right through Eli's chest.

CHAPTER THIRTY-FOUR

Cacy stood shivering in the Veil with Rylan, her clothes still soaked and sticky with Eli's blood. A void of sorrow surrounded her, a blanket of numbness, waiting to smother her. But she couldn't let it suck her in completely just yet, because Eli still needed her. Her eyes met Rylan's. "I have to find him. I need to be the one to guide his soul."

Rylan nodded, lines of stress etched deeply into his face. "I'll find Shauna and guide her."

"Are you going to call Aislin?"

Rylan arched a brow. "If Aislin is involved, I don't think that's a good idea. She's off tonight, anyway. I'll tell her tomorrow. And"—he gave Cacy a searching look—"I want you to call me later. Don't make me worry about you."

Cacy gave Rylan's hand a squeeze. "Thanks for trying to save him," she whispered, tears filling her eyes.

He hugged her and kissed her cheek. "I will never forgive myself for being too late. When I find Shauna, I'll try to find out how she could have done something like this. I'll find you answers, Cacy. I know it won't fix anything, but—"

"Thanks, Ry," she tried to say, but it came out as a breathless sob. She stepped away from him and watched him open his Scope and step through.

Cacy flipped her Scope, focused all the pieces of her broken heart on finding Eli, and opened an intra-Veil portal. She wasn't surprised when it revealed a completely unfamiliar place, and she stepped into the dusty wasteland without hesitation, desperate to spend a few final moments with Eli before having to send him on.

She stood high atop a hill. Sunbaked dirt stretched for miles in all directions except one. The full moon hung above the burned-out city of what she assumed was Pittsburgh, glinting off the shattered windows of skyscrapers. She didn't want to know what she would see if she climbed out of her Scope and into the real world. Poverty, disease, violence . . . Eli's toughness was proof enough that it was a rough place, rougher than anything she'd encountered in Boston.

"Eli?" she called, turning in place. "Are you here?" A trickle of dread snaked through her mind. Was she too late? Could he have become a Shade so fast? Was he out there somewhere, lost in the labyrinth of the city? Or had another Ferry come to claim him? Several Ferrys from the Boston area covered this part of the country. They could have felt the pull and beaten her here. She put her hand over her mouth to hold in her sob. She might never know what happened to him. She might never get to tell him how she felt.

"He's not here, my dear," said Moros as he materialized in front of her.

She took a wary step back. She could do nothing to Moros. He was too powerful. But she looked forward to the day the Keeper of Hell came for him. She wanted a front-row seat to that show. "You have serious balls coming here and talking to me," she spat.

He nodded. "You have every right to be angry."

"Anger doesn't begin to describe what I feel toward you. Get away from me." She turned to walk down the hill toward the edge of the city.

"We have business, Cacia," he called after her. "There are much more pressing things to attend to in Boston."

"Fuck off," she replied.

"Eli is at the hospital."

She stopped in her tracks and looked over her shoulder. "I know. Dec took his body to the morgue."

"You will find more there than his body." He inclined his head toward the city. "And you will find nothing down there but dozens of rabid Shades who will tear you limb from limb, steal your Scope, and use it to unleash themselves upon the hapless population of Pittsburgh—as if those poor souls need one more tribulation."

Moros was right next to her now, the tremendous heat of him making her sweat even in the chill of the Veil. As much as she wanted to punch him, if he was right about Eli's soul being somewhere else, she had no reason to be here. She felt mostly dead now. There was little left of her but a ragged, empty shell. And now that Eli was gone, it was like all the stitches had been ripped out of her heart. Like all the places he had healed after Moros's touch had been torn open again.

"Why?" she whispered. "Why did you touch me when you had no intention of holding up your end of the deal? You were my father's friend. Why would you do this to me?"

Moros sighed. "It was selfish of me to touch you. But I am a selfish creature, and it was a temptation I could not withstand. You feel things so intensely, and experiencing what was *meant to be* through your perspective was a rare delicacy. You had quite a future ahead of you."

"Wise of you to use past tense." Right now, it didn't feel like she had any future worth living.

The smile on his face would have rendered him entirely angelic if it hadn't been for the gleaming white tips of his fangs. "I am not the villain you think I am. I am responsible only for my failure to realize the danger, in my arrogant refusal to recognize that some of my Kere dared to work against me. But I did not Mark your man, Cacia, or any of the others. Nor am I a threat to Galena. Your father demanded to meet with me about her, but he never had the chance. I wasn't sure which side he was on. When I touched you, I felt the depth of your respect for your father, the power of your conviction, the certainty that protecting Galena was the right thing to do." He reached toward her, but then let his hand fall to his side again. "Even though I had already made my vow to protect Galena, you made me sure it was what I absolutely needed to do, no matter the cost."

Cacy stared at him, agape. "But if Eli wasn't Marked by *you*—"

"Yes. At least one of my Kere is rogue. I do not know who. *Yet.*" His voice was full of sorrow and rage at the same time.

"But you know the future. Can't you see who it is?"

He shook his head. "I can only see the future of humans, Ferrys included. Most of them, at least." Something both intrigued and regretful glinted in his gaze. "The Kere are not human. Not after they become mine. So when their futures interlace with humans', it is too hazy for me to see. I have blind spots. And sometimes, the future completely disappears."

He cleared his throat. "Something has happened. A fundamental departure from what has been fated. My sisters are enraged. They can feel it, like what is *meant to be* is being ripped away from *what is*. They sent me to Boston to find out why. But day by day and person by person, my future-sight is failing me. Your future disappeared completely a few minutes ago." He smirked, and she wanted to punch him so badly she had to fold her arms over her chest and hold them there. "Right now, I am as blind to the future as you are, but I suggest we get back to Boston and face it, before it is stolen from us entirely."

Her father's words rang in her head: *Protecting the future is more important than righting the wrongs of the past.* If she wanted to honor Patrick Ferry, she would focus on protecting Galena, even if it meant working closely with the Lord of the Kere.

Without another word, she turned her back on Moros, pictured the hospital, and opened a portal to the alley beside the emergency department entrance. She left Moros standing in the wasteland by himself. It didn't matter. He could be at the hospital, or anywhere else, for that matter, at the speed of thought. One of the dangerous powers of the Kere. Standing on the squashy gray pavement, she flipped the Scope and climbed into the inky, humid darkness.

When she stepped out of the alley, still wearing her blood-soaked clothing, Moros appeared next to her. She jerked to the side to avoid touching him. "If you're worried about Galena, shouldn't you be looking out for her?" she snapped.

He gave her a sad smile. "She is here."

Cacy's heart sank. She would have to comfort Galena now, when all she wanted to do was to collapse onto the floor and cry herself dry. She took a breath of briny, saturated air and stepped through the hospital doors. The sign for the morgue pointed to a side door that led to the temperature-controlled basement of the hospital, and Cacy began to walk toward it.

Moros hooked his long-fingered hand around her upper arm. "That's not where he is."

Cacy's heart beat like it had been jump-started. "What?" Dec had pronounced him dead a few minutes after arriving at Rylan's office. Could he have been wrong?

"I am quite certain we will find Eli among the living." Moros gave her a sidelong glance as he strode through the waiting room. The bedraggled would-be patients sat huddled in plastic seats, all waiting their turn to see the doctor for various ailments. From the smell, at least a few of them had fallen into the canal. Luke the Ker lounged at the edge of the room, his arm around an emaciated young man delirious with fever. He sat up a little straighter when he saw Moros. The humans also seemed to sense that death was walking among them, and instinctively made way as Moros walked by, drawing their arms and legs into their seats like turtles pulling into their shells.

The emergency department doors slid open as Cacy and Moros approached. A nurse looked up as they walked by but didn't stop them. Maybe she thought Cacy, covered head to toe in Eli's blood, was in need of immediate care.

Dec was leaning against the wall outside Operating Theater Four, his head bowed, his arms folded over his chest. He raised his head and met Cacy's eyes. He looked over his shoulder, into the room behind him, and back at her. Then he shoved himself off the wall and came toward her. "Galena's with him," he said slowly. "I'm sorry, Cacy. I had no idea this would happen." He gave Moros a chilling look.

Her heart, now making up for lost time, beat with the rhythm and cadence of a jackhammer. "He's alive?" she asked softly.

"In a manner of speaking," said a low, rough voice, one she would recognize anywhere. She stepped around Dec to see Eli standing in the doorway, leaning against Galena. He was pale from loss of blood, and wearing a set of scrubs instead of his ruined street clothes. His head hung low, like he was too exhausted to hold it up.

Cacy rushed toward him, all her words deserting her, driven forward by pure emotion. He was alive! And somehow, he was up. He was walking. Had she just imagined how badly injured he'd been?

He raised his head.

In the second before he blinked and squeezed his eyes shut, his eyes flashed red.

She froze, everything dropping into place.

Eli was a Ker.

The man she loved was no longer a man. He was a killer.

And if he was a Ker, it meant something else, something she'd never considered.

To become a Ker, a person had to have taken a life. And usually more than one. Moros accepted no one into his ranks who was not already a killer. But Eli . . . he couldn't be. How could this have happened?

Cacy put a hand to her stomach, feeling the loss of Eli all over again. As she stared, Eli kept his gaze focused on Galena, like Cacy wasn't even there. "Come on," he said to his sister. "I need to get out of here."

Galena nodded, clinging to him tightly, and allowed him to lead her past Cacy, Dec, and Moros. As if they were invisible.

Cacy turned to watch him walk away. Her arms rose from her sides automatically, reaching for him, but her feet were rooted in place. She glanced to the side to see Dec staring after them as well. Moros chuckled. "I guess they need some family time."

"You bastard," Cacy and Dec both whispered at the same time.

"Ferrys," Moros hissed, rounding on them. "Your self-righteous attitudes are entirely provincial and completely tiresome. By all rights you should be thanking me. Instead, you curse me. You would rather his body lie rotting in the basement morgue? I can arrange it if you like." His eyes burned crimson.

"Eli isn't a killer," said Cacy softly. "I don't understand how you did this to him."

Moros threw back his head and laughed. "Cacia, you are very naive. Eli will be the perfect Ker. He not only has the instincts of a killer—he has proven himself quite decisively."

Dec narrowed his eyes. "He was in the army. He was trained to be lethal in the line of duty. But that doesn't make him a murderer."

Moros nodded. "He *was* a soldier, but that's not what I'm talking about." He eyed Cacy. "He never told you about what happened to him and his sister?"

"Of course he did," Cacy snapped. "He was nearly killed. He feels awful about what happened to Galena. I don't think he'll ever forgive himself for it."

Dec's brow furrowed as his gaze shifted back and forth between Moros and Cacy.

Moros leaned back against the wall. "That's not where it ended, my dear. That was only the beginning."

"What are you talking about?" But she had a feeling she knew. It had been written in the tension of his body, in the hard stare as he told her what had happened, in the barely caged wildness he carried inside.

Moros seemed to see the dawning realization in her eyes, because he smiled. "Yes. You understand. Eli has respect for life, but only when that life respects those he loves. In the year after the attack on Galena, Eli systematically stalked the men who raped her. He hunted them in the streets. He cornered them one at a time. And he murdered every single one."

CHAPTER THIRTY-FIVE

Eli held Galena tight as they rode home on the bus. His chest was aching again. The look on Cacy's face when she'd seen his eyes . . . it had said everything. Her expression had changed from joy to horror in a split second.

Now they were standing on opposite sides of a bottomless chasm. And this was how it would be. Forever. Unless it got worse, and the way his luck was going, it probably would.

By the time they reached the apartment, Galena was barely able to walk. Eli wasn't surprised at her exhaustion. She'd been hysterical when she arrived at the hospital. Fortunately, he'd already been up and walking around. Dec had chased away the medical staff to give him space and time to pull himself together. Eli suspected there were significant bribes involved. He wasn't sure why the Chief had helped him, but there was no denying he had.

Eli had bolted up from death, every cell on fire, his vision stained red. Dec had taken one look at him and knew exactly what had happened. He hadn't let Galena into the room until Eli had managed to calm down. As he had, his eyes had gone back to normal, fading back to green as he watched in the mirror. But it was still right there, just behind his eyes and beneath his skin—the shrieking, rending rage, the desire to tear the world apart. He had barely held himself together as he walked away from Cacy.

In fact, he was barely holding himself together now. He hugged Galena and went to his room, where he stared out the window, thinking about how many things had changed in the last twenty-four hours. He'd started out the day with a fragile hope, which had been realized in the most powerful, ecstatic way. He'd thought that making love to Cacy was the first time of many. He'd been amazed at the strength of his feelings and at the intensity of hers.

But now he was a servant of death. A pawn in a game he didn't even understand yet. A creature with powers he could not control. Capable of doing damage he wasn't sure he could stomach. And the worst thing of all?

His feelings for Cacy hadn't changed.

That hurt the most. He'd hoped he would see her differently now that Moros had taken possession of his soul, but one look at her had dashed his hopes.

The roar built inside him, starting at the very center of his gut and roiling up, rising before he could stop it, molten and deadly, uncontrollable and unrelenting. He clenched his fists and gritted his teeth. He closed his eyes, and all he saw was crimson. Then a sound forced his mouth open and threw his head back. It tore through him like it came from somewhere else, shattered him like he was paper-thin, shook him like an earthquake. It went on and on, a howl of pure, unadulterated fury and grief.

And then it fell silent.

He opened his eyes.

He was no longer in his room.

He was in the Veil, standing next to a fruit stand, on a street he recognized as one about two blocks from the EMS station. He flinched as he uncurled his fingers and saw sharp claws where his fingernails had once been. He ran his tongue gingerly over his canine teeth, which had elongated into fangs. Here in the Veil, he couldn't hide the fact that he had become a monster.

Eli turned in place, wondering how on earth he'd gotten here. A fiery stab in his arm drew his eyes to his skin. As he watched, a name appeared, scrawled in spidery black letters. *Yang Bao-Zhi*. It meant nothing to him.

A face flashed in his mind, heavily lined, like someone had carved the years into the man's flesh. Eli blinked. The image was detailed, etched deeply into his brain. Eli didn't recognize him, but he had to find this Yang Bao-Zhi. The need was like a pull deep within his bones.

Eli sank into an alley and closed his eyes, feeling the tug of the real, warm, messy world as it yanked him from the Veil. People bustled by on the street in front of him. The road was choked with cars and AVs. Standing at the fruit cart in front of him was the old, stooped man he'd seen in his mind. The man handed a woman a bag of vegetables and held up a duct-taped portable scanner for her to swipe her phone over.

Eli's feet carried him forward automatically. His hand stretched out in front of him before he could stop it. He had to touch this man. It was the only way to get his face out of his mind, the name off of his arm.

Yang Bao-Zhi blinked his heavy-lidded eyes and smiled as Eli stepped from the alley. His eyes widened slightly as Eli's hand settled on his shoulder and squeezed for a moment before falling away. Eli looked down at the palm of his hand and was almost surprised it wasn't glowing red-hot. The man hadn't acted like he was burned, but—

Yang Bao-Zhi's mouth opened in silent surprise. He clutched at his left arm and stumbled to the side, knocking several bunches of radishes to the ground. Eli lunged forward, instinctively trying to help, but someone grabbed him firmly from behind and yanked him back. He spun around to see Trevor looming in the alleyway.

"Don't draw attention to yourself." His hand gripped Eli's arm tightly, and the world turned gray.

"Trevor? What are you doing here?" Eli gasped, looking up to see Trevor's eyes glowing red.

"Helping you," Trevor muttered as he pointed to Yang Bao-Zhi, whose shadowy form lay still on the sidewalk, a bright orange circle and *X* standing out starkly on his shoulder, right where Eli had touched him.

Eli's stomach turned. "Did I do that?"

Trevor nodded. "You did your job." His fingers closed around Eli's wrist, and they both watched the name fade from Eli's skin, leaving only an itchy tingling.

"Oh God," whispered Eli. "That guy didn't do anything wrong. Why was I supposed to kill him?"

Trevor shrugged. "The dude's time had just come, man. That's how it works. Looked pretty quick and painless to me. You must have some compassion in you."

Eli winced as he stared at his victim's sightless, glazed eyes. "This is what it's like? This is what I have to do?"

"You'll have more control over it as you get more experience. At first it just sort of happens. You didn't come here on purpose, right?"

Eli looked around. "I was standing in my bedroom, and then I was here."

Trevor smiled sadly. "Looks like Moros gave you an easy one to start off with. Some are harder. Especially the children."

Eli's mouth dropped open. "Are you serious?" He wouldn't be able to do it. He would refuse.

"You have to do your job, Eli. You won't like what happens if you don't. Trust me," Trevor said, patting Eli's back with a very hot hand. "But this is why I'm a paramedic. It makes me feel like I can balance out the things I do. I think you'll feel that way, too."

Eli stepped back, glad for the silence and invisibility the Veil offered as he freaked out. "How long have you been like this?"

"Since the late twentieth century. I know what I'm talking about." He folded his massive, muscular arms over his chest. "I haven't lost my humanity yet. And I won't."

Trevor sounded like he was trying to convince himself, which didn't make Eli feel better. Right now, the only thing keeping Eli from going straight to Moros and begging to be put down was Galena. He'd lost his soul. He'd lost Cacy. The only thing left was to keep Galena safe. He turned away from Trevor, wanting to get back to his sister, but realized he had no idea how.

Trevor beckoned him back. "Don't go anywhere yet. You have to wait for your commission."

A glossy, swirling ring appeared across the street, first tiny, then growing. A Ferry was coming through a portal.

From the shadowy body of the dead old man lying prone on the sidewalk, another old man rose, this one more colorful and solid. This version of Yang Bao-Zhi was alive, and there was no Mark on him.

Eli staggered back as the old man's soul drew itself up straight and smiled. "I'm sorry," Eli choked as he stared at his victim. "I shouldn't have . . . I won't . . ."

"The Kere serve a purpose," barked Trevor, stepping in front of Eli and blocking his view. "You serve a purpose. Death isn't evil. It just *is*. And we are all part of the process. Cacy is, too," he added gently.

Eli shut his eyes tight. He didn't want to think of her, and he didn't want to know what she thought of him now. She'd told him he was a good man, and now she would realize the truth.

"Leave me alone," he growled as he backed into the spongy alleyway, breathing hard, the pain in his chest tearing at him, splitting him open. It felt like Moros had replaced his soul with broken glass. He slid down the squishy brick wall of one of the buildings, focusing as hard as he could on being as far away from Trevor as possible.

When he opened his eyes, he was back in his apartment.

He lurched to the bathroom and retched into the toilet. With his back against the wall and his knees bent in front of him, he sat on the cool tile floor until he caught his breath. After rinsing his mouth, he stared at his teeth in the mirror to make sure they looked normal, then checked on Galena. She was sleeping soundly, so he went back to the bathroom to take a shower before the water switched off at four. He was scheduled to work in a few hours, and as much as he dreaded the thought of facing Cacy, he would go. Because if he was going to continue living, if he was going to try not to become a true monster, he at least had to do some good.

CHAPTER THIRTY-SIX

Cacy sat in the back of the limousine, staring out at the canal without actually seeing it. She had to be at work in a few hours, but she didn't want to think about it. Would Eli even show up? And did she want him to?

She'd been obsessing over that last question for the past few hours, and she had yet to come up with an answer. She shivered in the air-conditioned chill of the backseat and wrapped her arms around herself, but it did nothing to mend the gaping gash in her heart. Every time she closed her eyes, all she could see was Eli's face as he turned away from her at the hospital. It was as if, when Moros took his soul, he had also taken all of Eli's feelings for her.

She sniffled and tucked her hair behind her ear as the driver pulled up to the Psychopomps Inc. building. This time, when he offered his hand, she took it and let him drag her up. She walked forward unsteadily, realizing she hadn't slept since the day before. At some point, she would crash. But she had to meet with Rylan now. She had some questions.

Rylan was standing in the lobby when she arrived. He frowned when he saw her and held his arms out. She stepped into them and let him hug her, but she didn't have the energy to hug back. He held her shoulders and looked down at her. "I'm so sorry, Cacy. About all of this. Word reached me that Eli is a Ker now."

Cacy bit her lip to hold the sob inside. She nodded. Rylan crushed her to his chest again, so hard she could barely breathe. "I've arranged for a meeting with the Keepers of the Afterlife," he said, his deep bass voice vibrating in her ear. "Moros is going to be punished for what he's done. It's time for the Keepers to put him down. They should have done it millennia ago, and I got the sense they're eager for any excuse to do it now. And we're going to be the ones to make it happen, Cacy."

"Moros didn't Mark Eli."

Though she'd mumbled the words against his chest, Rylan heard her loud and clear. He tensed and tipped her chin up. "Who told you that?"

"He did."

Rylan stepped back quickly. "You talked to him *again*?"

"When I went to guide Eli's soul, he was there. He said there's a rogue Ker on the loose, and he plans to find out who."

Rylan's face flushed. "And you believed him?"

Cacy looked away, her eyes sliding over the vacant reception desk. Pictures of Shauna with her parents and friends still lined its surface. "He told me he planned to let Galena live."

Rylan coughed out a bitter laugh. "You're very gullible, little sister. We have ample evidence against him. Look what he did to Eli. For all we know, he's responsible for Father's death. So I wouldn't be surprised if he got to Shauna."

Cacy walked forward and picked up one of the picture frames. She stared at the bright, innocent smile of the round-faced young woman. "What could have made her want to hurt Eli?"

Rylan sighed. "She confided in me about a month ago. She's been secretly dating a Ker. It would have enraged her parents." He joined Cacy at the desk and picked up a graduation picture. Shauna beamed at the camera, her arms wrapped around her mother and father. "Maybe the Ker she was dating was just following orders, or maybe he was rogue. Either way, there's a good possibility that he convinced her to do it. To get to *me*. To us." He frowned at the happy young girl in the photo. "She could have done it all, Cacy. She could have bribed someone to delete the video of the attack on Father. She was good friends with Chad—she could have asked him to stop the car by the Common and could have paid someone for the killing. She knew where Debra and Peter were and could have worked with her boyfriend to Mark and guide them to the Afterlife without anyone knowing it."

Cacy wasn't sure Shauna was capable of such serious master-minding. She took the picture from Rylan. "Did Shauna say anything when you escorted her soul?"

Rylan's lips became a tight white line as he shook his head.

Cacy swallowed hard over the lump in her throat. "Did she end up in Heaven?"

Rylan looked at the floor and shook his head again.

The picture frame fell from Cacy's numb hands and hit the floor with a clatter. "Do her parents know?"

"I couldn't lie to them," said Rylan solemnly. "They had to know why I would take the life of one of the Ferrys, why I would do something so extreme and permanent. It hasn't happened in decades." The Charon was the only one who could discipline the Ferrys, and the only one who could execute one of them if they wore the Raven Mark on their skin. If he wielded the weapon, the wounds wouldn't heal.

Rylan touched his Scope. "Aislin is particularly furious. She doesn't believe Shauna committed this crime, even though you and I both saw it with our own eyes."

Cacy looked down at the frame, the digital image of Shauna's smiling face now flickering with static. Could Aislin have convinced Shauna to kill for her? Had Aislin given her the gun? "Are the police investigating?"

"Of course," said Rylan, kneeling to pick up the picture. He leaned over and dropped it into a wastebasket. "They said I wouldn't be charged. It was obviously a justifiable homicide."

Cacy put a hand to her stomach, which was feeling distinctly rebellious. "I'm sorry, Rylan. I don't think I could bear to kill someone and then send them to Hell."

He shrugged. "It was necessary. Now. How are you? I felt awful when I heard about Eli. Making Eli a Ker was just about the most evil thing Moros could have done."

Cacy nodded, but she was surprised at how wrong it felt. She knew she should be horrified, but every time she tried to summon up that feeling, all that was waiting for her was relief that Eli was still on Earth. Still existing where she could see him, where she could touch him—not that he'd let her. But no matter what he had done, and no matter what he did now, she couldn't make herself wish he was gone.

"I'll take care of this, Cacy. I'm going to ask the Keepers to fold the Kere into the Psychopomps empire. To put them under my supervision. I swear to you, I'll root out the evil ones, and if you want me to, I'll have Eli sent away. I'll fix all of this for you."

Cacy took a step back from her older brother, her heart constricting. "I have to get to work." She didn't want Eli anywhere but next to her, but there was no way she was going to argue with Rylan now.

Rylan took her by the shoulders again, his dark eyes boring into hers. "Don't worry about this. But stay away from Eli. The Kere are devious and sadistic—even before Moros takes their souls. Eli is obviously not the man you thought he was. Don't let him hurt you. Please." He chuckled drily. "You haven't been listening to me lately, but do this for me. His loyalty is to Moros now, not to you or the Ferrys. He's dangerous."

Cacy nodded, if only to escape the laser beam of his gaze. "Don't worry. I know."

CHAPTER THIRTY-SEVEN

Eli walked into the garage slowly, focused entirely on staying calm. He'd called the Lord of the Kere before leaving home and made sure someone Moros trusted was watching over the apartment and the lab, guarding Galena from anyone who would try to hurt her. Eli would have done it himself, but the past few hours had been hell on earth, and he felt like a brick of C-4, ready to explode at the slightest trigger. He'd been yanked into the Veil once more as soon as he'd left home, names appearing on his arm like someone had carved them there, faces appearing in his mind like they'd been stamped on his brain. And the only way to make it stop was to touch the people whose faces he'd seen. He was drawn to them, almost magnetically, and found himself stepping in and out of the Veil with only a thought, with just the push of an instinct that was now buried deeply within him.

He'd walked behind the young couple for nearly an hour, unable to stomach causing the deaths of these two innocent people. But the names and faces of Karen Pitts and Daniel Bateman were burrowing a hole right through him as he watched them stroll obliviously down the street, window-shopping, holding hands, and leaning in to kiss every so often. To Eli, it was beyond painful, for so many reasons. They were young. Karen had stylishly spiky brown hair and was wearing a green dress that could barely contain her voluptuous body. She carried a matching beaded purse that glittered under the streetlights as she walked. Daniel was stocky and fit, his reddish hair buzzed close to his head. Eli wondered if he was in the military.

Unlike the old man, this pair hadn't yet had a chance to live their lives. It seemed so unfair. And it reminded him too much of what he'd lost. He could picture walking with Cacy like that, holding her hand, pulling her close every few blocks to taste her lips and inhale her spicy scent. It was all too easy to imagine, and it cut through him like a scalpel, bringing with it fresh jabs of agony that added to the very real, gut-wrenching pain he was now feeling. Because every moment he held back and refused to Mark the couple, the pain became sharper, hotter, until it felt like someone had set his insides on fire.

Finally, he couldn't take it anymore. Biting down hard on the inside of his cheek, he ran forward and pushed the couple, laying his hands on their shoulders and bursting between them like a levee break. Ignoring the girl's surprised cries and the guy's shouted threats, Eli kept sprinting like something was chasing him until he stumbled over his own feet and went flying. But instead of hitting the ground, he hit his own bedroom floor, where he lay, stunned and panting, for less than a minute before bolting for the toilet to heave. Fortunately, Galena had already gone back to her lab for the night and hadn't had to witness her brother falling apart.

As he rode the bus to Chinatown, he wondered what had happened to the couple, if they had succumbed to heart attacks like the old man. That wouldn't really make sense, but all the same, Eli hoped Karen and Daniel had a few more hours together, maybe had a chance to make love one more time. He prayed that when the end did come, it was quick, taking them both at once so neither had to endure the knowledge that the other was lost.

Rig 436 was parked in its usual spot, and when Eli saw Cacy's bowed head through one of the small side windows, his breath caught. Her eyes were red-rimmed, and there were circles beneath them. Her beautiful face was pale and drawn, like she'd lived a decade in the last twenty-four hours. She looked like how he felt.

It didn't make him want her any less.

Someone bumped into him from behind, and Eli swung around with an instinctive growl.

Len smiled his ugly smile and held up a bottle of Powderkleen. "My rig needs a spit shine, Sergeant. Since you and your partner injured me in an unprovoked attack, it's the least you can do."

Eli was certain he felt his fingernails elongating and sharpening. "I'm busy. Sorry." He made it two steps before the night supervisor's broad hand closed over his shoulder and spun him around. Len's eyes widened as he stared at Eli's face, but Eli couldn't make himself care. He drew back his fist—

"Stop!" shouted Cacy as she shoved Eli, breaking his laser focus on tearing Len apart. She whirled to face Len. "Clean your own fucking rig," she barked. "Ask my partner to do your dirty work one more time and I will hurt you in a permanent way."

Len tried to sneer, but he'd gone pale. His mud-colored eyes darted back and forth between Eli and Cacy. "You two fucking deserve each other," he said hoarsely, then turned and stalked away, still clutching the bottle of Powderkleen.

Eli's gaze was fixed on the floor as he drew deep breaths through his nose, determined not to let Cacy see how close he was to ripping the arms off that asshole's gorilla-like body. He knew that his eyes were glowing red and if he lifted his head, she'd see him for the monster he was now. He couldn't bear it if she looked at him the way Len just had.

The screech of the wireless alert jerked Eli's head up, and to his relief, the world wasn't stained red. He sprinted for the rig, Cacy right next to him. Their shift had begun.

Over the next several hours, they went on five calls, never looking at each other, never speaking apart from their communication over patients. A badly broken leg. A nasty bolt-gun injury. A heart attack. A car accident. A near electrocution. Each time they pulled into the hospital bay with a live patient, Eli breathed a sigh of relief.

But on their sixth call of the night, what he saw on the videowall caused his stomach to drop. Twisted metal jutted up from the sidewalk in jagged spires, and people were gathered around it, shaking their heads and screaming. "One unit to the corner of Oak and Ash. Construction-site accident. Two reported casualties. Fire crews on scene."

"Eli." Cacy's voice cut him like a whip. "Get your ass in gear. We're up again." She ran for the ambulance.

Just as Cacy fired up the engine, he swung himself into the passenger seat and fastened his seat belt. She stomped on the gas, and the ambulance lurched forward, its sirens wailing.

It was the first time he'd really looked at her since the shift started, and now he was unable to tear his eyes away. Her hair was in a high ponytail, cascading down her neck in thick waves. He remembered what it felt like to bury his fingers in those silky locks. He remembered it brushing over his chest as she crawled up his body.

Then he remembered that he'd never feel those things again, and that gave him the strength to look away.

The streets of Chinatown streaked by, the residents walking the sidewalks like life was normal, like it could go on that way forever, like the messengers of death didn't walk among them. He had forgotten how that felt; even when he was human, he'd carried an awareness of death with him every day.

Cacy glanced at him from out of the corner of her eye. "I was surprised you came in today. I figured you'd want to watch over Galena now that you know—"

"Now that I know someone's trying to kill her? Moros has one of his personal guards watching her while I'm at work."

Her knuckles were white on the steering wheel. "And you trust him?"

Eli sighed. "I don't think he would have gone to the trouble of making me a Ker and keeping me around if he wanted to kill Galena." He stared down at his hands, squinting at them in the glare and flash of the street signs and headlights, wondering if he was imagining the shadows of razor-like claws cast across the dash. He crossed his arms and tucked his hands against his sides.

"This one looks bad. Are you up for it?" she asked, showing she knew him well enough to understand he was close to the edge. Her voice was even, but he knew *her* well enough now to understand she was working hard to keep it that way.

"I'll be fine," he answered as casually as possible. "I'm the s . . ." The words died on his lips. He wasn't the same, and they both knew it. "I'll be fine."

Cacy blinked rapidly and nodded. "Good. Get your gloves on and get ready."

Eli silently obeyed, wondering if she shuddered with disgust as he brushed past her, focusing his attention on his work so he didn't have to see it if she did. Cacy pulled the rig up to the curb and joined him in the back, her movements precise, quick, and calm. He couldn't help being haunted by her intoxicating scent. Then he opened the rear door and saw, lying on the sidewalk, a very familiar-looking beaded green purse.

He and Cacy hopped down from the back of the rig, and the firefighters cleared a path for them through the crowd. One of them explained what had happened: A crane had broken loose from one of the upper floors of the apartment building at the corner. It had fallen several stories, dragging with it the attached load of steel beams. All of that had landed on the sidewalk, and bystanders said there were at least two people buried in the rubble.

The firefighters had already shifted several of the beams and part of the crane wreckage using their ladder truck as well as some of the construction equipment on the scene. Cacy made a sound low in her throat as she reached the edge of the wreckage and saw what awaited them. She shouldered a burly firefighter aside and knelt by a limp, crushed arm. The hand was upturned, fingers curled in on themselves like a dead bug, sparkly green fingernail polish chipped and flecked with drying blood. Cacy took a pulse and shook her head. "Where's the other? You said there were two."

Eli stepped back, his chest caving in. He had done this. He had somehow caused this disaster and brought about the deaths of this young couple. Karen and Daniel. Their names echoed in his head.

A cool hand closed around his wrist, and he jolted back into awareness to find Cacy looking up at him with a solemn expression. "Two fatalities. I need your help to load them up. There were a lot of close calls, but no one else was hurt."

She squeezed his arm, and somehow her touch made it possible for Eli to get back to work. He and Cacy carefully loaded up the almost unrecognizable bodies of the couple while the firefighters continued to clear the rubble. The clang of the rear doors closing had a disturbing finality to it.

Cacy was quiet on the drive to the hospital and didn't once glance over at him. Which was good, because one look from her and he might have disappeared, might have wished himself deep into the Veil, far from anywhere she'd ever think to find him. Not that she'd look. How could she be anything but glad if he disappeared? He rubbed at that now-familiar pain in his chest and wondered if his missing soul was like a phantom limb. Maybe it would hurt him for the rest of his existence.

At the hospital, they unloaded the bodies and delivered them to the morgue. Cacy drove them back to the station. As soon as she parked the rig, Eli was up, planning to grab the cleaning supplies and sanitize the rig to keep his mind busy. But Cacy put her hand on his arm as he tried to get out, and he froze.

"We have other things to do," she said softly, looking at him like he should know what she was talking about.

She sighed. "I have to go guide those souls, Eli. I can feel them waiting for me. And I can tell by the way you're acting that you Marked them. You should come, too."

He slumped in the seat. "Why? Don't you think I've done enough?" he asked bitterly.

"No, I don't think you have. You have to come get your commission."

"I don't want it."

Her fingers tightened over his arm. "You're coming," she said fiercely. "That recovery took forever, and our shift's almost over. I'm clocking us out early. Wait here. And don't you *dare* disappear."

For some reason, he obeyed her.

She came back less than a minute later and practically dragged him into the back of the rig. She unsnapped her Scope from the chain around her neck, opened the portal, and held it out. "Get in there. Unless you want to travel on your own?"

He could have, but he wanted to spend every possible second in her presence. He poked his head through the portal and stepped into the squishy, chilled gray world of the Veil. Cacy followed him. She opened another portal, and both of them stepped out into a street. Karen and Daniel were standing next to a storefront. It was a bakery, and in the window was a ridiculously enormous wedding cake. It was the store they'd come out of when Eli first started following them. He'd never felt more vile.

Cacy walked up to them. "Hi, folks," she said cheerfully. "I'm here to show you where to go."

She flipped her Scope so that the set of scales was facing up and brushed her thumb over its surface. Blinding, shimmering white light appeared at its center, and Cacy smiled. Eli watched her with a hopeless hunger, wishing he could smother his desperate desire to touch her.

She stepped in front of the couple. "You're going to love this," she said with a wistful expression.

She pulled her Scope wide, and Karen and Daniel gasped, their faces lighting up as they saw where they were going. They hugged each other tightly, tears of joy streaming from their eyes. Daniel took Karen's face in his hands and kissed her gently. "You first, baby. I'll be right behind you."

Cacy held the Scope for Karen, lowered the ring over the woman's body, and held the ring in front of her so she could catch the heavy gold coin that came flying out a second later. Then she turned to Daniel, who thanked her and stood still as Cacy lowered the ring over his head and captured the coin that flew out in his wake.

Cacy compacted the Scope down to pendant size and snapped it back onto the chain. She flipped one of the coins at Eli, and he caught it by sheer reflex. It chilled his palm and felt like it weighed a thousand pounds.

His reward for being a killer.

Judging from the frustrated look on her face, Cacy was reading him like a book. "You have to stop beating yourself up and get used to this, Eli. This is what we do, and it's not wrong or bad. Do you know what happens to people who are fated to die but don't? Have you thought about that?"

Eli shook his head. He hadn't had much time to think about anything.

"They rot inside," she said. "They become like living corpses, unable to accomplish anything, unable to love, unable to be happy, unable to do good. They clog and warp the future, because they aren't part of it. What we do is necessary. We make what is *meant to be* happen. You're part of that now."

"Want to trade jobs?" Eli snarled, shocked by the sick, hot anger rising within him. Her compassion was almost more painful than disgust or hatred would have been.

She seemed to sense that, because she got right in his face, and even in the Veil her eyes sparked with vivid color. "Do you want me to feel sorry for you? Look, I *am* sorry. You got handed a truly shitty deal. And I am going to live with the fact that it is entirely my fault for the rest of my existence. But now you have a choice. You can choose to be miserable, or you can choose to fight your way through it. You can choose to be connected, or you can choose to be isolated. You can choose to be evil, or you can choose to be merciful. It's up to you."

Eli stepped back, needing space. It wasn't that she was yelling at him; it was that her scent was making him crazy. "It's not up to me to be merciful," he said. "Apparently, if I am, people will turn into walking corpses, and I'll walk around feeling like my insides are going to explode. For all I know, they *will* actually explode. Moros doesn't seem like the kind of guy to mess around with."

"That's not what I meant. You do realize you were merciful to that couple, right?"

He tilted his head up and stared at the moon, low and heavy in the gray-black sky. It was tinted with red, and he knew his eyes were probably glowing bright and evil. He turned his back to her. "I killed them. A young couple, blissfully happy and planning the rest of their lives together, and I *killed* them."

He flinched as she put her hand on his back. "It was quick. They probably didn't see it coming. They didn't have a chance to get scared. Death was instantaneous, and they were together. There's nothing more merciful than that, Eli." Her fingers curled into his uniform.

Eli's breath was coming hard and fast. He could feel her behind him, her body close to his. He folded his arms over his chest to keep himself from embracing her. "It doesn't feel merciful."

"That's because you're still thinking like a human. But you're not human anymore."

"I know!" he roared, his control snapping completely. He spun around. "Look at me, Cacy. Don't you think I know that? I'm a monster now." He laughed, and even to him, it sounded insane and brutal. "I was a monster before, too. You just didn't know it."

CHAPTER THIRTY-EIGHT

Eli tried to tear himself away from Cacy, but she was ready for him. She clung to his uniform, knowing he could disappear forever if she let go. "You aren't a monster, and you never have been. You protect the people you love. You'd lay down your life for them. I know that's the only reason you became a Ker. I know you."

Eli flashed his teeth at her, his canines sharp as daggers. "*I* don't know me, Cacy, so how can you? What I do know is that I'm dangerous." He stared down at his clawed hands and muttered, "I think I've always been that way."

He backed up, but Cacy followed him. "Why? Because you took the law into your own hands in a city where there's been no actual police force for at least ten years? You took the guys who raped your sister off the street."

"Permanently," he snapped.

"Yes," Cacy agreed, "because they hurt her. And they'd probably hurt other women in the past, and they were probably going to do it again." She'd thought about this a lot since Moros had told her. At first, she'd been stunned. Eli had seemed so gentle. He saved lives. But Pittsburgh was lawless and violent, and he'd struck back against that violence, unwilling to allow men who committed such brutal acts to roam free. She couldn't blame him for that.

She reached for his hand, and he jerked it away, but he stopped backing up. She knew she was getting to him. "You were dangerous before you became a Ker, Eli. You've always been dangerous. That doesn't mean you're evil. It means you're powerful."

He shook his head like she wasn't hearing him. "Look at me now," he said raggedly, spreading his arms and letting her see his claws. "Why are you even here with me? I'm a Ker. You hate the Kere. I've heard how you talk about them . . . us."

She shook her head. "I don't hate the Kere. I hate creatures who revel in the suffering of others. But you don't. You never have. I could never hate you." She took a quick step closer to him, enough to feel the heat rolling off him. His eyes were blazing red, like embers in a fire. And . . . he was still Eli. Still beautiful. Still looking at her like he'd die for her if she'd let him.

"When Moros took your soul, did he take your heart, too?" she asked.

His arms dropped to his sides. The glow in his eyes faded a bit. "No," he said hoarsely.

She inched closer, prepared to tackle him if he tried to disappear. "You still feel something for me."

He looked away, refusing to meet her eyes.

"You want me." She put her hands on his chest, but only had a moment to savor the heat, because he jumped back like she was the one who'd burned *him*.

He jabbed a finger at her. "Don't. Don't push me, Cacy. I don't want to hurt you."

She closed the distance between them quickly. "You won't hurt me."

His hands closed over her arms, holding her away from him. "Stop."

Her fingers closed around the front zipper of her uniform, and she slowly drew it down, enough to reveal her throat and the swells of her breasts. She shivered in the chilled air. "You won't hurt me," she repeated, her breath coming quicker as she watched his glowing eyes catch fire again, now glazed with something more than anger. Desire.

She smiled, hope blossoming in her heart. After seeing what he'd done tonight, how he was desperate not to hurt anyone and how he refused to let the Marked suffer in their deaths, she knew he was good. And she wanted him as badly as she had before. He was scared. He needed her to stand by him now, and she trusted him enough to try. Her fingers played with her zipper as she watched him. "Should I keep going?"

He ran his tongue along his bottom lip. "You don't want to do this."

"Was mind reading another nifty power you got when you became a Ker?"

He frowned. "No."

She pulled the zipper down another few inches, and Eli's fingers tightened around her arms. "Then you don't know what I want. Good thing I do." Another few inches.

He pulled her to him, enveloping her in heat despite the frigid air of the Veil. His arm swept around her back, and he lifted her off her feet, up to his waiting mouth. Cacy wrapped her arms around his neck and held on tight as he kissed her like he was starving for her. She ran her tongue over his fangs, reveling in his wildness, desperate to show him she wasn't afraid.

Because she wasn't. Not much, at least.

She could feel something coiling beneath the smooth surface of his skin, a barely restrained chaos, ready to explode. Whether in passion or destruction, she wasn't sure. It wasn't because he was a Ker now. That was just part of Eli. Becoming a Ker had only intensified it, but it hadn't changed him. And his feelings for her hadn't changed, either. She could feel it. She could taste it. She ran her hands over the muscles of his back and wrapped her legs around his waist as Eli's fingers curled over her thighs and held her against him.

She was hit with a blast of swirling wind, first cold then hot. Eli's grip on her tightened. She opened her eyes and saw that, somehow, he'd transported them from the Veil to his bedroom. Without lifting his lips from hers, he reached out and yanked the zipper of her uniform all the way down. His hand cupped one of her breasts, raising beads of sweat wherever he touched. She pulled her uniform open even more, needing to feel his heated mouth on her body.

He didn't disappoint her. He ripped her uniform off her shoulder, tearing the fabric down her arm, something no normal human could have done to bulletproof material. His mouth closed over her nipple, and he sucked hard, and Cacy didn't try to hold back her cry. It felt like everything inside her was being drawn toward him, into him, and that was exactly where she wanted to be. She buried her hands in his hair and held on tight.

Then one of his teeth scraped roughly against her breast, and she flinched. Eli reared back like she'd slapped him, his eyes flashing red, the glaze of desire bleeding into a look of horror. He set her on her feet and took a few steps backward, his chest heaving. "I'm sorry," he rasped. He put his hand over his mouth as he stared at her chest.

Cacy looked down at the red mark on her skin. It had surprised her more than it had hurt her. "I'm all right. Come back here."

She reached out to him, but he was running his fingers back and forth across his teeth like he believed he still had fangs. Cacy knew if he bolted now, he'd never come back; of this she was certain. He'd be convinced he was nothing more than a monster, and she would lose him permanently.

Slowly, she finished unzipping her uniform, peeling it away, never taking her eyes off his. She unlaced her boots and kicked them off, then pushed the uniform down her hips and legs before stepping out of it. Eli watched with hooded eyes, his hands fisted at his sides.

"Come back here," she said again, now standing naked before him.

He tore his gaze from her and held his hands up in front of him, staring at his fingers with a grimace. He was still getting used to being a Ker, going in and out of the Veil, appearing human in one place and inhuman in another. He looked convinced that he had claws, but outside the Veil, his hands were just ordinary hands. Hands she desperately wanted on her body.

"I shouldn't have brought you here," he said in a low voice.

She leaned back on the bed and lay on her side, propping herself up on an elbow. "Then why did you?"

His breath hitched as she drew her heel along the sheet, arching one of her knees, opening herself to him. She'd never felt this vulnerable, but she'd also never wanted anyone more. He remained frozen in place, trembling with tension. He was right on the edge of giving in; all he needed was a little push. So she trailed her fingers from her chest to her belly then between her legs. Even from across the room, she saw his pupils dilate as she stroked herself, imagining what his touch would do to her. "I want you here, Eli. Don't make me do this by myself."

CHAPTER THIRTY-NINE

At the sight of Cacy on his bed, running her fingers through the slick pink flesh between her legs, the thread holding Eli to his logic snapped. All his arguments about why being with Cacy was *a terrible idea* and *doomed to failure* became white noise in his head, drowned out easily by one thing: the need to bury himself inside her body.

He made it across the room in two long strides. His molten hands closed over Cacy's hips and flipped her over onto her stomach. He yanked down his own zipper and ripped his arms out of his sleeves, craving the feel of skin on skin. With his uniform hanging from his hips, the hot, rigid length of him pressed between the soft mounds of her ass, the tattoo of the raven on her back undulating as she pushed herself up on all fours and writhed against him, Eli was lost in a haze of passion. The only thing that mattered was now. This. Her.

"Eli," Cacy begged. "Now."

His fist slammed onto the bed next to her shoulder as he wrapped an arm around her waist and pulled her back against him. His hand stroked down her belly and delved between her legs, following the same path her fingers had taken seconds earlier. Cacy put her hand over his, urging him on, until he circled her clit and then slid a finger inside her, groaning at the sensation. She wiggled against him, deliberately provoking him in the sweetest way. His entire body was vibrating with tension; it rippled through him as he arched over her and ran the head of his cock along the seam of her body. He drove himself inside her in one deep, devastating thrust that lifted her knees from the bed. She was so soft, so slick, surrounding him with heat, sending shocks of it through his belly and legs. Lost in that feeling, Eli opened his eyes.

And saw red eyes peering back at him in the window glass, just like they had the night he'd found Cacy in the Veil. He froze. It was his own reflection.

Then Cacy ground against him, erasing coherent thoughts from his mind, forcing him to close his eyes as lightning strikes of pure pleasure hit him hard. He gripped her hips and relentlessly pumped in and out, chasing only feeling. Cacy cried out, and her fingers curled into the sheets. But when she tried to look over her shoulder at him, he bent over her, bracing himself with one arm. "Close your eyes," he whispered in her ear as he pulled back. "Don't look at me."

"I see you better than you see yourself," she replied, shoving her hips back as he slid inside her once again. Her body clenched around his, and they both moaned. He wanted to argue, but he couldn't think past the mind-blowing bliss that made him desperate with the need to move, to thrust, to ignite.

Eli buried his face against her neck, cursing and apologizing with each breath, his pace becoming more urgent. Cacy met him stroke for stroke, demanding more of him, refusing to let him pull away again. Refusing to accept any less than everything he had. She reached up and folded her arm around his neck, slippery with sweat and taut with barely bridled energy. She wove her fingers through his hair as they moved together; every time he flexed forward, she bowed her back, inviting him all the way in. He inhaled the scent of her, now deepened by heat and want, and drew his tongue along her neck just to taste her skin.

Her inner muscles drew tight around his shaft as her hand slid down his arm, guiding his hand between her legs. She pressed her palm over his, spreading his fingers, letting him feel where they were connected by the wet slide of his body into hers. She turned her head and nuzzled against his cheek.

"Do you feel this?" she said softly as she drew his fingers back and forth against the meeting of iron and silk, hard and soft, all soaked with the heat of desire. "This is what you do to me."

And then she looked into his eyes . . . and didn't look away. "Don't ever stop," she gasped as he hit her deep. Cacy's lips parted and she arched back. Eli covered her mouth with his, kissing her hard and absorbing the hitching sound of her pleasure, letting it reverberate all the way to his bones. Letting it drive him wild. He reared back as his body took over completely, giving in to the powerful, merciless rhythm of his hips, the invasion of her soft flesh, the maddening cadence of her moans, the frenzied grasp of her hand as her nails scraped along his hip, pulling him closer, urging him on.

The heat came from deep within him, that hidden place that had always been there, that he had never admitted to. It welled up, drawn to the surface by the tight clutch of her body, the relentless motion of her hips. It simmered at the sight of her hands fisted in the sheets, the sweat glistening along her shoulders where the wings of the raven were spread in flight. The pressure of it built with the feel of her—her full breasts bouncing in time with his thrusts, her nipples taut as he rolled them between his fingers. *Almost there . . .*

Cacy's muscles locked beneath his hands as an orgasm rolled through her. She gasped his name with every fierce spasm of her body. And it was exactly what he'd needed to ignite. He slammed into her and roared with his release, shaking the walls and windows, sending tidal waves of heat through the room. Cacy undulated against him as he gushed inside her, wringing every last shred of pleasure from both of them.

Eli came back to himself slowly, his body tingling with the aftershocks of his climax, his throat raw, his chest heaving. He rolled to his side and pulled Cacy with him, tucking her against his body, unable to believe her response to his loss of control.

She hadn't pushed him away. She had demanded more.

He bowed his head and kissed her shoulder, letting his gaze linger gratefully on the creamy hue of her skin. He pressed his forehead to her shoulder blade as relief washed over him. For a few moments there, he was convinced he'd turned into an animal, a raging storm that would destroy anything in its path, including the woman in his arms. But that wasn't what had happened. She had weathered it—no, it had gone far beyond that. She had controlled it, controlled him, but not by trying to hold him back. She had set him free. She had been there with him, as wild as he was and just as strong. And now he was lying here, nearly paralyzed with the power of his feelings for her. He spread his fingers over her chest, pressing his palm between her breasts where her heart beat rapidly.

She sighed and placed her hand over his. "It's yours, you know."

"I don't deserve it."

She turned to face him and threw her leg over his hip, drawing him to her. Her hand stroked down his cheek as she looked into his eyes. "I don't believe in deserving. You haven't deserved most of what has happened to you. But it happened anyway. So did we. We happened, Eli. I'm so thankful for that. I love you."

Eli stared at her, rolling her words over in his head. "Would you mind saying that again, please?"

She smiled, her full lips curled in that painfully sexy way. "How much will you pay me?"

He kissed her as his body awakened again, intoxicated by the heady ring of those three words in his mind. When she felt the hard jut of his erection against her leg, she made a little sound of surprise. "Oh, that was quick," she breathed. "In that case, I think we can work out some sort of payment plan."

He made love to her slowly this time, gently, whispering his devotion against her skin, worshipping every part of her. It was like floating in a warm sea, bathed with the sun, weightless and peaceful. He'd never had that feeling before, that sense of being carried, lifted up and yet completely surrounded, caressed but not shackled. As he lost himself in her again, letting her body undo his control, letting her words of love devastate him, he realized what the feeling was: *happiness*. Even now, with his life transformed, his soul taken, his will not entirely his own, he was happy.

Because of Cacy. This amazing woman who had saved him from himself. Her heart was his. In that moment, as she arched beneath him, her lips parted, her sweat-damp hair spread across his pillow, as he was rocked to the core by the force of his love for her, he vowed to spend the rest of his existence earning the right to call her his.

They came together, holding on tight, trembling with the release. Cacy collapsed against his chest as he rolled onto his back and cradled her head with his hand. He was still panting, but he could feel her muscles going loose with exhaustion. "Are you okay?" he asked.

"Never better," she mumbled. "I just . . . need to . . ."

She drifted off with a sigh, never finishing the sentence. The slow, even rise and fall of her chest told him she was asleep. It made him smile, that she felt safe enough to pass out on him. He welcomed the responsibility as much as the delicious, warm weight of her body and the tickle of her hair on his chest. He ran his fingers through the silky strands and kissed the top of her head. "I love you, too," he whispered.

Fiery pain shot up his arm, a now familiar call to action. He glanced down at his arm to see a name appearing in spidery black scrawl. *Lori Gaugin.* "No," he breathed. "Not now." But the face in his mind erased his bliss, blotting out everything else.

Still, Eli didn't move, focusing his gaze on Cacy's delicate fingers, which spread across his chest possessively.

The pressure built in his gut, that need to find his victim boring its way through him, causing him to tense to keep from groaning with the agony. "Cacy?" He didn't want to leave her like this.

She whispered his name in her sleep but didn't move. He shook her gently, trying to rouse her, but it was no good. Finally, he gave up, silently promising her he'd be back soon. He edged out from under her and yanked on a pair of sweats and a T-shirt, determined to be back and naked with her again in a matter of minutes. He let the pull of the Kere tug him into the Veil somewhere near downtown. He immediately walked forward, stepping into the real world, already looking for the woman whose face was newly stamped on his brain.

Lori Gaugin sat in her car, which was pulled to the side of the road near a busy intersection. She frowned as she opened her door and looked down at her flat front tire.

"Dammit," she snapped.

Eli walked toward her, determined to end this quickly. He reached out to brush her shoulder, the pressure in his body ratcheting to nearly unbearable levels. He shouldn't have denied it for this long.

A blonde woman appeared from nowhere, as if she'd stepped through a curtain of invisibility. Her long red-lacquered nails scraped up Lori Gaugin's back, causing her to spin in place and look around. Eli blinked as the blonde woman disappeared.

Lori took a step backward, still searching for the person who'd touched her. Her eyes met Eli's.

And she was run over by a passing taxi.

Eli stared helplessly as she lay crumpled on the road, where another car rolled over her legs. She shrieked in pain, fully conscious, her eyes round with terror and glazed with agony. Eli instinctively moved forward to help her, but a hand closed around his neck and yanked him to the side. He stumbled, gasping as the icy air of the Veil surrounded him.

When he turned, the blonde was standing in front of him. She wore a skin-tight shirt, a short skirt, and high heels. Her red-lacquered claws matched her eyes.

Eli recognized her. She looked different here in the Veil, and far more vicious, but there was no doubt it was the woman who'd tried to buy him a drink the day he'd died.

"What's up, gorgeous?" The woman smiled. "I'm Mandy," she said, her voice raspy and low.

Eli rubbed his neck, and his hand came away dripping with blood. She held up her claws and waved at him. "This could have turned out differently if you'd only let me buy you that drink." She pouted. "I hate to damage anything so edible-looking."

She lashed out so quickly he barely saw it happen. He looked down to see his blood splatter onto the soft gray sidewalk, from four deep gashes beneath the shredded fabric of his T-shirt.

A growl rolled up from his throat as his own claws lengthened. This woman was a Ker, but obviously not his friend. In fact, Eli was certain she was the one who had Marked him that day. She had been in the bar, too, just after he'd left Moros. She had put her hand on his chest, right where Cacy had seen the Mark.

That meant she was the rogue. She was the one who was after Galena. And now she had Marked Eli's victim, leaving him with Lori Gaugin's face in his mind and name on his arm, his need to Mark still unsatisfied. He snarled and bared his teeth at Mandy, a familiar rage building in his chest, almost overcoming the awful pressure twisting his insides. "Try that again."

She grinned. "So brave. So stupid." Her claws came rocketing toward him, but he caught her wrist and twisted her arm behind her. She kicked at him with her spiked heels and raked long furrows down his shins. Something silver flashed in front of his eyes, and a sharp pain stabbed through his throat, distracting him for a moment, which was all she needed to break loose from his hold.

She took a few steps back, licking her lips. He staggered forward, nearly doubling over from the now-unbearable pain. It felt like someone had cut him open, shoveled hot coals into his body, and sewn him up. She watched him with a knowing smirk. "You didn't Mark your kill, my friend. So disobedient of you." Her blonde hair bobbed around her shoulders as she nodded toward the street. Traffic was piling up, and a transparent crowd of onlookers surrounded the wounded woman, whose screams were so loud they could be heard in the Veil. She was dying. Slowly. Painfully.

Mandy nodded, like it was her intention for the woman to suffer. Eli suddenly understood why Cacy was suspicious of the Kere. As if to drive the point home, Mandy lifted her fingers to her lips and licked his blood from her fingertips with obvious relish. Her glowing red eyes lit on his. "And now you've stolen a Scope. You've only been a Ker for a day, and look how much trouble you're in. Moros will not be pleased."

Through the haze of his agony, Eli raised his head, finally noticing the cool, heavy weight cinched tight around his neck. Somehow, Mandy had looped it over his head. "Who did you take this from?"

"Let's say it's a fitting trophy for you to be found with. Now, I'm off to deal with your sister." She winked at him and disappeared.

Eli focused everything he had on getting back to his apartment, on getting to Galena and Cacy before Mandy could hurt them. But all he could see in his mind was the dying woman, and all he could feel was the burning pressure building inside his body, slowly reducing him to ash.

A shrieking growl spun him around, his eyes skimming the street and sidewalk. There, half a block away, a shadowy creature was limping toward him, its arms outstretched. A Shade.

Moros had told him the Shades would attack a Ferry to try to climb back into the real world, and Eli was wearing a Scope around his neck, the perfect invitation to target him. He tried to rip it from his body, but his own claws were so long and his fingers so clumsy he almost tore his own throat out.

"Shit," he said, stumbling back, burned by the blood gushing from his chest. His legs crumpled beneath him. He landed on the sidewalk on all fours and began to scramble toward the dying woman, thinking that maybe if he touched her, the pain would stop and he could fight back, and then he could get back to the two people in the world who mattered most to him. Even if, at the moment, he couldn't quite remember who they were.

He half slid, half crawled along the gelatinous sidewalk, punching through the soft surface of Lori Gaugin's car, nearly drowning in the suffocating jellylike mass before emerging from the other side. He landed in a sprawl a few feet from the crowd, who were mere shadows in the Veil. The Shade shrieked again, the wet slap of its feet against the sidewalk spurring him to action. It would be on him in a few seconds. He stretched his hand out, but it passed through Lori's transparent body, the lurid orange Mark of death right in the center of her back. She wasn't dead, so she wasn't solid in the Veil. He needed to be in the real world to touch her. He closed his eyes, trying to get there, but a body landed on his back, knocking him onto his stomach.

"It's mine, it's mine," chanted the Shade as its spindly, slimy gray arms wrapped around his neck.

Eli arched his back and flipped the Shade over his shoulder. It was a female, with long patchy red hair, bone-white skull showing through the bare spots. He sat back as it rolled toward him. "Shauna?"

Oozing blue eyes blinked at him. "I killed you," she grunted. But she'd stopped grasping at him. Her mouth opened and closed a few times, like she was trying to decide what to say. Her jagged teeth protruded from her mouth. Some of them had fallen out, and a clear fluid leaked from the corners of her lips.

Eli tried to remember everything he knew about the Ferrys, but he could barely push any words that weren't *Lori Gaugin Lori Gaugin Lori Gaugin* past his lips. "Didn't"—*Lori*—"one of your family come"—*Gaugin*—"to guide your soul?"

Shauna looked down at herself, her dress covered in greasy patches of corpse wax, her skin sagging from her bones in loose, fragile folds. She was rotting alive, a fact of which she seemed keenly aware. Her decaying fingers reached up to touch her face. "I ran from him here in the Veil. It was all his idea. He told me to do it. He said you were dangerous and a threat to our family. He said he'd tell my parents about my boyfriend. I wasn't supposed to die."

Eli grunted as another bolt of fire struck inside him. He'd scarcely heard a word she said. His arms gave out, and he hit the sidewalk, Lori Gaugin's face crowding out all his other thoughts.

Shauna leaned toward him, giving off the sick-sweet smell of putrefaction. "Mine. I need it."

Eli tried to fight her, but he could barely move. She removed the Scope from his neck and hugged it against her rotting breast, cooing to it. Then she turned to him, her streaming, nearly lique-fied irises focused on his. His fingers twitched in agony as he stared helplessly at her. He was supposed to be doing something. He was supposed to be somewhere else. But all he could think was *Lori Gaugin Lori Gaugin Lori Gaugin*.

Lori Gaugin . . . He swore he could see her right in front of him, sitting up, getting to her feet. He grabbed for her, but his shaking hand missed her legs by several inches.

A bright white light nearly blinded him. It got bigger, shining like the full moon, then disappeared abruptly.

His pain disappeared, too. Eli ran his hands over his ravaged neck and chest, still weak but no longer in agony. He pushed himself up. Shauna the Shade was standing in front of him, a Scope in her upturned palm. She had guided Lori Gaugin's soul to Heaven, cutting off his bone-deep compulsion to Mark, saving him from being reduced to cinders right there on the sidewalk. In the space now available in his head, Cacy's delicate face appeared. Next to her was Galena. And next to her was Mandy, lacquered claws reaching. Eli closed his eyes, needing to get back and make sure that image never became a reality.

"Wait. I need your help," Shauna lisped. One of her teeth fell out and landed on the sidewalk. "Please." She grabbed his arm in a shockingly strong grip while she brushed her thumb over the etched scales on her Scope with her other hand. Another beam of sparkling light shot up from its surface. "Tell my parents I love them and that I'm in Heaven. Please take my Scope to them."

When he nodded, she opened the Scope wide and stepped through, leaving it to fall to the sidewalk. His heart crashing within his ravaged chest, his thoughts racing, Eli grabbed the Scope.

Someone had blackmailed Shauna into killing him. Someone had given Shauna's Scope to Mandy. And that someone wanted Galena dead.

Cursing, Eli focused everything on getting to Galena.

CHAPTER FORTY

Cacy opened her eyes slowly, shedding the thick blanket of sleep that had enclosed her. The last thing she remembered was the most intense orgasm of her life, one that had sent her spinning and falling, so deeply in love she knew she'd never resurface. She'd fallen asleep in Eli's arms, thinking that was the way she wanted to slumber from now on.

She stretched leisurely, relishing the pleasant soreness. It meant Eli was real. That they'd made it through, that they could be together. She ran her hand down her body, the scent of him stamped on her skin, the feel of him echoing in her memory. She reached for him, wanting it to be more than a memory.

Eli wasn't in bed.

She sat up quickly. Their uniforms lay in a heap on the floor. The sheet was tangled around her leg and hanging over the edge of the bed.

A distant pounding shot her heart rate through the roof.

"Who is it?" Galena's voice called from the living room. She sounded nervous.

Cacy bolted from bed and grabbed her uniform. She wrenched it onto her body with desperate tugs, struggling with the torn sleeve, not wanting to be found naked in Eli's room. For half a second, she considered stepping through her Scope, but she paused before she got it open. Something wasn't right. She peeked out of Eli's room and saw Galena in the living room, her bag on the counter and her keys in her hand, like she'd just gotten home. Before Cacy could say a word, Galena dropped her keys in her bag and tapped the screen of the video door monitor. "Who is it?" she asked again.

"It's Cacy's brother. Please let me in, Dr. Margolis. I'm here to make sure you're safe."

And with that, Galena opened the door and let the Charon in. Cacy tried to push down her rising alarm as she walked into the living room to see Rylan shaking Galena's hand. If he had come here in person, something serious had happened.

Eli's sister looked startled when she caught sight of Cacy, and Rylan's friendly smile disappeared. "I thought I told you to stay away from him," he said to his sister. "Why didn't you listen?"

Galena frowned. "Um, it's nice to see you again, Mr. Ferry, but if you and Cacy want to talk, maybe you should—"

Rylan waved his hand. "No. It's all right." He tilted his head and gave her a sheepish look. "You know how protective brothers can be, right?"

"No idea what you're talking about." Galena chuckled, but there was an air of uneasiness to it. She glanced at Cacy like she was hoping for an explanation.

Cacy held her torn uniform closed and ventured farther into the room. "What's going on, Ry?"

He sighed. "I've been trying to track down the rogue element in Moros's ranks, and I think I found it. Galena's not safe here."

Galena gave Cacy a frightened look. "Where's Eli?"

No idea. But he'd probably gotten called into the Veil to Mark someone. "I think he just stepped out for a bit," Cacy said. "He'll be back soon."

Rylan ran his hand through his dark hair. "Galena, we need to get you to our corporate headquarters. I've got a car outside." His gaze darted about the room, like he was afraid of an ambush.

"But if she stays here, she's guarded, Ry. Eli said it was safe."

Rylan's eyes locked with Cacy's. "You have no idea how deep this goes." He shook his head. "You don't even know who's in control."

Galena looked back and forth between Cacy and Rylan. "You guys are scaring me." She pulled out her phone and hit a button. "I'm calling Eli."

Rylan opened his mouth to say something, but shut it again when the ring of Eli's phone came from his bedroom. Galena ended the call, her brow furrowed. "He always carries his phone," she said in a shaky voice.

Cacy stepped forward and stroked Galena's arm. "Maybe you should go with Ry, and I'll wait for Eli," she said. "We'll meet up with you there." As soon as Galena left with Rylan, Cacy planned to step into the Veil and find Eli. She had no idea how long he'd been gone, but Marking didn't take more than a few minutes. He should be back by now.

Rylan was still looking around nervously. He held out his hand to Galena. "Dr. Margolis, please come with me. Your safety is crucial. I—"

Mandy the Ker appeared right in the middle of the living room, a few steps from Cacy. Galena whirled to face the woman and let out a horrified scream.

Hanging from Mandy's clenched fist was a head, its wavy dark hair tangled in Mandy's red fingernails. Rylan rushed forward and put his arms around Eli's sister, shushing her. He glared at Mandy. "You disposed of the *traitor*?" he asked.

As Cacy looked at the head, she recognized the distorted features of the dark-haired Ker who'd been at the fund-raiser. "Yeah," Mandy said. "The rest of him's still wandering the Veil, wondering where the hell his brain is." She chuckled, but then sobered as Rylan gave her a murderous look. She tossed the head behind a chair in the corner, and Galena screamed again.

"Oh my God. I'm being so rude." Mandy wiped her bloody palms on her skirt and approached Galena, offering her hand. "So nice to meet you. I'm Mandy."

Galena shrank against Rylan, looking first at the blood smears all over Mandy's skirt and hands, and then to the blood on her lips.

Realization hit Cacy like a speeding AV. She bolted forward and stepped between the Ker and Eli's sister. "Don't even try to touch her!"

"Cacy," chided Rylan. "Mandy was just trying to be—"

"You try to keep me away from Eli, but you're fine being friends with *this* Ker?" Cacy yelled at Rylan. "What the hell is going on?" She turned to stare daggers at Mandy. "You were trying to Mark her, weren't you?"

The blonde Ker took a few lazy steps back, running her tongue along her bottom lip. "Ask your big brother, Ferry."

Galena gasped, but before Cacy could turn around, she felt something hard nudging the back of her skull. "Get out of the way, Cace," Rylan said softly. "I don't want to shoot you."

"He really has a gun," whispered Galena. "Cacy, do as he says. Please."

Cacy turned around slowly, her hands rising in surrender, her mind reeling with disbelief. "What are you doing, Rylan?"

"Making the hard choices," he said through clenched teeth. He kept the gun pointed at Cacy's face as she backed up slowly, then he wrapped his other arm around Galena's neck. He pulled her tight against his body.

"Ry? Let her go. Father didn't want this. You know that."

"He's not the Charon anymore."

A horrible thought nearly made Cacy retch. "Please tell me you didn't have anything to do with his death."

"You don't understand, Cacy. Father had grown weak since your mother died. He was so focused on making it to Heaven that he'd forgotten about his responsibilities to the Ferrys. To *us*."

"But they were the same," she argued. "He wanted us all to do the right thing. He cared about people more than money."

Cacy grimaced when Rylan's grip on Galena drew a strangled whimper from the struggling woman's throat. "Come on, Ry. Let's do as you said. We can go back to Psychopomps. We can talk with the others about what to do." Anything to buy time. Where the hell was Eli? *Had Mandy done something to him?* "Please," she said, her voice shaking. "Let's talk this through. Just like we always have. You and me, Ry."

Rylan shook his head, and his smile was sad and brutal at the same time. "Home invasions are tragic but so common these days." He brought the gun around and pressed it to the side of Galena's head. Cacy's blood turned cold. "I could have made this better for you if you'd let me, Cacy. But you didn't listen to me. You weren't *loyal* to me. You've left me with no choice."

His gaze found Mandy's. "Let's get this done."

"About time," Mandy said, starting for Galena.

Cacy leaped forward and barreled into the Ker, knocking her to the floor. Cacy yanked her head up and slammed her fist into Mandy's face. Mandy clawed and flailed. Then a blast of cold stole Cacy's breath, and she looked down to see Mandy smiling up at her, fangs glistening. She'd brought them to the Veil.

"I've always thought you were an entitled little bitch," she snarled. Then she lunged at Cacy.

As her back hit the spongy ground, Cacy caught Mandy's wrists, and she kicked out, nailing her in the stomach. She twisted behind Mandy, who screeched and struggled, digging her claws into Cacy's arms, shredding skin and muscle. Cacy's arms began to go loose and weak. With fumbling fingers, she wrenched her Scope from her neck and flicked it open wide, then threw the ring around both herself and Mandy, dragging them back into the real world, where Mandy's claws and fangs were nonexistent.

"Mandy!" called Rylan as he struggled to keep Galena under control, his gun still pressed to her head.

"If you want me to Mark her, take care of your fucking sister! You're the only one who can end her life," Mandy yelled. She and Cacy hit the hard floor of the apartment, sending Cacy's blood splattering across the tile. Mandy started to crawl toward Galena, hand outstretched. Arms trembling and spasming, Cacy struggled to her feet and threw herself on top of the Ker. Even if Mandy dragged her back into the Veil and tore her apart, there was no way Cacy was going to allow her to touch Galena.

"Dammit, Mandy," shouted Rylan. "If you want me to take care of her, get up and hold her still!"

Mandy's fingers burrowed into the deep gashes she'd opened in Cacy's arms, and Cacy's hands went numb. As soon as Cacy let go, the Ker was up and behind her, entangling her arms with Cacy's so that Cacy was facing Rylan. "Whatever you say, baby," Mandy huffed.

Still holding Galena tightly, Rylan aimed the gun at Cacy's chest. "I'm sorry," he whispered. "I love you."

Cacy closed her eyes.

A deafening crack and an inhuman roar shook the room.

Cacy blinked. She'd expected her world to end, but she was still being held tightly in Mandy's grip.

Eli stood in front of her, facing Rylan, shielding her with his body. His neck was torn open. Blood ran down the back of his shirt in thick crimson stripes. His broad shoulders sagged, and he stumbled back a step, rocked with the impact of the bullet that had been meant for her.

"Cacy?" he said.

"I'm okay," she whispered.

Eli drew himself up and leaped at Rylan.

CHAPTER FORTY-ONE

Before Eli could make it across the room, Rylan fired two more shots. Eli staggered back, slipping in his own blood, which was now dripping down his legs and pooling around his bare feet. He steadied himself and took a few more heavy steps toward Rylan, who was having trouble holding Galena still. She was struggling fiercely, her eyes wild, clawing at Rylan's face and arms, dropping her legs out from under her so he had to fight to hold her up, making it impossible for him to aim his weapon steadily.

Rylan put his gun to Galena's head. "Stop. Both of you."

"You can't kill her unless she's Marked," Eli rasped. "You can't kill me, either."

Rylan gave him a hard smile. "I'm a merciful man, Eli. I wanted to make death instantaneous and quick for her. But if you force me to, I can just ravage her brain. Is that what you want?"

"You won't do it." Eli braced his hands on his thighs, determined to stay upright. Behind him, he could hear the sharp bursts of Cacy's breath as she struggled with Mandy. He forced himself to stay focused on Rylan.

"You're up against a wall, Rylan," Eli said. "I know you don't want a war with Moros. You understand the politics better than I do, but I know he's committed to keeping my sister safe, and he doesn't mess around. If you let Galena go, we can end it right here." Eli put everything he had into making those words sound convincing. He prayed Rylan would listen—and do as he asked—before Eli collapsed. His body was at war with itself, getting torn apart as quickly as it could knit itself back together. He wouldn't die like this, but he might lose his ability to fight.

Rylan's lips were pressed into a tight line. "I have every intention of ending it right here." He shoved the muzzle of the gun harder against Galena's temple.

Then a glossy portal opened behind him. A hand shot out of it, knocking the gun away from Galena and punching Rylan in the side of the head. Eli staggered forward to catch his sister as Dec climbed from the portal, trying to wrench the weapon from his brother's hand.

Nearly blacking out from the rending pain in his chest, Eli dragged his sister away from the fight, down the hall toward her room. As they staggered together, Eli noticed Galena's wide, glazed eyes. He knew that look. She wasn't really seeing him. She was reliving the worst night of her life. "No no no no no," she whispered, sounding a million miles away.

As he opened the door of Galena's room, Eli heard an agonized scream.

Cacy.

He lowered Galena gently to the floor. "Stay here, G. Don't move." Eli stumbled back down the hall, his heart erratically pounding, valiantly circulating what was left of his blood. He had to get to Cacy. He couldn't lose her now—

The first thing he saw was her wound, traversing from shoulder to belly, revealing muscle and bone beneath. And then he saw Cacy's mouth, open in a silent cry of pain, blood trickling from the corners of her lips. Mandy held her by the throat, smiling evilly as blood gushed from her nose. She ripped Cacy's Scope from her hands and hurled it across the room. Eli lunged for Cacy and Mandy, but they disappeared.

Before he could focus and get himself into the Veil, a bullet whizzed past his head. He ducked instinctively and turned to see a completely bizarre sight. Declan Ferry was behind his brother—who appeared not to have a head. Dec had gotten his Scope over Rylan's head and cinched it tight around Rylan's neck, so part of the Charon was in the real world and part of him was trapped in the Veil, blinding him. Despite that, Rylan lashed out with strong kicks and punches, and he still held the gun in his hands. Eli's cry of warning came too late, as Rylan swung the weapon around and fired right at Dec.

The Chief smashed into the counter and hit the floor with a nauseatingly heavy thump, blood already haloing around him as he clutched at his neck. Eli barreled forward and hit Rylan with his shoulder, sending him crashing against the wall. Eli ripped the gun from Rylan's hands and shot the Charon in the chest.

Rylan sank to the floor, clutching at his wound, his head still invisible and the Scope still clamped around his neck. Eli knelt clumsily next to Dec, ripping his shirt and pressing it hard against the Chief's neck. Dec tried to hold the cloth with shaking hands. "Galena," he gasped, desperation in his pain-filled voice.

"She's okay." He pressed his hand over the Chief's cold fingers. "Will you heal?"

Dec's gaze darted to his brother, who was stirring weakly. "Not if . . . he . . . doesn't . . . want . . ."

"*Rylan* has control over that?"

"He's the Charon," Dec whispered.

Eli wanted to roar in frustration as he watched Dec's blood drip from between his fingers. "I have to get to Cacy. That Ker dragged her back into the Veil. She's ripped open."

"Go, Eli," Dec gurgled.

Eli squeezed the Chief's shoulder and stood up, silently vow-
ing to return as soon as he could to help the Chief—assuming he
was still alive.

"Where is Cacy?" a high, taut voice asked. Eli turned his head
to see Aislin step through her Scope and into the room, her pale-
blue eyes sweeping across the apartment.

"You didn't see her in the Veil?" Eli asked, his heart sinking.
Mandy could have dragged her anywhere in the entire world.

Cacy didn't have her Scope, and she was badly wounded. She
wouldn't be able to get back without help.

Aislin shook her head, already striding across the room to
kneel next to Dec. She stroked his hair, her face taking on a soft,
tortured look. Her pale-pink lips brushed his cheek, and she whispered something in his ear. He nodded, a weak, barely perceptible
movement.

Aislin got to her feet, walked over to Rylan's writhing—but
already healing—body, and unsnapped the heavy Charon's Scope
from the chain around his neck. She stood up straight, staring at
Dec as she unsnapped her own, more delicate Scope, tucked it into
her pocket, and replaced it with the ornate Charon's Scope. "You're
not going to die, Declan," she said.

Dec drew a shuddering, gasping breath, like he was surfacing
from too long underwater.

"I'll be back for you," she said quietly. Her eyes met Eli's, cold
and calculating. "Where is Galena?"

Eli hesitated. Everyone wanted Galena, and he had no idea
who to trust. "I'm not your enemy, Eli," said Aislin. "I never have
been. Your sister needs to be protected until this is over, and I'm
going to make that happen."

Something in Eli's chest loosened. Cacy might be suspicious
of her sister, but given everything he'd just witnessed, she seemed
like his best ally at the moment. "She's in the bedroom."

"Go after Cacy. You're the only one who can find her."

Eli shook his head, his helplessness strangling him. "I don't know how."

She pointed to her Scope. "We can only use this. But you can use this." She touched her heart. "You have instincts now. You have enough power to find her. Please hurry. My sister needs you."

Eli turned away and closed his eyes. He thought of Cacy, her beautiful face, her full lips, her mischievous smile, that dusting of freckles over her nose. In his mind, he reached for her, stretching across the distance between them to feel her, touch her, run his fingers over her skin. He recalled her scent, that spice, her voice, sweet and tart.

Nothing happened.

He grimaced and forced himself to picture her as she had appeared to him just now, pale and bleeding and torn. Her chest laid open, her arms splayed. Her eyes wide, blood dripping from her mouth. The pressure rose within him like lava, shooting through his veins and singeing every cell, dragging his strength up from a well deep inside him, from the place where he kept it hidden and caged. It snapped and crackled like electricity, painting his world red, leaving him with only one need. One thought.

Take me to Cacy.

A blast of cold hit him, but the heat rolling off him burned it away instantly. He opened his eyes. Cacy was feebly trying to crawl away from Mandy, but her arms and legs were too weak and uncoordinated to get any traction. Eli didn't know where they were, but he knew it wasn't in Boston or Pittsburgh. It seemed like they were in some barren desert plain, with no buildings or people for miles.

"Enjoy your stay in Kansas," Mandy taunted as she raised her arm, claws flashing under the white sun.

Eli's crimson world narrowed to a point, focused completely on Mandy. His fangs cut at his lips; his claws drew his fingers wide. And he attacked.

Mandy spun, her eyes widening until Eli could see his own horrifying reflection in them. He landed heavily, crushing her to the ground, slashing her neck and chest, piercing and tearing her flesh. Eli's head buzzed with the savage need to destroy the Ker who'd hurt Cacy.

Mandy slashed and bit at him, but it didn't slow him down. With one brutal twist, he wrenched Mandy's head from her neck. He dropped it to the squishy dirt and turned to Cacy, who was facedown and unmoving.

"I've got you," he whispered as he turned her over, tears burning his eyes as he saw her ravaged chest, ribs exposed and raw. Her skin was gray. Her eyes were closed. Eli folded her limp body against his chest. Her head lolled in the crook of his neck. "We're going home now. I'm going to take you home."

Cacy moaned softly, swamping Eli with the sweetest relief. He kissed the top of her head then pictured his apartment and focused on getting back to Galena. The warm air of his bedroom greeted them a second later. He laid Cacy on his bed, brushing off the sheet that still hung over the side, and reached for his med kit. If this was anything like the last time she'd been injured, she would heal. But even if her skin knit back together, she had lost so much blood. Her lips were tinged blue, and her breaths were shallow and fast. Brain damage might be a possibility if he didn't act quickly.

Her uniform peeled away easily, shredded as it was. Eli grabbed his last vials of self-perpetuating saline and plasma and injected them into her arm. He brushed his fingers along her temple and gently kissed her. Then he ran his lips along the light-blue vein pulsing beneath the skin of her neck.

"Come back, Cacy. I miss you already," he whispered in her ear.

She drew a shivery breath. Eli closed his eyes and bowed his head, touching his forehead to hers. He reached down and took her hand, and she squeezed his fingers. For all her weak grasp, the power of his relief nearly carried him away again.

Galena's scream pierced the quiet. Eli bolted from the bed, crashing through his bedroom door so hard it came off its hinges. Aislin lay sprawled on the floor at the threshold of Galena's bedroom, clutching at her head. And Rylan was opening Dec's Scope to step into the Veil—with Galena.

Eli caught the edge of the Scope just as Rylan lifted it over his head. Rylan's eyes sparked with madness as he tried to keep his grip on the Scope and on Galena. As Eli reached for his sister, Mandy appeared at his elbow, her head oddly tilted, the bones of her neck poking through skin just barely knitted together, the whites of her eyes stained red. Her hand shot out to touch Galena, but Eli kicked her away. He and Rylan fell over a chair and hit the floor, each scrambling for the Scope.

"Galena?" Eli shouted. He had to focus all his strength on fighting Rylan, whose determination had made him strong, but he needed to know where his sister was.

Out of the corner of his eye, Eli saw Mandy get up and lurch toward Galena, who was backing down the hall. "Keep away from her, G! Don't let her touch you!"

Eli tried to get up, but Rylan slipped the open Scope over Eli's forearm and snapped it shut, using it like a pair of handcuffs. "It's better this way, Eli," said Rylan, eerily calm. "She would have cost us too much."

Eli punched Rylan in the face with his free hand, cutting his knuckles on Rylan's teeth. Rylan grimaced and held on tight. Mandy was steps away from Galena, reaching out with lacquered nails extended.

"*Stop.*"

The voice thundered through the room, shaking Eli to the bone and stopping his heart. His body obeyed the voice with complete submission. Mandy seemed affected in the same way. She sank to one knee inches from Galena, clutching at her chest. "No," she gasped, her eyes bulging. "This shouldn't be happening."

As Eli faltered, Rylan delivered a punishing kick to his ribs, knocking him to the floor. Rylan wrenched the Scope from his hand as Eli tried to breathe, paralyzed by that voice and its sweeping command.

Moros stepped out of the void right next to Galena, who barely seemed to notice his arrival. His eyes lit on Aislin, who was shaking her head and sitting up unsteadily. Then he bent down to scoop Mandy from the ground, cradling her in his arms. "My poor darling."

Eli nearly choked on his dread as every cell in his body screamed. Moros was on Mandy's side? He was standing right next to Galena, who could be Marked in an instant. And Eli couldn't do anything about it—with one word, the Lord of the Kere had immobilized him.

Moros raised his head, as if he'd heard Eli's thoughts. "Carry on," he said.

Eli's head buzzed as oxygen rushed to his brain and muscles, and his heart began to beat once more. Mandy also sucked in a desperate breath, her broken bones creaking.

"Who is responsible for this chaos?" Moros asked. "Who did this to Mandy?"

"I did," said Eli, struggling to push himself up, his limbs tingling painfully.

"He attacked the Charon," rasped Mandy, her voice distorted and thick. "He should be put down."

"Is this true?" Moros asked, his eyes now glowing bright red.

Eli nodded as if his head were under the control of a puppeteer.

Moros opened his mouth to say something, but his attention was drawn to Rylan, who had suddenly pulled his Scope wide—seeking his escape hatch into the Veil.

"I can follow wherever you go, my friend," the Lord of the Kere said softly. "So I suggest you stay and help us figure out what's happened here."

Rylan hesitated, but he didn't close the Scope.

Moros let Mandy's feet slide to the floor, still holding her against his chest. She snuggled in, shooting Eli a smug look. Moros used his teeth to tug the glove off his left hand. "Eli, come here."

His heart hammering, his mind raging, Eli stepped forward, unable to stop his body from carrying him toward his new master.

CHAPTER FORTY-TWO

Cacy was awakened by the raw protests of her lungs and limbs, which hurt almost as much when they were healing as they had when they were first torn open. She was back in Eli's bed, and the spent saline and plasma vials next to her pillow filled her with hope. Eli had been here. Had he stopped Rylan and Mandy?

Voices in the hallway drew her unsteadily to her feet. She winced at the strain on her barely closed wounds. She wrapped the sheet around her body and walked to the doorway in time to hear Mandy accuse Eli of attacking Rylan. Cacy had to get out there. Mandy's accusation would mean one thing: Moros would have to execute Eli. Attacking any Ferry was a punishable offense. Attacking the Charon was an automatic death sentence.

"Mandy is the rogue," Cacy said as she emerged from the bedroom, leaning heavily against the wall. Galena was crumpled in a nearby corner, and Aislin was next to her looking even paler than usual. Mandy was locked in Moros's embrace at the end of the hallway. And Eli was a few feet away from Rylan but shuffling hesitantly toward the Lord of the Kere, as if he wanted to run in the other direction but couldn't.

Mandy jerked in Moros's arms like she was trying to escape into the Veil. "Be still," Moros ordered, and she obeyed.

Cacy shifted her gaze back to Rylan. She had always looked up to her eldest brother, had always believed he was a good man, like their father had been. But the truth was that he'd hurt so many people. He'd *killed* so many people. People she loved. And so, as much as she hated the words, as much as they hurt to say, she said, "And Rylan is a traitor."

"She's lying," said Rylan. "She's only interested in protecting her lover."

"No, she's right," Aislin said, slowly walking over to her sister. She laid a cool hand on Cacy's bare shoulder, then gave Moros her ice-princess stare. "Besides, Rylan is no longer the Charon. *I* am."

She touched the ornate Scope at her throat. Cacy's mouth dropped open.

Moros also seemed caught by surprise. "You—"

Rylan pointed at Aislin. "You can't become the Charon by stealing what's mine."

Aislin's eyes narrowed. "While you have been conspiring with this Ker," she said as she gestured at Mandy, "I have secured the confidence of our board. Declan is also supporting me. Cacia?"

Cacy looked up at her remote, beautiful sister. She was just as ruthless as Cacy had always believed, but apparently in the service of what was right. What was *meant to be*. She nodded. "I'll support you."

Aislin inclined her head toward Cacy and glared at Rylan. "All that is left is Moros's consent to officially recognize me as the Charon."

She turned to the Lord of the Kere. "Rylan abused his power and neglected his responsibility. He and Mandy conspired to murder our father. They murdered our employees, Debra Galloway and Peter Lambeau, as well as our family friend and lawyer, Albert Knickles. They also murdered Eli, using one of our young cousins, Shauna Ferry, as their pawn. And after forcing her to commit this abominable act, Rylan executed her." Aislin's voice shook as she spoke of Shauna. Then it became flinty again. "Rylan is clearly unfit to be the Charon. Do you accept me as his replacement, Jason?"

Moros's eyes flashed. "Well played, my dear. I have no objection." He turned to Rylan. "By the way, I have been called to appear before the Keepers of the Afterlife to answer the charges you have brought against me. I'm looking forward to seeing you there."

Rylan went pale. "We can work something out. I can rescind the charges."

Moros laughed. "Oh, no. I wouldn't miss this summit for anything in the world. I'm sure the Charon will *allow* you to attend." He looked down at Mandy, and his face shifted into real sadness. "You've been bad, darling, but so clever. I never thought it possible that you would betray me."

"I was misled," whispered Mandy, shaking now. "He manipulated me."

Moros *tsk*ed and clutched her tighter. "Ah, but there are limits to your cleverness. I am sorry it ever had to come to this."

Before Mandy had a chance to struggle or scream, Moros laid his bare hand on her cheek. Mandy's eyes went wide, and so did her mouth, opening and closing like that of a hooked fish. Her smooth skin cratered and turned ashen, aging decades in seconds. Her emaciated hands, lacquered red nails long and sharp, scrabbled at Moros's arm, trying to get him to release his grip, but he held her tight, gazing at her with his burning red eyes.

A moment later, he let her go, and she crumpled. Blonde hair scattered across the floor as her skull hit the tile and shattered, the ashes of her incinerated brain swirling on the air. Rylan stared at her remains with a stone face. He showed no emotion at all.

Moros brushed his hands together, clapping the dust of Mandy off. "Eli, come here."

Cacy threw herself between Eli and Moros, shoving Eli back as hard as she could. "Don't touch him," she shouted, digging in her heels and wrapping her arms around his waist as Eli pushed against her. "Aislin, *please*. Say something."

It was the first time in years she'd asked her sister for anything, but she was desperate. Eli looked down at her as he took another step toward Moros. "I'm sorry, Cacy. I have to obey him."

"Jason," said Aislin quietly. "The Ferrys have no quarrel with Eli."

Moros turned to look at Aislin over his shoulder. "Are you certain? By rights he should be punished for his assault on your esteemed brother."

Aislin stepped carefully over Mandy's ashes and bones. She pointed at Rylan. "I no longer consider him my brother," she said in a sorrowful voice. "Not after he murdered our father."

Rylan pulled his stolen Scope wide again. "I won't stand here and listen to—"

Dec snatched the Scope from his older brother's hand, then slammed his fist into Rylan's face. "That's for shooting me," he muttered as Rylan sank to the floor.

Pale and drawn, Dec swayed in place. It looked like the events of the last hour had sucked the life out of him. His gaze traveled right past Cacy and landed on Galena, whose slender arms were wrapped around her knees.

Moros chuckled. "Ferrys, your family politics are astounding. Very well. Eli, come with me."

Cacy's grip on Eli tightened, but she couldn't stop him from taking another step. "But—"

"I'll be all right." Eli's arms went around Cacy. He drew his fingers along the slope of her collarbone, over a streak of dried blood.

Cacy glared at Moros. "I want him back."

Moros smirked. "Such a fierce little thing. Your father would be proud."

Right before Moros disappeared from sight, that smirk softened, and Cacy realized he had sincerely meant every word.

Eli kissed her forehead. "Get some rest, and . . ." He threw a glance at Galena.

"I'll take care of her," Cacy promised.

Eli squeezed her hand. "I love you, Cacia Ferry."

He disappeared.

CHAPTER FORTY-THREE

Eli materialized in the hallway of his apartment, exhausted but relieved. After a brief meeting, Moros had released him. He must have known that Eli was desperate to get back to the two women he loved.

"She's sleeping," said a male voice from the living room. Dec was sitting on the couch, his tablet phone in his hand.

Eli moved quietly into the room to stand in front of the Chief. "Moros has assigned two of his personal guards to watch over her," Eli told him. Protecting Galena now would be a few of the most intimidating-looking Kere that Eli had ever seen.

Eli was glad, because Galena wasn't out of danger yet. She might never be. Not as long as she threatened the income of the Kere and the Ferrys. But Moros seemed determined to use his own guards to keep her safe, and Eli was now a part of that elite group. Eli had been told he would have more power to choose his own assignments as long as he consented to take care of personal business for Moros as well. It sounded like a fair trade.

Eli looked Dec over. The man had recovered from his wounds and changed his clothes, but he still looked thrashed. "You don't have to be here, Chief."

"Call me Dec," the Chief said wearily, setting his tablet on the couch and rubbing a hand over his face. "I had a friend of mine—Dr. Romero—make a house call to evaluate Galena. Rylan didn't hurt her." He winced. "Not physically, at least."

Eli's chest ached as he glanced over his shoulder at Galena's closed door. "Today probably brought everything from her past to the surface again."

Eli turned back to find Dec's ice-blue eyes steady on him. "She was barely responsive," Dec said quietly. "Dr. Romero gave her a light sedative, just so she could sleep." He sighed. "I don't know much about what happened to you guys, but she was so scared. I-I didn't feel good, leaving her alone. Though I'm not sure she even knew I was here."

Eli wondered if he was imagining the sadness in Dec's eyes. "She'll need time," Eli blurted out, not completely sure why he'd said it.

The Chief didn't look away. "Would you like to know the last thing my father ever said to me?" When Eli didn't respond, Dec continued. "He said, 'Protect her, and you protect the future.'"

"And you think he was talking about Galena?"

Dec picked up his tablet and got to his feet. "I had no idea what he was talking about until I heard Galena speak at the fund-raiser. But after that, I had no doubt."

Eli stared at the Chief. He didn't trust easily, but Dec had saved Galena earlier, nearly dying in the process. "She's guarded by Kere," Eli said, "but . . . I don't want her to be alone if she wakes up."

The corner of Dec's mouth twitched. "And you want to go to Cacy."

Eli bowed his head. Now that he knew his sister was safe, he didn't just *want* to go to Cacy, he needed it.

"I could stay for a while," offered Dec. "You guys are scheduled to work tonight. If you want to see my sister before your shift, you'd better get going."

Their eyes met, and Eli had the sense there was a lot more to be said between them but that now wasn't the time. "Thanks. I'll see you later. If she wakes up—"

"I'll call you immediately."

"I'm grateful." Eli closed his eyes and thought of Cacy. He appeared in her bedroom and inhaled deeply, drawing in her spicy scent.

The sound of the shower drew his attention. A strip of warm yellow light glowed from beneath the closed door of Cacy's bathroom. Eli's groin stiffened as he imagined her in the spray of the hot water, covered in soapy lather, her hands sliding—

Cacy shrieked, her feet slipping out from under her as Eli appeared behind her. He caught her around the waist, spluttering as the hot spray hit his face. "Eli?" She was already laughing.

"Uh, yeah. Sorry about that." He looked down at his soaked clothes. "I've got to learn to control myself."

Her hands were tugging off his shirt, and he raised his arms to accommodate her. It landed with a wet slap on the floor of the stall.

"I take it you don't mind?" he asked.

She kissed his chest and nipped the tight nub of his nipple, drawing a deep groan from him. "Are you kidding?" She raised her head and pulled his mouth to hers, kissing him fiercely, letting him know she'd been worried sick but was trying to cover it. She stood on her tiptoes to press her forehead to his. "You're *here*," she whispered, the smile on her face piercingly beautiful.

He wrapped his arms around her slick body and relished the feel of her breasts pressed against him. That increasingly familiar feeling—the one he'd only known since meeting Cacy—rose within him. *Happiness.* It rolled through his chest where his soulless heart beat, washed over the past he'd tried to keep hidden, and filled his mind with hopes of a future spent protecting and loving her.

"Oh, yes," he said as he leaned in to kiss her again. "I'm here."

EPILOGUE

Jason Moros allowed himself one last look at the city. The view from this penthouse had long been one of his favorites. Boston spread out before him in all its messy, unseemly glory—and the Psychopomps skyscraper was only a block away, its sleek facade kissed by the mist that rose off the canals. He stared at it, wishing that the simple act of staring could give him the answers he so desperately needed now. But nothing could, it seemed. In fact, with every day that passed, he appeared to be losing his grasp, even on things he'd thought he understood.

His fingers slid over the engraved metal case in his pocket. The surface was warm to the touch, heated by the human soul trapped inside. A small, bitter smile crept onto his face. His newest Ker was complicated to say the least. Inextricably tied by the heart to a Ferry, of all creatures. The choice to change Eli had been an impulsive one, but for now, their interests were aligned.

Moros closed his eyes. A visit to his sisters was long overdue, and perhaps they could help him puzzle out how one of his Kere had operated without his direction and knowledge. He shed the warmth of the physical world and entered the Veil. This world between worlds was his true home, his birthplace. He bowed his head and allowed the faint rustling whispers to tug him along.

"We were wondering when you'd show up."

Moros opened his eyes. He was in a vast space made of polished travertine. Atropos stood in front of him, a sickle in her hand, the curved blade ending in a razor-sharp point. Her heels were almost as sharp, and her simple black dress fit her like a second skin. Like his other sisters, she looked no older than midtwenties, but she was as ancient as Moros. Her thick black hair was held away from her face by golden bands, and her brown eyes were brimming with accusation.

"I've been a bit busy," he said, offering her an embrace.

She sniffed and turned her back. "As if we're not busy all the time."

"And have you been busier than usual, darling sister?"

She looked over her shoulder, her eyes narrowed. "What are you implying?"

"Nothing at all." He looked up at the massive gossamer tapestry a few feet above their heads, lit by the stars above. Though it looked like a jumbled, holey, chaotic mess, each stitch had been planned. Some bits of it sparkled or glowed while others had become dead and gray. Atropos reached up and sliced away one such thread, and Moros felt it in his gut, the prick of another soul to reap. Usually the feeling was fainter than a prickle of static, a sensation he'd long since learned to ignore, but whenever he was near Atropos, it stabbed him a little deeper. A face and a name flashed in his head, and he pushed that knowledge outward, into the Veil.

Somewhere, a Ker was feeling the call of death.

"I came for help, not to argue," he said, weariness seeping into his voice. "I've been called before the Keepers, and though I did not sanction a single unauthorized Marking, they'll still want an explanation from me. It could affect us all."

"But mostly you," Atropos said, whirling the dull gray thread between her fingers. "Come. Clotho and Lachesis have missed you far more than I."

They walked beneath the shimmering fabric, which flexed and rippled like a living thing. Beyond the bounds of the tapestry were the lush apartments where each of the siblings, including Moros, kept their private sanctuaries, but straight ahead was the massive loom, the divine machine that churned out the endless fabric of life.

On the other side of the almost-transparent cloth, a shadow bobbed along. Moros and Atropos made their way around the loom to greet its owner. Lachesis paced toward them, her steps precise, her back rod-straight, her blonde hair cut so close to her head that from a distance she looked bald. She had on a skirt-suit that reminded Moros of something Aislin Ferry might wear, so prim and proper, and it made him smile in spite of himself. Lachesis clutched a measuring stick tightly in her grip, as always, and her brows were drawn together. But when she saw her brother, her face split into a grin that made her blue eyes sparkle. She closed the distance between them quickly and dove into his arms. "I've been thinking about you," she said, pressing her cheek to his.

He released her reluctantly. She and Clotho were the only two beings in the universe who would touch him willingly. The weight of it, the warmth . . . Moros looked away as loneliness sank its teeth deep. He forced a smile onto his face. "I've been thinking about you, too."

He'd opened his mouth to say more when Clotho stepped out the front door of her apartment, her loose, flowing gown fluttering around her ankles. She was still twisting her brown hair into a knot at the back of her head, preparing to sit at her wheel and spin out the thread of each soul's life.

"Brother!" she called out happily. "I thought you might have abandoned us."

"It's not affection that drives him to visit," muttered Atropos.

Lachesis tapped her sister on the arm with her measuring stick. "Don't be rude. We're all trying to figure out what made it possible for the Ker to go rogue. Our brother's got to face it out *there*, so why wouldn't he be concerned?"

Atropos brandished her sickle. "Then help him figure it out," she snapped. "I have work to do." She gave Moros one last searing look and stalked away, her heels clicking on the stone tiles.

Clotho *tsk*ed and enveloped Moros in a hug. He stroked her face, treasuring the comfort of her soft skin against the backs of his fingers.

"Remember the knot of uncertainty we discussed?" he asked. "I know the thread you weave sometimes contains them, but this one . . ."

Clotho bit her lip. "The soldier? The one in Pittsburgh?" She smiled when he nodded. "You let him live."

Lachesis nodded knowingly. "Much to Atropos's disgust. She'd sliced away his thread, and I had to weave it back onto its new path."

Moros removed the case from his pocket. "He's mine now."

Lachesis pulled a shimmering thread from the pocket of her suit. "This is his. Atropos claimed it had turned gray. She sliced it from the fabric."

Moros watched the gossamer thread sway as it dangled from Lachesis's grip. That was Eli's life. It had been entwined with so many others, but now it had been pulled from the tapestry, along with Moros's knowledge of what was meant to be. "He wasn't supposed to die, and you know it. *She* knew it, too."

Clotho frowned. "Atropos only makes the cut. She doesn't decide who lives or who dies." Her eyes strayed along the path where their sister had stormed away. "It's part of what makes her so angry."

"And might she have taken matters into her own hands a time or two?" Moros whispered. "Something is happening. I don't know what, but—"

"That something is *you*, unable to control your own monsters!" Atropos peeked around the edge of the loom, her face a mask of fury. "You're just here to find someone to blame. Create order in your own house before you lay this at my doorstep." She waved her sickle at them and disappeared.

A second later, Moros felt another stab, this one like a knife twisting behind his rib cage. Another face, another name, another Ker sent into action.

Lachesis stroked his arm. "We don't know any more than you do," she said quietly. "The strands keep falling away, slipping loose of the tapestry all around the thread that belongs to Galena Margolis." She gestured at a silvery strand that wound its way along, entwining with a few Moros knew quite well. But along its path in the near future, in the fabric that had emerged from the loom and hung heavy over the floor, jagged holes had begun to grow where the tapestry had once been tightly woven. The shimmering thread looked so vulnerable, so easy to slice away.

Lachesis's eyes shone with tears. "I'm doing my best, Jason. I monitor every knot, every joining, every stitch I make, but I can't stop it. Someone is acting outside our authority."

Clotho put her arm around her sister, but her dark gaze was on Moros. "Right now it's just a few threads, but if it gets worse . . ."

The entire tapestry might unravel. Especially considering how many threads of life Galena's was destined to intersect. Not just some of them. Virtually *all* of them. As brilliant as she was, the woman had no idea of the power of her discoveries—not just what she'd already done, but what she was meant to do in the future. And as tempting as it had been to wipe her from the Earth, as much as an enemy of death as she was, Moros had realized he'd be signing his own execution order if he hurt her. He'd made his vow to the Keepers as part of the treaty—he would not divert from the path of fate, nor would his Kere. And although he knew that a few unsanctioned Markings here or there could go unnoticed, the same was not true if Galena were Marked. If her thread was cut away, it was possible the fabric of life would fall apart completely. No more order, no more fate. Instead, randomness.

Atropos had been right; the Keepers would come after him first. Their hatred of him was miles deep and millennia old. That didn't mean his sisters weren't in danger, though.

He shook himself out of his reverie. "Who could be doing this?" he asked. "Have you seen any of the others?"

Lachesis and Clotho shook their heads. Most of their siblings had long since faded from memory to myth, allowing themselves to bleed into abstraction. Humans were so good at causing strife they no longer needed Eris to do it for them. They were too riddled with envy to require anything more from Nemesis, and so full of lies they did not require Apate's lessons of deceit. But could these siblings still be skulking in the Veil? They would be unaffected if the fabric of fate and destiny disintegrated. In fact, they might enjoy it. Could one of them be the cause of these problems?

Because Moros didn't believe for a minute that it started and ended with Rylan and Mandy.

"Where would we have seen them? You know we never leave our domain—and we rarely have visitors," Clotho said, tucking a stray brown lock behind her ear. "Have you checked your trunk? Are all the souls of your Kere present and accounted for?"

Lachesis tapped the case in his hand. "Aren't they the ones causing the problems? Money is nothing to us, nothing to our siblings, but for your death-bringers, it matters quite a lot."

His sisters' voices had been gentle, but their doubt made his teeth clench. Everyone believed he and his Kere were evil. The Keepers had always looked on them with contempt. Hearing that his sisters believed the same was too much. He took a step away from them, certain his anger was making his eyes glow with ruby fire. His hands fisted over his clawed fingertips. The frustration made him want to tear the cloth from the loom and toss it onto a fire, heedless to the consequences.

"I'll be in my apartment," he said quickly, then strode toward the building that rose up from the vast island of travertine tile. He strode into his sanctuary, the home that held his favorite possessions, mostly gifts and mementos from true friends and comrades long since dead. A soft sofa sat in the corner, a book lying pages-down on one of the cushions. And along the back wall, the trunk that contained every single soul he'd ever taken.

Minus the ones he'd destroyed, of course.

Still holding the case containing Eli's soul, Moros pulled his key from his pocket and slid it into the heavy lock. He opened the trunk and peered inside. The souls oozed along like translucent multicolored serpents, each one unique. Trevor's was a pale green shot through with shimmering threads of blue. Luke's was a deep, bloody crimson spotted with black.

Mandy's lay still at the bottom of the trunk. It was yellow, glinting with pinprick dots of indigo. Moros had always found it far more exquisite than the woman herself, and perhaps he had been deceived by that beauty. Somehow, Mandy had Marked soul after soul without his knowledge. He hadn't felt it at all. Could she have done that of her own free will? He hadn't thought it possible.

But if it were, it meant the Kere could rebel. It meant he wasn't in control. And if that were true, and if the Keepers of the Afterlife realized it, Moros knew that the deepest pit of Hell awaited him. He reached into the trunk, and the souls wriggled away from the intrusion. He grabbed the limp soul of Mandy, and it turned to dust in his grasp, just as her body had.

Then he opened the case. Eli's soul nestled inside, sapphire blue. No spots. No streaks. Just vibrant, solid color. He gently lifted the soul from the case and placed it inside the trunk, where it slithered along like the rest, testing the boundaries of its new for-ever home. He stared down at the animated pieces of all the Kere at his command. He had chosen each and every one of them, and it didn't matter that there were several thousand in the trunk—Moros knew they were all accounted for.

So either the rogue element was within his very ranks, or one of his siblings was acting outside the bounds of fate, which Moros and his three sisters served as a matter of survival. The rage roiled inside him, millennia of slavery winding their way through his unforgiving memory. He had come so far. Enough to taste a certain kind of freedom. Not pure, but delicious nonetheless. And now everything he'd fought for was threatened.

He leaned over the trunk. "Behave," he growled. As if they sensed his presence, his voice, the writhing souls went still, some of them trembling slightly. He smiled, running his tongue along his fangs.

The Lord of the Kere closed the trunk and willed himself out of the Veil.

ACKNOWLEDGMENTS

Writing often starts out as a solitary pursuit, but in the case of this book, it was a shared effort all along. So first and foremost, I want to thank my agent, Kathleen Ortiz, for encouraging me to branch out and try my hand with this genre, for being such a great advocate and strategist every step of the way, and for finding the best possible home for this book.

Which brings me to the team at 47North: Thanks to David Pomerico for enthusiasm from the get-go, and to Jason Kirk for taking the wheel. To my copyeditor, Elizabeth Johnson, thanks so much for being meticulous *and* fun. And of course, unending gratitude goes to my developmental editor, Leslie "Lam" Miller, for being wise, for making me laugh while making me better, and for teaching me the difference between Scotch and Irish whiskey. Lady, I owe you a Jameson.

I want to thank my writing friends and beta readers, especially Brigid Kemmerer, Jaime Lawrence, and Justine Dell, who read early versions of the manuscript and provided both the encouragement to go on and the criticism I needed to make it better. I also want to thank Lydia Kang for sitting next to me on this roller coaster. Being an author is weird, and I know you'll always understand.

Thanks to my colleagues, and especially Anne-Marie Bora for sharing my love of romance. Thanks to my parents for cheering me on. Mom, thanks for reading this with your critical romance reader's eye, and Dad, thanks for not reading it, because that would probably be sort of weird. Gratitude goes to my husband for taking everything in stride. And to my kids, thank you for tolerating my spaciness and for finding me at least mildly interesting some of the time. I adore you guys.

ABOUT THE AUTHOR

Sarah Fine is a clinical psychologist and the author of the Guards of the Shadowlands series (*Sanctum*, *Fractured*, and *Chaos*), as well as other young adult novels. She was born on the West Coast, raised in the Midwest, and is now firmly entrenched on the East Coast, where she lives with her husband and two children.